Praise for these award-winning authors

New York Times **bestselling author**

Heather Graham

"Refreshing, unique…
Graham does it better than anyone."
—*Publishers Weekly*

"A writer of incredible talent."
—*Affaire de Coeur*

USA TODAY **bestselling author**

Merline Lovelace

"Merline Lovelace rocks!"
—*New York Times* bestselling author
Mary Jo Putney

Merline Lovelace delivers "thrilling adventure
and wonderful romance in perfect measure."
—*Romantic Times*

USA TODAY **bestselling author**

Ann Major

"Want it all? Read Ann Major."
—*New York Times* bestselling author Nora Roberts

"Ann Major sets our senses on fire…."
—*Romantic Times*

HEATHER GRAHAM

New York Times bestselling author Heather Graham has written more than ninety novels, several of which have been featured by the Doubleday Book Club and the Literary Guild. There are more than twenty million copies of her books in print and she has been published in more than fifteen languages. Heather lives with her husband and five children in Miami, Florida.

MERLINE LOVELACE

A career air force officer, Merline Lovelace spent twenty-three years in uniform. She's served at bases all over the world, including tours in Taiwan, Vietnam and at the Pentagon on the Joint Chiefs of Staff. She has produced one action-packed sizzler after another and now has over twenty published novels. Merline lives in Oklahoma City with her husband, where she is working on her next novel.

ANN MAJOR

lives in Texas with her husband of many years and is the mother of three grown children. She has a master's degree from Texas A&M at Kingsville, Texas, and is a former English teacher. She is a founding board member of the RWA and a frequent speaker at writers' groups. Ann loves to write; she considers her ability to do so a gift. Her hobbies include hiking in the mountains, sailing, ocean kayaking, traveling and playing the piano. But most of all she enjoys her family.

HEATHER GRAHAM
MERLINE LOVELACE
ANN MAJOR

THE ULTIMATE TREASURE

Published by Silhouette Books
America's Publisher of Contemporary Romance

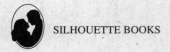 SILHOUETTE BOOKS

THE ULTIMATE TREASURE

Copyright © 2003 by Harlequin Books S.A.

ISBN 0-373-21858-3

The publisher acknowledges the copyright holders of the individual works as follows:

BETWEEN ROC AND A HARD PLACE
Copyright © 1993 by Heather Graham Pozzessere

DREAMS AND SCHEMES
Copyright © 1994 by Merline Lovelace

WHAT THIS PASSION MEANS
Copyright © 1987 by Ann Major

CONTENTS

BETWEEN ROC AND
A HARD PLACE

Heather Graham

To Doreen and John and Baby Westermark,
with lots of love and best wishes.

One

"Captain! We've caught more than fish in the net, sir!"

Roc Trellyn strode forward on the deck of the *Crystal Lee,* his bare feet silent against the wooden planking. They were between the Florida peninsula and the Bahamas, the weather was warm and balmy, and he was clad in nothing but a faded pair of blue cutoffs. As befit a man who spent the majority of his life on the water, his bare chest and arms were deeply bronzed; even the dark hair on his chest was bleached until the tips were golden.

He was a tall man, lean, hard and well muscled, a swimmer, a diver, a sailor. He was dark, with jet black hair, a little shaggy since they had been at sea for several weeks now, and his face was just as bronzed as his shoulders. His features were striking, saved from true handsomeness by the rugged edges brought on by constant exposure to the sea and sun. His cheekbones were high, his nose straight, his mouth broad and generous, sensual. Against the utter darkness of his face, however, his eyes were a brilliant, steely blue. He was a man it was impossible not to notice.

"Captain!" The call came again even as he reached the pile of netting and fish on the forward deck of the *Crystal Lee*. It was Bruce Willowby who seemed so concerned, his first mate on this and most cruises, his best friend on and off the ship, though his entire crew was small and close-knit. Bruce and he had majored in marine biology together at the University of Miami, and ever since, they had cast their fates to the wind together. Bruce was tall, lean, with sun-bleached white-blond hair, also shaggy now, and almond-shaped dark eyes.

The entire crew of the *Crystal Lee* had gathered around the netting, alerted by Bruce's calls. Connie, Bruce's sister, their best cook and a skilled diver, was standing by his side. Connie was a pretty woman, with her brother's platinum hair and beautiful dark eyes. Then there was Peter Castro, half Cuban, half Irish-American, dark and green-eyed, small and wiry, a whiz with sonar equipment. Completing the crew were Joe and Marina Tobago, husband and wife, Bahamians, and two of the best divers and swimmers he had come across in all his life. When they had spare time in the evenings, Roc liked to race Joe Tobago. Sometimes he won. A lot of the time he lost. And Joe would tell him in his melodic singsong that he was getting old and letting himself go slack. That, of course, always spurred him on, and he usually won the next race. He wasn't slipping all that badly, he would assure Joe in return.

Except that maybe he was.

Hell, he had to be.

Because Bruce was right. He had just hauled up a hell of a lot more than fish.

Something, no some*one*, was struggling in the netting. Oddly, the entire crew had stepped back. It was their surprise, he was certain, that had caused them to do so.

He stood dead still himself, at first. Then he realized not just what but *who* he had caught. She hadn't seen him yet.

He stepped back, moving to stand on the first of the steps leading to the helm, out of the woman's line of vision, and motioned to Bruce, who lifted a curious brow at him. He waved a hand, indicating that they should release her from the netting, though it would be a grudging effort on his part.

Bruce shrugged, then lifted the netting that had entangled the woman.

And from his vantage point, Roc saw her. Really saw her.

A silent whistle echoed in his head.

She hadn't changed.

Just what had he pulled up from the ocean's depths? A ghost from the past? A siren from the sea?

She was kneeling on the deck, so he couldn't really see her height or size, but he didn't need to. She was tall and slim and elegantly, sensually built. Her hair was dripping wet, plastered against her face and head, so he couldn't really judge its color now. It didn't matter. He already knew it. When that hair dried, it would be the color of sunlight. Not pale, but golden, with specks of red fire.

She was still the most exquisite creature he had ever seen.

Her face was lifted as she stared at Bruce. It was stunning in its perfection. Her cheeks were high and classical, her nose small and straight, her lips richly defined, rose-colored against the elegant tan of her flesh. Her face was a perfect oval, her eyes very large and wide-set, framed by high brows and velvet lashes. He could see the color of her eyes clearly, furious and flashing, an aquamarine to rival the most glorious waters of the Caribbean.

He'd seen them flash that way before.

This time, however, her angry stare was directed at Bruce; she seemed to have taken him as the one in charge.

She pointed a finger at him. "You, sir, should be arrested and put under lock and key! How dare you!"

Bruce stepped back in surprise. He had obviously been taken in by her heart-stopping beauty. Poor Bruce. Ah, well, he was a big boy. And he had realized that Roc had recognized her. In a few minutes, he might put two and two together himself.

"Lady, you're in our net—" he began.

"Exactly! I'm in your net!"

Bruce—ever the gentleman—moved to try to help her up.

She didn't want help. She shoved his hand aside, struggling on her own power.

Ah, and there she was, at her full height, all five feet eight inches of her.

A sudden pang swept mercilessly through Roc's heart. *No, she hadn't changed.* She was still perfect. And it wasn't because she was clad so scantily; her bathing suit was actually a rather subdued one. It was a black one-piece, low-cut in the back to her waist, with French-cut thighs.

It was the way she wore what she wore.

She was slim, but extremely shapely. Her legs were long and finely muscled, her waist very slim, her hips just perfectly flared, her breasts just perfectly...

Perfect.

Roc crossed his arms over his chest, surveying her as she surveyed Bruce.

Despite her startling beauty, he sure as hell didn't need this. He was having enough trouble with his latest venture without adding a problem like this. She was a pain. And she was trouble. Definitely trouble.

A niggling suspicion tore at his mind. Had she been sent to spy on him? To see just what he was up to with the *Crystal Lee?*

His eyes roamed up and down her. She *was* perfect—perfect bait. As stunning as ever a silver fish was as it wriggled on a hook, a lure to bring in the big catch...

Bruce was still staring at her. Just staring. Roc was tempted to walk over and snap his friend's gaping mouth shut, but he didn't want her seeing him, not yet, so he resisted the temptation.

"Oh!" she cried aloud in exasperation, the fury flashing even more brightly in her eyes. "What in God's name is the matter with you? How can you be so entirely careless?"

Bruce found his voice at last. "Lady, what are you talking about? I can't even figure out where you came from! We're moving in deep waters. We're not in swimming or diving areas, we're—"

"The type of fishing you're doing kills hundreds of marine mammals yearly!"

"I've never caught a marine mammal in my life!" Bruce assured her quickly.

"You've just caught me!" she exclaimed. "And I'm just about the same size as a small dolphin."

Oh, lord. So she was supposed to be a bleeding-heart liberal, or something of the sort.

Was it true?

Roc doubted it.

Oh, not that she didn't care about the dolphins. She did. She loved the water, almost as passionately as he did. Maybe more so.

But had she come here because of the dolphins?

No. He was absolutely sure of that.

And he *had* caught a marine mammal—when he wasn't even a fisherman.

But she knew that. She just didn't know yet that this was his ship. That he was captaining the voyage.

She was here to discover just what he—or the *Crystal Lee*—was up to. Well, maybe, he thought grimly, just maybe, she was going to get her chance to find out.

Bruce was looking over her head now, to the helm. Roc made another motion. Bruce stared at him, confused for a moment. Then he shrugged. Roc was obviously up to something.

Suddenly Bruce smiled.

Roc wondered if his friend had just figured out who their beautiful mermaid was.

"Ma'am, if you have a problem with us, you'll have to take it up with the captain."

Ah, there they went, those perfect brows of hers, flying up in surprise.

"You're not the captain?" she said to Bruce.

He shook his head.

"Then take me to him—immediately."

"Ah, I don't think he's quite ready to receive company yet. Maybe you'd like a cup of coffee or tea, or a soda? Even a beer?"

"I don't want anything to drink, thank you. I just want to see the captain, have my say and get back to civilization!"

"We are civilized here, miss…?" Connie murmured with a sniff.

She glanced at Connie. "I'm sorry," she said quickly. "I'd just really like to speak to the captain and get back." She flashed them all a beautiful smile. Ah, here it came, the charm. "I really am sorry. I was just so frightened. If I've been rude to you all, I didn't mean to be. It's your captain with whom I have a fierce disagreement."

She didn't yet know just how fierce! Roc thought.

Then he decided it was time to disappear into the captain's cabin. The *Crystal Lee* wasn't all that big—it was going to be difficult finding privacy, but he meant to have a little of it.

Silently, he turned, padding across the decking to the large cabin in the far aft of the ship. He could hear the others talking as he quietly opened the door and slipped into the cabin. "You come, missy," Marina Tobago was saying, slipping a chestnut arm around her shoulders. "I make the most wonderful coffee in the entire world. It will make everything look a little better."

Marina was going to take her into the galley and central living quarters. Fine. All the sonar and other special equipment was below deck, wedged in between the crew quarters. Space was of necessity tight on the *Crystal Lee,* but she was a beautifully built vessel, so well designed that Joe and Marina had their cabin, Connie had her own smaller place, and Peter and Bruce shared the larger living quarters just beneath Roc's captain's quarters.

He sat behind the antique ship's desk he had managed to procure for the *Crystal Lee.* Damn. He was still amazed. How could *she* be here? Maybe he shouldn't have been so amazed. She was, after all, her father's daughter.

And it still seemed that his heart was being squeezed, just a little.

No, a lot…

How long had it been?

Nearly three years. She hadn't changed.

Had he?

Sometimes it had felt as if she had aged him an entire decade.…

Maybe several.

He reached absently into his bottom drawer. There was a bottle of special dark Caribbean rum there. He didn't open it often. Not on a trip like this one.

Tonight...

Tonight he needed a drink.

He set the bottle on his desk and reached for a tumbler, then discarded the idea and took a long swig out of the bottle. Whew. It burned. Hot and sweet, going down. Warmed his heart. Melted away the pain.

No, not really.

There was a quick tap on his door. Bruce entered. His eyes were wide, his manner excited.

"I've got it!" he said. "It's her! Right? Ms. Melinda Davenport. I can't believe I didn't see it right away, except that in most of the pictures, she's *dry*. She does look a little different, soaking wet and all. Damn, I'm sorry. I didn't mean to be so slow-witted!"

Roc shook his head. "Bruce, you weren't slow-witted. How could you have been expected to know? I almost stepped on her before I realized it myself."

Bruce shook his head. "God, but she's beautiful!"

Roc nodded wryly, then looked meaningfully at Bruce. "But watch it. She's treacherous. Cunning. Don't forget, she's old man Davenport's daughter. She can be vicious. Hard as nails. Tough as leather. As charming as formaldehyde!"

Bruce grinned. "She sounds like the Wicked Witch of the West."

"And don't you forget it!"

"Want to get her off the ship fast, huh?" Bruce said.

Roc leaned forward, grinning. "Not on your life!" he exclaimed softly. "Hey, the way I see it, this was no accident. She wanted to come aboard. Well, she's here now. She can just stay a while."

Bruce frowned. "Won't that be kidnapping?"

"She came aboard my boat."

"Well, we did pull her up in a net."

"And she slipped herself into that net on purpose, I assure you."

"Sounds like you really dislike her!"

"She's absolute trouble," he promised.

Bruce shook his head again sorrowfully. Then he arched a brow. "By the way—did you ever actually get a divorce from her?"

Roc started.

Had he?

No, actually, he hadn't done anything. But surely she had. Old man Davenport would have seen to that! Roc was always at sea. He'd never been served any papers, but then, he wouldn't have been around to receive them. The way things had ended had been so furious and wild....

"Wouldn't that be something?" he murmured.

"What?"

He grinned. "If our little imposter is still my wife!"

Bruce smiled in return. "Well, it might help out in case of a kidnapping charge!"

Roc sat back, remembering his brief and stormy marriage. The wildness, the fights...the lovemaking.

A searing jolt seemed to rip right through his body. He gritted his teeth, leaning back again, and swallowed another long draft of good Caribbean rum.

"Why don't you bring the lady in?" he suggested. "The captain is ready to be met."

Bruce flashed him a quick salute and hurried out. A second later, the cabin door opened and she came on in.

Melinda. Melly...

She was drying, and drying nicely. Connie had supplied her with clothes, white baggy pants and a white tailored shirt with short sleeves. The tails were tied at her waist in a knot.

Her hair was drying. Long, wavy, spilling golden over her shoulders. She wore no makeup at all. Melinda had no need for it.

She strode in, already having taken a deep breath and ready to vent her anger on the captain.

But even as she stepped in, he was rising. And before she could speak, he was smiling, greeting her smoothly.

"My, my. *Ms.* Davenport. To what do we owe this very strange, er, pleasure?"

The air rushed out of her. Aquamarine eyes lit on him, amazed.

But was she as amazed as she seemed? He doubted it.

"You!" she breathed.

He arched one dark brow. "These are my waters," he reminded her politely. "They always have been."

Her lips seemed to be trembling slightly. But was it for real?

He lifted a hand. "Do come in, Ms. Davenport." He paused, cocking his head, staring at her. "It is *Ms.* Davenport, isn't it? You did divorce me, I assume?"

And then he knew. Instantly.

She paled to the color of snow.

She had never divorced him.

She had probably just assumed that he had divorced her, the way he had assumed...

Oh, no. This was rich! Really, really rich!

He started to laugh, the sound deep and husky in the small room. "So it isn't Ms. Davenport! What a startling surprise. Almost as surprising as pulling one's ex-wife up in a fishing net at sea. Except you're not my ex-wife."

"And you're not a fisherman!" she lashed out, at last finding breath again.

"Right," he said, his laughter having faded, his voice tense. He set his hands on the table, leaning across it as he demanded, "So just what are you doing on my vessel, Melinda?"

"I was caught just like a dolphin because of your absolute carelessness—"

"Wrong!"

"Damn you!" she cried, striding across the room, ready to accost him—until she realized just how close she had come.

Close enough to touch.

He could see the pulse beating at the base of her throat. The rise and fall of her breasts. Just as she could see the ripple of his naked chest with every breath of air he took.

She shook her head, the movement a little wild. And just a little…desperate.

Melinda, beautiful in white, golden hair cascading over her shoulders, aquamarine eyes a damp, gemstone fire. Chin held high. Always held so high.

"You're not going to believe a word I say to you, no matter what. So why don't we end this impossible situation right here and now?"

He sat back in his chair, controlling the wild rush of emotions surging through him. "This impossible situation?"

"Me. Here."

He shook his head, as if trying to understand her better. "Melinda, you connived your way aboard my vessel."

"I was caught up in your—"

"No, Melinda, I don't think so."

"How can you not think so? I was in your net—"

"Yes, but I think you ended up there on purpose."

"You would!" she cried. "You would never credit such a thing to your own inability—"

"Ah. And it just happened to be *my* boat you came upon, eh?"

"What does it matter?" she cried. "Just take me to port. Any port! Then this will all be over and done."

He smiled at her. Just as pleasantly as he could manage.

"But I'm not ready to head in to port."

"I am."

He rose again, striding around the desk, pausing just before her. His smile deepened. "But I'm the captain, Ms. Davenport. And what I say goes."

He walked past her, heading for the door.

"You can't possibly mean to keep me a prisoner on this boat!" she cried.

"Prisoner!" he exclaimed, swinging around. "Oh, you are mistaken!"

"Then you will take me to port—"

"Sorry!" he informed her. "But please, think of yourself as a guest, not as a prisoner!"

"You son of a—" she called after him.

He closed the door on the last word, then leaned against it, smiling. But it was a painful smile. Then he turned back, opened the door, and grinned.

"Since we are still married," he offered politely, "you're more than welcome to share the captain's quarters. I mean, you did come aboard to discover just what's going on here, didn't you? What better way to make discoveries?"

He knew her. He knew her well. So he shouldn't have been surprised when the bottle of fine Caribbean rum came flying his way.

Thankfully, he was quick.

He closed the door, then heard the bottle clank against it.

Once again, he smiled.

The bottle hadn't broken.

But then his smile faded. The rum hadn't eased a thing. He seemed to be burning inside and out. Giant fingers had closed around his heart.

There had been a time when he hadn't thought her tough at all. And never had he seen her as a witch.

There had been a time when those eyes had lit on his with sea-green passion, when the golden threads of her hair had curled over the bronze of his chest, tangled in his fingers. When those perfect legs had entwined with his own. When they had lain beneath the stars, feeling the swell of the sea beneath them, dreaming...

There had been a time.

But that had been long ago now.

And though she might still be his wife, she was definitely old man Davenport's daughter.

And she had come here to spy; of that he was convinced.

And there was only one thing he could do. He had to make damned sure that she didn't return with any information whatsoever.

And there was only one way to do that. He had to make sure she didn't return. Not until he had made his claim.

However long that took.

Melinda... Aboard this boat. Day after day.

Torture!

He gritted his teeth. All right. So torture it would be. But he was going to make damned certain that it was torture for both of them!

Two

He was gone.

Melinda sank into the chair behind the captain's desk and realized that she was shaking. She gripped her fingers together, trying to stop.

So, this was his boat! She should have known, she had suspected, but still, she hadn't really been prepared....

With a soft groan she let her head fall to the desk. She had wanted it to be his boat. Face it, she had wanted this to be his boat, even if she actually *was* spying in a way. This time, if she could, she would make sure that things went the way they should have gone before. She owed him that much.

Was that *really* why she was here? she mocked herself.

Wasn't she still just a bit...a little bit...in love with him?

Not that it mattered. They might still be married—and that was truly a shock!—but the way he had looked at her had clearly indicated that he felt he had brought a shark on board.

Her fingers were starting to tremble again. Well, what had she expected? That he would welcome her with open arms after what she had done?

On the other hand, he was the one who had walked out.

After she had taken her father's side. Against him, against her husband, and even Jonathan Davenport admitted now that he had been wrong, that he should have given credit where credit had been due....

It was all so long ago.

But she'd never managed to convince herself that it was over, she realized. She'd been so naive, so foolish—and so wrong in so many ways. She could clearly remember her fury that he could say anything ill about her father. In fact, she could remember how angry they had both been, the words that had flown, the accusations, the recriminations. Then she could remember being in his arms, believing that he had listened to her, that he had understood, that everything would be all right. She could remember the tempest and the sweetness of making love....

And she could very clearly remember not believing that he was really leaving when he walked away the next morning. He had asked her to come, of course. She just hadn't believed that he would really go.

And she hadn't seen him since.

At first she'd thought he hadn't changed, but now she knew he had. He was three years older, wiser, determined, confident and very set in his ways. His hair was a little shaggy; he wasn't getting it cut very often. He had probably decided that he just didn't have the time. If he was on a quest...

He was definitely on a quest. Her father had said that if anyone could find the *Contessa Maria,* it would be Roc Trellyn. Of course, Jonathan was looking for the ship, but he hadn't been the one to plant the idea of trying to find out if Roc was in pursuit of the elusive galleon and, if so, how he was doing. It was Eric who had rather offhandedly given her the idea one night when they had all been in that little pub in Key West.

"There's no doubt Trellyn will be after this one. He's always been convinced that the *Contessa* went down between Florida and the Bahamas, no matter how the scholars have insisted that she went down closer to Cuba. This new evidence must have him dancing for joy. I'll bet he's out there right now, in one of those supposed *fishing* boats, searching his little heart out. Oh, to be a fly on that boat! But then again, Melinda, you could just ask your ex what he knows and what he's up to!''

He'd given her one of his lazy half smiles. Eric was very good at lazy half smiles.

She admitted that he was an attractive man, tall, blond, tan, lithe and muscled, and charming in his own way. He worked with her father on and off, moaned and drank beer with her father on and off. She'd tried to like him, tried to date him, and sometimes she'd even enjoyed herself. But she'd kept her distance from him, all the same. They'd danced, they'd kissed—but she'd managed to stay out of bed with him and still retain the friendship or flirtation or whatever it was. She had created the distance, though she hadn't really known why. Or else she'd never admitted why until now.

It all came back to Roc.

He wasn't Roc.

No one was. She'd learned that painfully in all the long and lonely nights since he had left. She had never known, never imagined, the torture of lying alone at night, remembering him, the hard-muscled length of his body, the whisper of his breath, the excitement of his touch, the magic of his kiss. The simple sweetness of falling asleep in his arms, of dreaming there, of awakening to find herself still held so tenderly.

Her fingers started shaking again despite her efforts to still them. His passions always ran so deep. He had loved the sea, the water, diving, the hunt, the adventure.

And once upon a time he had loved her. She had lost that. And she could probably never have it back. It had been a mistake to come, and she should leave as quickly as possible. She had to get away from him. It hurt more to be near him than it did to be away. She had betrayed him. Once he had loved her so deeply, but now he seemed to despise her with the same fierce energy. She couldn't let herself dream about what had been....

Because it was gone. All gone. All that remained was the look he had given her tonight. As if she were a cobra with a forked tongue.

She shivered suddenly, looking around the cabin. Was she

locked in here? He had said that he wouldn't take her to port, so what did he mean to do with her?

Maybe he was waiting for her to go to him, to beg for mercy. Never! She hadn't completely lost her pride.

And her fingers were still shaking. She didn't really know him anymore. Didn't know his heart or his feelings—or if he was sleeping with the very pretty blond woman she had seen on deck.

So what should she do?

Wait. She just had to wait. Eventually he would come back. He had to, didn't he?

"So that's Melinda Davenport," Bruce said, shaking his head. He'd been standing by the port side railing when Roc came slamming out of his cabin.

Roc breathed deeply, studying his first mate, determined not to reveal the turmoil of his emotions to anyone, especially his best friend.

"Trellyn," he said softly.

"Trellyn?" Bruce's eyebrows shot up.

Roc shrugged. "It seems she never divorced me."

"Oh. Well, surely you two can rectify that. Next time we pull into Fort Lauderdale or Miami, you can see an attorney."

"Right," Roc agreed. He walked to the rail, his fingers curling around the polished wood as he looked out to sea.

He should head for port right now. Get her off the boat. The *Crystal Lee*'s sixty feet didn't provide enough room for the two of them to be together.

"She must be spying for her father," Bruce surmised.

"Must be."

"So, we get rid of her quickly, right?"

"We should."

"But we don't?"

Roc spun around and leaned against the rail, crossing his arms over his chest. He was definitely feeling a little malicious. "She wanted to come aboard. We'll keep her aboard for a while."

Bruce shook his head. "You're the captain."

"Right."

"She is Davenport's daughter."

"Right. But she's on *my* boat. And, startling as it seems, she's still *my* wife."

"You mean that you're still in—"

"I'm not still anything," he said impatiently. "But I'm not sailing into any port, either. We were scheduled to dive tomorrow—we'll dive."

Connie came around the corner, looking at them both with grave concern. "So you do know her?" she asked Roc.

"Know her?" Bruce snorted. "Inside and out!"

"She's my ex-wife," Roc told Connie.

"Only she isn't his ex anymore," Bruce said, shaking his head worriedly again.

"How can you suddenly undo being an ex?" Connie asked.

Peter Castro came around the corner next. "You get married again," he told Connie. He looked at Roc. "*¿Que pasa, Capitano?*"

"You married her again already?" Connie asked, totally confused.

Bruce gave her an amused look. "Connie, don't be so dense. He never divorced her. She never divorced him. And neither one of them ever stays on land long enough to read a newspaper or collect the mail, so they both assumed they were divorced."

"Davenport's daughter!" Peter said with a soft whistle. "Well, she's spying. She has to be."

"We have to get rid of her," Connie said.

"He doesn't want to," Bruce said mournfully.

"But she's obviously come to see where you're searching! She'll go back and tell her father, and they'll both be after the *Contessa Maria* right where we're looking," Connie told Roc, her brows furrowed.

"Don't let her take you for a ride, my friend," Peter warned him.

Roc sighed, irritated. "She isn't taking me anywhere. And she isn't going to tell her father anything, because I'm not letting her go back to him until after I've made my claim."

Connie gasped. "Can we keep her that long? Isn't that kidnapping?"

"She did come aboard voluntarily, right?" Roc said.

"Well, technically, we did haul her up in a fishing net," Bruce reminded him.

Suddenly Roc smelled smoke. The others smelled it at the same time. "Dinner!" Connie cried. "Oh, no! Marina asked me to watch the potatoes!" She whirled around, running down the deck to hurry down the stairs to reach the galley.

"I think," Roc said, "that dinner seems to be more than ready. We should go eat."

"But what about...your wife?" Bruce asked him.

"She's not locked in. If she's hungry, she'll find her way to the galley."

"She could find her way to a lot of other places."

"Not with all of us up and ready to stop her."

"Are we staying up all night?"

"I'll see that she doesn't go where she shouldn't," Roc said softly.

"Oh," Bruce murmured. "Oh..."

"No *oh!*" Roc said wearily. "I'll just be keeping my eye on her."

"Be careful now."

"She's five feet eight and maybe a hundred and thirty pounds. I've got five inches and eighty pounds on her. I'll be all right."

"Right. And fire coral looks delicate and beautiful, but touch it, and you've got one hell of a burn!"

"Bruce! I left the lady, remember? I'll be all right." He refrained from mentioning that it had half killed him to do so and only his pride had kept him from going back to her.

He should just have dragged her along. After all, he was bigger, as he had told Bruce.

He might have carried her away....

But he couldn't have changed things. No amount of anger or muscle could have swayed her from her father.

Bruce studied him and grinned. "Well, I wouldn't be all right if she were in *my* cabin. I would never sleep. I'd sit there all night and—ouch!'' He broke off as Peter's elbow connected with his ribs. ''Hey!''

''She's his ex-wife, not yours!'' Peter reminded him pointedly.

''Not an *ex,* remember?'' Bruce insisted in return.

Roc let out a groan of exasperation. ''She may not be an ex, but my days with the Davenports are long over. Let's have dinner.''

''Without her? We're really going to let her starve?'' Bruce asked unhappily.

''It's my guess she'll come prowling out in a few minutes. It will be hard for her to do much spying if she just hides out in my cabin, right?''

Bruce shrugged.

''Let's go.''

In the galley, Roc sat at the big boothlike table that ran down half the port side length of the combined galley and dining room and found Marina Tobago staring at him with her dark, soulful eyes as she set bowls of potatoes and vegetables and plates of grilled grouper on the table. He smiled as he sat, and didn't say anything. Peter slid in near Roc. Connie set the salad on the table and sat down, too. Bruce cleared his throat and took a seat opposite Roc. Joe Tobago, tall, burned bronze, sat down next to Bruce. ''Eh, Captain. Roc, my friend!'' he said softly, his Bahamian singsong accent pleasant and melodious. ''Just what do we say if this mermaid from the sea talks to us?''

It was finally too much. Roc started to laugh. ''I don't know. It depends on what she says. Joe, if she wants to discuss the weather, discuss it. If she asks how you cook your grouper, Marina, just go ahead and tell her. If she wants to know anything about our boat or our search for the *Contessa,* tell her that she has to come to me. If she offers to help with the dishes, let her!''

Marina grinned. ''Davenport's daughter does the dishes?''

''She's very good aboard a boat,'' Roc said, the words softer than he had intended. But she *was* good. Melinda loved the water. She loved the reefs, loved snorkling and diving for treasure. She could handle herself in any motorboat or sailboat; she loved to fish—and she had never shirked a bit of the cleanup in anything. He supposed he had to credit Davenport for that. Despite their differences, there were many things Roc had admired about the man. He didn't have a prejudiced bone in his body; he judged both men and women on their abilities. He demanded as much from himself as he had asked from any of his crew, and if he had ever been more demanding of anyone, it had been Melinda. In many ways, she was like her father. She loved adventure, loved people and was always intrigued by anything new and different. She would taste any dish of food, dive into any treasure hunt—just as she had dived into his net!

He shrugged, still determined to give no hint of emotion. "She knows what she's doing. If she gets in your way, just put her to work."

"We're diving tomorrow, though," Connie said worriedly. "We haven't come up with anything but that old World War Two hunk on the sonar. Nothing to prove. But still, she's going to know where you go in, and if we find anything..." Connie trailed off and paused a minute. "Well, her father was awfully quick to steal a find from you once before!"

"I told you, we don't let her go until the claim is made," Roc reminded her.

"And how do we manage that? Sit on her? At some point we're going to have to make port for supplies!"

"I'll handle things!" he said softly.

Marina sniffed audibly. The table fell silent. "Who's going down tomorrow?" Peter asked.

"Marina and Joe can stay aboard, the rest of us will dive. Then Connie and Bruce can stay aboard the next day, and I hope we'll have something to show for our efforts soon."

"You're still convinced we're looking in the right place?" Joe asked.

"More convinced than ever," Roc said firmly.

"Roc," Joe said softly, leaning forward with a piece of fish speared on his fork. "I trust your judgment, but why can't we find anything with the sonar equipment?"

Roc shrugged, stretching across the table to pour iced tea into his glass. He had nearly grabbed one of the icy beers in front of him, but he had already swallowed a fair amount of rum—instant reaction to Melinda. He wanted his wits about him for the rest of the night.

"I've always been convinced that the *Contessa* went down here. Everything I've found convinces me that they were much farther north than the historians have argued when the storm first hit. Now those letters from that sailor to his sister have been uncovered, and he was convinced that they were farther north than their captain believed, and that's what he put in the letter. Anyway, I have a hunch. I had it the minute I first heard of the *Contessa*. She's within ten miles of us here, I swear it. And I'm going to find her."

"And everyone else in the world is going to be on top of us very soon, now that the letter's common knowledge," Bruce commented.

"Like our...guest," Connie said.

Roc smiled and looked at Marina, who had taken her place beside her husband. "If she does ask you about the grouper, make sure you tell her, OK? It's absolutely delicious, Marina."

"Thanks, Captain," Marina told him. Her eyes were still worried.

"Actually, I think she *should* do dishes, don't you?" he asked Marina.

"I don't mind—"

"Stowaways should work, so I've always thought."

"But," Connie reminded him, "she hasn't shown up to have dinner, so how can we make her wash the dishes?"

"Hmm. That is a dilemma," Roc agreed. "All right, well, we'll wait until she actually eats a meal to make her wash the dishes. How's that?"

"We'll see," Marina commented. She reached across the table and tapped his plate. "If it's so delicious, eat."

"Yes, ma'am!" Roc said, and speared a big bite of grouper. He chewed it, swallowed and smiled. "I'm eating!"

He finished his fish quickly, talked idly about the dive as he ate his salad, and then pushed the potatoes around on his plate—

Connie had forgotten to keep her eye on them, and they did have a slightly burned taste. He drained his tea, then rose, thanking Marina again, repeating that the meal had been excellent. He set his dishes on the small counter by the small sink and very small dishwasher, then made his way up the steps to the main deck.

Well, Melinda hadn't appeared for dinner. Maybe she'd managed to carry a stash of candy bars in her bathing suit or something.

Maybe she was afraid of his crew.

No, not Melinda.

Maybe she hadn't been ready to face him again yet, and then again, maybe she had been waiting for an invitation, for him to come back, to beg her to forget his bad manners and please grace them all with her presence.

No way.

Pride must cometh before a fall, but it was a hell of a good thing to cling to. He wasn't begging Melinda Davenport—Trellyn—to do anything. Not again.

He had begged her once. He'd begged her to come with him. And either she hadn't believed that he would really go...

Or else she hadn't cared.

He leaned over the rail, looking out at the coming night. The sun had nearly set. The sea was dark, mysterious. The air was cool and light and refreshing on his cheeks. There were just the remnants of the sunset on the horizon, beautiful streaks of gold and red and rust. The anchor had been cast, and they were stationary, just rolling slightly on the gentle waves. It was a beautiful night, a spectacular one, really.

A lot like the first night he had seen her.

He'd had a month off from working for Davenport and had been working with Bruce and Connie on his own when he'd received a message from Davenport. He was ready to start up again, and if Roc could meet him in Largo on the following Friday, Davenport would appreciate it. He, Bruce and Connie had just finished bringing up the personal property of a Connecticut man whose yacht had gone down in the Florida Straits, so he wouldn't be leaving in the midst of anything, and working with Davenport was an incredible experience. He always learned something new.

In Largo, Jinks Smith, Davenport's cook and all-around man, came to pick him up in Davenport's dinghy. Davenport's boat was anchored just out of the harbor. Roc had climbed aboard, completely unaware that anything—everything—was about to change in his life. He was wearing cutoffs and sandals, and his gear was in a pile in front of him, when Davenport came out of the main cabin, greeting him with a warm handshake, telling him about the treasure they would be hunting for in the ensuing months.

Then he had met Melinda.

The sun had been like this. And she had been a dark silhouette against the blazing red horizon. All he had seen at first had been her lithe shape. She had been a shadow moving with sensual grace across the bloodred horizon, reaching her father, slipping her arms around him. Then she had been a shadow no longer. She was wearing a two-piece suit, a figure-hugging bikini. He could remember the color, brilliant aquamarine, like her eyes. She was exquisitely shaped. She'd just finished diving, he imagined, because her hair was still wet, only a few long strands dry and flying free to catch the dying sun.

And she was hugging Davenport....

A spiral of jealousy had curled into Roc's stomach almost instantaneously, since he hadn't known, at that first meeting, who she was. Jonathan Davenport was an even twenty years his daughter's senior, a man of forty-one that year, and as Roc knew that his employer had a daughter but had never seen her, he'd assumed that Melinda was the older man's latest fling. He had to admit being a little resentful that Jonathan could acquire such an elegant young creature.

But then Jonathan had quickly disentangled himself from her and introduced them. "Roc, meet my daughter, Melinda. She'll be with me from now on. Melly, Roc Trellyn. He's my right hand. You two be sure to get along with each other now."

She'd been right in front of him. Blue-green eyes, dazzling, her hair like endless waves of gold in the firelit sunset. He'd never been shy with the opposite sex; he'd had his share of relationships, and he'd imagined that at his age—twenty-eight, back then—his head controlled both his heart and his loins. He'd kept his affairs unemotional because he'd never met anyone who fascinated him more than the lure of the sea.

But that had been before Davenport's sea-siren daughter. His head hadn't had a chance against his heart and his loins.

She looked at him. Just like a princess from the sea.

Those aquamarine eyes touched his with instant challenge. She reached out a delicate, golden hand and touched his, then pulled quickly away. "How do you do, Mr. Trellyn."

Her voice was cool, completely disinterested. She turned back to her father, apparently annoyed that they were not alone. "I didn't realize you were busy, Father. I think I'll shower now. We can talk later, when you're not involved with the help."

If she'd slapped him, she couldn't have made her feelings any plainer.

In fact, come to think of it, he'd been itching to slap her back at the time.

However, he'd managed to keep his cool, though Davenport had been furious with her for her lack of manners. He'd apologized to Roc, explaining, "My ex-wife, her mother, was just killed in an accident. It's no excuse for her behavior, really...." He shrugged. "I've had her with me often over the years, of course. She's a phenomenal diver, you'll see. She's out of college now, and she'll be with us full time."

Full time. Full torture.

Well, the sea siren had been nothing but a bitch to him, so at first he had managed to steer clear of her easily enough. She barely spoke to him, and when she did, it was in a condescending tone. But once, when they'd made port in Jamaica, he'd left the ship in a suit and tie, having met an old friend from his University of Miami days on the beach earlier and made plans to go out. He hadn't returned until the next morning. She had been helping Jinks serve breakfast, and his eggs had landed right on his lap.

"Sorry!" she told him.

What a lie! He'd leaped up, the hot food beginning to burn through his swim trunks.

"Let me cool you off."

And she had, dousing him with a pitcher of water.

Perhaps he'd lost it a little bit there. He'd gripped her by the upper arms and told her quite frankly that she was a spoiled little brat, and if she did something like that to him again, he would damned well see that she had a burning rear end.

She turned the color of flame, wrenched free from him and disappeared. Jinks had been there, but it seemed he never said anything to Davenport about the incident.

And neither did Melinda.

Two days later they clashed again. Melinda had gone down to a wreck and stayed too long. The others had been concentrating on a map. Roc—who, despite himself, always had half an eye on her—was aware that her tanks held only thirty minutes of air.

He went down quickly himself, only to find her trying to free a gold chain from some twisted metal. He caught her hand, and she spun on him, shocked, furious. He pointed to her watch, and she wrenched free, clearly furious with him.

And then her air gave out. She began to struggle, and he forced her to share his air. Finally, slowly, once she calmed down, he led them to the surface.

Well, needless to say, she hadn't thanked him. She was furious and convinced that, if he'd just left her alone, she could have surfaced on her own.

He could have throttled her then and there, but instead he somehow managed to swim away.

And he still kept quiet to her father.

Then, after the next day, it didn't really matter, because that was the day they came into Bimini and stayed at the huge hotel by the casino. He'd taken his key from the desk and gone up to his room to start putting his things away. But when he went to put his shaving equipment in the bathroom, he found the shower occupied. Melinda was just stepping out of it, blond hair damp, curling slightly around the perfect oval of her face. His eyes, of course, didn't stay on her face. They fell. He felt the tension she always aroused in him tighten and spiral incredibly. Damn her. She was a witch. He couldn't begin to understand the attraction, and he forced his eyes back to hers.

She snatched up a towel. "How dare you?"

"Me!" he snapped. "I was given this room!"

"Well, I was given it, too, so you can just get out. Anyway, I don't believe you! How can you just stand there? My God, you did this on purpose—"

"Get off it, princess! I'd just as soon burst in on a barracuda!"

He'd managed to turn around and stride to the bedroom, gritting his teeth, feeling every muscle in his body clench with fury…and frustration.

But then something amazing happened. He heard his name spoken very softly.

"Roc?"

He turned. She was wrapped in a huge white towel, and she was staring at him, a liquid glimmer in her beautiful eyes.

"I'm—I'm sorry. I've been wretched to you since you came. I didn't mean to be, and I apologize. It's just that you're so close to my father, and I need him now, and I—" She paused, a bit of a smile curving her lips. "I was jealous."

His stomach knotted. She was beautiful and vulnerable and suddenly as soft as silk. He knew right then that he was in trouble. He should stay exactly where he was, tell her that he accepted her apology and that he was sorry about her mother, and then he should walk out as quickly as possible. If he didn't he would be trapped. For eternity. He would taste her sweet forbidden fruit and find himself hopelessly drugged on it.

But there were tears in her eyes. And he felt compelled to walk forward, compelled to take her into his arms. "I'm sorry," he heard himself saying very softly. "About your mother. You have behaved abominably, though, so I can't apologize for my own behavior." She almost smiled. His arm was around her, and somehow he swept her up to his lap, and she leaned against his shoulder. "Your father told me about your loss."

"Did he tell you everything?" she whispered. "That Mother was drunk? That she caused the accident?"

"No," he murmured.

Her pain seemed to streak through him. "I tried!" she whispered. "I tried for so many years! But she kept—drinking. I must not have been there enough. I must have been a rotten daughter—"

"Hey, hey! Stop that! Melinda, you can't blame yourself, and no one else can blame you, either. You have to be sorry, you have to miss her, but you have to remember that alcoholism is a disease!"

Her eyes looked into his, so naked, so vulnerable, so trusting. Then she was sobbing softly, and he found himself kissing those tears from her cheeks. "It's all right, it's all right...."

Her arms were tight around his neck. The towel she was wearing was slipping away, and he was still clad in nothing but trunks and sandals, and the fiery pressure of her body was against his, her naked breasts a torment against his chest, the nipples so hard, tempting his flesh. Then his kiss found her lips, and she returned it passionately. Her mouth parted for his, and his tongue delved deeply into the sweetness of her. Deeply, deeply...

He was losing himself, and it didn't seem to matter. The towel was gone completely, having fallen somewhere, and they were stretched out on the soft, comforter-covered bed. She seemed to know exactly what she was doing, returning kiss for kiss, her fingers moving sensually over his shoulders and back. His kiss began to stray, finding the wonderful silken texture of her throat, closing over her breasts, tasting, taunting. She pressed against him, soft, sweet, yielding, so enticing, her body arching to his touch.

He was fascinated by the woman he held in his arms, tempted beyond measure. He couldn't taste enough of her as his lips and tongue traveled the length of her, resting intimately here and there. Her fingers remained upon him, her touch erotic, her cries compelling, her warmth exciting and inviting. She writhed, twisted, called his name....

He could have drowned in her more swiftly than he would

have been lost in any sea. The scent of her hair, of her flesh, drove him wild. Yet with all the hunger he was slow, wanting her to want him with the same fierce fever. And it seemed that she did.

He didn't take her until he couldn't bear the aching a minute longer. And when he did, he was stunned, but it was too late. He could have shot them both before he could have risen and left her. She was stiff, startled. She had known, of course, but perhaps she hadn't realized *exactly* what she would feel, or that something so incredibly sweet could suddenly be so incredibly painful. But she clung to him, gritting her teeth, and he whispered to her, softly, gently, kissing her, caressing her. And in time she was with him again, the anguish having ebbed, the fire having been lit once again. A blaze so fierce...

When it burst upon him, he felt almost as if he'd never made love before, it was so volatile, explosive, shattering, sweet, to be with her. Yet even as the sheen of heat cooled on his body, he was ready to kick himself. Davenport's daughter. He'd tried so damned hard...

Bull.

He'd wanted her, needed her, from the first moment she had moved so gracefully into his life. But she might have told him, warned him, said something. So he was a little bit angry with her, and when the wonder and excitement were gone, she got angry, too, telling him that she'd had the right to choose to be with him, the right to choose not to be with others.

"You don't owe me anything," she assured him, trying to drag the covers around herself. She could be so damned dignified when she chose.

"It's not a matter of owing!" he said angrily. "It's a matter of—"

Of what, he wasn't sure.

"You can't be afraid of my father!"

"Of course not!"

She swallowed hard, looking away. "I knew I wanted you!" she whispered very softly. "I was horrible because of it. The night you stayed out, I was so jealous, that was why I—"

"What?"

"Well, it was why I dumped the eggs on you. And the water, of course. I didn't want you—out with another woman."

He started to laugh then. Intrigued. And in a matter of minutes she was in his arms again, and the magic was still there, stronger, greater.

She didn't want to say anything to her father right away, so they didn't. But by the end of a week, the lying, the not speaking, bothered Roc. He told her that it was going to be all or nothing. He loved her, he believed that she loved him, and they were going to be married.

She had no argument with him. She smiled, her beautiful eyes so dazzling, and she leaped into his arms. In all of his life, he had never been so happy.

But things change....

Leaning against the rail now, Roc realized that the sun had finally gone down. Stars were appearing. The night was blanketed by darkness, all color gone except for that spattering of stars.

"That was then and this is now!" he reminded himself.

He turned. The boat was quiet. He'd been standing at the rail forever, and they'd all let him be. There were no more sounds of clanking dishes, footfalls or conversation.

They'd all gone to bed, he surmised, leaving him to his thoughts.

So now what was he going to do? Bright guy. He had left Melinda in his cabin. There was a nice comfortable bed in there...with Melinda in it.

The thought made his pulse quicken, and he almost groaned aloud. Comfortable, all right. Sometimes he could forget the fights, but he had never managed to forget the feel of her at night, the silken softness of her flesh, the feel of her hair, long and lush and taunting against him. Her curves, her derriere thrust against him, the fullness of her breast in his hand...

Bright, bright boy. He'd even gone to college! Then he'd gone and stuck his ex-wife in his own comfortable cabin, where she was probably sleeping like a kitten while he stood out on deck in the middle of the night in torture.

No, she wasn't sleeping. Not like a kitten. Not at all.

From his position by the port side rail he could see the door to his cabin. Moving back a hair, he could still watch and yet be fairly certain that he couldn't be seen in turn.

Yes...

It was cracking open. The door to his cabin was cracking open.

And there was Melinda. Looking out carefully. Listening. She was very still for several long moments. Then she slipped into the pale starlight and paused, listening and waiting again.

She still looked like a sea sprite, slim and elegant, so innocent in white, that cloud of golden hair gleaming even in such dim lighting. Her delicate face turned, her head cocked. At last she seemed satisfied and headed for the stairway to the living cabin.

Slowly, silently, he followed her.

Was she hungry at last? Trying to raid the galley now, when the crew were resting?

No...

She was hungry, all right, he thought angrily. For information. Little witch! She was heading swiftly down the next ladder, down to the lowest deck.

Down to where they kept their sonar equipment.

He followed, still in silence. Waited until she stood right before the equipment, studying it, leaning closer to carefully view the screen.

He came up behind her, stopping just an inch away from touching her.

"Looking for something?" he whispered politely.

A gasp seemed to choke her. On instinct, she started to run.

On instinct, he went after her, catching her when she reached the ladder, pulling her down.

She lost her balance, and he lost his.

And they crashed together to the floor.

Three

Perhaps he should have felt some sympathy for her—despite his efforts to swing around as they fell, she hit the floor first, with him stretched out on top of her. And they landed hard, but she didn't cry out. She simply stared at him, furious and outraged, in the strange green light from the sonar equipment.

He should have felt some sympathy—except that she had been spying.

He didn't ease his weight completely off her, but he did slide to one side, resting an elbow comfortably on the floor while he smiled at her, his eyes slightly narrowed.

"Isn't this romantic?" he said softly.

Her teeth ground together audibly. "Romantic? You're breaking every bone in my body."

"Imagine. If you'd kept your bones where they should have been, they'd be in no danger of breakage now."

"Would you get off me, please?" Aquamarine eyes flashed with fury into his.

His smile deepened as the rest of his muscles stiffened. Maybe he should move. He could feel her warmth, each subtle shift of her body. As furious as he was, he still felt the urge to throttle her being overwhelmed by the urge to strip her then and there and make love to her by the ethereal green light.

"Spies have been hanged throughout the centuries, you know," he informed her politely. "Tortured, and then hanged. Or maybe shot."

"I wasn't spying."

"Oh, right. You were looking for the head."

Her eyes flashed again, and she shoved her hands against his chest. Determined, he didn't move.

"I could kick you!" she reminded him.

"I know," he replied. "Forewarned is forearmed." He shifted his weight over her body in such a way that she couldn't possibly move enough to do him any real harm.

"Roc—"

"Melinda."

She inhaled deeply, then exhaled on a long note of exasperation.

"You've been spying, Melinda."

"I was picked up in your net—"

"You swam into that net on purpose. You knew exactly what you were doing. You were fully aware that this boat was out here searching for the *Contessa,* and I'm willing to bet you even suspected it might be *my* boat. Of course, if it hadn't been, I can just imagine the sweet smiles and wide-eyed innocence you would have given the captain—any captain, from a toothless old salt to a green-behind-the-ears young lad. Then you would have set to until you knew exactly what the crew had discovered, at which point you would have brought all the news back to Papa. Of course—"

He broke off at her sudden flurry of motion, as he felt the sudden sting of pain and heard the crack of her palm against his cheek.

He stroked his cheek, his eyes on fire as he stared at her.

"Davenport must be getting pretty desperate!" he said softly. "He was willing just to drop you off in the middle of the ocean and assume that you'd make it safely aboard in a fishing net!"

She was aiming at him again; he knew it. This time he caught her hand before it could fly. There seemed to be a glistening of tears in her eyes when she retorted, "This has nothing to do with my father! He didn't let me out to swim into any fishing net!"

"Oh, Melinda! I know you're half fish, but don't expect me to believe that anyone just swam this far out—"

"I didn't say that! I said my father had nothing to do with this. It was my idea."

"To come spy?"

Every sleek muscle beneath him seemed to tighten. Once again, he could hear that furious grinding of her teeth.

"You're not going to have any canines left," he warned her. "And if I remember correctly—"

"I never bit you!" she lashed out.

"Well, we do have different memories of our relationship, don't we?" he asked politely.

She surged against him in a sudden, strong fury. She was very slim, but wiry, and she nearly toppled him.

Uh-uh. He wasn't moving.

"If you don't get off of me...!" she raged.

"What *are* you going to do?" he inquired. "Call Daddy?"

"Off!" she demanded, grasping the bare flesh of his arms, nails digging as she shoved at him.

He caught her wrists. Stared into her wild eyes. "How about asking politely?"

"You are a hateful human being."

"That's not asking anything, and it's not in the least polite."

"I'm warning you—"

"And I'm warning you, Melinda," he said impatiently. "This is my boat. You're a damned stowaway and spy, and I should have you arrested."

"I wasn't spying—"

"Well, there's a head in my cabin, and the galley is on the deck above us. What could you possibly be doing down here?"

"Looking for the radio," she said.

"Have to tell Daddy you're safe?" he asked.

She ignored that. "Would you *please* be so kind as to let me up?" she asked.

He thought that one over. Anger wasn't helping him. Maybe it was just making things worse. Being this close to her seemed to tie his muscles in knots, boil his blood and cause a definite rise in his libido.

He couldn't stay where he was much longer. Not unless he wanted her to know just how exactly and completely she was on his mind—and in his system.

"That was fairly polite," he acknowledged. He got swiftly to his feet and reached a hand down to her. She started to rise on her own, but he impatiently grasped hold of her wrist with a little growl and dragged her up. Maybe it was better; maybe it was worse. The twelve inches between them now didn't seem like much at all. He wasn't touching her, but his body could still feel the warmth where they had been touching. He was suddenly more aware of her sweet, clean scent. Connie's soap and talc, he thought, but scents were different on different women, and this was all Melinda.

"May I use the radio?" she asked.

"No. But I will radio your father for you."

He started to walk by her. Maybe she had miscalculated; the radio was at the helm. Or maybe she *hadn't* miscalculated. She had come down here to check out his progress before going to the radio.

"Roc, if you'll just let me call myself—"

"I told you, I'll do it."

"But I wasn't with my father!" she cried softly.

He had reached the first rung of the ladder, and he paused, hearing a note of desperation in her voice.

And also a note of the truth.

He stared at her.

"All right. So just who did drop you off in the middle of the ocean, assuming that you'd be picked up okay?"

She hesitated. "Does it really matter?" she finally asked softly. "If you'll just let me use the radio—"

"No, I just won't," he said flatly. He left the ladder and came back to stand before her. "Who were you with?"

"It's none—"

"Who?"

"Eric Longford," she said in a rush.

Longford.

Great waves of heat and fury suddenly came sweeping over him, like a massive tidal wave.

Longford.

He hated the man. Eric Longford was a tall, tanned beach bum, in Roc's opinion. He hadn't ever had two thoughts of his own, but he somehow managed to be in the right places with the right people at the right time to make a decent living from the sea. Roc and he had always been civil to one another in company, but the tension had always been there between them. Roc had always considered the man dangerous. The type to create huge waves right where the signs commanded *No Wake!* He was a careless diver, never gauging his time and oxygen. He was completely heedless of the delicate coral reefs around Florida and the Bahamas, casting anchor anywhere.

And worst of all, he was a womanizer who had always had his eye on Melinda, and Roc would have thought she had the good sense not to become involved with such a man.

"Eric Longford?" he repeated, trying to fight the fury that continued to wash over him. Had Longford already been in bed with his ex-wife?

No, not his ex. His *wife!*

He wanted to kill the man.

She must have seen it in his eyes, because she backed away from him. "It isn't what you think—" she began.

"How do you know what I think?" he grated out.

"Not that it matters!" she suddenly lashed back. "You walked out on me—"

"No, lady, I didn't walk out on you. You chose another man over me—it happened to be your father, but you made the choice just the same. And now—*Longford!*"

Her hands on her hips, she stood very tall and straight and regal and faced him. "You've been sailing around for three years now without the least concern for my welfare, and I'm sure you have no intention of giving me an accounting of how you spent your time. For the moment, you've chosen to keep me a prisoner on this boat. Therefore, you owe me the courtesy of letting me use your radio.''

"I owe you the courtesy?'' he exclaimed, his hand clenching into a fist. He raised it, swore suddenly, then turned around and slammed his hand into the wall.

His damned knuckles hurt like hell.

"Yeah, let's radio Longford!'' he said. "The ass left you in the middle of the ocean, crawling into another man's net, but by all means, let's let him know that you're all right!''

"I told you,'' she said very softly, and there was a note of pleading in her voice, "this was *my* idea.''

"Maybe I was off before. Way off. Your father would never have let you pull such a dangerous stunt!''

She backed away again. "Roc, please—''

"Is your father somewhere out there, too?'' he asked her impatiently.

"I don't—''

"Bull! Is he out there?''

She turned away, glancing at the sonar screen. "I, er, I think so.''

"Fine. We'll radio your father. He can call Longford if he wants.''

He reached for her hand, unaware how angry he still was until she cried out at his touch. He forced himself to ease his hold on her.

"Come on!'' he commanded.

"I am coming,'' she returned stiffly. "Where else would I be going?'' she asked with aggravation.

"And shush up, will you? I have a hardworking crew, and they're sleeping.''

"You're the one who's shouting!''

Shouting. He wanted to shout. Scream. Tear his hair out. Tear *her* hair out. Smash Longford right in his tanned jaw.

He dragged her with him up to the living cabin, where she seemed to pull back.

Maybe she could catch the delicious aroma of dinner, still in the air.

Good. He hoped she was absolutely starving.

He pulled her out to the main deck, then directed her to the steps leading to the helm. She climbed as quickly as she could, all too aware of the angry man behind her.

He joined her a minute later, pushing her aside so he could take a seat in the captain's chair and pick up the mouthpiece for the radio. He switched it on, found his frequency and identified himself as the *Crystal Lee*. He stared at Melinda. "What's your father sailing on these days? I heard he just bought a new boat."

She was silent.

"Melinda."

She sighed. "I believe he's on the *Tiger Lilly*. But if you'd just let me do this myself—"

"I won't," he assured her. He flicked the radio on, identified himself once again and called the *Tiger Lilly*.

A few minutes later he heard Davenport's fuzzy voice. "Roc?" He sounded puzzled.

"Yes. I wanted to let you know I have something of yours. Over."

There was silence, then static.

"Melinda? Is it Melinda? Over."

"She'll be with me for a while. She's fine."

He was startled when he *thought* he heard a sigh of relief. "So she is with you. Over."

"Yes. Over."

He looked at Melinda, waiting for Davenport to make some protest, to tell him that he would be motoring his way over in the dead of night to pick up his daughter. Instead, Davenport sounded relieved.

"Melinda's alone? Over."

"Yes. Over."

Another sigh of relief. Roc sat back, staring at Melinda. She was very tall, straight, still. Staring at him with her blue-green eyes glittering, her chin high.

Then he realized something that almost made him smile. Davenport hated Longford almost as much as he did himself. Old man Davenport wasn't upset that Melinda was with him, because it meant she wasn't with Longford.

Longford...

Just thinking the name made his teeth grind together, his muscles tighten. He wanted to know just what she'd been doing with the man.

No, he didn't want to know.

Yes, he did. He wanted her to tell him that it had been entirely innocent!

"Melinda, what in God's name—" Davenport began suddenly, and if he hadn't been so angry himself, Roc might have found his old mentor's outburst amusing, just as it was amusing when Melinda snatched the handheld mouthpiece and shouted quickly, "I'm a grown woman, Dad!"

She was still staring at Roc, who smiled. "Over," he said.

"What?"

"It's a radio communication. You should know that. Tell him 'over.'"

"Over!" she snapped.

There was still silence. Then some static. Then Davenport's voice, amused again. "You're after her, eh, Roc? Over."

"After her? Over."

"The *Contessa*. Over."

"Just searching around, like always. Over."

"Well, good luck, then. Until we meet again. Take care of her for me. Over."

Roc set the mouthpiece into its socket and studied Melinda. "Well, at least he isn't too concerned."

"If you'll excuse me," she said coolly, "it's very late."

Her chin high, nose in the air, she swung around like nobility to slide gracefully away.

He was still sitting in the broad captain's chair. So she thought she was about to disappear? Not on her life.

"Wait a minute!" He reached out, fingers curling around her wrist forcefully. "I did not excuse you!" With a flick of his arm, he dragged her back until she was directly in front of him, still standing, but between his knees.

"What now?" she enunciated crisply.

"I don't trust you, that's what. We'll go down together."

She lifted her arm, indicating the bronzed fingers that remained wound around her wrist. "I can only go so far, you know!"

He released her and stood so quickly that she jumped back, her temper growing.

"I already know you're carrying sonar equipment and that you're looking for the *Contessa!*" she exclaimed in exasperation. "And even if I weren't here and hadn't seen anything, it wouldn't have taken a genius to figure that out! You were the one who always insisted that the *Contessa* was out here, remember? All I've done—"

"Is come aboard to see if I've found her or not, and if so, get away fast enough to turn her over to your father—or Longford!"

"How dare you?" she demanded furiously.

He shrugged. "Mabye you're in business for yourself now."

He knew Melinda. He should have been prepared. Maybe he was prepared; maybe he just wanted her flying into his arms.

She did. Fists flailing, she was a whirlwind, striking out at him. He caught her quickly, crushing her against his body so she couldn't inflict any damage.

Her head fell back. Aquamarine eyes touched his, glistening. Damage...

Without moving a finger, she could inflict it. And despite the torture, he was glad to hold her. Glad to feel her crushed against him.

"I'm not working for anyone!" She exclaimed angrily to him. "And if you weren't such a great ape—"

"You'd beat the truth into me?" he queried.

He was startled by the sudden passion in her voice. "Yes! Yes, that's exactly it. But you are an ape, and I'd appreciate it greatly if—"

"Longford?" he grated out suddenly.

"What difference does it make to you?" she cried in exasperation. "You walked away! You walked right out—"

"No, it wasn't exactly like that. Damn you, Melinda!"

"You left me!"

"No, you left me."

"I didn't move!"

He shook his head. "You didn't have to move. You left me. Geography had nothing to do with it, did it?"

She jerked away with such force that he found himself releasing her. Her back was to him, her head bowed, her hair streaming golden down her back in the moonlight.

"It really is late," she told him.

He bowed, indicating the stairs. "Please, you first."

He couldn't keep the bitterness out of his voice. She swung around, her head high again. "You aren't planning on throwing me down the ladder?" she inquired coolly.

"No. When I find some, I'll just throw you to the sharks. Though I doubt if they'll bite. Like recognizes like, you know."

"Really? Well, here's hoping *you* do fall to them, Captain Trellyn. Sharks can get into a frenzy and feed on each other. I'm sure you know how that works."

He stared at her, suddenly sorry. What should he do? Should he tell her he was so furious about Longford that he couldn't begin to be civil?

No, he didn't dare reveal that kind of emotion to Melinda.

He lifted his hands. "You're right. It's late. How about a truce for what remains of the night?"

She looked at him suspiciously.

He sighed. "I'm serious. I apologize. I'm not tossing you down any ladder, or to any sharks. They might come down with massive indigestion. No, no, just teasing, honest! I wouldn't want to let you go back to your father or Longford in anything less than the absolutely perfect shape in which you arrived."

"Roc Trellyn, if you—"

"Down, Melinda. I'm trying to stop. I'm tired. I wasn't expecting you, so you can't expect my manners to be great. Let's get some rest. Maybe things will improve tomorrow."

She stared at him for a moment, then turned and silently started down the ladder. He followed her.

She headed away from the galley and toward the captain's cabin.

He was right behind her.

She entered his cabin and started to shut the door quickly, but he caught it.

She stared at him. "You did tell me I was supposed to stay in here," she said.

"That's right." He forced the door open and followed her in, then closed it. She backed away from him, right into his desk, her eyes narrowed.

"If you think you can just—"

"Melinda, go to bed."

"You must be joking!"

"About what?" He sat in the chair, hiking his feet up on the desk, folding his hands in his lap and staring at her curiously.

"You're sleeping there?"

"Right here," he said lightly.

She bit her lip, lashes sweeping over her eyes for a minute.

Then she swung around and approached the bunk. It was broad, very comfortable. No room for complaint.

She stretched out, fully dressed, and turned her back on him. Then she swung around and stared at him again within a matter of seconds.

"This won't work."

"I'm very comfortable." He congratulated himself on being one hell of a liar.

"It's a big boat!" she told him.

"I've promised my crew that I'll be responsible for you and your whereabouts."

"Where can I possibly go—"

"Back down below. To the sonar, to our maps and plans."

"I was just—"

"Looking for the radio. I still want to know where you are."

"If I were to move—"

"From right here, I'd catch you!" he said softly.

"But I'm not—"

"Good. Then we can both get some rest."

She expelled another sigh of exasperation, staring at him hard.

"Good night, Melinda."

She swung around once again, her back to him. "This will not work!" she insisted again.

She sounded almost as desperate as he felt.

He leaned his head back. The chair was hard. Uncomfortable. He stared at the bed. Her hair was dry, falling all around her in golden waves. She was curved, tempting, soft, provocative....

He sighed.

She was right. It wasn't going to work. And now...

He clamped down hard on his teeth, swallowing a groan. Damn it!

He was going to sleep!

Despite the fact that the elegant beauty who slept just an arm's reach away in his bed was still his wife...

And despite the fact that he loved her still.

Four

He must have slept at some point during the night, because how else could he have woken up in such terrible pain? His neck hurt, his back hurt—hell, his whole damned body hurt.

And there she was. Sleeping just as sweetly as could be, all sprawled out, a vision in white and gold, arms embracing both his pillows, body cushioned by his mattress, one he'd ordered special, since he spent so much time on the boat.

Swearing softly, he rose, then banged his knee on the desk and swore again. Finally he stared at her.

She was still asleep. She didn't move a hair.

He couldn't take it. Muttering beneath his breath, he stumbled out on deck, where he ran right into Connie, who was heading into the galley in her bathing suit and white robe.

"Good morning!" she said cheerfully, then backed away. "All right, so it's not such a great morning. But I've got the coffee on already. Maybe that will help. Then again, maybe not."

"Coffee sounds great," he muttered, walking past her to the port side of the boat.

"Where are you going?" she called after him.

"For a swim!"

"Now? The sun's barely broken. It will be cold."

"Good!"

He took a swift running leap up to the rail and plunged over.

Salty water greeted him. Nice and cold this early in the morning, even here in the Florida Straits. He plunged downward and downward with his dive, not fighting the momentum. A few seconds later he gave the water a firm shove and broke the surface once again. He swam hard toward the ship, feeling the familiar movements remove some of the aches in his muscles.

It was all her fault. Life had been going all right. At least he'd been sleeping.

Now she was sleeping beautifully while he had suffered the tortures of the damned all night. He didn't feel as if he'd slept a wink. He felt as if he could bite.

He would damned well like to run into his cabin, pick up his sweetly sleeping little beauty and throw her overboard into a nice, crisp awakening!

He reached the aft ladder, twelve feet from the rear of his cabin, and found that Connie was there to greet him once again, this time with a cup of steaming black coffee in her hands.

He accepted it gratefully and leaned on the rail, dripping beside her.

"Well," she said softly, "we thought that maybe you'd gotten lucky last night." She caught his glance and amended her words quickly. "Well, I mean, we thought that maybe there'd been some kind of a reconciliation. But the way that you woke up..." Her voice trailed away, and she looked out over the sea. "It's going to be a great day. A beautiful day for diving."

He grunted his agreement, staring out toward the horizon. For those who had actually slept through the night, it probably was going to be a beautiful day.

Connie started to say something else, but he raised a hand to silence her, then pressed his temple with his thumb and forefinger.

"Did you drink too much?" Connie asked solicitously.

"No, I didn't drink enough," he replied softly. He slid off the railing, slipping a hand around her shoulders. "Did you say breakfast is on? Maybe we should head into the galley while it's still edible.''

''Edible! Oh, the bacon!''

Connie went racing ahead; he followed more slowly.

Maybe breakfast would improve the morning.

Then again, maybe the morning was just doomed.

He seemed to be looking her way.

Melinda instantly dropped the curtain over the porthole again, sitting back on the bed, her heart beating too quickly, then seeming to become very heavy and fall into the pit of her stomach.

They'd looked so close, the two of them, so natural together. Connie handing him coffee, his fingers brushing hers as he took the cup. Then the soft conversation between them, their heads bent, nearly touching.

Melinda inhaled deeply and fought the sudden threat of tears. Well, what had she expected after three years? She'd had him once. And she'd lost him.

She lay back on the bed, still feeling an overwhelming sense of loss. She closed her eyes and wished that it weren't quite so easy to remember the past.

She would never forget the very first time she had seen him, standing beside her father. So tall, so dark, built like steel. She'd never seen a more arresting man, nor had she ever met one who seemed to make her feel quite so young or insecure. Her father seemed to live by his word—Roc Trellyn had been all that Jonathan had talked about since she had come to live with him. But she hadn't wanted to hear about anyone else, not then. She had been too wrapped up in herself, in her own guilt. She hadn't caused the accident....

But she hadn't been home when it happened, and that had added to the guilt. If she hadn't been out, she might have stopped her mother. At least that time. If she had just done something, she might have changed things. She couldn't manage to put her feelings of absolute failure into words, but of all people, her father should have been the one to understand how it was possible to love her mother for being sweet and beautiful and witty—and hate her at the same time. Sharon Davenport had died two days before her thirty-ninth birthday.

Melinda hadn't been able to talk to anyone, but at least, in her father's company, there was someone who had known Sharon, known her well, loved her. Jonathan was someone who could understand, someone she had needed badly at the time. He was removed, of course. He'd been gone for seven years. But he had still cared. He'd still felt the pain.

Melinda had been jealous of Roc Trellyn from the very first time she saw him.

And she had also been absolutely fascinated.

He was older than the college boys she had been dating, seven years older than she was. He was striking, and so assured, mature, his voice deep and strong, his eyes touched with wisdom. He was so handsome, broad at the shoulders, muscled in the right places, slim in others. She wanted to keep her father away from him, but she wanted to be near him herself.

Somewhere along the line, she realized that she simply wanted him. And then the fear of wanting someone so much—especially Roc Trellyn, who seemed to have someone waiting at every port—added to her discomfort. She didn't keep her distance any longer; she seemed intent on picking fights, on making sure that he saw that though others might faint at his feet, she couldn't care less.

But then there had come that day when they had been inadvertently thrown together in the same room, when she had felt his eyes on her, felt the length of her body burn from head to toe. She hadn't known what she intended at first—only to apologize. She had been rotten, she had tried to irritate him, and she had also tried to make sure she didn't pull any of her little tricks in front of her father. Maybe she couldn't have him, but at least they could be friends.

But then he had talked to her, as even her father hadn't talked to her, and it felt as if the weight of the world had been lifted from her shoulders. She could remember staring into the depths of his blue eyes, seeing the passion in them, hearing him reassure her.

Then she could remember wanting him once again. And, at long last, having him...

She trembled suddenly and leaped up from the bed. She strode quickly to the not-so-small head in the Captain's cabin and stood beneath the shower, anxious for the water to wash over her.

There had been no one in the world like Roc. No one to hold her, reassure her, love her. No one with his gently spoken wisdom.

And then again, no one with his shouted commands when he was on to something!

No one more stubborn.

No one fairer to a crew, more willing to listen.

Stop! she warned herself. She didn't dare fall headlong into the trap of wanting him again, of loving him....

Then just why was she here? she challenged herself.

To make sure that the big claim was his this time, that he found his *Contessa,* that she helped to make sure he wasn't cheated a second time....

Because she knew now that her father had been wrong, that Roc's accusations had been hard, but that he had been right to walk away. She hadn't known it then, though; she hadn't seen it. Her father had given Roc his start, trained him like a son. She had only seen Roc turning his back on her father after all that. It had never occurred to her that Jonathan might be wrong, that Roc's words might be true. She simply hadn't been capable of believing any ill of her father. So now...now she had to make sure things did go his way. He had always said everyone else was wrong about the *Contessa.* And he had been right. Now the world would soon be congregating in this vicinity, seeking the lost ship. But by all rights she should be Roc's. Melinda was a good diver, and she really could help.

And was that all she wanted? To fix things? she taunted herself.

No...

She had always wanted Roc. And she still did.

But it was too late. She had known it when she watched him sitting on the rail, his fingers curled around the cup of coffee another woman had given him. Their heads had been bowed, close together. He had laughed softly, touching Connie's shoulder with obvious affection.

Well, what had she expected? It had been a long time. Three years since he had left.

She'd never, ever realized he really meant to go. He'd held her so tenderly that night, made love to her so passionately. And then he had been gone....

And she hadn't been able to believe the ache, the void, the pain.

Only pride had kept her from going after him, that and the fear that he wouldn't want her again once he had left her behind.

The water was still running. She turned it off quickly, stepped out of the shower stall and shivered. Three years, and here she was, in his cabin, a most unwelcome guest—or a prisoner. It all depended on which way one chose to look at it.

And once again he'd managed to walk away. The thought brought tears to her eyes, and she quickly blinked them away.

Well, she wasn't staying in this cabin any longer, not unless he wanted to slide a bolt across the door.

And she could smell the tempting aroma of bacon. It made her stomach somersault as she realized just how long it had been since she had eaten.

She quickly donned her borrowed clothing again, then found his brush on the back of the sink and borrowed that. When she was done, she rummaged until she found an extra toothbrush in a case, and then she stared at herself in the mirror. Her eyes were too wide, too lost, too frightened. She lifted her chin. Better, a little better.

Then she took a deep breath and turned, determined. It was time to face the sea beasts!

Breakfast was on the table, a huge plate of bacon and sausage, muffins, toast and rolls, eggs scrambled with peppers and tomatoes. Despite the food, Roc had his maps out, ten of them in a bound roll. With his finger he traced a course from their position in the Florida Straits past Andros in the Bahamas and onward to a few of the smaller islands. "Now watch," he murmured, flicking the first map over and showing the group a more detailed map of the area, one that identified all the smaller islands, inhabited and not, and the reefs around them, with emphasis on the ones that jutted into the water with little warning, causing danger to ships. "She's here, right around this reef, and as soon as we've cleaned up, that's where I want to head. Joe—" he began, then broke off.

Silently, lithely, she had come into the galley. Bathed, freshened, smelling as sweet as a field of roses, her beautiful face scrubbed clean, her golden hair a mane around her shoulders, Melinda had made her way to them at last.

She ignored him at first, greeting Connie with a cheerful, "Good morning!" Then she looked around at the rest of the crew, her smile in place. She extended a hand to Bruce. "Well, I suppose you all know who I am, and in a rather strange way we've already met, but I'd like to make a few amends and do it a little bit better, if you all don't mind. I'm Melinda Davenport—"

"Trellyn, isn't it?" Connie asked softly.

Melinda flushed a lovely shade of rose. It only added to her charm, Roc decided. "I'm not really sure," she murmured, and hurried on, flashing Connie another smile and starting with Bruce.

"You're Connie's brother, Bruce. She told me that last night, while I was borrowing her clothes. And you...?" she inquired politely, facing Marina and Joe.

She had such a sweet smile on her face. They must all be thinking that he was either a complete bastard or a huge fool not to have managed to get along with her. In fact, they all looked a little hypnotized.

It was time to cut in.

"Joe Tobago and his wife, Marina. And Peter here rounds out my crew. Now if you're—"

"I'm starving," she said softly, smiling once again. "It smells absolutely delicious in here."

Marina nodded, and Bruce suddenly leaped up. "Sit down. I'll get you coffee."

"How nice, thank you, but I can see the pot on the stove. I'll get it myself."

She did so, walking toward the stove, finding a cup, helping herself. She came back to the table and looked down at the map. Roc clenched his teeth and carefully rolled up the lot of them.

"Excuse me," she said softly. "Deep dark secrets."

"You're a spy," he reminded her politely.

"A prisoner now," she said lightly. "Aren't prisoners supposed to be fed?"

"Bread and water," he said flatly.

"Please, sit!" Marina said, casting Roc a stern gaze. "You must be starving. You ate nothing last night. The plates are there, help yourself."

"Thank you," Melinda said, and did so. Roc leaned back. She was comfortable. Just as comfortable as she had been last night, while he had suffered the tortures of the damned in a hard chair. "I do apologize if I was rude to you yesterday," she told Bruce.

"Oh, it's all right, really. You *were* in a net—"

"Enough!" Roc said irritably. "She was caught in a net because she meant to be there. Marina, is there any more coffee over there?"

"Aye, captain!" Marina murmured, going for the coffeepot. Roc stared hard at Melinda, who stared back innocently.

"You look extremely well-rested," he commented.

"It's a very comfortable cabin."

"Bathed and fresh."

"The water pressure in your shower is magnificent," she replied politely. "And I took the liberty of borrowing a toothbrush from the pack of extras under the sink. There were a number of them."

Um. He wasn't the one who kept all the extra toothbrushes aboard, Marina was. But they were kept under the sink in his cabin simply because he had the most room. But he knew that

Melinda must be wondering just how often he entertained in his cabin to keep such a collection of extra toothbrushes.

Good. Let her wonder. He had his own tortured thoughts to live with.

Longford!

Damn! He wanted to gag each time he thought the name. Wanted to pick her up and shake her...

He stood quickly, nearly knocking into Marina and the coffeepot she had just brought so she could pour him more coffee. "Bruce, we need to get under way. Let's pull anchor and start moving."

"Aye, captain!" Bruce agreed.

He paused to let Marina finish filling his cup, and by then Melinda was ready with one of her innocent questions. "So you're diving today? Where are we heading?" Aquamarine eyes, wide, innocent, looked around the cabin.

They'd all nearly dropped their tongues on the floor over her—Bruce, Peter, even Joe. And somehow she seemed to be gaining the sympathy of the women in the crowd. Roc waited for one of them to tell her exactly where they were going to look for the *Contessa*.

But they all seemed to have retained some sense of loyalty. There was silence in the cabin.

He smiled, leaning toward her. "You're not supposed to tell spies what you're up to and where you're going, Ms. Davenport."

Bruce nudged him. "Trellyn," he whispered. "She's still a Trellyn, isn't she?"

Roc raised himself up, meeting her eyes. "I'm not so sure she ever was!" he exclaimed softly; then, despite the liquid beauty of Melinda's eyes, so determined upon his, he swung around to leave the cabin.

She jumped up, following him. "Roc!"

He paused at the steps leading to the upper deck, looking back. They still had an audience.

"What?" he asked impatiently.

"Let me dive."

"You must be insane."

She threw up her arms. "What am I going to do?" she inquired almost desperately. "I'm a prisoner here. Where can I go with any information? Who can I tell?"

"There's still a radio on this boat!" he reminded her.

"And you won't let me use it."

"I won't always be aboard—"

"But your crew—"

"Don't know you—and your loyalty to your father—quite the way I do, Melinda!" he reminded her softly. So softly that their audience couldn't hear him.

It was almost amusing. The whole group of them suddenly seemed to lean forward en masse, trying to catch his words.

"I told you, my father—"

"Right. Longford let you out in the middle of the ocean. That's even worse."

He spun around, determined not to be stopped.

"Roc—"

He swung to face her once again. "Go do the dishes!" he snapped irritably.

She stared at him, her fingers clenching into fists at her sides, her chin still high, her eyes more dazzling, but damp, as if she might really care.

He'd seen those eyes look like that before....

She turned around, and he did likewise, a little blindly, hurrying up the steps to the deck. He headed for the anchor winch and automatically set it in motion, rolling up the heavy anchor from the bottom of the sea. Bruce was quickly there beside him. "Take her up!" Roc said, leaving him to finish the task while he climbed to the elevated helm to stare out at the horizon.

He'd been careful in the last week. He knew right where he wanted to search, but he didn't want to anchor too near the spot by night, and he had changed his anchorage every night so as not to arouse suspicion in those who might be watching him.

Obviously he had been found anyway. Melinda was aboard.

But he hadn't been discoverd actually diving, and that, at least, was good.

Bruce called to him that the anchor was up, and he flipped on the switches for the motor, idled a moment, then took the big wooden wheel and started a course toward the Bahamas, toward a deserted island near the southwest section of the Northwest Providence Channel and a treacherous reef that had once caused danger to the great ships seeking the riches of the New World.

The *Crystal Lee* was a smooth-running, fast boat, and he quickly felt the cool rush of the morning air touching his face, sweeping back his hair. The sun was rising now; it was going to be a hot day, just barely cooled by the sea breezes.

It felt good to stand against the soothing, salt-laden wind. It helped to clear his mind after his difficult night, and it seemed he reached his destination far too soon.

He cut the motor and called down to Bruce to cast the anchor. They were off the reef by a good fifty feet, but the water here was still no more than fifty or sixty feet deep. He hurried down from the helm, only to discover that Melinda was there with the others, dressed once again in her black bathing suit, waiting patiently.

"Bruce, you've checked the tanks?" he asked his friend, staring at Melinda all the while.

"Joe and I did. Checked and rechecked."

His equipment was on the deck. Joe Tobago, who would be staying aboard, reached for Roc's tanks and mask and helped him into them. Connie and Bruce had helped each other, and there was Melinda, giving a hand to Peter.

Roc thanked Joe briefly and accepted his flippers, then found that Melinda was staring at him. "You're not diving," he said curtly.

"But—"

"Go—"

"Don't tell me to go do the damned dishes! I already did them. You can ask Marina!" she informed him in a vehement rush.

"You're still not diving!"

"You can't keep me out of the water!" she cried.

He looked over at Joe. "If you see another boat, any boat,

near us, lock her up somewhere. It could be Longford trying to pull her back out of the sea.''

''Roc, you have no right—''

''I have every right!''

He didn't wait for her reply but sat on the edge of the boat, then rolled backward into the water, setting his mouthpiece into place. Seconds later he was alone, accompanied only by the lulling sound of his regulator as he breathed in and out, sinking lower and lower into the sea. The blue and green seemed to close around him, and the cool, floating feeling that he loved so much entered into him, easing tension swiftly from his limbs. God, it was wonderful. It was another world, where all the rules changed and a man became nearly weightless, where the sweet sound of silence blanketed the harshness of the world above the surface.

He was nearing the reef, with the highest point jagging up to about fifteen feet below sea level, when he heard a sudden whooshing sound.

Another body in motion in the water near him…

Like a small dolphin.

Or a five-foot-eight-inch woman.

He turned his head. There she was. No tanks—neither Joe nor Marina would have betrayed him so far—no mask, no flippers. Just Melinda, with her incredible swimming skills and her near record-breaking ability to hold her breath.

She was swimming below him, golden hair following in her wake. She was as graceful, as fluid as any fish or creature of the sea, and truly, at that moment, she might have been a mermaid, a siren, one of Neptune's daughters, reigning supreme in the beautiful blue-green waters.

Damn her hide!

He plunged downward, swimming after her. She had gone past the reef, over to the other side, where the World War Two shipwreck lay strewn about.

Even as he pursued her, she disappeared inside the hulk.

''Melinda!'' He started to scream her name, nearly choked, then swore at himself for being a fool.

Then he started after her in furious pursuit.

Five

He followed her across the rusting hull and in through a door that hung eerily on half of its hinges. The sunlight that had streaked through the beautiful blue-green water was dimmed within the confines of the rusted old hulk. Crossing a deck filled with cramped living quarters, he came to the point where damage and time had worn the downed ship completely in two. There was a near-barren expanse of sand, with just a few areas of haphazardly thrown seaweeds, coral and delicate, beautifully colored little sea creatures. The rest of the rotten ship had fallen over the shelf and lay another twenty feet deeper, about a hundred yards away.

Melinda was just disappearing over the ledge that led that twenty feet downward.

He caught her halfway down. She stared at him furiously, trying to shake free. How long had she been holding her breath now? It was uncanny.

He forced her to take his mouthpiece. She inhaled a vast supply of air, then tried to escape his hold once again, but he held onto her tightly. He pointed to the surface and let her know that he was taking her there—whether she wanted to go or not.

He gave a good kick, and they went shooting upward together.

His legs brushed hers in the water, and he was startled by the erotic impact that slight touch seemed to have on him. She was sleek here under the sea. Tempting, even as he longed with all his heart to wring her neck.

They broke the surface, and he spat out his mouthpiece. "What do you think—"

"I'm not diving, I'm swimming!" she said irritably.

"What you're doing is dangerous, and you know it!"

She was silent for a moment, her lashes sweeping her cheeks. She knew it was dangerous to crawl around the old hulk the way she'd been doing. She could too easily become trapped by some falling piece of rot.

She opened her eyes again, staring straight at him. "Then what you're doing is dangerous, too!"

"But I have air tanks—"

"And you should still be with someone."

"Well, if I weren't following you around, I *would* be with someone!"

"If you don't let go of me, you're going to drown us both!"

"Ah!" he exclaimed, but his hold on her didn't ease in the least. "That's it. I've got it now. You're not a spy. You're just here to torment me to death so your father—or Longford—has time to move in for the find!"

"I'm not tormenting you—you're tormenting me. And if you'd just let me help you...I'm a damned good diver!"

"Out!" he told her, giving her a shove toward the ship.

"You don't rule the ocean!" she cried, treading water.

He lunged toward her. She started swimming again, at first slipping easily away, since she was unencumbered, but then the added power of Roc's flippers kicked in, and he overcame her about halfway between where they had been and the *Crystal Lee*.

"I said, out of the water!"

"And I said it's a free ocean!"

"Not while you're on my boat."

"I'm not on your boat, I'm in the water."

"If you don't quit arguing with me, I'll haul you out of the water and—"

"Oh, big talk! You wouldn't dare. Your crew would mutiny!"

"I dare just about anything, and you ought to know that by now, so there's just one question left—is that a challenge, Ms. Davenport?"

She jerked free of his hold, trying for a deep dive that would bring her back to the coral shelves, but he caught her first. With a firm hand on her arm, he started swimming hard for the *Crystal Lee*. She was strong, struggling and wriggling like a game fish on a line. But he reached the boat and the ladder, thrusting her toward it, then grabbing hold himself to force her ahead of him. Joe and Marina were on deck, anxiously waiting. Melinda leaped easily aboard, then disappeared into the captain's cabin with a quick nod to the others.

Roc struggled up more slowly, because of his gear. Fine, she was in his cabin. They would have a little privacy.

Right. With everyone on board listening just a few feet away!

"Eh, captain, I give you a hand!" Joe said, quickly coming over to take the tanks.

Roc ripped off his mask, breathing deeply, trying to control his temper. Even as he did so, Connie broke the surface, calling out, "We're coming up. It's a wash so far, Roc. We haven't found a thing."

He gritted his teeth. What was Melinda up to? He hadn't realized it, but an hour had gone by, and she had kept him occupied all that time.

Was that her job? To sabotage his search?

He started for the cabin, but Melinda suddenly burst out of it, a towel around her shoulders. Her eyes met his, and he almost smiled.

He knew her so well.

She'd run to the cabin first for protection. Then she'd realized that it was the one place where he could get her alone—and where she couldn't bat her lashes in hopes of help from the others.

He was still staring at her when Peter and Bruce crawled aboard, too, releasing their tanks, pulling off flippers and masks.

"Nothing," Bruce muttered disgustedly.

"Well, not nothing," Peter said with a shrug.

"We found some skulls," Connie informed him. She shuddered a little. "Eerie. I never came across part of anyone who'd ever been living before."

Bruce leaned against the wall of the elevated helm. "But not a darned thing on the *Contessa.*"

"Actually," Melinda said softly, and suddenly all eyes were upon her, "I think I might have found something. Perhaps it did belong to the German ship, but it seems like it might come from before that...."

Roc, no less amazed than everyone else, watched as she slipped a long sand-encrusted item from the side of her leg, held there by the elastic on her bathing suit.

He strode quickly across the deck. She held it out to him, one brow lifted in a definite challenge, her lip curled into a delicate smile.

"What is it?" Connie cried.

"Tableware of some kind," Melinda said, her eyes still on Roc. He hadn't taken the piece from her; he hadn't said a word.

She extended it to him. He wondered if it was like some kind of an olive branch.

For a long moment he didn't reach for it. Damn her. Down there with no tanks, with him following her, dragging her up.

And she was still the only one among them to come up with anything that might have even a remote possibility of coming from the *Contessa.*

"Roc?" She said his name softly, questioningly. He wasn't even sure the others could hear her.

He took it from her at last. It was heavily encrusted with sand and growth, but he had a hunch. She was right. He didn't think that a relic from the German boat would be so heavily encrusted. It was heavy in his hand, too—and not just from all the sand.

Just as he had always had a feeling about the *Contessa* being in this area, he now had a feeling that the object in his hand was from the lost ship.

"I'll take a look at it," he said, his eyes on hers. "Just where did you pick it up?"

She shrugged, then shook her head. "I'm not sure. I'd have to go back. I'd be more sure, of course, except that I wasn't paying attention at the time. I thought a shark or something was following me. Of course, when I turned back, I saw it was you, but I was nervous and, naturally, forgetful."

"Naturally!" he muttered, and spun away from her. Ignoring all of them, he hurried down the steps to the galley, then down the second flight to the equipment room below. He drew out a cloth and set the long object on it, then found a small mallet and painstakingly began to chip away at some of the growth.

It was a slow task. It required infinite patience. And he was good; he usually had all the patience he needed.

But he wasn't alone. One by one, they all followed him, Bruce and Connie, Peter, Marina and Joe and, *naturally,* Melinda.

There just wasn't enough room for the whole lot of them to sit there breathing at him.

With a sigh, he looked up. "Give me a little air, okay? I'll report the minute I know something."

Joe, always the wisest and most levelheaded of the group, nodded.

"Eh, 'e's right! 'E can't breathe down here. Wife, come on. Let's lie in the sun a while, eh?"

Marina quickly went up. Joe arched a dark brow at Connie. A little unhappily, she went. Then Peter, though not without saying, "Call me if you need me." Bruce shrugged and followed them.

Only Melinda remained.

He stared at her.

"Well, I did find it," she said softly.

"But you were on my expedition," he reminded her.

"Just as you were on my father's expedition—" she began.

"No! *Not* just as I was on his expedition, and if he ever chose to tell you the truth about it, you just might believe that. But it's too late, isn't it, Melinda? You simply chose not to believe in me—not to come with me. But I'll tell you what, if this proves to be a piece from the *Contessa,* I *will* do something for you that your father didn't do for me. I'll credit you for the dive!"

He was sorry for his outburst the moment it was finished. She stood very straight, without moving. She seemed to have gone pale beneath her tan, and her lashes had fallen over her marvelous aquamarine eyes. He saw the pulse beating at her throat. Indeed, he saw too much, because she was in that black bathing suit of hers that was not an erotic creation at all—except that it was on Melinda, and he could see the shapely, golden length of her legs and remember, could stare at the golden length of her neck and hunger. Could look at her lips and want to leap up, forget the past, forget the *Contessa,* forget even that there were five other people aboard the boat, and certainly forget himself...

"I don't need credit for the dive," she said with quiet dignity. "It's just that I did find the piece, and I'd like to see if it's worth anything or not."

He stared at the piece in his hand, then chipped at it again. His fingers were shaking.

He looked at her. "Melinda, give me a few minutes on my own. Let me get closer to the piece itself; then you can come back when we get to the cleaning."

She lowered her head again, then nodded and turned, and he found himself watching her every movement as she crawled up the ladder.

Back, buttocks, legs.

He tried to stare at the piece. His fingers were still shaking. His body felt as hot as molten lead, as tense as piano wire.

He sat back, seething, wanting to wring her neck again.

Wanting her.

He looked at the piece, trying to concentrate. He needed her off the boat. He closed his eyes for a minute, willing his hands to be still. He went back to his task, slowly, carefully, chipping away.

He hit the right place. Barnacles and grit broke away in his hands. He leaped up, going to a cabinet for cleaning solution, then dipping some onto a cloth and rubbing at the piece.

It began to gleam a beautiful silver. Carefully, he rubbed farther.

Finally he sat back, staring at it. Then he leaped up again, finding a magnifying glass, studying the piece with high excitement.

It was a spoon. Elaborate, definitely Spanish, definitely very, very old...

From the *Contessa*. It had to be.

He studied the design on the piece, then set it down very carefully. He picked up his copy of the ship's manifest and leafed through it quickly.

Eighty-eight silver spoons had been aboard, crested with a likeness of a crown.

He looked at Melinda's find again. Once more his fingers began to shake. They were close. So close. The *Contessa* was here—somewhere....

He stood quickly, carrying the spoon with him, climbing to the galley deck. He started to shout, then realized that they were all there, seated around the galley table, looking like a troop of puppies at the pound that hadn't been adopted. Connie and Melinda were sipping tea; Bruce and Peter had beers. Joe was just sitting there drumming his fingers on the table, and Marina was behind him, her arms around his neck.

"My lord, this looks like a wake!" he said.

They turned, leaped up as one.

He produced the spoon.

"I checked the manifest. Looks as if this is definitely the real McCoy."

Connie let out a wild shriek and kissed Bruce on the cheek, Marina threw her arms around Joe, and Peter rushed forward to pump Roc's hand.

Roc stared over Peter's shoulder at Melinda, who just stood there alone, very quietly, aquamarine eyes steady on his.

"So you've found her!" Peter said. "The *Contessa!* Just like you always knew you would."

"*We've* found her," Roc murmured. And he walked forward, placing the spoon on the table in front of Melinda, his eyes still hard on hers. "Actually, Melinda found her, so it seems. Congratulations, Ms. Davenport."

He left the spoon sitting there, then turned and walked out of the galley, heading up the steps, anxious to get on deck, to feel the breeze tear through his hair, cool his face.

He set his hands on the port side rail. He should be ecstatic. Not that one spoon was proof positive of anything, but since he had always thought the *Contessa* was somewhere near here, it did seem like an awfully good indication that they had almost found the whole treasure.

So why didn't he feel ecstatic? His fingers curled tightly around the rail until the veins in his hands stood out. He looked down at them and released the rail quickly.

Maybe a shower.

He moved away from the rail and headed into his cabin. He kept the water chilly, then hot. He scrubbed his face, his hair, and reminded himself that when he reached land he really did need a haircut. The steam rose around him. He was using way too much hot water. At the moment, though, it felt good. It was easing the tension from his muscles.

He started, hearing, just above the rushing water, his cabin door opening. Hands that had been sluicing soap over his shoulders suddenly went still.

"Who the hell is it?"

There was silence for a moment.

"Who the hell—"

"It's me!" Melinda announced. "Damn, you're the one who insisted that this place be my particular prison."

"What?"

He'd heard her. At the moment, though, her words didn't make any sense.

She came closer. Looking over the glass enclosure of the small shower stall, he saw that she had come unhappily to the doorway.

"I said that you were the one to insist that your cabin was my prison! I'm sorry! I didn't mean to interrupt you. I was just going to take a shower. I didn't realize that you were already there, captain!" She offered him a quick salute, looking as if she were quite ready to flee, and not nearly so confident as she tried to sound.

But Melinda was always confident....

"I'll be out in a minute."

Suddenly the door to his cabin burst open, and Connie came rushing on in. "A picnic, that's it! A barbecue! We need to celebrate, and Teardrop Isle isn't a twenty-minute ride away. What do you think—oh!"

Bless Connie. When she was excited, she didn't see a thing, not a single thing even if it was right in front of her face. It had taken her that whole long speech to realize that Roc was in the shower and Melinda was standing in the doorway.

"Oh. Oh, I am sorry! I didn't realize. Forgive me, I—"

"Connie, damn it, there's nothing to forgive you for!" Roc grated in exasperation.

"I didn't mean to make you mad—" she began again, looking from Roc to Melinda, then back again.

"I'm not mad!"

"Then why are you shouting?" Connie demanded.

"You *are* shouting," Melinda told him with a shrug.

He placed his hands over his face and groaned softly. "Get out of here, both of you, please. Connie, I'm not mad, and a picnic sounds just like a little hunk of heaven. Melinda, the shower and the cabin will be all yours in just ten minutes. Now—out!"

Connie turned and fled instantly. Melinda stood there staring at him, aquamarine eyes glittering with anger.

"You just scared that poor girl half to death."

"She's not scared. She knows me too well for that."

"Really?"

Was there perhaps a touch of jealousy in the inquiry? Hard to tell. She had that regal look about her, chin high, eyes flaming, hair a fantastic golden mane. She leaned against the door frame, arms crossed over her chest, totally defiant. Well, why shouldn't she be? He never had seemed to carry out a threat with her. Except once.

He inhaled slowly, deeply. "She knows me well enough to get the hell out when I ask her to!" he snapped.

"Ah, yes, the great captain speaks! Let's all jump quickly or else walk the plank!"

"Out," he warned her.

She arched a brow.

The water seemed to have grown hotter and hotter. "If you're not out of here in thirty seconds, you'll be joining me for a shower," he warned.

"I'm simply trying to make the point that you can't yell at people and scare them just because *you're* in a foul mood because *I* found the proof *you* were looking for."

"Ten seconds."

"Roc, I told you—"

He pushed open the clouded shower stall door, and her eyes widened considerably. She stared at him quickly, hastily, from head to toe.

"Wait a minute—" she began.

"Time's up," he promised.

Well, she had surely seen him. All of him. Maybe it had even stirred a few memories.

What those memories were, he couldn't be sure, because she had turned to flee.

Too late. He had warned her.

His hands landed on her shoulders, and he spun her around, bending and throwing her over his shoulder.

A shriek left her, faint because he had left her so little breath with which to protest.

She was light, he thought. Despite her shapely, muscular strength, despite her five feet eight inches, she was light when he lifted her.

Skeins of soft golden hair tumbled over his naked back and shoulders. Teased his buttocks and beyond. Her fingers gripped his bare flesh as she struggled to escape.

He almost groaned aloud, it ached so to touch her, aroused things already aroused, things she surely had already seen, and yet, to his amazement, things that could feel an even greater call to hunger.

Touching her...

It was a mistake!

He walked quickly, intently to the shower stall and set her on her feet under the still rushing water. The water poured over her golden hair, soaking it, plastering it around her face. She stood beneath the heavy spray, gasping, steadying herself with her hands on his shoulders.

She looked into his eyes, her own burning. "You son of a—"

"You said you wanted a shower!" he reminded her, catching her hands, taking them from his shoulders. "Enjoy!"

He turned swiftly, closing the shower door behind him. Still dripping, he grabbed a towel and stepped into the cabin, swallowing hard, trying not to shout out loud. He dried himself in a fury, stepped into briefs and shorts, muttering beneath his breath all the while, furious with her, furious with what she could do to him.

He stared at the bathroom door. He was dressed now. Sort of. Halfway composed. And fair was fair.

He strode across the room, throwing the door open. As he had suspected, she had apparently been certain that he was gone.

She had stripped off the black suit with its sexy, nonexistent back and French-cut thighs. It was flung over the door of the stall.

She was facing the flow of water, scrubbing her face.

The misted panel of the shower door did little but add a fascinating intrigue to the shapely structure of her body. Naked, she seemed a work of art, her back so long, so beautifully curved, her hips flaring, her derriere rounded and perfect, legs so willowy and long....

She swung around, her eyes meeting his and widening. "What—" she began.

"Thought you might be needing a towel!" he called out in a light tone, tossing his own on the hook. "Go right ahead. I didn't mean to interrupt you!"

His hand on the doorknob, he started to walk out, then paused for a second. "Gaining a few pounds, eh?"

It was a lie. She hadn't gained an ounce.

"What?" she demanded.

"Nothing."

"Will you get out?" she demanded.

He grinned. "Yeah, sure."

She spun around, reaching for the faucet, shutting the water off instantly.

He was going to leave. He was really going to leave. He meant to leave.

It was just that his feet wouldn't obey his mind's command.

He strode toward the stall instead, throwing the clouded glass door open once again.

And he reached for her, hands circling her waist, drawing her against his naked chest. He felt the thunder in her heart.

Felt the fullness of her breasts, the torment of her nipples grazing across his flesh, felt himself fitting against her despite the cutoffs he had donned.

She felt it, too. Everything. The stroke of flesh, the hardness of muscle—and of...other things.

Those beautiful eyes filled with alarm. Her voice was meant to be tough, filled with bravado. But her words faltered. "What the hell are you doing, Roc?"

What the hell *was* he doing?

"I forgot to thank you for sharing the spoon," he said softly, and before she could protest again, before she could move, he held her even tighter.

He'd been aching to do this. Dying to. He caught her chin with his free hand, lifting her face to his. Touched her lips with his own, covered them, engulfed them. Softly at first. Then with force, demandingly.

A protest sounded in her throat as his tongue parted her lips, her teeth. She squirmed in his hold, the movement of her breasts across his chest delicious.

His tongue slipped deeper into her mouth. Tasted, explored, played.

Her fingers froze on his upper arms. She was still, crushed against him, her heart hammering, slamming....

What in hell are you doing?

The question rose with cruel torment in his own mind. He had wanted to touch her; he had done so. And awakened all the fires of hell inside himself.

Damn...

He broke the kiss, met her blazing eyes. "Thanks," he forced himself to say softly. "Thanks very much."

"Damn you, Roc Trellyn!" she cried. "Get out!"

"Ms. Davenport, I am gone!" he promised.

Then, blindly, he managed to step from the shower stall.

And this time he left not just the shower but his cabin, swearing violently to himself that in the future he would remember to lock the damned door.

Six

Long after Roc had left the cabin, Melinda remained in the shower stall, shivering. Damn him. She had known what it would be like if he touched her again. She kept trying to tell herself that she was here because she owed him, but she was really here because she wanted him. But wanting was so foolish, so wasteful...so painful.

She should have kept her distance; she needed to be careful. She couldn't run around throwing out brash challenges, because...

Because she was the one who was going to get hurt. All over again.

At last she managed to reach for the towel he had tossed her way. His towel, she thought, roughly rubbing herself dry with it. Something of him seemed to linger about it, his clean scent, his...

She threw the towel aside, then realized she had nothing to wear except for the black bathing suit she had just discarded, the only piece of clothing aboard the boat she could call her own, or the white outfit she'd borrowed from Connie, but it was already feeling awfully grungy.

Well, she could always find something of his. After all, she had to have something to wear.

She bit her lip, feeling the shakes start again as she thought of the way he had kissed her. It had been more than a kiss. Roc could always make it more than a kiss. Somehow he kissed with all his body, and she felt all of his body with all of hers, and...

She could remember so clearly the feel of him. The hardness, the hunger, the sweet fire that seemed to sweep from him to her no matter how she tried to fight it.

And yet he had managed to set her aside and walk away. Just as he had done three years ago.

And here she was, back again.

Because I was wrong! she cried in silent anguish to herself.

It would serve him right, she thought, if she just waltzed out on deck stark naked and apologized for being a prisoner without any clean clothing. He was hardly sparing much thought to such matters. She would have been in dire trouble already, if it weren't for Connie.

Connie, who was so sweet, so nice. And who made Melinda so jealous.

She squared her shoulders and swallowed hard. Now, as to the matter of clothing...

She sighed deeply, fully aware that she wasn't going to prance anywhere naked.

Yet even as she stood there, wrestling with the dilemma, the pretty blonde with the enormous brown eyes tapped on the door to the cabin and stuck her head in. Melinda snatched the cast-aside towel from the floor and smiled wanly at the other woman.

"Thanks for coming. I was just looking at my limited wardrobe, and I think I definitely give new meaning to the words, 'I don't have a thing to wear.'"

Connie smiled. "I rather thought that. It's lucky we're about the same size, although, of course, you're taller. Actually," she mused, stepping back, "you're a lot more somethinger in a number of ways."

Melinda raised an eyebrow. *"What?"*

"You've—you've just got a lot more shape."

Melinda was startled by the strange compliment. "Connie, trust me," she murmured in turn, "you're not lacking a thing. You're a beautiful woman, and you must know that."

Connie seemed equally startled. "Really?" she murmured.

Melinda frowned, amazed. "Really. Don't these goons around here let you know it now and then?"

"Well, Bruce is my brother, Joe is married, Peter is busy all the time, and..."

"And Roc?" Melinda asked softly.

Connie's lashes lowered. "Roc is a courteous man," she replied. "A busy one, too. And the boss."

And anything more? Melinda longed to ask, but she refrained. Roc was usually courteous. And he could be very kind. She should know that better than anyone else alive. He had dealt with her so gently—even when she had been entirely rotten to him—once she had admitted that she was hurt, lost and in pain.

And then I managed to lose him, she reminded herself.

She lowered her lashes quickly, gritting her teeth for a moment. She was going to get a grip on this thing. She should never have come out here.

And she would be an absolute idiot to let him get close to her. In his eyes she had betrayed him. He would never forgive her. And if he did touch her, it would be only to taunt her, as he had today.

He had proven how easily he could walk away. Twice now. No matter what she felt for him, she wasn't going to let him get close again.

She still loved him, but she couldn't afford to be used by him. And, God help her, maybe she was better off with him thinking she had come to spy. If he mistrusted her, held her an arm's distance away all the time, it would be much better.

Maybe I shouldn't have picked up the damned spoon, she thought. It had angered him somehow. He didn't believe she meant for him—*wanted* him—to make his claim.

Maybe that was good, too.

Roc had been right about the *Contessa* all along. She could remember sitting with him one night when they had taken one of her father's boats out alone for a weekend, just to be together.

She'd made dinner, the moon had risen, and she'd come out of the galley after cleaning up to find him with a book in his hands, a book on the *Contessa*. Somehow she had ended up curled in his lap, listening to him.

"They're all wrong, you know. Look at the course she took! She's here, right between the Florida coast of the old U.S. of A. and the Bahamas. She's right here under our noses!"

"Why hasn't she been found, then?" Melinda had asked, smiling, humoring him.

And he'd kissed her. "Because we sometimes lose sight of the treasures right beneath our noses!" he had assured her. And then they hadn't talked about it anymore, because he had kissed her, and they had stared up at the stars and the night, eventually becoming lost in each other....

That was then, she reminded herself. And this was now.

And Connie was staring at her, reminding her that she had been in the middle of a conversation when she had lost herself in the past. Thinking back to that conversation she realized that Connie, almost unbelievably, didn't seem to be very confident about her beautiful blond appearance.

"Well," Melinda murmured, smiling at Connie again, "they're all goons if they don't take the time to notice now and again that you're a lovely woman. And I'm extremely grateful for the loan of clothing."

"It's hard to bring your own when you're planning on getting scooped up in a fishnet, huh?"

Melinda stared at Connie, wondering if there was rancor in the question. But she saw only amusement in the other woman's eyes, then found herself smiling in return.

"Right," she agreed.

Connie lifted her hands. She was carrying a bundle of clothing.

"More goodies. A few are from Marina—she has a few things I'm missing. Like boobs," she said a little mournfully, and Melinda laughed.

"Hey, yours are just fine. Remember that one day most of the world's big-breasted women will be sagging, but you'll keep a nice shape your whole life."

Connie laughed. "I'll try to look at it that way! Anyway, there's a whole lot of stuff here—bras, panties, shorts, shirts, a few beach cover-ups. Not more than a few days' worth, but we have a washer and dryer in the galley, and Marina says just throw your laundry to her whenever you want."

"Thanks," Melinda said softly.

When Connie threw the pile of stuff on Roc's bunk, Melinda studied her for a moment, her heart racing.

The woman just couldn't be having an affair with Roc. She wouldn't be so blasé about a suddenly returned ex-wife—who wasn't really *ex* at all—sleeping in Roc's cabin if there had really been anything between them.

"May I ask you a personal question?" Connie said, hesitating.

"Ask anything you like. Whether you'll get an answer or not…" Melinda said, and shrugged.

Connie grinned. "Are you spying? Did you know that this was Roc's boat? I mean, the dolphin thing—"

"I love dolphins!" Melinda promised vehemently. "And I *am* involved with a number of groups trying to educate fishermen in ways *not* to snare them and yet still manage to make their living from the sea."

Connie laughed. "Oh, I believe you love dolphins. I love them, too. So do most people. But, well, what were you *really* doing in our net?"

Melinda hesitated. "I had an idea that this boat wasn't a real fishing vessel. I thought that it might be searching for the *Contessa*."

"So you *were* spying!"

Melinda shook her head. "Not really. I want Roc to find this treasure. I don't know if you can believe me or not—I certainly don't expect you to—but I want this claim to be his. I'm not working for anyone."

"Not even your father?"

Melinda grinned. "You don't know my father, Connie. He

doesn't need anyone spying for him. He'll do his own searching, in his own way. Except that I think—"

"Yes?"

Melinda shrugged again. "Actually, I think my father wants Roc to make this claim, too. Maybe we owe him. Both of us."

Connie watched her for a moment. "Actually," she said after a moment, "I *do* believe you." She turned, then paused at the cabin's doorway. "Hey, get dressed. We're taking the dinghy over to the island as soon as Roc brings the *Crystal Lee* a little bit closer in. It's a celebration!"

Connie left, closing the cabin door behind her. Melinda went to check out her new wardrobe, and chose a checked crop top and navy shorts. She felt the boat getting underway even as she buttoned her last button.

She turned to the dresser by the wall near the captain's bunk and found Roc's brush. She hesitated a minute, then began to stroke it through her drying hair. It took some time to work out the tangles. When she finished, she set the brush down and stared at her face, at her still too-wide eyes.

Don't look vulnerable! she warned herself. More than that, don't *be* vulnerable.

But she was.

They all seemed to think that she was protected by some kind of armor, that Davenport's daughter had to be as tough as nails. Well, good, let them think it. She did wear armor—her pride.

But there were chinks in that armor. Lots of them.

The boat had come to a stop again. She felt the rocking movement as it settled.

Roc shouted to someone to cast the anchor. Connie shouted to someone else to come help her with the bags.

Melinda set the brush down and hurried out, determined to help Connie.

After all, they were celebrating tonight.

It wasn't really night. It was the most beautiful time of day, the very beginning of sunset.

They brought the dinghy over to the uninhabited island just

as the sun dipped to the water, throwing rays of gold and vibrant red across the blue of the sky and that of the sea.

Barefoot, like the rest of the group, Roc jumped into the water to drag the dinghy ashore. Peter leaped out swiftly after him, reaching in to grab a few of the bags Connie and Marina had packed. The rest followed quickly. Roc noticed that Melinda was fitting in annoyingly well, just as if she had been hired to hunt for treasure the same as they had been.

With the dinghy pulled up on shore and the others starting to dig a pit for the fire, he paused for a moment, staring from the beautiful sunset to the scene before him, Melinda down on her hands and knees alongside Marina, scooping up the sand and getting ready to lay the coals they'd brought.

The tension was getting to him again.

Her outfit didn't help.

She should be dressed in rags, ill-fitting things like potato sacks.

No, not even potato sacks could make her look unappealing.

But they wouldn't be as bad as what she had on. Short, *short* blue shorts, and a blue and white checked midriff thing that barely covered her. It hadn't been so long ago, of course, that he had seen her in nothing at all, so it was easy to imagine what lay beneath the wisps of clothing.

He gritted his teeth.

His ex-wife—all right, his *wife*—was definitely managing to create havoc in his life.

He kept staring at her, watching as Bruce said something, to which she smiled quickly in return.

The poor boy was going to trip over his own tongue if she kept smiling at him like that.

Roc started to walk a little way down the beach. When he stopped, he sat with his feet in the water, looking out on the horizon.

They'd spent so many nights like this, under red and gold sunsets, staring out at the endless sea.

Strange. Once he had known the lure of the sea was so totally in his blood, he'd never expected to meet anyone like Melinda.

A woman who could live happily and easily aboard ship, swim like a fish—and look like an angel. He'd been sure he was meant to be a loner, but then he'd met Davenport's daughter....

Not that things had been smooth. Melinda had always been determined, as he was reminded again and again now. They'd had a tendency to fight over the fact that she could be reckless—especially when she was determined. He'd hauled her out of the water a few times when she'd gone on some search alone, and they'd both yelled and argued, and he'd usually won, because he'd been right. But he'd also had his ways of making it up to her softly in the darkness, where the anger that had spurred him so hotly became a passion made all the sweeter by what had gone before.

And so things had gone—until the wreck of the *Infanta Beatriz.*

Like the *Contessa,* she had sailed for the New World from Spain. Legend had it that she sank off the northern tip of Cuba, and it was rumored that if she were found, she would yield little, because she had gone down in shallow waters and been stripped of her wealth long ago.

Still, Roc had read everything he could about her, fascinated by the promise of an unusual horde of jewels that might—or might not—have been aboard.

He had talked with Jonathan Davenport about the ship, had thrown all his enthusiasm into pleading that they hunt for her.

Davenport had been unconvinced, so Roc had spent his free time searching for her, out on his own.

The lure hadn't really been the value of the treasure, nor even the idea of showing off what he had steadfastly sought and discovered, despite the skepticism of others.

After all, in the end, he dived for the love of diving, not for gain. Like any hunter, his thrill was in the chase.

But he had by chance been with Davenport when he discovered a lady's chest from the ship, deeply encrusted, yet yielding a startling cache of perfect golden coins. He had barely managed to clean a few when he discovered that Davenport had called a press conference and laid claim to the *Infanta Beatriz.* And when

Roc protested in anger, Davenport insisted that the search vessel had been his—damn the long days Roc had searched alone!—and that Roc was simply working for him. He had known, of course, that they were looking for the ship.

Despite the fact that he had refused to do so.

Roc could never forget the anger he'd felt. Or what had awaited him after he'd hurried to his cabin, assuming that Melinda would be equally outraged.

Oh, she had been outraged, all right. But not on his behalf. It *was* her father's ship, she insisted.

"How can you be so ungrateful? Everything you've done, you've done with my father!"

"Melinda, he didn't want to be bothered with the *Infanta*. He did everything he could to keep me from even looking for her!"

He could still remember her behavior that night. She had undoubtedly overheard the wild argument between her father and her husband, but she had simply showered, then sat before the small dressing table in a white terry robe and brushed her hair. She had barely turned when he had walked in, instead meeting his eyes in the mirror.

He should have known then. She might be his wife, but first and foremost she was Davenport's daughter.

"Roc, what difference does it make? His find, your find. There will be more ships—the sea is littered with them."

He had walked over to her then. "No more ships together," he said softly. "We're leaving in the morning."

She'd set the brush down at last. "Don't be ridiculous! Of course you'll find more ships together. My father's humored you all along, searching for the *Beatriz*. Roc, you have to give him his due. I think—"

"I think your father's mad that I was right, and he just can't admit it."

"And I think you're acting like a spoiled two-year-old. My father said he gave you his blessing, that he traveled where you suggested, that he put as much energy into the search as into any other. My father—"

"Your father is a liar and a cheat—"

Suddenly she was on her feet, her hand cracking across his chin. He couldn't remember having been more furious in all his life, but he managed just to catch her up, his fingers wound around her wrists, and tell her succinctly, "I'm leaving first thing in the morning. You have tonight to decide if you're my wife or his daughter."

She paled at that. Her head back, her eyes sizzling, she insisted, "You have no right to walk out! I *am* your wife—but I'm his daughter, too."

"We're leaving."

"We're not! You'll make up in the morning."

"No, Melinda, we will not. I'm leaving."

And he was. He knew it with complete certainty. Everything inside him ached as if a limb were being detached. Davenport had been his boss, his mentor, his best friend—and his father-in-law. But he couldn't accept what Davenport had done. He was too damn good at what he did to be ridiculed—and then used.

"Are you with me?"

She'd wrenched away from him, and he had known her answer. She wasn't with him but with her father.

The ache within him deepened. He had loved her. Really loved her. Loved her raw determination, her wild reckless spirit, the way she was so swift to teach others, to help them, to give to them. So aloof at times, so independent, and yet so quick to come to him, to curl against him and trust in him, to dream with him beneath a star-laden canopy over a gently rolling sea.

No more. Her trust was in her father.

So this was it. Their last night.

He was still seething with anger, besieged with pain. But she stood with her back to him, her shoulders square, as if determined to keep the argument going.

But he knew it was over. He walked across to her, lifted her hair, kissed her neck. She turned to argue; he slipped his hands beneath the neckline of the terry robe and sent it floating to the floor. She opened her mouth to speak, and he closed it for her with the seal of his own. For brief seconds she was rigid.... Then she returned his passion wildly, sweetly.

Perhaps she was trying to convince him to stay.

Just as he wanted her to ache in the night once he was gone.

He didn't sleep. He rose at dawn and packed his belongings, leaving most of his equipment. She was still asleep. He sat by the bed and woke her at last, feeling once again as if he were losing some piece of his body. Perhaps his heart.

Perhaps his soul.

She woke slowly, eyes so beautifully dazed, body sleek, hair tumbling all about her.

"Are you coming?" he asked simply.

"You can't just walk out on him!" she cried, aquamarine eyes suddenly wide and ablaze.

That was it. He turned and started out the door.

"Don't you ever, *ever* come back!" she cried fiercely.

He turned once. "If you decide to choose me over your father, you're welcome to come after me."

"You're really leaving? Just like that? After all that he's done? After last night?"

"Yes."

Her chin went up. "I hate you!" she whispered fiercely.

Her lower lip was quivering, the sheet falling from her shoulders. Her eyes were glittering. With fury? With tears?

He dropped his bag and found himself beside her again, taking her into his arms, unable to keep from touching her. Her fists slammed against his shoulders and his back; then her fingers began to dig into his flesh. "I hate you, I hate you, I hate you!" she cried. But she held him. Held him as he kissed her, touched and savored the length of her, tried to tell himself that there were other women in the world. He knew that he had come back this time because he couldn't bear to go, that he had to remember her, each curve of her, each taste of her. Yet, once again, the passion and the fury were finally spent. And she whispered softly, "I couldn't believe that you would really leave me."

"I'm not leaving you. I'm leaving your father."

She went still, then became a whirlwind of motion, sweeping

the covers around her, drawing to the head of the bed, staring at him with eyes as hard as gemstones. "You mean that you—"

"Melinda, I've said it a dozen times now. I'm leaving! I'm leaving your father's employ, I am not leaving you. If you insist on staying, you are the one who is leaving me."

He turned his back on her; he had to. He dressed methodically, not turning around.

"I hate you!"

The words burned into his back.

"Melinda—"

"If you're going, go. Get out!"

He reached for her, but she jerked farther away, as if she could merge with the wall.

"Go!" she whispered.

It was the only thing left to do. He turned, and that time he left for real. But all the while he walked down the dock, he prayed that she would appear behind him, perhaps yelling, perhaps indignant, telling him again that he had no right, telling him anything, trying to convince him to stay.

But she didn't appear. Still, they were in Key West, and he made his every move for the next few days just as obvious as possible. Anyone could have found him—if they had wanted to.

Melinda hadn't wanted to.

I hate you, she had said. Words of passion, of anger, spoken in a rush. She couldn't have meant them.

But perhaps she had.

Because two days later her father's ship headed out to sea, and Melinda sailed with him.

He hadn't seen her since. He'd heard about her, of course. She'd made a few finds of her own over the last few years, and every time her father was mentioned, she was, too, of course. The press loved Davenport and his beautiful daughter. Everyone loved a mermaid.

He pulled himself to the present and discovered that the sun had nearly set.

They'd gotten a nice fire going on the beach, and its yellow flames were competing with the colors in the sky. Roc frowned suddenly, staring past the fire.

Joe had the grill set up over the coals in the sand pit, and Connie and Marina were busy setting fish fillets and chicken pieces atop it. Peter was stirring some concoction in a pan at the edge of the heat, and Bruce leaned back on a bunched-up towel, a beer in his hand, supervising the lot of them.

"Careful with the fish now, Marina. Those fresh fillets don't need more than five minutes a side!"

Marina's dark eyes rolled his way in warning.

Roc leaped to his feet, aware that Melinda was nowhere to be seen. He strode to the fire. "Where is she?" he asked, a scowl knitting his brow. He was amazed at the worry, the fear, the anguish, that had seized hold of him.

Bruce seemed startled by the tension in his voice. They all stared at him for a moment.

"She just went for a walk around the island," Bruce said. "There's nowhere for her to go from here, Roc. I mean, she can't possibly be reporting to anyone."

"No, the little fool could be in the water again!" he muttered darkly. "Which way did she head?"

Bruce pointed down the beach to his left.

"The waters are calm, not much current, and the cove on the other side is well protected," Marina reminded him quietly.

He nodded briefly, then turned and started down the beach.

His strides were long. There wasn't much daylight left. The red streaks were now being overtaken by the darkening grayness of the swiftly coming night.

They simply didn't know her. It was one of the things they had fought about the most. She always taught others never to siwm or dive alone, but she seemed to think herself invincible, and whenever she was upset, which undoubtedly she was right now, she always seemed to go straight for the water. There were so many dangers at night. On a dive in the daylight, they both knew how to deal with curious sharks. But at night, there could easily be some hungry predators ready to find her appetizing.

Makos, lemon sharks, hammerheads, blues and more frequented these waters.

He lengthened his strides. His heart thundering, he passed a big clump of trees, but he didn't see her yet. He walked over a sand dune and into a cove protected on all sides by brush and hills of sand. It was getting so damn dark!

"Damn her!" he muttered, his fear increasing. He looked up at a sudden fall of light. The moon had been up, big and full already, even while the last vestiges of day remained. It had been hidden by a dark cloud, which now had drifted away.

He saw her at last.

She was there, just staring out to sea. Tall, slim, alone, her chin high, her shoulders straight, her back to him.

It was how she had looked that last night. So determined to stand against him.

And just as he had wanted to touch her that night, he wanted to touch her now.

No. Just as he had *wanted* her that night, he *wanted* her now.

Fool...to think he had left all that behind.

He found himself walking silently down to her, pausing for a moment just behind her as the breeze lifted her hair.

He stepped closer. Her shirt left her shoulders bare, and his left hand settled on her upper arm, while his right hand lifted the wealth of golden hair from her nape. He pressed his lips to the flesh he'd bared, breathing in the sweet scent of her.

She stiffened slightly. Shoulders so square, back so straight. She was probaby going to spin around and slap him any second....

But she didn't. His kiss moved from her nape over her shoulder, the tip of his tongue searing her flesh.

He felt the hunger in him. Felt the slight trembling that had begun in her...

"Roc," she murmured softly, starting to shift.

"No," he murmured, not willing to listen to any protest. His fingers caught the elastic of her borrowed shirt, and he tugged it downward, baring her breasts. Arms laced around her from behind, he cupped her breasts with his hand, callused flesh rounding over her nipples. She moaned softly as he continued to caress her. Kiss her. Slowly, so slowly. Savoring each sweet, erotic brush of his roughened hands over her silken skin.

He eased the shirt down farther. Over her midriff, still touching, still stroking. He found the waistband of her navy shorts, the button, the zipper. He opened both, his hand sliding down against her belly, then farther still, fingers brushing over the soft golden triangle there.

A strangled sound escaped her. He pressed closer against her back, his kiss finding her ear, her throat.

"Don't deny me!" he whispered harshly, feeling again the tempest of her trembling. Feeling the rise of his own hunger, the burning...

"The others—"

"They won't follow, I promise."

She was silent as he tugged on the shirt, her shorts, the panties beneath them. Slid them downward until they fell to the beach. She slipped her feet gracefully from the puddle of clothing, one at a time, then stood very still, the moonlight beaming down upon her shoulders.

At last she turned into his arms. Facing him. Naked once again.

"This is a mistake..." she began gravely, aquamarine eyes a tempest of confused longing.

"I've made lots of mistakes," he assured her, then reached for her once again, sweeping her into his arms to lay her down upon the cool welcoming sand. His arms around her, he kissed her lips passionately, fully, tasting, exploring, demanding, fueling the blaze within him.

His lips left hers, and she stared into his eyes, her lips still slightly open, damp, her breath coming too quickly, the rise of her breasts incredibly seductive in the ethereal glow.

"Now you're supposed to walk away!" she charged him.

He shook his head slowly, eyes roaming over the length of her, from the perfect beauty of her face to the exquisite shape of her hips.

"No," he said hoarsely.

"Maybe I'm supposed to walk away this time," she suggested softly.

Again he shook his head.

"No way—wife. No way."

And then his lips touched hers again.

Seven

——

She'd felt him behind her, of course, long before he had touched her. His footsteps on the sand had been nearly silent, but she had heard him, sensed him. She had known he was there, standing behind her, watching her, waiting. Thinking.

Thinking what?

That she had come back into his life in a fishnet to spy on him?

No, not at that moment.

At that moment she'd felt the tension, the heat, the electricity. She'd known that they weren't going to argue. That he was going to come closer.

And she hadn't moved.

Somehow she had known that he would touch her again. And some inner voice had shouted, warning her not to trust him.

But she had ached for his touch for too long to be denied now.

No matter what bitterness lay between them, no matter what anger, what distrust... No matter what, when his hands fell upon her flesh, when his lips pressed against her nape, there was something infinitely tender about his touch, as if he were awakening her from some deep sleep. As if she had been waiting all these years.

Perhaps she had been.

Odd, how the sand was suddenly so cool beneath her, hard packed, endlessly white and clean. She saw his eyes above hers, as passionate and determined as his voice had been, their color cobalt in the moonlight, dark with intensity. A great shivering suddenly seized her. The sand was actually cold, the air cool, yet her flesh felt as if it had suddenly caught fire....

Then she felt his lips again. He seemed to kiss her forever, only his mouth touching hers, leaving the rest of her body cold once more, like the sand, waiting, aching, needing more.

Suddenly his lips broke from hers. She was more aware than ever of the chill of the sand beneath her body, and she could hear the surf pounding relentlessly against the beach. She opened her eyes and saw the moon, wondering fleetingly if he hadn't left her again after all, if his anger and bitterness weren't so great that even now he could walk away. An awful anguish filled her, an aching that brought tears to glisten suddenly in her eyes.

Then, without warning, she wasn't cold or empty anymore. He had left her merely to shed his clothes. Now the feel of his hot flesh brought a startling heat and fulfillment as he settled over her, his fingers entwining with hers, his eyes searing hers with dark cobalt fire once again.

"Damn, but it's been a long time," he whispered, the words husky. "A long, long time..."

Eons, she might have whispered. Far too long a time...

But she didn't dare. She didn't dare speak at all, and even if she had wished to, no sound would have come to her lips. She closed her eyes again, aware now of the rough texture of his legs, his chest. Aware of his sex, so hard against her flesh...

He shifted, his knee parting her thighs. Her eyes flew open again, and she saw that he was poised over her, waiting.

Her eyes met his, and then suddenly, shatteringly, he was inside her. Sound at last left her lips, a soft, startled cry that seemed to give him pause until she dug her fingers into his shoulders, arching swiftly against him, taking, wanting, giving, needing to love and to be loved.

The moon seemed to burst, a sudden gleaming splash of color against the dark sky.

Her memory had failed to recall just how wonderful this could be. His touch, his strength, his tenderness. The sheer ecstasy of feeling him gloved within her, moving, igniting a burning, racing fire, a magical heat that filled her and tore through her, spiraling deep to reach her core...

No, memory could never serve.

He kissed her lips, her breasts, caressed her, held her. And all the while he moved within her, each thrust bringing her closer and closer to cataclysmic wonder. His hand curved over her buttocks, pressing her even closer to him, driving his thrusts even deeper inside her, touching her within and without. Even in the breeze they both glistened, the sheen of passion gleaming on their bodies, echoing the warmth that burned inside. She scarcely breathed, yet she gasped for breath. She closed her eyes to feel the intensity of the moment, then opened them again and saw the tension in his face, corded in his neck, rippling in his arms. His lips bore down on hers once again; then he stiffened, thrusting so deeply into her that she thought she would die. But she didn't die. Sweet deliciousness seemed to sweep throughout her as fulfillment, wild, volatile and shattering, burst upon her at last. For long moments she was only dimly aware of him, holding her tightly, then quivering with the power of one final thrust before falling to her side.

She shivered suddenly in the chill that raced through her with the warmth of his body gone.

He lay there, too, just breathing.

Then suddenly he sat up, arms clasped round his knees, staring out at the dark surf.

"Damn!" he muttered softly.

She gritted her teeth tightly together, fighting the new wave of hot moisture that rose to her eyes. Three years, then something so sweetly magnificent, and all he had to say was *damn?*

She started to rise. He had already gotten to his feet and reached for his shorts. Now he tossed her the checked midriff top and commanded roughly, "Get dressed."

She caught the blouse, staring at him with a fury so great that she was able to blink away the tears.

"I'd fully intended to dress!" she assured him. "You're the rudest man I've ever—"

The shirt fell to the sand as he suddenly jerked her to her feet. They were both naked in the moon glow, and she felt thoroughly chilled as his eyes bore down into hers.

"The rudest man you've ever *what?*" he demanded. "The rudest man you've ever slept with? Was that it? I imagine Eric is far more polite. Was he at your side like that when he *politely* suggested you dive in the ocean and find out what I knew about the *Contessa?* Did he suggest you go this far?"

"*What?*" she gasped, unable to believe what she had heard.

She jerked free with a sudden burst of power that surprised even him, then took a swing at him, but he was ready. Yet even as he caught her wrist and dragged her against him, she slammed his chest with her free hand, still struggling fiercely, pitting all her weight against him.

"Little witch," he muttered fiercely, trying to catch her wildly swinging hand, stepping back, hitting a dune—and falling.

They both went tumbling over in the sand, rolling.

Melinda caught herself and tried to struggle up, but he was straddling her.

"Don't you touch me—"

"Melinda—"

"I mean it!" The tears had risen to her eyes again; she couldn't hope to blink them back now.

"Damn it, Melinda, I wish I could believe—"

"I don't give a damn anymore what you believe. Get away from me. Leave me alone!"

He didn't leave her alone. His eyes were as deep and furious as her own, and he didn't budge from his intimate perch atop her.

"Would you like to tell me just what your relationship is with him?" he demanded fiercely.

"No, I would not!" she retorted furiously. "You've decided what it is—I have no intention of telling you a damn thing!"

He sat on his haunches, arms crossed over his chest. She tried to struggle up, but with his legs still locked around her hips, it was impossible.

"I'm going to scream any second," she promised him. "Then I'm going to scratch your eyes out. Then I'm—"

"Longford," he interrupted smoothly.

"I'm going to gouge your chest, and if that doesn't move you, I'm going to bite."

He arched a brow. "How hard and what?" he inquired politely.

"Oh!" She took a swing, but he caught her, leaned low against her.

She spoke through gritted teeth. "I'm really going to hurt you in a minute."

"You really hurt me three years ago," he said softly.

"You walked out."

"You refused to come with me."

She closed her eyes. "I'm going to knock your lights out in about thirty seconds."

He leaned even closer, his chest hair teasing her naked breasts mercilessly. "Not a chance," he assured her.

"Please move!" she grated.

"I want to know about Longford."

"Are you going to believe what I say?" she demanded.

He sat back again, staring at her. She trembled slightly. It was so strange. Three years apart and less than twenty-four hours back together, and now they were arguing naked in the sand.

The naked part was all right.

The things he said were not.

"Look at me," he said very softly. "Meet my eyes. I'll believe anything you say."

She hesitated. Her life really wasn't any of his business. She certainly didn't want to give him any power over her, and she was damn sure *he* hadn't been living her ridiculously celibate life.

But he was determined. Relentless. And perhaps even passionate in his pursuit of what he wanted to know...

"There's nothing between Eric Longford and me," she told him, her eyes steady on his, "other than dinner now and then, a few diving trips, and conversation."

He didn't move. Not for the longest time. His black lashes fell for a moment; then his eyes were hard on hers once again.

"Really?"

"I just told you—"

"Sorry."

"Now, if you'd please—"

"In a minute."

"What?"

"What was that comment about?"

"What comment?" she cried, beginning to feel desperate.

"That I was the rudest man you'd ever slept with."

Anger filled her again, and she gritted her teeth. "You're the densest man I've ever met!" she exclaimed. "I never said that. *Never!* I didn't say the word *slept* at all, and you never gave me a chance to finish the sentence. You're the rudest man I've ever met. *Met!*"

He seemed unaffected by her anger, holding her still. "So who have you been seeing?" he demanded.

"None of your business. And if you don't—"

"Who?" he persisted.

"Let me up!"

"Answer me."

"In about two seconds, I will begin to scream!"

He shrugged. "You won't get a whole lot of help if you do. I have a very loyal crew. Now tell me who, Melinda."

She stared at him, aware of the hard sand beneath her, aware of the power of his thighs and the intimate way they rode her hips. She was aware of the cool air on her body, hardening her nipples, of the very *naked* way he was straddling her...

"No one," she muttered.

"Who?"

"No one!" she lashed out more angrily. "Now will you please—"

"You mean to tell me you haven't...dated seriously? In all this time?"

"If you mean, have I slept with anyone in all this time, the answer is no. Now, damn you, this is supposed to be a barbecue, not *True Confessions!* If you'll please—"

He stood, reaching a hand down to her and drawing her to her feet. She tried to walk by him to retrieve her clothing, but he held onto her wrist, pulling her back.

"So just what were you doing out on the ocean with Longford?"

"Diving."

"And he just left you stranded?"

She sighed. "Yes. I thought the *Crystal Lee* might be yours, and if not, she was someone looking for treasure, not a fishing boat."

"What if she had been a drug runner? What if she hadn't been mine? What if she had belonged to someone ready to slit your throat for getting in his way?"

"I can take care of myself."

He groaned. "Right. Just dive into a fishing net. Age isn't doing a damn thing for your common sense."

"And it hasn't improved your manners."

"Your recklessness—"

"Isn't your concern!"

"Actually, it is," he said softly, releasing her at last as his eyes met hers with cool speculation. "It seems that until we manage to do something about it, you're still my wife."

"Don't let it concern you."

"But it does." His eyes dropped to study the length of her, causing a rush of blood to bring a crimson tide to her flesh.

His eyes met hers again. "We'd really better get dressed. My crew may be around any minute now."

"Would they follow their great leader if he'd given the impression he was out for privacy?" she mocked.

He shrugged. "By now, they may think the sharks have already eaten us both. Get your things on. Someone might be along any second."

She turned away from him, quickly picking up the few pieces of her clothing and shimmying into them. She didn't look his way.

When she did, he was clad in his shorts once again and walking the way he had come, calling over his shoulder, "I'm sure dinner is on. Let's go back."

"Maybe I'd rather go for a swim!" she retorted.

Then she made the mistake of turning away from him.

Footsteps came pounding toward her. He could run as fleetly as he could swim. She found herself gasping for breath as he swept her off her feet and into his arms. "No night swimming alone, you little idiot. Damn it. You are the most headstrong and reckless female I have ever—"

"Slept with?" she suggested.

He was silent for a second. Then a slow grin curved his lip. "I was going to say *met!*" he informed her.

He started walking back along the beach. For a moment Melinda let herself be carried. It was nice. So nice.

Then she looked up at him, determined. "So who are *you* sleeping with these days?" she asked, trying to keep her tone light.

He looked down at her, mischief burning in his eyes. "None of your business," he said softly.

She stiffened. "You hairy son of a sea serpent!" she cried angrily, shoving at his chest until he half set her down, half dropped her.

"Hey!" He caught her arm when she would have run past him.

She faced him, her hands tightening into fists at her side. "You sat there and forced me to tell you all about my life, and now you tell me that yours is none of my business?"

He cocked his head, thinking for a moment. Then he shrugged. "That's right," he told her. And he was the one to walk away then.

She ran after him. "Roc, you bas—" she began, but his finger fell on her lips.

His eyes were intense and his voice husky when he promised

100 BETWEEN ROC AND A HARD PLACE

her softly, ''I'll tell you this. I have never, never slept with anyone like you in all my life. Never. Now, come on—Ms. Davenport.''

She spun around quickly, startled by the effect his words had on her. Once again, she was just a breath away from tears. She was in better shape when he was being rude, when he was angry, making demands!

She walked quickly, keeping several feet in front of him. When she finally saw his crew, Connie was anxiously pacing before the fire, Marina staring into it, and Joe, Peter and Bruce were looking in the direction from which she and Roc were coming.

Guilt plagued her. They were all worried. And wondering, of course, if they should be saving their leader—or leaving him to his, er, private recreation.

Connie stopped pacing. The three men tried to look in different directions.

''Something smells wonderful!'' Melinda called out, only a slight tremor in her voice. Dear lord. She could feel crimson color flooding her face again. Did everyone know exactly what she had been doing?

Roc was closer behind her than she had suspected. She nearly jumped when he said, ''Well, did you all start eating yet? What are we waiting for? Connie, is there a cold beer for me?''

''Sure!'' Connie called. ''We—uh, yeah, well, we kind of waited. The fish was too tempting, though. Marina's got more. We'll put it right on.''

Roc shook his head, accepting the beer Connie handed him. ''The chicken's fine for me.''

''For me, too,'' Melinda echoed quickly.

''There's plenty more,'' Marina offered, her dark eyes giving away no hint of curiosity.

''We'll have it another time,'' Melinda promised, trying to sound cheerful.

''Catch!'' Roc called suddenly, throwing her a can of beer. She caught it swiftly, wondering just what Roc had told these people about her.

They'd definitely known he'd had a wife. And that she was old man Davenport's daughter.

They'd all been wary enough of her, certainly.

The barbecue was delicious, and the night was beautiful. One by one everyone came to sit around the fire. The orange flames snapped and crackled against the ever-darkening night.

Roc was across from her. She was half listening to one of Bruce's tales about a ghost ship that sailed the Atlantic when, in the very middle of the story, she found herself distracted again with an inner trembling.

How could she be sitting here so calmly when they had made love in the sand such a little while ago? When he had accused her of such awful things, when he had nearly walked away, when he had made her tell him everything.

She was a fool.

She could still close her eyes and feel his touch....

And, looking across the fire, she could see his shoulders glinting copper in the fire glow, see his eyes, which met hers now and then, still questioning.

She had told him the truth, yet he still seemed suspicious.

"Oh!" Connie gasped, letting out a little scream and jumping up.

A branch had fallen where she had been sitting. A very small one.

Bruce burst out laughing. "Connie!" he admonished his sister.

"Well, it scared me!" she snapped. She stared at her brother, shaking a firm finger at him. "You were sitting there talking about bony fingers and suddenly—" She broke off. "Where did that branch come from?" she asked, frowning.

Melinda turned around. The trees were some distance away.

Peter stood, as well, shrugging. "The wind must have carried it from those trees over there."

Connie shivered, staring at them. "Bony fingers, dead eyes!" she muttered. "It's like they're looking at us, isn't it?"

Roc moved to stand behind Connie, staring off at the trees, too.

"You feel eyes in the darkness?" he asked, but his tone wasn't as light as Bruce's. Melinda stared at him, wondering what he could possibly be thinking.

"It's late," Connie murmured.

"Very late," Marina agreed, rising and immediately and efficiently beginning to gather up the dinner things.

Without comment, the others began to help her. Melinda gathered the utensils, while Roc and Peter made sure the fire was completely out. With very little conversation, everything was gathered and brought to the dinghy.

The same efficiency made cleanup equally quick when they returned to the *Crystal Lee*.

When they'd finished, Marina told Melinda good-night and left her in the galley.

Alone, Melinda hesitated, then climbed to the deck. She could hear Roc discussing the next day's dive with Peter and Bruce.

She didn't feel like seeing them all again, so she hurried silently to the captain's cabin.

She hesitated for a long time, then stripped and hopped in the shower, washing away the sand that still clung to her.

When she came out of the shower, the cabin was still empty. She hesitated again, then turned off the light on the desk, crawled into the captain's bunk and lay there listening to the cacophony of her own heart.

Minutes later, the door to the cabin opened. Moonlight filtered in, and she saw Roc silhouetted there, the light gleaming on his shoulders, his face in shadows.

His thoughts in darkness.

Then he entered the cabin, closing the door behind him, moving like a cat in the night, silent, graceful.

She nearly gasped when she realized that he was standing by her side.

"Sleeping?" he asked softly.

She shook her head, then wondered if he saw the motion. "No."

"You've waited up?"

"I—I showered. The sand, you know."

"Umm. The sand. I haven't showered. Should I?"

She felt her heart slamming again. "Your life is none of my business, remember?"

"So I shouldn't shower?"

She smiled suddenly, her lashes sweeping her cheeks. "It's entirely up to you."

"Ah. So I'm not welcome."

She scooted over toward the paneling, running her hand over the empty expanse beside her.

"No," she said very softly, "you're very welcome—with or without sand."

They were the last words she spoke that night. In a matter of seconds he was stretched beside her, warm, electric.

And the sand didn't matter in the least.

Eight

The next day they explored the same area again. Melinda seemed drawn to it, Roc realized, and though they still hadn't found anything, he was more than willing to go with her instincts.

So far, she'd found the only real clue to the *Contessa.*

She was ahead of him today, moving with tremendous ease and grace before him in the fascinating if sometimes eerie world of the sea. The coral shelf to their left housed a wild variety of creatures. Huge, slow groupers—two of them, maybe four hundred pounds apiece—were staring at them with glassy eyes. Just beyond the big fish there was a plateau of anemones, with pretty, bright orange and white clownfish—tiny as fingertips—darting swiftly within their hosts' wavy fingers, luring prey for the anemone that supported the fish.

They passed a pair of yellow tangs, brighter than sunlight. Yet even as they passed the tiny creatures, Roc suddenly became aware of something much larger looming in the water.

Instinctive wariness held him still as he watched, but experience told him the creature wasn't a shark. Just ahead of him, Melinda, too, had gone still, watching, waiting.

Then the creature came into full view, and Roc grinned around his mouthpiece. They were being visited by a dolphin.

That the curious mammal was swimming near them was not an unusual experience. Dolphins were common in these waters—both the mammal, like their friendly visitors, and also the very edible, much smaller and brightly colored dolphin *fish*—but as often as Roc had seen them swimming near him before, he had never seen one behave quite like this. The animal swam straight to Melinda.

He saw her eyes widen behind her mask. She arched a brow to him, then reached out.

Just like a puppy or a kitten, the dolphin seemed to want to be scratched.

Melinda's hand moved gently, knuckles stroking down the creature's throat and downward to its belly. Her air bubbles rose around them both. The dolphin arched its body and plummeted in a smooth dive beneath Melinda. Roc swung around just in time for it to come up on his other side, staring at him with dark eyes, like a precocious youngster who had managed to trick his parents.

He'd swum with dolphins before, having studied them as part of his major in school. They were, in his opinion, absolutely incredible creatures, amazingly intelligent and definitely capable of affection. In captivity, those individuals born and raised with human interaction could display a startling ability to form friendships with man. But in all his days of diving on the ocean floor, he'd never seen one come quite so trustingly close in the wild as this fellow was doing.

He wondered if perhaps the animal hadn't belonged to an aquarium or private study facility, then somehow found its way to the ocean, because it wasn't just being friendly, it wanted to move right in.

Roc reached out a hand, too, touching the dolphin. It edged closer to him, accepting his touch, moving just as if it wanted to be scratched once again, like a cat curling up on its master's lap before a roaring fire.

Melinda swam around, fascinated, running her hand down the dolphin's back once again.

Roc motioned her to move on, curious to see what the dolphin would do.

It followed them.

They spent several minutes swimming around the edge of the World War Two wreck again, crossing through skeleton doorways, over chunks of metal long grown over with seaweed and coral, their new friend following them.

It was a fascinating dive, but one that was yielding nothing, Roc decided wearily a few minutes later as he checked his watch.

He caught up with Melinda and tapped on his dial to show her they were running out of time. She seemed surprised and looked as if she were about to move onward again. He shook his head.

She nodded, and they started toward the ship, the newfound friend still following them.

As they neared the *Crystal Lee,* Melinda paused again, stroking the dolphin. She stared at Roc, and he could see her smiling around her mouthpiece. He shrugged. The dolphin swam around them again, and he reached out, stroking it. Then he gave the water a flippered kick that brought him to the surface, where he spat out his mouthpiece and swam the fifteen feet that brought him to the ladder at the back of the boat. Wrenching off his flippers, he crawled aboard. Bruce was there instantly, taking his tanks and mask as he slid them off.

"Well?" Bruce said anxiously.

Roc shook his head, watching for Melinda. If she was staying down to play with that dolphin...

But just then she broke the surface, quickly swimming toward the boat, reaching the ladder, shedding her flippers, crawling aboard. She ripped off her mask as Roc caught her tanks.

"It was wonderful!" she cried excitedly.

"You did find something!" Bruce exclaimed.

"A dolphin!" Melinda replied, happily nodding her head.

Bruce frowned instantly, staring at Roc. "A dolphin?" he whispered, deflated.

"It was wonderful!" Melinda repeated.

Bruce looked at her as if he wondered what she had been breathing out of her tanks. "But, Melinda, there are lots of dolphins in this area. You must have seen them before."

She sat on the edge of the boat, squeezing the water out of her hair, shaking her head. "Bruce, never in my whole life have I seen one like this. Tell him, Roc!"

A smile curved his lips, and startling warmth swept over him, a tenderness. Her enthusiasm was contagious, her fascinated pleasure with the creature something so warm and real that he found himself wanting to sweep her into his arms then and there.

He leaned back instead, arms crossed over his chest, and shrugged. "I think our friend below must have had human contact before. Perhaps he belonged to an aquarium or private researchers. He is—" He paused a moment, looking over at Melinda; then he grinned. "He is pretty wonderful."

Just as he finished speaking, Joe and Marina, who had also been diving, broke the surface behind them, coming aboard.

"Eh, mon! You never seen such a fish!" Joe exclaimed, coming aboard. "He thought he was my poodle!"

Melinda laughed, staring at Bruce. "See!" she charged.

With the Tobagos aboard, Connie came hurrying out of the galley, and they were all together at the bow of the boat, Connie and Bruce listening to the others' tale about the dolphin.

"I'd love to see him!" Connie exclaimed.

"He'll probably swim around again," Bruce said.

"But maybe he won't," Connie worried.

"He may already be gone," Roc warned.

"I'll go see," Melinda volunteered quickly. She stood, poised to dive off the edge of the boat. Roc told himself that he really had no right to stop her. She wasn't wearing a mask, fins or a tank, but she didn't need them for what she wanted to do. If the dolphin was around, it would play with her right on the surface.

She arched a brow at him, a small smile curving her lips. An invitation.

He shrugged, then leaped up with her. His fingers curled

around hers, and they jumped from the bow together, plummeting swiftly downward into the temperate waters.

It was there—their new mascot—the dolphin waiting just as if it had known that they would come back to play with it.

Melinda caught hold of its dorsal fin, and the creature took her for a swift ride, striking out away from the boat, then swiftly turning and bringing her right back to where they had started from. She grinned at Roc, blinking against the salt in the water, then jackknifed her legs to bring her to the surface for air.

He followed her. With both their heads breaking the surface, Melinda shouted to Connie, "Come on down! He's here!"

"Bruce, please, let's go see it. We've got enough tanks."

Bruce grumbled, but he was already getting the tanks that would allow himself and his sister to dive. Treading water now, Roc called out to Melinda, ten feet away, "Okay, Ms. Davenport, can we let the others play with your sea beast now? We're turning into raisins here."

She hesitated, as if she were about to protest, then lowered her lashes swiftly and agreed.

Funny behavior for Melinda. She'd been with him for three days.

With two incredible nights between them now....

And she'd been an angel, never disagreeing with a single captain's command.

"Why are you staring at me like that?" she demanded.

"I'm wondering what you're up to," he called honestly.

A flash of fire touched her eyes, but she didn't reply; instead she swam to the boat, crawling aboard easily, even as Connie toppled smoothly backward over the edge, wearing her gear.

Roc followed, but more slowly. When he crawled aboard the boat, she had already disappeared. Joe and Marina were still seated on the bow, discussing the extraordinary behavior of the dolphin. Roc caught Joe's eyes, and he knew his friend instantly realized that he was wondering where his wife had disappeared to so quickly.

"She said she had a chill, boss man!" Joe said softly, a

slightly wicked gleam in his dark eyes. "She needed a warm shower and a hot cup of coffee."

Roc nodded, staring at Joe warily, sliding down beside Marina. So she had a chill. Great. He'd just had to say something to ruin things when they were going incredibly well....

But why?

He was startled by the swift pain that seemed to seize him, just like a knife in the chest. It was frightening. And he hated like hell to admit fear. But Melinda was here. Spending her days with him.

Spending her nights with him.

And in those days and nights, it was so easy to go back, to pretend they had never been apart. There were even moments when he could forget that his wife had chosen her father over her husband....

Then there would be those other moments, moments when he would wonder what she was doing there. She had, after all, more or less leaped aboard from Eric Longford's boat, and her father was still Jonathan Davenport.

She had definitely been stunned to discover that she was still legally married to him, and yet...

There were the nights.

He did seem to have the good sense to keep his mouth shut when they were in bed together, but at other times, the bitterness remained. The mistrust. And then he just had to ask what she was doing here. They were on a treasure hunt. He needed to be on the alert. Yet every moment he was near her, his guard relaxed a little bit.

So there was the possibility that she could be sleeping with him by night, searching with him by day... and radioing to her father during any private moment she might be able to sneak!

Well, the future remained to be seen. And if he hurt her with his suspicions, then he was sorry, but then she damned well deserved them.

He realized that Joe and Marina were staring at him, and he scowled.

"My friend," Joe said softly, "I suggest we go ashore for a break."

"A break!"

"We need supplies," Marina told him. "We're nearly out of sugar and coffee and detergent."

"We're low on gas," Joe added.

"And," Marina added, "a night in Nassau might do us all good. Dinner at a restaurant."

"Dancing," Joe added.

Roc sat back, lifting his hands, then letting them fall again. "We're on the brink of discovery—" he began.

"And growing more and more frustrated every day," Joe reminded him. "We know we're in the right place. We're staring straight at the answer—we just haven't touched it yet. Maybe we need to close our eyes, take a break and look again."

Roc started to protest again, but he fell silent instead. Frowning, he thought over Joe's words. Maybe his friend was right. They were staring at the answer. They couldn't see it. Maybe they needed to look away.

"All right," he said quietly. "It should be about two hours into Nassau Harbor. We'll go for tonight—we'll leave by ten tomorrow morning. Marina, that will give you time for shopping and a little R and R."

Marina smiled. "Plenty of time."

"I think—" Roc began, and then he broke off.

"You think what?" Joe asked.

Roc shook his head.

Melinda.

Bring me to a port, any port, she had told him. But she had been determined to come aboard his boat, and now she had even been diving with him, and he would be damned if she was going to get the chance to rejoin her father and dive these waters with him.

Or with Eric Longford.

"I think I need a cup of coffee myself," he said, and stood, then strode toward the steps that led to the galley.

The breeze and sun had dried him by then, and he hurried downward in his damp trunks and bare feet.

Melinda wasn't in the galley.

He strode to the stove and poured himself a cup of coffee, quickly swallowing a sip of the hot black liquid. He swallowed more, wondering what would happen when he reached New Providence, Nassau Harbor, and let his wife reach civilization and a telephone.

And access to the world, if she chose...

He crossed the galley and left it behind, coming to the main deck and swiftly dispensing with the fifteen feet to his own cabin. He threw the door open and entered, closing the door behind him.

Melinda was sitting on the bunk, clad in a white terry robe, towel drying her hair, which she had evidently just washed. She smelled clean, redolent of fresh soap and shampoo. With her hair sleek and wet and pulled back, her eyes were startling against the golden tan of her face.

She stared at him as he entered, watched him warily as he crossed the room and sat on the opposite end of the bunk, leaning against the wall.

"What?" she asked at last, an edge to her voice.

"What are you doing here?" he asked her.

Her lashes fell over her eyes. When they rose again, their aquamarine depths were blazing.

"Sleeping with you for all your deep, dark secrets!" she snapped.

He reached for her, catching her wrists, drawing her close, causing the brush to fall from her fingers. She didn't protest, didn't fight him or say a word. Her chin remained high, her shoulders straight—her eyes afire.

"Damn you, Melinda."

"Isn't that the answer you want?" she demanded.

"I want the truth!" he shouted; then he gritted his teeth, aware of how loud he had been and equally aware that he didn't want anyone else knowing his affairs.

She pulled free of his hold, rising, walking across the cabin as if she had to keep her distance from him. "It doesn't matter what I say to you now," she told him. "I keep thinking that it does, and I even think that whatever the future brings, these days have been…worth the price. Then I look at you, and before you even speak I see it all in your eyes—I've just come to get whatever information I can and bring it back to my father. And Eric."

Her words were so cool, so controlled. He liked her anger better. At least there was passion in it, emotion, a link between them that erupted into more.

He hated her words. He wanted to dispute them.

But they were true.

He stood and walked across the cabin to her, opening his mouth to speak. It would have been easier if she hadn't smelled so delicious. If he hadn't hungered for her for so long. If he didn't know that she was naked beneath the robe, and if he didn't know just how sweet and tempting and stunning that nakedness would be…

"No!" she whispered suddenly, backing away from him. He was amazed to see the glaze of tears in her eyes, when she had been so cold.…

"No what?" he demanded.

She shook her head. "I know…I know that look in your eyes," she murmured as her lashes fell, and against her tan there was a sudden touch of rose. "And it's not…"

"Not what?"

She shook her head again. "You can't do this!" she whispered frantically. "You can't accuse me of everything in the world and then decide that none of it matters if you want to…"

"Make love," he finished roughly. He wanted to push her away, but even more than that he wanted to sweep her into his arms. He threw his hands up in the air. "Damn you!" he whispered. Then he repeated it again raggedly, "Damn you! I can't help it, Melinda, what do you want from me? You chose another man over me—"

"My father—"

"It doesn't matter—you were my wife!"

She swung around, turning her back on him.

He watched her for a moment, aching to touch her, but somehow he managed not to.

"Well," he said softly. "The ball is going to be in your court, Ms. Davenport. We're spending the night in Nassau."

She swung around, staring at him. "What?"

"We're spending the night in Nassau. Of course, if you do disappear and find your way to your father—or Longford—I will manage to find you and wring your neck."

"By what right—"

"You're still my wife!"

She started to walk past him, heading for the cabin door, her strides determined. He caught her arm.

"Let me go," she demanded, her eyes wild.

"I don't think so."

"I don't need to be near you and your—"

"Why are you here, Melinda?"

She jerked away from him. The glaze of tears was in her eyes again. "Has it ever occurred to you that the entire world isn't black and white, Captain Trellyn? Maybe my father was wrong, maybe he even hedged the truth with me—"

"Lied."

"All right, damn you, maybe he lied. He was wrong, he didn't do something that was great, but his transgression against you didn't turn him into a dangerous and evil man!"

"What are you saying to me?"

"Maybe I was wrong, maybe he was wrong, maybe you were wronged. But you weren't perfect in all that happened, either. You walked in and asked me to turn my back on my father—"

"He was wrong!"

"He was still my father!" she cried.

His fingers were wound so tightly around her wrists that he was surprised she didn't cry out. He forced himself to ease his hold. "So why are you here?" he demanded.

"Because we were *wrong!*" she cried in exasperation, trying with no success to free herself from his touch. Her head flew back, her eyes a sea of blue-green fire once again. "Because on this one,'' she gasped, ''I figured I owed you. I wanted you to make this claim. I wanted you to find your *Contessa*.''

She trembled with the passion of her words, with the fury of them, with the emotion of them. He tried to stiffen his shoulders, tried to retain rational thought. It was all drifting away in his hunger to slip his hands over her bare shoulders, to force the terry robe to fall to the floor. But his fingers were trembling as he held her, and he gritted his teeth hard.

''So, Ms. Davenport, when I pull into Nassau, you'll be staying with me? My wife, in my room?''

''Yes, your wife!'' she snapped out. ''But you don't even call me by my name anymore, it's always *Ms. Davenport!*''

Startled, he nearly stepped back. He *had* been calling her Ms. Davenport almost continually since she had come aboard. Maybe it had been a defense mechanism, part of the wall he had erected against her. But now...

Now it surprised him that she had noticed, and that it had apparently bothered her.

Anger drained from him as he stared at her taut, strained features and dazzling eyes.

''All right, Mrs. Trellyn,'' he said very softly, ''when I pull into Nassau, are you sharing a room with me? Perhaps dinner and dancing ashore? Or will you be leaving at the first opportunity?''

Her lashes fell swiftly.

''Melinda!''

Her eyes rose to his again. ''Yes!'' she hissed.

''Yes, *which?*'' he demanded hoarsely.

''I'll be staying with you!'' she cried angrily. Her lower lip was trembling. ''I told you, I'm here to see that you make your claim, that...''

Her voice trailed away, but it didn't matter. He set his forefinger on the trembling curve of her lower lip and stared at it, fascinated.

Then, at long last, he gave in to temptation, slipping his hands beneath the terry robe to her bare shoulders, touching the smoothness of her skin, causing the robe to fall to the floor. He moved his finger so that his lips could touch down on hers, then cradled her in his arms, kissing her passionately.

For one brief moment, she was stiff. Resisting him...

Then her arms curled around his neck, and he threaded his fingers through the drying strands of golden hair that waved over her shoulders, entangling them both. She was flush against his body, the tips of her breasts hardened cherry peaks against the dark hair on his chest. He groaned aloud, kissing her, tasting her, feeling the fullness of her lithe form against his, feeling the desperate rise of heat and hardness within himself.

Her lips broke from his suddenly, her fingers trailing over his shoulders as her mouth touched the furiously pounding pulse at his throat. She lowered herself against him, lips, teeth and tongue playing over his chest, fingers rubbing his muscled flesh, his nipples, the lines of his ribs. She followed the curve of his body still lower; then her fingers were around the elastic rim of his trunks, sliding them down over his hips. He stepped instantly from them, kicking them aside.

She dropped suddenly on her knees before him, and he gasped with the shattering sensation that filled him like lightning when she took him in her hands, stroking, touching him.

Lowering her golden blond head, she stroked him anew.

The world exploded, or perhaps it was only himself. He bent down, sweeping her up, his lips covering hers as he carried her swiftly to the bunk, setting her there, straddling her, then lying at her side, the pulse that had guided him before now beating a thousand times harder, pounding within his head, his heart, his loins.

His mouth found hers again. Left it. Touched down upon a very delicate vein at her throat. His eyes met hers again. They seemed so liquid, so beautiful, so mesmerizing.

"I..." she whispered.

"Yes?" he demanded huskily.

Her eyes closed against him. "Want you," she said very softly.

"Well, *Mrs. Trellyn,* you've got me!" he assured her huskily.

Indeed, she had him....

He stared over the length of her. The slim, shapely, so damned perfect length of her. His hands covered her breasts, encircling them. His head lowered, and he tasted the tips with his tongue, cherished their fullness with fiery liquid caresses. Her fingers dug into his hair, danced slowly over his back, dug again as she groaned softly, shifting beneath him.

He spread his hand over her abdomen, seeing the bronze of his skin against the pale flesh that was normally covered by her bathing suit. He pressed his lips there. Circled his tongue around her navel. Inched downward against her, watching his fingers as they entered the golden blond triangle above her thighs. Felt her move and shift and writhe beneath him.

He shifted his own weight up, parting her thighs fluidly, his knees between them. Then he lowered his head, stroking and touching and laving with a searing, wet, intimate desire.

She shuddered, gasped, cried out. He rose above her, taking her into his arms, sinking deeply within her until she shuddered anew, all the while whispering her name....

Minutes later, hours, moments—he didn't know which—the whole of the world seemed to explode again. She trembled wickedly within his arms; then they drifted to earth, and her trembling became shivers as the cool afternoon air settled over bodies that had burned and now grew chill. He held her close, tenderly, neither of them speaking for the longest time.

Then he realized that she was staring at the paneled ceiling above them. He stroked her cheek, and she turned toward him, her eyes damp.

"What is it?" he asked her softly.

She shook her head.

"Melinda?"

"I..."

"What?"

Her lips moved; and she shook her head again, her lashes falling quickly over her eyes. "I swear," she murmured. "I want to help you stake your claim."

Silently he cradled her against him once again. He stroked her hair and felt the rocking of the boat.

Then he groaned.

"What?" she asked him softly.

"Well, if we're going to make Nassau tonight, I'd better get moving."

He rose. She curled his pillow to her chest, staring at him with a troubled gaze.

"Why are we going to Nassau?"

"Marina needs some supplies. And she also thinks we can't see the forest for the trees."

Melinda nodded, understanding with no more need for an explanation.

"I'm going to shower," he told her.

She nodded again. He started toward the head door, wishing he could stay in the bunk with her.

Yet suddenly more anxious than ever to reach Nassau. A luxury hotel room for the night. A great dinner somewhere, and then the night ahead of them. In an air-conditioned room, maybe with a bottle of champagne at their side...

"Roc!" she called after him.

He paused, turning. She half rose, watching him with eyes that had gone dark with emotion again, tense, passionate.

"I meant what I said. I told you the truth. I want *you* to make this claim."

He walked to her and kissed the top of her head, then looked into her eyes again.

"You know what I want?" he asked her softly.

She shook her head, and he kissed her lips lightly.

"Well, I very much want you to be *Mrs. Trellyn* tonight," he told her.

She searched his eyes.

"Well," she murmured lightly. "It seems you've got me."

So it seemed....

He managed to turn around again, and this time he made it to the shower.

After all, the night loomed ahead....

Nine

The first time Melinda had entered Nassau Harbor, she had felt a strange affinity and affection for the place. She'd been a little girl that first time, spending the summer with her father. The summers had been magical times to begin with. The year had always seemed so hard, so strained. She loved her mother, but she never really knew her, so she would sit throughout the year dreaming about the summer, about sailing on her father's boats, racing the wind, or motoring through the waves on one quest or another, but always following the lure of adventure. He had brought her to many of the islands in the Bahamas, the heavily populated ones, the not-so-populated ones, even the uninhabited ones. She had learned very early to love the tranquil azure waters, the gentle, laid-back singsong of the people, the sun that shone so frequently and so fiercely, the magical beaches and the lure of the reefs. She loved so many of the islands. But sometimes, she thought, coming here was the best of all.

Nassau, the hub of the Bahamian island of New Providence, was definitely filled with tourists and tourist attractions, but it always seemed to carry a little bit of the past with it, a charming past, filled with the nice and the not so nice, but even the shadowy realms of the past seemed to add to the draw of the place.

In her day, Nassau had been a haven for countless pirates. She had harbored smugglers, thieves, murderers and more, and she had survived them all.

Coming in was always beautiful. Giant cruise ships often lingered in the harbor while their passengers were off motorcycling or shopping, visiting forts, or sitting in quaint little restaurants for tea. In the downtown section many of the buildings were from the colonial period, painted in soft pastels that seemed to beckon the traveler from the sea.

It was a comfortable place for American citizens, with easy customs procedures, and Roc dropped her and all the crew except for Joe Tobago on the dock to acquire rooms for the evening while he cleared the *Crystal Lee* for the night and made provisions to obtain gas and a few other necessities for the boat.

Marina, with relatives in town, shooed Melinda, Bruce and Connie on to check in to the hotel they had chosen, telling them that she was going shopping for bargains, and that she and Joe would see them at dinner.

"Let's walk along Bay Street a little bit," Connie suggested as they stood on the dock.

Bruce groaned.

"All right," Melinda quickly agreed.

"How about I go get rooms, and you two go walking?" Joe suggested.

Connie grinned. "Great!" she told her brother.

So she and Melinda did just that, jostling with the tourists through the straw market, where Connie found a new hat for the endless days on the *Crystal Lee* with the sun beating down, and then they wandered past hawkers with their wares to Bay Street, where the shops were indoors, often air-conditioned, and offered many exotic and expensive perfumes and imported wools and clothing, as well as more touristy goods.

Melinda waved a perfume bottle beneath her nose in one store and discovered Connie behind her, sniffing as well. "That's wonderful! What is it?"

"Something native, I think. Umm, here. They call it Passion Flower," Melinda told her.

Connie picked up the vial, then surveyed the shelf. "They have bath oil, perfume, dusting powder…the works." She picked up Melinda's wrist where Melinda had dabbed the perfume. "Oh, wow, this smells great on you."

Melinda shrugged. "I'm just window-shopping," she told Connie.

"But it's—" Connie began, but she stopped short. "Oh, I know. You don't have your wallet, But I have mine—"

"Connie, I'm not going to borrow money from you."

"But I have one of your husband's credit cards."

Melinda's brows shot up in surprise. Connie shrugged and explained quickly. "We all have them. He's extraordinary to work for. He's great about giving credit to everyone, about sharing all our finds—and he still covers expenses. None of us abuse the privilege, you know—"

"Connie, I can't imagine you abusing anything!" Melinda assured the pretty blonde quickly.

"This perfume is great. And you should get it. Let me put it on his card."

Melinda shook her head. "No."

"He's your husband—"

Melinda shook her head emphatically. "Connie, honestly, neither one of us knew it, so it doesn't count."

Connie grinned suddenly. "You know, you're not half the shrew you're supposed to be. Not that Roc ever said anything about you, you know. But we all kind of knew the story. And I didn't mean that. About being half a shrew. You're not a shrew at all, but even other divers are kind of in awe of your abilities, and I guess men think a woman has to be tough and—oh, wow, I'm not getting myself out of this at all, am I?"

Melinda, grinning, shook her head.

"I'm buying a pack of this stuff, from the soap and bubble bath on down."

"Not for me."

"For you. On your husband's credit card."

"But—"

"Well, you are sleeping with him again, aren't you?" Connie demanded.

This was absurd. She felt like laughing while she turned every color of crimson, also while turning swiftly around to see just who else might have heard Connie's question.

"Connie—"

"Trust me! He won't mind."

There was no stopping the woman. Melinda stayed with her to make sure she didn't buy out the store; then they left, and in the next shop Connie found a bikini she thought would be perfect for Melinda. She also insisted that Melinda couldn't keep diving in the same bathing suit over and over again, so in the end, Connie bought the suit, but Melinda insisted that she would pay her back just as soon as she got hold of some of her own money.

"Roc pays really well—"

"So does my father!" Melinda assured her.

They spent another hour poking around as if they were tourists. Melinda discovered that though Connie had been to Nassau a dozen times, she'd never managed to hear much of its history, so Melinda told her about the wild pirate days. The island had been in bad shape when Woodes Rogers, the first royal governor of the Bahamas, arrived in Nassau in 1718, determined to make it a decent place to live. He was so determined that he made the pirates clean up the island, even managing to make a few of them clean up themselves.

They wandered past some of the beautiful buildings from the late 1700s, and Melinda told her that many of the American colonists who had been loyal to Great Britain during the Revolutionary War had hurried here once their cause had been lost. At last they turned toward their hotel.

Bruce met them in the lobby. He'd already showered and shaved and settled in, so it seemed, and he was just waiting to give them their keys before moving out to the terrace for a few drinks beneath the coolness of the ceiling fans. Connie promised to join him shortly, and Bruce shrugged. "We've got dinner reservations in the Turtle Room for eight. Just be there," he warned.

Melinda and Connie left Bruce in the lobby, then parted from each other in the elevator. Connie got off on the second floor, and as the elevator took her up to the seventh floor—the highest—Melinda mused at Roc's choice. He tended to like things that were old and atmospheric, but this was one of the new hotels, beautiful but modern.

When she turned her key in the door and entered her room, she paused, biting her lip, all at once understanding his choice.

The room was heaven.

Huge windows overlooked the harbor and the beautiful old buildings, the whole bustle of the place. There was a door to her left leading to a spacious bathroom, and the king-size bed was to the right of the magnificent windows, while there was a huge Jacuzzi to the left of them. A wet bar flanked the rear wall, while a large-screen TV and video system was set across from the bed.

"Wow!" she murmured softly.

She dropped her duffel bag of borrowed belongings and walked over to the tub, reading the instructions on how to use it. It was wonderfully tempting. She set the water and the temperature, then brought over a few of the Passion Flower bubble cubes. She was just about to strip and plunge in when there was a soft knock on the door.

She opened it to find a bellman there with a package for her.

"There must be a mistake—" she began.

"No, ma'am. Your husband sent this. There's a card."

"Oh!" she murmured. Where was Roc? And what was he up to now? She felt a too familiar trembling seize hold of her. Some moments could be so perfect. So unbelievably perfect. Then she would see his eyes on her, see the suspicion in them, and she would wonder—no, she would know!—that he doubted her again, and her heart would sink, because she was so afraid that he could never really trust her again.

"Oh," she said again, taking the package from the man. "I'm so sorry," she said awkwardly, "I don't have a cent on me at the moment. If you'll give me your name—"

"I'm all taken care of, lady," he assured her swiftly, with a wide smile. "Enjoy."

She closed the door, studying the package. Then she walked to the bed and ripped the paper off with a burning curiosity.

It was a dress. The fabric was a wild mixture of exotic colors, turquoises and blues and greens, fashioned into a strapless creation with a short flared skirt. It was made of the softest silk, with a petticoat to go under the skirt. There were also a number of skimpy silk panties in the bundle, and a pair of white sandals.

And a note.

Size 7 on the dress, 8 on the shoes. I'm sure memory serves me correctly. Please accept these, as I'm anxious for Mrs. Trellyn to appear tonight in her own clothing, and they are offered with all good heart. See you soon, Roc.

Melinda set the package down softly, her fingers moving over the cool silk. It was a beautiful dress, and it would be perfect for her. He'd always had an eye for clothing.

"Offered with all good heart..." she whispered aloud. "And what do you think that means?" she asked the dress. "I'm not after a present—I'm after a lifetime!"

She set the dress down, certain that it wasn't proper to accept such a present from a husband she had just discovered was still hers.

Or was he?

She clenched her teeth tightly, wondering if she wanted a relationship that was constantly embittered by suspicion and feeling a moment's desolation as she wondered if there could possibly be any way back.

Yet that afternoon...

Things could be so wonderful. Maybe she did have a chance. She'd tried so hard not to respond to many of his comments. Just as she'd tried so hard that afternoon not to let the words slip from her lips. *I love you...*

She had been so close to whispering them, so close to giving away the truth—along with her heart, her soul and her pride. It had to wait, she knew. Had to wait until he believed in her again.

Until maybe he could fall in love with her again. She'd revealed a great deal about how she'd spent the time they'd been apart from one another—and he hadn't told her a thing.

She sat at the foot of the bed, feeling overwhelmed for a moment. Then she looked at the tub, filled with Passion Flower bubbles, and she stripped off her shorts and shirt and stepped in.

The water was hot. She winced, then felt the steam crawl all over her. It was a delicious, soothing feeling. She sank down, closed her eyes and appreciated the sheer physical comfort, then opened her eyes again and appreciated the size of the tub. It was oval, surrounded by beautiful tile and handsome brass racks for towels and robes, and small brass shelves for soaps and shampoos. The bubbles broke around her, their sweet scent rising to her.

Please, God, she thought suddenly, don't let me fail him. She closed her eyes, thinking again of the night when he had left, how she had been so certain that he wouldn't go....

Her father had told her within a few weeks that he had colored the truth a little and that she should give Roc a call.

She'd been so hurt then. Devastated. And determined that no one would know.

Then again, what she had said today had been the truth. Her father had behaved badly, though he wasn't a bad man. He had loved Roc like a son, taken him beneath his wing.

"Stubborn!" she said softly.

She closed her eyes again, savoring the heat. Then she heard a key twisting in the lock, and she looked up quickly. The door opened and closed.

Roc was there.

He strode in, surveying the room swiftly. He was clad in cutoff jeans and a plaid denim shirt and brown scuffs. His hair was too long and delightfully askew over his forehead.

She felt that trembling begin inside her again. Then the aching. The longing.

She had loved him so much. She still did.

"Like it?" he asked her, throwing his duffel bag down on the end of the elegant king-size bed.

"It's great," she said, her arms stretched out on the tub's tile rim, a small sea of bubbles around her.

He walked over to the plate glass windows to see the view of the city, now darkening with the sunset and coming to life with artificial light.

"Thanks for the dress," she told him.

He spun around. She thought again how much she liked every little thing about him, the stubborn curve of his chin, the inky color of his hair, the vivid blue of his eyes. The handsome breadth of his shoulders beneath his shirt.

He arched a brow. "Do you like it?"

She wanted to say something flippant, but only nodded.

Suddenly he started undoing the buttons of his shirt, then gave up and wrenched it over his head. He kicked off his sandals and unzipped his fly, stepped from his shorts and briefs and walked over to the tub.

She bit her lower lip, fighting the wave of hot shivers that seized her. He was entirely bronzed—except for that white streak around his hips and sex—and there wasn't a half-inch on him that could be pinched. Muscle corded his throat and shoulders and even the flatness of his belly.

She lowered her lashes quickly, wishing he didn't affect her the way he did, almost wishing she had kept her distance.

He might want her again. Wanting was easy enough.

But she wanted more. She wanted him to love her. She didn't want to be his wife because they had both forgotten to get a divorce—she wanted to be his wife because he loved her still.

As much as she loved him.

There was no way to tell him that now. Too much lay between them.

But as he sank into the water with her, an easy smile rose to her lips.

"The dress is great," she heard herself saying huskily. "Thanks. I mean, under the circumstances, I really don't have much to wear. I'll pay you back—"

"You're crew at the moment," he told her. "You don't owe me anything." He winced briefly at the heat of the water, then slid over to sit in front of one of the jets. She saw the tension ease from his face as he said, "Ah!" softly.

"Well, we'll see," she murmured.

His eyes had been closed, his head back, resting on the tiles. He opened them suddenly.

"Have you tried it on?"

"Not yet. I saw the tub and..."

He grinned, lacing his fingers behind his head, leaning back again. "Definitely inviting."

She nodded.

He frowned suddenly, inhaling deeply. He arched a brow at her. "What am I bathing in?" he asked.

She grinned. "Passion Flower," she told him.

He groaned.

"You don't like it?" she whispered. "Connie thought it was great. In fact, Connie told me that as crew, I could buy some and put it on your credit card."

He was silent, but his grin deepened, and his eyes were on hers. "I like it on you."

"Do you always buy bubble bath for your crew?"

"Depends on the crew member."

She started to rise, but he swiftly moved a foot, and to her surprise she found herself falling back into the slick tub.

"To the best of my knowledge, you're the only crew member for whom I've ever purchased bubble bath."

She sat still, staring at him. A moment later she felt his toes again, inching along her calf. His eyes met hers, and he smiled wolfishly.

Then she felt his toe along her inner thigh. Her upper thigh. Touching her intimately.

"Roc..." she whispered.

He grinned and came across the tub. "We've got to make love," he assured her, straddling her in the swirling water. "After all, we both smell like Passion Flower!"

She started to laugh, but then his lips sealed her laughter in her mouth, and the fullness of his body filled her with the same steaming heat that lapped around her. Her laughter was swallowed by the ecstasy that filled her, the hunger, the sweet delight. And eons later, when darkness filled the room and she lay dazed and sated and serene in the security of his arms on the expanse of the huge bed, she heard him sigh.

"I had Bruce make dinner reservations for eight. I think I'd best shower off my perfumed bubbles before we meet the gang, eh, Ms. Daven—Mrs. Trellyn?"

She felt tears sting her eyes and nodded in the darkness, hoping he didn't notice them.

He left her, striding toward the shower.

She waited a few minutes, then slipped in with him, her bar of Passion Flower in her hand while he used the soap provided by the hotel.

He looked curiously at her.

She shrugged. "Well, it worked once!" she said mischievously.

She found herself in his arms once again. "Melinda, the scent is nice. Sexy. Alluring. But you know what?"

"What?"

"You don't need a single whiff of it!"

His lips touched hers.

Why, in God's name, had they stayed apart so long?

She drew away from him, trembling again. "Dinner, eight o'clock," she reminded him.

"Eight o'clock," he agreed.

She stepped out of the shower, leaving him there. She made good use of the rest of her Passion Flower assortment, the talc and the body lotion. Then she slipped into a pair of the new silk panties, the elegant strapless dress and the sandals. When he emerged at last in a towel, she was brushing her hair and awaiting his appearance.

"Wow," he said softly.

She twirled for him. "You've always had great taste," she assured him somewhat primly.

"Yes," he said softly. "I have, haven't I?"

She started to smile as he walked over to her, then kissed her lightly. "Why don't you go on down before I get too tempted not to dress? I'll bet Connie's anxiously awaiting you by now."

"I'll wait," Melinda told him.

He groaned. "No, do me a favor, get out of here!"

She smiled, finding it very hard to leave. "All right," she told him at last. As she walked toward the door, she could feel his eyes upon her. She paused, turning back. *I love you!* she nearly cried, but she held back the words. "We'll be waiting," she told him.

She left him then, and hurried down to the Turtle Room. It was easy to find their table; the others were all there, Bruce handsome in a casual white suit, Connie lovely in a crimson flower creation, and the Tobagos a very striking couple, he in casual beige, she in striking red.

"Come, sit!" Marina called across the room to her as she entered. She hurried to their table. Bright tropical flowers adorned it. When she sat, she discovered that Connie had already ordered her the house specialty to drink. She wasn't at all sure what it was, but it was a soft orange color, and filled with pineapples and cherries and oranges. She took a sip and found it a little sweet, but good. Across the room, a calypso band was playing. The night seemed so easy, so perfect.

"Turtle steak is the specialty," Connie told her over the music.

Melinda made a face. "I've had it before. Not my favorite. I can't help feeling sorry for the turtle."

"What about cows? Have you ever seen animals with more soulful eyes?" Connie demanded.

Melinda laughed. "I don't dare think about it!" she admitted.

A moment later Roc arrived. He was wearing a light blue sport jacket and a striped shirt, no tie and darker trousers. Somehow, despite the fact that he'd packed in a duffel bag, he appeared pressed and relaxed and very handsome, his jacket emphasizing the striking color of his eyes.

He drew out the chair next to Melinda. "Have we ordered yet?"

She shook her head. "Dolphin?" she suggested.

He nodded. "The fish, of course. Not like our friend out at sea today. I learned something about him, by the way."

Her brows shot up.

"They call him Hambone. Everyone thinks he must have been in an aquarium somewhere. He's played with a number of the divers and spear fishermen around here."

"Maybe he'll stick with us!" Connie suggested.

"Maybe he's good luck," Marina said.

"Maybe," Roc agreed. Melinda felt his fingers squeeze her thigh. He reached over and sipped her drink, then made a face.

"What is it?"

"I'm not at all sure."

He grinned. Their waiter was there, and he ordered the dolphin oreganato and a beer. She ordered the dolphin, too. The rest of the table went for turtle steaks.

They talked about the dolphin, Hambone, and they talked about diving again, and Roc, his hand still resting lightly on her knee, mentioned that he was grateful for Melinda's finding the spoon, or else he would be worrying now that he was chasing a figment of his imagination.

His eyes touched hers. Cobalt. Warm.

It was a wonderful night.

They finished their food, then ordered exotic coffees. The band was playing, and people were dancing.

Roc stood at a slow number and reached down to her. She took his hand and rose swiftly, following him to the dance floor, where she leaned against his chest. His hand moved tenderly over the hair at her nape as they drifted together.

"Nice night!" he murmured.

"Very nice," she whispered against the fabric of his jacket.

Yet she had barely spoken when she suddenly felt him stiffen and go dead still.

Suddenly she realized that someone had tapped him on the shoulder.

"Excuse me, may I cut in, Trellyn? It seems you're dancing with a friend of mine!"

She instantly went cold, her hands growing clammy long before she looked up and saw Eric Longford standing at Roc's shoulder.

He was a tall man, nearly of a size with Roc, as broad shouldered, as well muscled, blond where Roc was dark, his eyes very light, his upper lip covered with a platinum mustache. Striking...

But not Roc! her heart cried out.

And then panic set in as she saw Roc's eyes. Saw him look at Eric, then felt the ice in his gaze. "Longford," he breathed very softly.

The music was still playing, but Roc wasn't holding Melinda anymore. His arms were crossed over his chest as he stared at Eric.

"Longford. Just imagine. What on earth could you be doing here?"

"Just trying to dance," Eric said, placing a hand on Melinda's shoulder.

She would have eased away—except that his was a powerful grasp.

It didn't matter.

Roc's hand suddenly fell on her other shoulder.

"Trellyn, I was cutting in—"

"But I'm not letting go," Roc said icily.

The tension was combustible. Melinda herself wanted to scream. She knew Roc, knew his thoughts.

He was thinking that Eric could only be here if she had contacted him, if she had told him where to find her....

But it wasn't true!

"Trellyn, Melinda and I—"

"Longford, what's the matter? Have you lost your comprehension of the English language? You're not cutting in. Not on this dance, partner!"

Now they each had one of her hands. And each started to walk in a different direction.

So this was to be her punishment for recklessness! Drawn and quartered on the dance floor, she thought in fleeting panic.

"Eric—" she began, determined not to let this get out of hand. She had to let Roc know that she hadn't contacted anyone.

Damn him! She was furious! No matter what, he doubted her so damned quickly!

"Wait!" she tried again, jerking furiously on both hands.

But before she could go any further, she felt another set of hands fall on her shoulders. And a third male voice suddenly intervened on her behalf.

"Gentlemen! Will both of you get your hands off my daughter?"

Her father. Oh, God.

Her hands were free. She spun around. Yes, he was there. As tall, as handsome as the other men. A little older, of course, and very dignified tonight, his bronzed face ageless, his eyes so like the color of her own, his hair bleached platinum from constant exposure to the sun. His eyes held a startling twinkle.

"Dad!" she gasped.

"Oh, sure—*Dad!*" Roc said softly.

"Nice way to greet me after all this time, Trellyn," Jonathan said irritably.

"We're making a scene on the dance floor," Melinda commented wryly.

"Then dance with me," Eric suggested, taking her arm. "Let them settle old grievances!"

"Eric, if you'd just—"

"Longford, damn it!" Jonathan said firmly. "I meant what I said. Get your hands off my daughter."

"Right," Roc agreed. He took her hand again and pulled. She flew from Eric hard against Roc's tense body.

"Now, Trellyn—" Jonathan Davenport began.

"Now, nothing!" Roc nearly growled. "You can both get your hands off my *wife!*" he commanded.

Then, before anyone had a chance to say anything else, he whirled, leaving the dance floor.

And very determinedly dragging Melinda right along with him.

Ten

In all his life, Roc couldn't remember being as fiercely angry as he had been when Eric Longford walked up and tapped his shoulder.

So she was there to help him! Right! And she'd just brought a few friends and close relations along for the ride!

The temptation to throw a fist into Longford's face had been overwhelming. Somehow, though, he had managed not to touch the man, despite his obvious anger.

Maybe that had had something to do with Jonathan Davenport's sudden appearance.

He couldn't deck them both.

And no matter how he itched to do so, he certainly couldn't deck Melinda.

And just when he had begun to believe...

"What in God's name are you doing?" she seethed at him.

What was he doing? He didn't really know. Just getting away from the entire situation as fast as possible before something did happen.

Just getting *her* away.

But as he stared into her features, pale and taut, he realized that Melinda was every bit as angry as he was. He'd dragged her from the floor, right past the dinner table, through the lobby and to the elevator.

"I've never seen anyone be so rude in my entire life!" she snapped angrily. There were people in the lobby, so she kept her voice down, but it carried a wallop of vehemence.

"Rude?" he said. *"Rude?"*

"That was my father back there—" she began.

"Oh, yeah, that's right!"

She jerked at her hand, but he had it in a vise, and he didn't let go.

"He's a salvage diver, just like you, remember? He spends a lot of time on the water, he was near here when we radioed, and Nassau is hardly a strange place to find him."

"How convenient."

She gasped suddenly, her eyes narrowing. "So I called him here, is that it? I wasn't allowed to use the radio alone, remember?"

"You could have done anything you wanted after your first day aboard. You seduced the entire crew the same way you seduced me."

She tugged hard on her hand. Too late. The elevator door had opened. He drew her through with him and punched their floor number.

He leaned against the back wall of the cubicle as it began to move, his fingers soldered to hers.

She stood very straight, outraged, indignant.

"If you think I'm going to share a room with you after the things you've been saying, you've lost your mind."

"If you think you're going back with your father or Longford, *you've* lost *your* mind."

"I didn't summon my father here. You can ask him."

The elevator reached their floor, and the door opened. Roc crossed the hallway, digging in his pocket for his key. Only when they entered the room did he release her fingers at last.

She walked farther into the room, giving herself some distance from him, and spun around. "I'm telling you—"

"Don't bother!"

He leaned against the door, staring at her, feeling a dull ache burning in his stomach, his heart. She was still crying innocent. But both Davenport and Longford were just below, and both of them had always been interested in the *Contessa.*

She admitted jumping into his net from one of Longford's boats. And tonight the tall blond man had been just itching to get his hands on her....

"I'm not staying with you," she told him quietly. She was standing very straight, her shoulders squared, her hair like spun gold tumbling around her shoulders, her eyes as bright as gems, her chin very high.

He wished the fire that was ripping through him would burn itself out. He wanted so much to take back his words. He wanted to believe her.

But he'd been burned badly before. He couldn't take any chances.

She'd done everything so smoothly. Arriving out of the blue—literally. Admitting she'd been on Longford's boat. Swimming with him—just swimming—and finding the spoon. Then continuing to search and finding nothing.

But now that she had her bearings...well, here they all were.

He shook his head, staring at her. "You have to stay here," he said flatly.

"I wouldn't stay with anyone who acted the way you have."

"Because you're so innocent. Because you're so anxious for me to lay claim to the *Contessa.*"

"Because your behavior is horrible."

He was still leaning against the door. It seemed to be giving him strength. "You said that you'd stay here," he reminded her.

"I'm not going to my father or—or anyone!" she snapped to him impatiently. "I simply can't stay with you after everything you've accused me of doing!"

He swept his arm out, indicating the still tousled bed where they had found a few precious moments of abandon.

"It's yours," he told her. "I've slept on numerous floors. I'll just take the bedspread and a pillow."

"I don't think you understand!" she exclaimed. "I don't want to be near anyone who's convinced that I'm such a horrible human being!''

"And I don't think you understand. You're not leaving."

She whirled around, heading for the glass windows to stare out at the city below. "All right, Captain Trellyn!" she snapped, her voice as cold as dripping icicles. "Fine. I won't leave this room. I'll finish the entire search without saying a word to another living soul. But you just keep your distance from me, do you understand?"

Keep his distance from her...

When he already hated what he had started, when he was ready to give up the whole damned hunt just to have her again, with no need to hold her, because she would stay of her own free will, just to be with him.

He felt ill, but stood straight, feeling very cold himself. So distant. That was what she wanted.

The phone rang suddenly, jarringly. Melinda jumped, then stared at it without moving.

It kept ringing.

"I'm certainly not going to answer it and give away the great secrets of the deep!" she exclaimed.

"Why not? It's your father—or your *dear friend* Longford."

She didn't move, so he crossed the room and yanked the receiver off the phone. "What?"

"'Hello' is the more customary response," Jonathan Davenport informed him lightly.

"'What do you want?' is far more appropriate under the circumstances. Although I'm assuming I know what you want. To speak with your daughter. Well, I'm sorry. She can't talk tonight."

Melinda was staring at him with a fury that promised to be explosive. Then he forgot about her, suddenly startled by Jonathan's response. "Can't talk to her, eh? Is she bound and gagged? Never mind, that wouldn't be your style. I just wanted to make sure she was all right."

"She's absolutely wonderful—for a woman wearing a gag."

"Why don't you meet me for a drink?" Jonathan suggested.

"Why?"

"Maybe you'd be willing to give me a chance to talk to you. Maybe you'd even be willing to give me a chance to apologize."

Roc kept staring at Melinda, stunned. Old man Davenport wanting to apologize?

It could be true. Maybe somewhere along the line he had decided that he had been wrong. Maybe he'd even told his daughter that he'd been wrong.

"Yeah," he said slowly. Melinda was stil staring at him.

"There's a small bar off the main lobby. I'll be there," Davenport told him.

Roc replaced the receiver, still staring at Melinda. He lifted a hand to indicate the room. "It's all yours."

"What are you doing?" she demanded, suddenly running after him as he headed for the door. Her eyes were suddenly anxious, the chill gone from her voice.

"Well, I'm not going out to get into a brawl with your father. Is that what you're worried about?"

She fell silent, staring at him.

"I won't be gone long," he said swiftly.

He turned and exited the room with long strides, then leaned against the door once he had closed it behind him. He waited for a long moment, wondering if she would follow.

But she didn't.

He found the bar easily enough, and Jonathan Davenport more easily. He was sitting on one of the bar stools—with Connie by his side.

They made a startlingly attractive couple, both slim and blond, both tanned. Jonathan, of course, despite the fact that he looked damned good for his age, was still a more mature individual, with his bronzed face and craggy features. But Connie was laughing delightedly at something he was saying, glowing, her velvet brown eyes wide and bright. She was very pretty in the crimson dress that enhanced her pale hair and darker eyes. And Jonathan *was* a handsome man.

Perhaps he needed to have been, to have something to do with the creation of his daughter.

Despite the age difference—at least sixteen or seventeen years—the two looked good together.

Then Roc scowled suddenly, wondering just what Connie was doing with the man. Where the hell was Bruce?

Bruce was her brother, not her keeper, he reminded himself, admitting that his mood was raw, his temper still frayed. Only curiosity had brought him here. At least Melinda couldn't go running out to talk to her father, since he would be talking to Jonathan himself.

Which left Eric Longford, of course.

And that called for a Scotch.

He walked across the crowded bar and slid into the seat on the other side of Jonathan.

Connie's brown eyes went very wide. "Roc! I was just—I guess the two of you want to talk. I think I'll take a walk through the lobby."

She leaped up, disappearing before either of them could protest.

Roc ordered a drink swiftly, then sipped it, staring at his old friend and mentor. He looked good. And clean living, Roc decided, hadn't done it.

"Sweet girl," Jonathan said lightly, referring to Connie.

"Little young for you," Roc commented.

Jonathan shrugged. "Maybe. But I always thought interests and compatibility were more important than age."

Roc lifted his glass to Jonathan. "That's because you're aging," he informed him.

Jonathan laughed, not offended in the least. He ran his fingers up and down his beer glass, staring at the amber liquid. "So she's bound and gagged, eh?"

"You don't want to run up and rescue your daughter?" Roc said.

Jonathan shrugged, turning to stare at Roc at last, his eyes so like his daughter's, determined. "That depends," he said.

"On what?"

"Is it true that my daughter is still your wife?" Jonathan demanded.

It was Roc's turn to shrug. "Well, Davenport, I never divorced her. So if she never filed papers against me, then she's still my wife."

Jonathan nodded. "Well, then..." he murmured.

"Well, then what?"

"Well, then—I'm not going to go up and rescue her. This is between the two of you."

Roc took a sip of his Scotch. "She was on one of Longford's boats when she dived into my net, you know."

Davenport seemed to wince. "She does have that reckless streak in her."

"She wasn't with you," Roc commented.

"Of course she wasn't!" Davenport replied indignantly. "I would never have let her pull such a stunt, and she would have damned well known it. She must have wheedled Longford—" He broke off, maybe realizing instinctively just how Roc felt about the other man. He shrugged again. "Well, she hadn't been with him long. We were in Miami together the morning before you called me, so they had just gone out on a day trip."

"I'll give you this, Jonathan, you do make more of an effort to explain her behavior than she does."

"Well, she didn't really know she had to explain her behavior, did she now? You two have been apart for a long time."

"It was her choice," Roc reminded him.

Jonathan nodded, his eyes downcast for a moment. "Her choice and my mistake then," he said, staring at Roc again. "I was wrong—the find was yours. Even if the salvage should have been shared, the credit should have been yours. Maybe I was just so damned irritated that you could be so right—and against all the odds I quoted you. Maybe I just couldn't believe that I could be so wrong. It's late. Too damned late for me, really, but not for Melinda...."

Roc felt his heart thundering. "What do you mean?"

"Well, you said it was her choice back then. It's her choice now, too, isn't it? And she wound up on your boat, right?"

"Coming from Longford's," he reminded Jonathan.

"Maybe you should think about this, then. Longford was always attracted to her, and she never wanted to give him the time of day. She was always polite, and I won't lie to you, we've been thrown together enough over the past few years. She's still polite. A friend. That's it.''

"Why are you telling me all this?"

"Because my daughter's bound and gagged up in your room," Jonathan said cheerfully.

Roc sat back, feeling a smile curve his lips, feeling as if the warmth of his Scotch had spread through his whole body, searing away the cold.

"She was in a rather bad position, you know," Jonathan said suddenly.

"Pardon?"

"Well, you put her in a rough position—a choice between her closest blood relative and the man she loved."

"She went for the relative," Roc said lightly.

"Well, there was a time when I was all she had. And, admittedly, I did do my best to sway her at the time."

"And now?" Roc asked.

"And now, well…" His voice trailed away; then he finished his beer and looked at Roc again. "Well, now I was just relieved to discover that she was on board with *you* and not Longford."

"So you'd be swaying her in my direction?"

Jonathan shook his head. "I've learned my lesson the hard way. I wouldn't sway anyone in any direction."

"Then—"

"She was in your damned boat, and she's in your room now, right?" Jonathan demanded.

"Bound and gagged," Roc reminded him.

Jonathan smiled. "I just wanted to let you know that a pig-headed treasure seeker was wrong once, and that I'm sorry. And that I hope you do find your *Contessa*. Although I hear you're well under way."

"She did get in touch with you, then—" Roc began.

"No." Davenport shook his head. He indicated the now empty seat at his side. "Your crew member was telling me that my daughter brought up a spoon from the ship."

Connie. Hmm.

"Yeah, Melinda brought up a spoon."

"She's a good diver. The best. Treasure what you've got."

Roc stood. Three years had been a long time. Davenport had changed. So had Melinda. And so had he.

"Thanks for calling," Roc said, setting a hand on Davenport's back.

Davenport grinned and nodded. "The best of luck."

"With the treasure? Or your daughter?"

"If you haven't seen yet that she's the real treasure, then you're searching in the dark, my boy."

Roc laughed. "I'll take that to heart, Jonathan. Good night."

He left the bar behind, anxious to return to his room. To the beautiful view, the clean white sheets, the cool air...

His wife.

If she forgave him. He'd been seeing only the awful vision of himself on the floor—the great whirlpool empty, the bed a haven of nothing more than ice for him.

At least they'd had a little time together before...

Before he'd acted like a Neanderthal, he admitted to himself, striding toward the elevator.

She might still be angry. Unwilling to forgive him.

But then, apologies weren't so hard. He'd just learned that from his father-in-law.

There was a sudden tapping on his shoulder, and he spun around. All the warmth that had been flooding him abruptly turned glacial.

Eric Longford. Very tall, beach-boy blond. Face knotted in an ugly grimace.

"You've got a lot of nerve, Trellyn!" he grated furiously.

"I've got nothing to say to you, Longford," Roc began. Then he saw that Melinda was not waiting for him upstairs. She was standing just behind Longford.

His heart sank anew, and his temper flared.

"Take a hike, Longford," he said, and started to turn. Melinda could go wherever she damn well pleased. He started toward the elevator.

"Not on your life, Trellyn!"

The hand hit his shoulder again, spinning him around. He tensed and ducked just in time to miss Eric's flying right fist.

"Damn it, Longford," he snapped, but Eric was swinging again.

That was the end of the line for Roc. He ducked and came up with a fast right hook himself, catching Eric right beneath the chin.

The big blond fell cleanly backward, out cold.

"Roc!"

It was Melinda, furious, falling to her knees by Longford's side. "Roc, this is no way—"

"Let's go," he told her, reaching down and catching her hand.

He dragged her to her feet. A crowd was milling, but luckily, most of the assembled people had seen Eric taking the first swing.

Someone else could pick up his nemesis. Melinda damn well wasn't going to do it.

He strode into the elevator with her. They were alone. The door closed.

Melinda spun on him. "You didn't need to knock him out! Hitting a man never solved anything—"

"He swung at me."

"You—"

"Twice! And you—what the hell were you doing downstairs with him?"

"What? Oh, all right, you idiot. I was down there trying to give him the most exact directions I could on right where I found the spoon!"

"Were you?"

She took a wild swing at him, but he caught her, holding her tightly in his arms. "Anyone would try to hit you!" she cried out furiously.

"What were you doing?"

"I wasn't even with him!" she cried out, struggling in his arms.

The elevator door opened. He kept a firm hand on her while

he fumbled for his key, found it, then ushered them both through the door.

He leaned against it again. "So, what were you doing downstairs?"

"I don't owe you an explanation. Your behavior just keeps getting worse and worse!"

He crossed the room toward her, and she tried to back away. "You keep your distance from me. I mean it!"

But he came closer, and she backed around the big whirlpool tub.

"You have no right!"

"I'm just asking!" he told her, coming relentlessly closer. He had to touch her again. They just couldn't waste such a great room....

"And I—" she began.

He caught her upper arms and pulled her against him. "What?" he asked.

"Connie called up and told me you were in the bar with my father!" she cried furiously. "I came down to make sure you were both all right!"

Tears glazed her eyes. Suddenly his mouth ground down on hers as his long strides brought them to the bed. Together they fell to the mattress, and it seemed as if they sank into an embrace of softness.

Her hands pressed against his chest. "Roc, you can't do this to me. It's not fair. It's not right. It's—"

"I'm sorry," he said softly.

"What?" Her eyes were very wide, so beautiful with their damp glaze.

How had he lived without her for so long?

He kissed her lips lightly. Caught her hand and brought it to his lips and kissed her fingers. "I'm sorry," he told her.

"But you'll be suspicious again—"

"I'll try not to be. Melinda, you just suddenly appeared back in my life when I'd nearly managed to get over you. My manners aren't great, and I might act like a bastard again."

"Then sorry isn't enough!" she charged.

"Melinda, damn it, I love you!" he cried. "Isn't that enough?"

She was silent. Not breathing. Then she whispered. "Oh, my lord…"

"Well?"

Her arms wound around his neck. Her lips touched his. Her tongue circled them, then dove into his mouth. She kissed him heatedly, passionately.

But he broke away from her, staring down at her. "Well?"

"It's enough!" she cried. "It's enough!"

His lips found hers once again.

And later, much later, she whispered softly to him, "Roc?"

"Yes?"

"I…"

"Yes?"

She rose above him, hair wild, eyes dazzling, her naked flesh warm to his touch.

"I love you," she told him. "I never stopped loving you. I tried, I tried so hard, but…"

His arm slid round her, and he swept her down beside him, then kissed her forehead.

Davenport was right. He would keep looking for the *Contessa*, of course. But he already held treasure in his arms. It was just a matter of keeping her now.

Eleven

"**A**ll right, get ready now...."

Melinda looked at Roc, ten feet to her left, then at Joe, ten feet to her right. Connie was another ten feet to Joe's right, and then Bruce was about ten feet away from his sister, and they were all treading water, waiting for Marina to give them the go sign.

"We're ready!" Roc called out, exasperated.

"Eh!" Marina cried, lifting her chin. "I am the starter here. Now, you men, mind you! The first one to touch the boat is the one who wins, eh?"

"We've got it, Marina!" Bruce called. "But we're all going to turn into prunes out here if we don't—"

"*Go!*" Marina cried.

Bruce, of course, was left to gasp in a breath before he could shoot through the water with his first stroke, already giving the others an advantage.

Melinda knew she was fast, but she wasn't quite as fast as Roc. She started out just a hair ahead of him, and she swam for all she was worth. She knew she was well past Connie and Bruce—she was even level with Joe Tobago—but just as she neared the boat—right when she was nearly touching it!—Roc pulled ahead strongly, beating her.

Gasping for breath, he held on to the ladder to the bow, shaking a raised fist in the air and letting out something like a victory cry. Melinda clung to the other side of the ladder.

"Beat you!" he told her.

She shrugged, grinning.

"Right! You beat your ninety-pound wife!" Marina chastised from above them.

"Oh, Marina, she's way more than ninety pounds!" Roc said, crawling out of the water.

"Hey!" Melinda protested.

"All right, maybe not *way* more." He leaped into the boat, offered her a hand and helped her aboard.

Joe crawled up behind her. "Ah, well, the lady has put me to shame!" he said, shaking his head and grinning.

Melinda smiled and reminded him, "But I didn't dive today, and you did." It was their first day back over the old World War Two wreck since they had left Nassau. They hadn't gotten out nearly as early in the morning after their night's stay as Roc had intended—partially because neither he nor Melinda woke until nearly noon, and then, since no one had bothered to inform them about the time, they proceeded to squander a lot more of it.

It had been nice squandering, Melinda thought.

But once they were up, Roc still had to see that provisions were brought aboard. There were lists to check and double-check, and it was dusk when they finally managed to leave Nassau Harbor behind.

This morning she'd been tired. But it didn't matter. For the moment she was content to merely cherish this time. She didn't know what her father had said to Roc—she hadn't had a chance to see Jonathan again. She was certain, of course, that her father felt just fine about the way events were occurring, though. If he hadn't, he would have been tearing down hotel walls. He and Roc were an awful lot alike when it came to their protective, macho habits.

She hadn't really said much more to Roc about the past, either. Maybe he still didn't trust her completely.

Or her father.

But though she thought it was understandable that she had taken her father's side on that long ago occasion, she had to admit that she had done so instantly and completely—she had never given Roc a chance at all. Maybe it took time to come back from something like that, although it seemed that at least they now had time on their hands.

He was still after the *Contessa*. Naturally. But he seemed to have slowed down just a little bit in his pursuit. They seemed to dally longer over breakfast, lunch, dinner. They stayed out on deck, staring up at the stars. They still woke with the dawn, but they didn't quite manage to rise with it, and the whole of the *Crystal Lee* seemed to be more relaxed.

Maybe there was still a barrier between them, though. Roc didn't talk about the future. No matter how close they were becoming, he was keeping a certain distance.

She might still be his wife. And she might be sharing his life, his bed and now, his work. But she didn't know what would happen when they found the *Contessa*—or failed in their attempt.

"Hey! How about a hand here?" Connie called, climbing up the ladder.

Roc quickly responded, then helped Bruce aboard behind her.

"I think we need a rematch!" Bruce complained.

"I think I had better start supper," Marina said.

"I think," Peter called from the helm, where he had been surveying the nearby waters with binoculars, "that it's time for a beer!"

Melinda grinned at him, then noticed that, despite the lightness of his voice, something seemed to be bothering him.

He came down a second later and joined the rest of them as they tramped into the galley, popping soda and beer cans, pretending to help Marina but really getting in her way.

"Melinda," Marina called to her. "Do you mind slicing some fresh vegetables?"

"Just tell me what you want sliced and diced," she said cheer-fully. "Other than the captain, of course," she added sweetly.

Roc offered her a warning frown, which she ignored, but as she sliced a carrot, she looked out the window and saw that he was standing beside Peter, staring out into the coming night with the binoculars.

Darkness seemed to fall swiftly that night. The sun had been setting while they'd been in the water, and then boom—it was dark. Melinda squinted, trying to see through the galley port-holes. There seemed to be a light out on the water.

She arranged the vegetables on the platter Marina had indi-cated, left Connie and Bruce setting the table and Joe Tobago marking one of the maps they were using for their dives.

Marina looked at her as she started out, and Melinda promised to be right back.

"Everything is nearly ready," Marina assured her. "Take your time."

Melinda nodded and went out on the deck, shivering a little as she came up behind Peter and Roc. She hadn't had a chance to shower and change yet, and the night air had quickly become chilly.

They were murmuring together, but they fell silent, turning as she reached them.

Roc's jaw was tight, a sure sign that though his words might not give him away, something wasn't to his liking.

"What is it?" she asked.

"Another boat," he told her.

She didn't like the sound of his voice. It had an edge to it. She felt a chill sweep over her, and she was instantly defensive.

He had no right to keep doing this to her.

"How amazing," she said coolly. "These are temperate, beautiful waters! Why on earth would anyone want to sail around here?"

Her sarcasm wasn't lost on Roc, who cast her a quick, warning glare.

"Well," Peter said, "she's keeping her distance now. Nothing more than a dot on the horizon for the night. We'll see what she does in the morning, eh, *mi amigo?*"

"*Si,*" Roc agreed. He had been in South Florida and among the islands constantly enough over the years to pick up both Spanish and island French. Then he said something else to Peter in Spanish—which Melinda didn't understand. He hadn't meant for her to understand, she realized angrily.

She gritted her teeth. She had been on the boat alone today for a while. Even Marina had joined the divers since Hambone, their dolphin friend, had made another appearance.

So here she was. Guilty again. No matter what. Roc was obviously thinking that she had climbed to the radio in her first moment alone. And summoned...?

Someone. Her father. Eric.

She swung around, having nothing else to say to either of them, though the sympathetic glance Peter had given her seemed to tell her that he was on her side.

Well, she didn't need anyone on her side. Because she wasn't guilty.

She started walking down the deck. "Melinda!" Roc called to her sharply. "I'd like a word with you."

"Later," she said coolly. "If you don't mind. I'm freezing, and I think I'll shower quickly before dinner."

She marched into the cabin, rummaged through one of Roc's bottom drawers for the strange clothing collection she was acquiring, grabbed a towel and stepped into the tiny shower.

She was grateful for the blast of hot water. She lifted her face to it, then nearly screamed aloud as the shower curtain came crashing open.

He was there, of course, cobalt eyes narrowed, hard.

"What was that all about?" he asked her.

She reached for the shower curtain, trying to wrench it back. His fingers remained tightly around it. "Do you mind?" she inquired tightly.

"I do," he assured her. "Why did you stomp off like that?"

"There's a boat out there. Of course I must have summoned it, right?"

"There's a boat out there. And I think it's your father's."

She gasped aloud, then tugged harder on the curtain. "You've spoken to my father since I have!" she said angrily. "Remember? I couldn't be trusted to talk to him!"

"But you two are very close," he reminded her.

She swore at him as he stepped into the shower with her, still clad only in his swimming trunks.

"Don't do this to me!" she charged him. "Roc, I'm warning you—"

The water splattered both their faces as he drew her into his arms, then took her lips with a very wet, hot kiss. His hands slid erotically over her body along with the water, cupping her buttocks, drawing her close to his half naked body.

She broke away from his lips, feeling the pounding of the water between them. "You don't accuse someone one moment—"

"I haven't accused you at all," he told her huskily. She heard a splatting sound and realized that he had dropped his trunks to the floor and she was suddenly in his arms again.

"You just said—"

"I said I think it might be your father's boat!" he told her firmly, cobalt eyes fiercely on hers.

"Because—"

"Because he's out there!" he exclaimed, aggravated. The water was still deliciously warm, cascading over them. He leaned her back against the wall, his kiss openmouthed, demanding. Both his touch and the falling water were instantly arousing, and she found herself breathless, still trying to argue, but forgetting what she was arguing about.

Suddenly his hands were on her hips and he was lifting her, then bringing her swiftly down on his sex, urging her to wrap her legs around him. Dizzy with the sweet sensations, she obeyed instantly, her arms wrapping around him as well, fingers digging into the wet thickness of his hair, then grasping his shoulders. A soft moan escaped her as he thrust swift and hard within her, again and again. He very quickly drove her wild, his speed and movement suddenly a tempest, one that burst upon her in a sweet, sudden, shattering moment.

Then she felt him easing her down against the length of him. She felt the water beating against her face and breast again. Her knees were steady, but that didn't matter; he lifted her out of the shower, wrapping her in a towel and holding her tenderly.

A moment later he glanced at his watch. "Damn," he murmured softly.

Her face had been burrowed against his chest. Now she looked up. Teasing eyes touched her own.

"I think we've missed dinner."

She grabbed his wrist, staring at his watch, and groaned, unable to believe that she had walked out of the galley to find him on the deck nearly a full hour ago.

"You seem to have a thing for making me miss meals," she told him.

"Pardon?"

"You did drag me away from my dolphin oreganato in Nassau," she reminded him, toweling dry quickly and trying to step around him.

"We weren't eating, we were dancing then, remember? And you were about to dance off with Longford."

She gritted her teeth. "I wasn't about to dance off with anyone." She walked past him to dress in the cabin.

He followed her out, but he didn't bother to dress, just stretched out naked on the bunk, watching her.

"I wonder why the hell he was there," Roc mused.

Her eyes quickly shot to him. "I'm telling you—"

"I didn't accuse you!"

"But every time something happens, you have one hell of a way of looking at me!"

"I like looking at you," he assured her.

She pulled on a long sleeved T-shirt over a pair of jeans. "Would you come on now, please? What is your crew going to think when we both disappear—"

"Oh," Roc said offhandedly, "they're probably going to think that we're having sex in my cabin."

"Roc, damn you!"

He started to laugh, leaping up. He set his hands on her shoulders and kissed her lips lightly. "I'll be right along," he assured her.

She nodded. But for some reason, she didn't like the look in his eyes at all.

No matter what his words were, the barriers remained.

And she had already risked so much of her heart again. She shivered suddenly, thinking that this had become so much more dangerous than it had seemed at the beginning.

After all, she had merely jumped into the sea and waited to be dragged up in a fishing net.

While now...

Now the stakes were very high indeed. Much, much higher than the riches of the *Contessa*.

She awoke ahead of Roc the next morning and dressed quickly. Finding herself the first one up, she started coffee and breakfast. She was already sipping coffee, the bacon was nearly crisp, and she'd managed a huge pile of scrambled eggs with peppers and mushrooms, when Marina came yawning into the galley, smiling delightedly, saying she would be happy to take over.

"Wake the captain gently with coffee!" Marina suggested, and Melinda grinned, then started to leave the galley.

"Melinda!" Marina said, calling her back suddenly.

She paused, curious, and turned. Marina was studying her gravely. "You're a real asset on board," Marina told her.

Melinda smiled. From Marina, it was quite a compliment.

"Thanks," she said softly.

She left the galley, bringing coffee to the captain's cabin for Roc. As she entered and closed the door behind her, she remembered how miserably jealous she had been of Connie. That hadn't been so long ago. Now Connie was proving to be a good friend.

And she was bringing Roc his coffee. Even if suspicion still lurked in those cobalt eyes...

She found him awake, leaning comfortably on a pillow, the

covers pulled to his waist. He smiled, just like a king, and she knew he had been waiting patiently and serenely for his coffee to arrive.

"Thanks," he said, reaching for the cup and pulling her down to sit by his side. "I like having a wife aboard. Coffee in bed. Sheer luxury."

"It wasn't so bad before," Melinda reminded him primly. "Connie brought you your coffee."

"But not in bed."

Melinda shrugged. "I think she would have if you had wanted her to."

"Maybe."

"I ought to pour this all over you!"

He laughed and offered her a sip. She took it. "You're a jealous little thing," he told her.

"Neither jealous nor little, remember?" she told him.

"Little to me, and I think that a little bit of jealousy is great."

"Feeds the ego, huh?"

He nodded gravely. "Your ego must be pretty nicely inflated, then."

She frowned.

There was more tension in his voice than she would have liked. "Longford! I really enjoyed decking that guy." He reached out and touched her hair suddenly. "I think that if he had ever touched you..."

"What?" she asked.

He shook his head. The look in his eyes made her feel warm. Nicely warm.

"Breakfast is nearly on. You need to get up."

"I am up," he said innocently.

She leaped away from the bed, laughing. "I really can't afford to miss any more meals or I *will* be a little thing!" she warned him.

"I'll be right along," he promised her, throwing the covers aside. She was very careful to keep her eyes on his. "Are you diving with me this morning?" he asked her.

"Yes."

"Good."

An hour and a half later, they were ready to start.

Peter was at the helm with his binoculars, but there wasn't another vessel of any kind in view this morning. It seemed that they were alone with the endless blue sky and sea, without even a cloud on the horizon.

Bruce and Connie went over the edge first, paired up for their dive. Melinda and Roc followed in a few minutes, entering the strange, exotic world that so fascinated them both.

They swam down to the ledge directly over the old wreck. Tangs and clown fish darted by, and a jellyfish floated eerily a distance away.

Something bright in the sand attracted Roc's attention, and he swam down to it, listening to the familiar sounds of his regulator and air bubbles. He felt a rush of water and turned in time to see Hambone making a dive behind him. He watched the dolphin, then turned his attention to the sand. He shot deeper, digging around one of the rusted masts from the World War Two ship.

Hambone dove by him again. A second later he looked just past the mast to see that Melinda was playing with the dolphin, stroking him, catching on to his flipper, taking a swim with him.

He looked toward the mast again, then dug around it some more. Nothing. He didn't know what he had seen.

He looked for Melinda again and saw her diving past a section of the bow of the ship. She disappeared, following the dolphin once again, so it seemed.

He sighed inwardly. He didn't like her disappearing. He quickly swam in her direction, his flippers shooting him swiftly through the water.

There she was, making a startling beeline to him already. He paused, ready for a collision with her, but the force of the water just brought her right to him, where she began trying to talk around her mouthpiece, letting out strange sounds in the aquamarine depths.

Then she lifted her hands. She was holding a small chest, so covered in soft green growth that it was amazing she had seen the thing. It was just the size of a lady's jewel box. Maybe a lady from a very different time...

He nodded to her, and they kicked the water, rising swiftly to the surface. He called out, and Joe was quickly there to help them from the water. He took the prize out of Melinda's hands while she climbed aboard, stripping off her equipment.

"Roc! It's something, isn't it?"

"Something? Of course," he agreed, taking the piece. It was eight inches along, he thought, four deep, four wide. The top was arched. He tapped on it gently and looked at Melinda.

"Brass, I think."

He turned and started down to the equipment room, finding a tiny wedge to set in the indentation he at last discovered in the chest.

Melinda was behind him, along with Marina and Joe. Peter was out on deck yelling to Bruce and Connie, who had just surfaced, to hurry in.

The chest popped open.

There was no dank green growth inside. The brilliance of the gems was startling. The small container was filled to overflowing with necklaces, earrings, brooches, pins.

"My God!" Melinda breathed.

Roc's eyes touched hers. "Quite a find!" he exclaimed softly. He shook his head. "How on earth do you do it?"

"How do you find the right stretch of ocean floor?" she asked him in return.

"I've got to match this with the *Contessa*'s manifest," he told her, "but I'm sure we've really made an incredible find."

"Then we stake our claim—"

"I want a better idea of where she's really lying, first," he said softly. "But this is the main step. We should be ready in another day or two."

"Hey, how's it going down there?" Bruce called down.

"We're coming up. Wait until you see this!" Roc replied.

They started up the stairs to the main deck. Suddenly they saw Peter's face right above them.

"And you," he warned softly, his voice tense, "should see what else we've discovered up here."

Roc looked at Melinda.

She felt that awful, awful cold again.

"What?" he asked Peter. "Another boat?"

"Not another boat," Peter said. "*Two* boats. And moving in very, very quickly!"

Twelve

There were definitely two boats very near them, one to the south, one to the north.

As Roc stood by the rail of the *Crystal Lee,* Peter handed him the binoculars, and he stared out.

Melinda saw him stiffen as he looked north, then seemed to harden to concrete as he looked to the south.

She didn't need binoculars to recognize either boat. It was her father's newest to their north. And it was Eric Longford's well-equipped search vessel to the south.

She was damned. He didn't have to open his mouth. She was already damned.

"Company," Peter said lightly.

"It doesn't matter anymore," Bruce said, standing close by Roc's shoulder. "We've got the spoon, and the casket. It's time to go ashore, fill out the papers and pull out the heavy equipment ourselves."

Roc lowered the glasses and pointed across the water. "They're already diving from Longford's boat," he commented. "And we still don't have a fix on the damned position of the *Contessa.* You know, it is amazing—*amazing!*—that after all these weeks, Davenport and Longford home in so exactly on our location.''

He wasn't looking at Melinda. He didn't need to look at her. There was an edge in his voice, cold, sarcastic.

For a fleeting moment she wondered just what in hell her father was trying to do to her. Then she felt a shivering deep inside. It seemed to start at the base of her tailbone, then send icy little fingers to curl around her heart.

She couldn't change things. She couldn't go back. Something had broken between them years ago, and now his barrier against her was always in place. He would condemn her at the drop of a hat.

She couldn't change it, and she couldn't live with it.

She turned away from the group. She had on her black one-piece bathing suit—exactly what she had arrived in. She wasn't going to fight with Roc anymore. And she couldn't plead with him anymore to believe in her. Maybe it was time to go.

"We're being radioed!" Connie called suddenly, hurrying up to the helm, Roc close behind her. Standing in the cool breeze below, Melinda couldn't hear their conversation. But a second later Roc came down, his face thunderous, eyes furiously dark and flashing. He didn't say anything at first, just stood by the rail, looking at Longford's boat.

Then he spun around, staring at Melinda. "It was for you," he told her very politely. "He says that he's here now, and has suggested that you might want to swim back."

Melinda felt the blood draining from her face, but kept her chin high. She shook her head. "I never—"

"Then there's your father, of course. Only one of them had to know where we are. The other one simply followed! Maybe you didn't call Longford. Maybe you just called dear old Dad."

"Roc!" Connie gasped.

"Roc, maybe—" Peter began.

"This is between us!" Roc snapped, staring at Melinda. "Damn it, don't you think I've wanted to believe all along? My God, she snapped her fingers and I was back like a puppy on a string. In all the seven seas, she's the only damn thing ever to undo me!''

He was clearly angry, but there was something else in his voice, too. Maybe an edge of anguish. But it didn't matter. He couldn't hurt the way she was hurting; he couldn't feel as if a knife had been thrust right down his gullet. Maybe she hadn't earned his total trust, but she didn't deserve this.

His eyes, burning ice, ripped into her. ''Well?'' he said, and suddenly his voice was soft.

Well. This was it.

''Don't you have anything to say?'' he suggested.

She walked the few feet across to him, her heart seeming to shatter into little pieces as she did so. She stopped right in front of him and met his gaze. ''No!'' she said flatly.

''Lord,'' he whispered softly. ''So you admit—''

She'd meant to leave with a little bit of dignity, but this was the wrong side of too much.

She swung at him without thought, her hand cracking against his chin. The sound was loud, and her palm was left stinging.

This time, she thought fleetingly, they had quite an audience for the death of their relationship. Now they would all know that she really was the Iron Maiden, the witch of the sea.

It couldn't be helped.

Neither could the tears that were stinging her eyes like acid.

Roc didn't respond to her slap other than to raise his fingers to his reddening flesh, though she couldn't really see his face; she couldn't see at all anymore.

She did know which way was north. She turned and headed down the port side rail, leaped up, then plunged into the sea.

She dived deep and swam a good distance beneath the water before surfacing. When she did, she heard him shouting to her.

''Oh, no, you don't! Get back here!''

She looked. He was poised on the rail, then leaping in after her.

She looked at her father's boat. It seemed to have moved farther away since she had entered the water.

She started to swim. She had a head start, and she was nearly as fast as Roc.

She swam hard, streaking through the water. Yet almost impossibly, two seconds later, Roc had reached her, his arm winding around her middle, sending the two of them plummeting into the depths.

He let go of her then, and she shot to the surface. He rose alongside her. She stared at him in disbelief, and then she saw the dolphin's fin.

Hambone. Hambone had come along just in time to give Roc a nice ride. And now that he had caught up with her, the same ice-hard look was in his eyes. "Back!" he told her.

"For what?"

"To finish this thing."

She shook her head, the tears stinging her eyes fiercely once again. "It *is* finished. It was finished three years ago. I was just too stupid to realize how final it was. I—"

"Back!" he insisted again.

"I'm not giving you any explanations—"

"You're not going to your father or Longford—"

"I *am* going to my father!" she cried. She turned, stroking determinedly through the water once again.

A hand clenched on her ankle, and she found herself jerked back.

The amount of struggling she was doing would have drowned anyone else, she thought, but not Roc. He'd managed to get a hold on her, and no matter how she twisted and flailed, there was only so much damage she could do. Gasping, choking, furious—but spent—she finally went limp in his hold. She didn't think she'd ever been so miserable in her life, feeling his touch, the power of his hands, and knowing that he wouldn't listen to her, didn't believe in her, and that somehow, though she still loved him despite her fury, she was going to have to escape him.

He reached the ladder at the bow of the *Crystal Lee*. She had very little choice except to climb ahead of him. Connie was there, her pretty face troubled, ready to offer a towel. Roc came up right behind Melinda; she felt him at her back. His hand fell on her shoulder, and she whirled. "Don't you touch me! Don't touch me, and don't speak to me! I've done all the pleading I can do with you. I've—"

"There are two boats right out there!" he roared.

She started to walk past him, but he grabbed her arm and swung her around until both his hands were clutching her upper arms in a relentless hold. "Tell me how the hell they got here!"

There was something desperate in his words, in his hold. He held her in a vice, but his hands and fingers shook with emotion.

"Go to hell!" she cried back.

"Stop!" Connie shrieked suddenly. She ran to the two of them, then stopped, biting her lower lip, her eyes miserable. "I did it!" she said. "Roc—I did it!"

"Oh, Connie! Don't!" Melinda whispered.

"Connie—" Roc began.

"You don't understand!" she said swiftly. She looked quickly from one to the other of them. She shook her head, looking into Roc's eyes. "I spent a lot of time with Jonathan Davenport the other night. In the bar, when you came in. And then later…" Her voice trailed away. Melinda felt her eyes widen. Connie? And her *father?* "Roc, if he's doing anything, he's trying to help you. He doesn't want the *Contessa,* he just wants to see that everything goes smoothly for you. And naturally he was worried about his daughter. He's just here to help. I'm sure of it! I'm sorry, Roc, I didn't mean to cause any trouble."

Roc shook his head, his hold on Melinda easing. "It's all right, Connie. We've both been seduced."

"Ahoy there!"

They all swung around, staring toward the bow, where Jonathan Davenport was now securing his dinghy, then reaching for the ladder. He was in cutoffs, bare-chested and barefooted, light hair in disarray over his forehead, aquamarine eyes very bright.

Melinda frowned at her father, then realized that he was a striking man and only in his mid-forties. Maybe he was just right for Connie, and Connie for him.

If any of them could survive the next few moments…

Jonathan stared across the bow to where Roc was standing

with Melinda. "She almost had you that time," he informed Roc matter-of-factly. "Am I losing my mind, or did you get a little help from a dolphin there?"

"I had a little help," Roc said.

"How's it going, kitten?" Jonathan asked his daughter softly.

"Kitten!" Roc snorted. He met her eyes. "Barracuda!" he assured her.

She kicked his shin. He winced, but offered no retaliation.

"Hi, Dad!" she murmured to her father. He could be off on his own, but he was standing here, just about doing somersaults to help her. She felt an overwhelming tenderness for him and wanted to hug him fiercely.

"Well," Jonathan said matter-of-factly, "I really wouldn't want to break up whatever it is that's going on here, but I think you should know that Eric has divers down below. Don't you have anything on which to base a claim?" he asked Roc.

Roc's hands eased from Melinda's shoulders. "Melinda has found a few things," he said. "But I still don't have a fix on the ship itself."

"Radar isn't yielding—" Jonathan began.

"Radar gives us a World War Two wreck," Roc said.

"Well, I've got a suggestion for you," Jonathan said. "I'll take Melinda back to my boat with me, along with another diver or two. Let me get back, looking as if I've just come to rescue my daughter from your clutches, then you hightail it into shore to make your claim. Melinda can go down and keep up the hunt. If you've come this close, it has to be right under your nose."

"I don't think Melinda will want to dive again on my behalf," Roc said smoothly.

"Yes, she does," Melinda announced icily. "Melinda is just dying for you to make this claim. She would give her eyeteeth to find the ship and cram it—"

"Melly," her father interrupted her swiftly, "there's not a lot of time left."

"I don't want her doing it!" Roc said flatly. "I'm not going to leave my wife out here—"

"I'm not really your wife anymore."

"Yes, you damned well are."

"I will not—"

"Excuse us for just one minute, will you?" Roc suddenly demanded of the group. With an exasperated sigh, he suddenly grabbed Melinda and dived into the water.

Their combined weight sent them both deeply downward; then he kicked strongly to break the surface again.

Sputtering, Melinda stared at him furiously.

"Damn you!" she cried. "You already half-drowned me once today! What more—"

"It was the only way I could think of to have any privacy!"

"Trying to drown me again?"

"I didn't try to drown you. I just tried to get you alone for a few lousy minutes. You won't listen!"

"*I* won't listen! Oh, that's rich. I've begged and pleaded, I've made a fool of myself. I've been honest—"

"Yeah! Right after you crawled out of that net, right?"

She ignored that. "You haven't listened to me since I came aboard, not once, no matter what I said."

"I'm trying to tell you that I'm sorry."

"But it doesn't mean anything!"

"Damn it, Melinda, you made mistakes, I made mistakes, but the point is—"

"You've made a hell of a lot more of them recently than I have!"

"Yes!" he agreed. "Yes! I have."

"I'm going to my father's boat, as he suggested. I'm going to find that stinking *Contessa* for you. And then—"

"Then you'll talk to me, or I'll abandon the damn thing right now and let Eric Longford have it!"

Staring at him, seeing the passion, the fury, in his eyes, Melinda knew that he meant what he said. Her salt-laden lashes swept her cheeks. Maybe he was right; maybe they both had to put the past behind them.

"All right," she said softly. "We find the *Contessa*. Then we talk."

He reached a hand across the water in silent agreement.

"I can swim very well myself, thank you."

"I know," he told her, but he caught her hand anyway, and a few very powerful kicks brought them to the ladder at the bow of the *Crystal Lee.*

"I don't quite get this," Jonathan Davenport said, reaching down to help his daughter aboard, his eyes looking over her shoulder and focusing on Roc. "You've spent years talking about the *Contessa.* Months searching for her. Weeks on the brink of discovery. And now she's right beneath your damn feet, and the two of you are wasting time arguing!"

"We're not arguing," Roc said.

"We're discussing," Melinda grated out.

"And?"

"Roc's going to take the *Crystal Lee* in. I'm coming diving with you."

"Fine," Jonathan said in a determined voice. "Let's get going, then, eh? Eric's got divers in the water, and who knows, when you lead a horse to water, sometimes it does drink."

"Roc, Bruce and I are going to dive, too," Connie said quickly, still wearing a look of guilt and apology.

Roc sighed with exasperation, his shoulders slumping. "It's fine, Connie. It's fine."

"Roc—" Connie began.

"Connie, let's go," Melinda told her.

She stared at her husband one more moment, gritting her teeth, fighting tears and the wild urge to fly across the few feet between them and throw herself into his bronze arms.

Not now. Not now! She was still aching....

She forced herself to turn away, but she could feel the heat of his stare as she climbed down the ladder to her father's dinghy.

Connie followed, then Bruce. Jonathan came last, picking up the oars, and sending them shooting across the water to his boat.

"Tanks!" Melinda said suddenly.

"You don't need to worry about a thing, I promise," her father told her.

"Melinda," Connie said suddenly, "I'm sorry. I'm so sorry."

"There's nothing for anyone to be sorry about at the moment. All's well that ends well, and we haven't finished this yet," Jonathan said.

"The *Contessa* is somewhere right beneath us," Bruce reminded them all quietly.

The oars slapped the water, and that was the only sound they heard as they finished the trip to Jonathan's boat. Jinks was there to help them aboard, waiting in the bow with diving tanks.

Her father had been awfully sure of himself, Melinda thought. And she almost smiled. Then a startling misery seemed to overwhelm her, right after Jinks, tall, gnarled, as gentle as ever, gave her a welcoming hug.

She found herself suddenly in her father's arms, whispering softly, "He didn't believe me. He didn't trust me, Daddy,"

Jonathan lifted her chin, and she saw the tenderness and determination in his eyes.

"He's just a little raw, Melly. He thought his wounds had healed—and then they were all opened up again. But it's going to work out."

"How do you know?"

"Because he loves you."

She smiled, unable to say anything in reply.

"Jinks, help me with my tanks," she said instead. "Do you have my favorite flippers?"

"Yes, Melly, that I do," Jinks told her. In a few moments she was suited and ready, so she sat at the edge of the boat, waiting for Connie and Bruce. She stared out at the *Crystal Lee*. Any second now, she would disappear across the blue.

And Melinda was suddenly very determined that when she returned, she was going to have the *Contessa* on a platter to hand to Roc.

"There's something funny about this regulator," Jinks told Jonathan, frowning over Connie's equipment.

"Then get another one," Jonathan said. Melinda smiled at her father. Safety was one of his major concerns. Like Roc, he had often been angry with her for her recklessness. But it suddenly seemed as if everything was taking too much time. "I'm going down," she said.

"Melinda, Roc doesn't like you down alone," Bruce began.

"You'll be with me in minutes!" she assured him.

"Melinda!" her father called, but it was too late. She had already gone over, shooting through the depths, ending up right by the ledge.

The water was exceptionally beautiful. The afternoon sun was shining through, and the bright, stunning colors of the sea life surrounding the coral were vividly there before her. She saw the ledge and the edge of the World War Two wreck that had been intriguing her. She had found the casket wedged beneath it.

She swam deeper, studying the ledge, then caught hold of a rod protruding upward from the ship and tugged on it. At first nothing happened, so, in exasperation, she tugged again. It gave. Not a lot. Just an inch. She clenched her teeth and pulled again.

Suddenly it came free in her hand, and she went pitching backward with startling force. Sand spewed up all around her. There was a groaning sound as part of the World War Two wreck broke free and went tumbling, in slow motion, over the edge of the shelf.

Her heart hammered as she fought to maintain her position in the swirling waters. She saw a board sticking out from the bottom and she caught hold of it.

Slowly, the water around her began to settle. She stared at her hand, trembling inwardly.

Then she stared harder. She was holding on to a piece of lumber with a jagged tear beneath it. A very old piece of lumber. And now, with the piece of the other ship having fallen away, she went deeper, keeping her hand on the wood and tracing it to its source.

She nearly jumped. She'd come across a figurehead. The features were marred, eaten away by time. But there was a giant head before her, with long waving wooden hair.

Her heart slammed against her chest. She had found it. The *Contessa*.

The sun above her was suddenly blotted out. Frowning, she looked upward.

A boat was blocking the light above. No...it wasn't a boat blocking the sun, not alone. There was something else going on. It was hard to see. The water still hadn't really settled. It was churning, it was dark, it was...

It was *red!*

She swallowed hard, nearly losing control over her breathing, as she slowly realized just what was happening.

There was a boat above her. And the water was red.

The water was red because someone was chumming the water, throwing out gallon after gallon of blood and guts and dead fish and trying to summon every shark in the vicinity.

Even as she watched, the sharks began to move in, creating a frenzy of motion. She felt ill. She'd never been afraid of sharks in the water before—she kept her distance from them, and they kept their distance from her. She'd never done much diving in waters where great whites were prevalent, and she'd never seen one, though she had encountered lemons, blues, tigers and hammerheads. Sometimes they showed interest, and someone in the party would usually butt them away with a shark stick.

Most shark attacks, she knew, came when a shark was confused and thought that a person was his natural prey. It was one of the reasons there had been so many great white attacks off the coast of Northern California. The sharks looked up and saw the surfers' arms and legs paddling alongside their surfboards and thought they were sea lions, the creatures' customary diet.

She had never been afraid before, not really. But she was terrified now.

They weren't that far above her. Not forty-five feet. And there were more and more and more of them.... Some small, perhaps six feet.

Some larger...perhaps ten feet or so... And all of them thrashing, hideously thrashing, swimming in a frenzy, even snapping at one another.

She stared at them horrified. One swam downward in a sudden

motion, then shot toward the food supply again. She edged against the body of the ship she had finally discovered.

Eric had discovered it, too, so it seemed. Or had been sure that she would.

Dear lord, she couldn't believe that someone she had known could want the treasure so badly that he would...

Murder her, she thought.

She had no defense against the sharks, none at all. And the water was growing bloodier by the second.

Eyes tearing, she fought the wild pull of desolation. It was so hard! All she could remember was wanting to run across the deck and throw herself into Roc's arms. She could remember the cobalt fire of his eyes. She could almost feel his warmth.

But she hadn't run to him, she had run away from him. She hadn't forgiven him....

And now maybe it was going to be too late. He would come back and find the pieces of his *Contessa,* all right. And he would also find the pieces of his wife....

She inhaled slowly, fighting desperately not to give way to fear. To hold on, to wait. She checked her watch. She needed to see how much time she had left in her air tanks.

Just then something bumped against her back with startling force, and in the bloodred depths of the water, she let loose a strangled scream.

Thirteen

It was amazing how quickly things could change. One minute he was feeling the warmth of the late afternoon sun touching his shoulders as he cranked up the anchor, his heart weighted down by the fact that he might really have gone and done it this time.

Time had taught him that pride meant nothing in the darkness of the night. Well, he should have learned his lesson better. He had walked away once, so sure that he had been betrayed, so righteous.

Well, hell, maybe he had been right. It just didn't matter a lot. This time, he'd been wrong as hell. That just didn't matter, either.

He didn't think he would be able to bear it if he lost her a second time.

Those were his thoughts—about losing her—when he suddenly saw Jonathan waving frantically to him. "Hey, captain!" Peter called out at the same time. "Holy Mary! Look at the water!"

He did. He looked and saw a growing pool of blood in the water.

His heart jumped instantly to his throat.

At the same moment he noticed that the third boat—the uninvited boat, Eric Longford's boat—had already taken flight, skimming rapidly away over the water.

Panic seized him as his mind conjured up a terrible picture of a diver caught in the blades of a motor, ripped to shreds, bleeding....

Bruce? Connie?

Melinda?

Oh, God...

Then he realized that Jonathan had brought his own vessel to life, and the boat was nearing him at a dangerous pace. Finally, just in time to avoid a collision, the motor was cut. He could hear Jonathan shouting.

"That bastard! That damn *bastard!*"

"What in God's name?" Roc shouted to him.

"He chummed the water! The idiot must have found something, and he's trying to stake the first claim. Look at the damned water! And Melinda is down there!"

Once again Roc's heart slammed against his chest. Hard. A second ago he'd been afraid of losing her. Now they could all lose her—for good.

Steady, capable Jinks, who'd been with Jonathan for as long as Roc could remember, was pulling out gear. For a moment, staring at his father-in-law's face, Roc thought that Jonathan was going to jump in without tanks or mask, he was so desperate to reach his daughter.

"Wait!" Roc cried.

"There's no time to wait!" Jonathan cried back. "She only has an hour's worth of air. I've got—"

"You've got to pull your boat around over there, away from all the blood. I'm going down for her."

"I'm going—"

"Damn it, Jonathan, face it. I'm the fastest, and probably the best."

"She's my daughter!"

"She's my wife!"

"Eh, my friends!" Joe Tobago interrupted swiftly. "Whoever goes down first needs to be prepared. It seems to be a group of blues, though I think I saw a lemon or two. Nasty sharks. Mr. Davenport, if you take your boat around, I can pull the *Crystal Lee* into the middle of the swirl, shoot a few, and keep the others busy so that perhaps Cap'n Roc can bring your daughter up to you, eh?''

"It's the best way, Jonathan!" Roc shouted.

Peter had tanks, fins, a mask and regulator ready for Roc even as they spoke. He'd also brought a weight belt, with sheaths for two knives, and two shark sticks—six feet each, and primed to give a shark a good electric jolt when the point punched into the animal's tough flesh.

In all his years as a diver, Roc had used the electric prods only twice. He'd never been big on shark hunts; he'd always felt they had their place in the sea. Now he prayed that Peter could shoot the whole lot of them. There were plenty of big, sharp-toothed fish in the sea.

There was only one Melinda.

He got suited up amazingly swiftly, with Peter assuring him that he would have a solid hour's air to share with Melinda once he'd reached her.

Once. Peter stumbled over the word a little, almost saying *if* instead.

Well, if he couldn't reach her, it didn't matter. He didn't want to come up alone. He knew that now. No matter what the future held, he wouldn't come back without her.

"I'm going over!" he shouted to Jonathan. "Get your boat into position!"

"Get clear of the blood!" Jonathan shouted to him.

He was clear enough of it. He was afraid that if he didn't get down swiftly, he wouldn't find Melinda in time. He raised a hand in agreement, then sat on the edge of the *Crystal Lee* and let the weight of his tanks take him backward into the sea.

He splashed swiftly into the water, then sank into the once azure sea. He allowed the impetus of his fall to take him downward quickly, ten feet, twenty, thirty....

Then he stabilized himself. He could free dive deeper without causing himself any pressure difficulties, but the last thing he needed now was a case of the bends. Encumbered with gear as he was, he tried a slower drift to the ocean's depths.

Peter, he saw, was already at it with his gun. One of the sharks, a blue, about five and a half feet long, had been struck through the head with a bullet, pulling it and the frenzied throng around it away from Roc—and away from the ledge where Melinda had gone down.

For a moment he found himself watching the tempest with an awed fascination. It seemed that along with the blood and chunks of fish guts Longford had cast into the water, he had left some big bait, too, split tunas, good-sized groupers. The whole conglomeration was now floating around in a sea of blood, eerie, half eaten, sightless eyes staring about.

The sharks turned on the shot blue, whose nervous system had been hit. It thrashed and jerked wildly in the water, like a robot gone amok.

Roc drew his gaze from the tempest going on above him. The sharks—dear God, twenty of them? thirty?—hadn't paid him the least heed as yet. They were intent only on one thing—food. Within minutes the blue was half consumed, dinner for its kind before it had even succumbed to death.

Roc pulled his gaze from the tempest and looked to the shelf below. That was where Melinda had found the casket. It was where she would go to search for the lost ship.

He dived quickly, then thrust himself quickly backward as a large lemon shark came nosing into view. Smooth, slim, sleek, it was veering away from Roc, then made a sudden turn into him.

He hit it with the prod.

The shark shuddered and turned instantly away.

Roc blinked hard and turned toward the ledge again, reminding himself that he needed eyes in the back of his head. He kept seeing that wounded blue in his mind, thrashing wildly about, then bitten to pieces....

It couldn't have happened to Melinda. He wouldn't believe it. He wouldn't allow it to happen.

He reached the shelf and turned toward the crimson waters,

trying to assure himself that no new predators were on their way toward him. The frenzy was still going on above him. As he watched, another shark went into a wild fit of thrashing, even farther away than the blue had been.

Peter had shot the creature, he was certain. And bit by bit, Peter was managing to draw the melee away from Roc.

And away from the shelf.

He pitched himself still more deeply downward, then saw the shelf loom into view. There was deep water to the left of it, he thought unwillingly. These were temperate waters. Makos, hammerheads and the like were known to frequent the area, though none of them had appeared as yet. And surely they were in far too temperate a zone for a great white to appear....

But they had appeared in these waters. Recently, actually.

He had to get a grip on himself. He had to find Melinda.

He swam swiftly alongside the shelf. Then, to his amazement, a wall of timber suddenly seemed to rise above him. He swam swiftly along it, certain that it had not been there before, that he had been to this exact spot and hadn't seen it.

He came upon a plaque. Grown over. Green with seaweed, laden down with barnacles. He ran a hand over it. Saw letters.

essa

He had found his ship, he realized.

A little late. Apparently Eric Longford had already found her, as had Melinda.

He shot down the length of the broken vessel, not giving a damn about it. He had to find Melinda. Panic began to set in as he realized that more and more sharks were congregating above, even if Peter was managing to move them somewhat.

He swam along the broken wooden bow. Ahead of him, he could see the outstretched, decaying arm of a figurehead. He swam hard toward it.

Suddenly he bumped into something coming around the edge of the ship.

And he saw, miraculously, that it was his wife.

She was about to scream. She had seen the sharks, of course.

She had seen the tranquil azure waters become a pool of blood. And she had assumed that he was one of the beasts.

The underwater world was known to be silent. It wasn't entirely true. He could hear her scream.

And around his mouthpiece, he shouted to her in turn. "It's me! Careful. Careful!"

Her eyes were very wide, terrified. Well, hell, he had felt that way himself. Yet at the sight of him, she seemed to feel better. She threw her arms around him, clinging to him.

He drew her closer. Held her there for a moment, trembling inside as he realized that while she was alive there was hope.

They had a chance.

But that didn't change the fact that there was a feeding frenzy going on directly above them, that other predators of the deep were hurrying to join in the tempest.

He realized suddenly that she was nearly out of air. He motioned for her to spit out her mouthpiece and take his. Then he shouted to her in the water. It would be just possible for her to make out his words if she tried.

"We've got to head north! To your father's boat. Do you understand?"

She nodded gravely.

He thrust one of the shark sticks into her grasp, then took the mouthpiece back, just as he was about to inhale sea water.

"Your tanks are no good. We have to share. Understand?"

Again, she nodded, then took a breath from his regulator before trying to talk to him. "Roc! It's the *Contessa!*"

"I know, I know. But we've got to get out of here."

She nodded. She did know. But she suddenly let the mouthpiece float between them for a moment so her lips could touch his.

She mouthed the words, *Roc. I love you! You came for me.*

He mouthed back to her, *I'd come for you anywhere!*

He set the mouthpiece between her lips, forcing her to inhale deeply. Then he took another breath himself and indicated the length of the hull of the *Contessa.* She nodded her understanding.

Slowly, carefully, they started down the length of it.

Halfway down, Roc spotted a curious blue. It was only about seven feet long, but it came very near them, fascinated by the call of the blood in the water.

He was ready, prodding the animal swiftly. It shuddered violently and moved off.

It wasn't big, Roc knew. Not by shark standards. But that didn't matter. It had rows of fantastically sharp teeth, and one bite from it...

Would have brought on a hundred more!

They were past it, though. Past it. No matter what happened, he couldn't give way to panic.

He reminded himself that there were researchers who purposely baited the water, anxious to study the creatures. Film crews sometimes went among them, filming events such as this. They survived because they kept cool heads.

And a cool head was what they needed now.

They moved slowly along the length of the ship.

How odd, he thought. After all this time, they had found the *Contessa.* And they were using her to make their escape from the tempest in the sea above them.

She was long, one hundred and fifty feet. She was also badly damaged. There really wasn't all that much left. A broken up hull, long covered by the wreck of a World War Two ship. The last vessel had fallen almost completely over the first one. Both of them victims of the sea.

Well, he was determined that they would not be victims, too.

He tried to peer through the water. It wasn't nearly as crimson here as it had been at the figurehead. If he looked ahead, he was certain he could see the outline of Jonathan Davenport's ship. But to reach it, they would have to leave the comparative safety of the decaying hulk of the *Contessa.*

He paused, forcing Melinda to take a deep draft of air. Then he indicated the ship, and she nodded. He pointed to her shark stick, and she nodded again. They had dived together so often before. Even now, Roc thought, they were a good team.

Back to back, they began a northward ascent.

A curious lemon, a small one, came unnervingly close. Roc prodded it. The shark veered away, but it didn't leave.

A second later another shark began milling uncomfortably close. A blue this time.

Then another blue. And another lemon. Circling them. Swimming away, coming back in again. Close.

Too close.

Too many sharks for them to prod off at one time.

Melinda seemed to sense his thoughts. She turned into him suddenly, taking air from him, then letting the mouthpiece fall. With the sea beasts all around him, she threw her arms around him again— And kissed him.

One last kiss.

Just then Roc felt a sudden thrust against his body. He waited for the rip of teeth, thinking that perhaps he could thrust Melinda upward if the creature had him. But he felt nothing.

Then again, he had heard that a shark bite was so swift and sharp that divers often didn't feel the teeth.

He looked down, expecting half of his leg to be gone. But his leg wasn't gone at all. And the sharks were backing away. Even in the midst of their frenzy, they were backing away.

Because Hambone had come.

The playful dolphin was beneath them now, circling slowly, then suddenly streaking through the water and butting against one of the sharks, which seemed to flop away through the water.

Hambone swam back to them, and Roc caught a firm hold on the dolphin's flipper. They began to move swiftly. He clung to the flipper and Melinda clung to him.

Miraculously Hambone brought them through the water as if they were flying, somehow knowing that they needed to go north.

Past the field of blood, ten feet from Melinda's father's boat, Roc released his hold on the dolphin's flipper. Moments later they broke the surface, not five feet from the boat.

"Thank you, God!" they heard suddenly.

Roc, spitting out his mouthpiece, looked up. Jonathan was at the edge of the boat, looking very old at that moment, and reaching down to help his daughter aboard.

"Melinda!" he shouted to her.

"Dad!" she cried back.

But she didn't take his hand, not right away. She ripped off her mask and stared at Roc. "Hambone!" she cried, then dived under.

Roc instantly followed his wife.

The dolphin had come back to them, swimming beneath Melinda, allowing her to stroke his back. To say thank you.

Roc reached out and touched the dolphin, too, staring into the dark eye of the gentle beast, trying to mentally communicate his own appreciation. Then he clamped a hand on his wife's wrist. They could thank Hambone further later. It was time for the two of them to get aboard.

A hard kick propelled them to the surface once again, and Jonathan was ready once again. He reached down and grabbed his daughter. Bruce and Connie were there, ready too, to pull Roc from the sea. In seconds he and Melinda were both free of their gear, encompassed in warm terry towels and holding steaming cups of coffee.

"You made it. You made it!" Jonathan said anxiously. "Thank God!"

"Thanks Roc," Melinda said, her smile beautiful as she glanced his way.

He couldn't take credit. Not under the circumstances. "Thanks to a dolphin!" he said softly.

"Thanks to anything!" Jonathan cried. "You weren't touched?" he said to his daughter. "Scratched, harmed—"

"Dad, I'm fine." She looked at her husband again. "I knew I'd be fine the moment I saw Roc's face."

She frowned suddenly and stood. Her towel fell from her shoulders, and she thrust her coffee cup to Bruce as she said, "Oh, my God. Roc! You came back for me! That idiot who nearly murdered us both is going to manage to make the claim on your *Contessa!*"

Roc stood, His towel fell, too. Then he thrust *his* coffee cup into Bruce's hands as he caught her in his arms, lifting her chin.

"Who gives a damn about the *Contessa!*" he told her. "Your father told me something once, the truest words I've ever heard. I could search the sea forever, but it wouldn't matter. I've found my treasure. If you'll just forgive me for being a doubting bastard, I swear I will never forget again that I have the greatest treasure a man can find—my wife."

There was silence on the boat. The dying sun was golden and orange, its rays streaking across the heavens and the seas. Then Melinda spoke at last. "Oh, my God! Roc, that was beautiful."

"Can we start out fresh?" he asked very softly.

"Yes!" she whispered. "Oh, yes!"

He kissed her. Kissed her as the last rays of the sun touched them. Kissed her until Jonathan cleared his throat at last.

"Well, that's lovely, you two, just lovely. But I might be able to add a wee touch of icing to the cake here."

Roc, his arms around Melinda, turned to his father-in-law. "And what's that, Jonathan?"

"Well, the *Contessa is* yours, my boy."

Roc arched a brow. "Jonathan, even if we tried to convince the authorities that Eric was willing to commit murder to stake his claim, we'd have one hell of a time proving it. In another hour, there won't be much sign of what happened here."

Jonathan smiled smugly, taking a seat on the rail.

"But you see, that slimy bastard is going to make it into port to discover that a firm claim has already been made on the *Contessa.*"

"*You* made a claim?" Melinda gasped.

Jonathan shook his head. Then he nodded. "Well, yes. And no," he said.

"You've gone and outdone me again," Roc said, but there was no anger in his words.

Jonathan shook his head firmly. "I made the claim, all right, Roc. But I did it in your name. I just happened to get lucky the day my daughter opted out on me and managed to get that slime to drop her off in the middle of the ocean. I made the same find

Melinda did, a few pieces of silverware.'' He shrugged. ''I hadn't actually found the ship, but…well, hell, it had to be here. So I made the claim, saying that I was in your employ for the time.''

Roc stared at his father-in-law. Then he threw up his hands. ''But if you made the find—''

''I didn't make the find! I still thought you were an idiot about the whole thing, but then, the last time I'd doubted you, well, I was proved a fool. In many, many ways,'' he added softly.

''But, Jonathan—''

''Roc, the find is yours. It always was. And there wouldn't be a damned bit of justice in the world if you didn't accept me as a crew member on this one.''

Roc had gone stiff. Melinda could feel it.

''I don't know, Jonathan. Thinking is one thing. Finding is another.''

But Jonathan stretched out a hand to his son-in-law. ''I have a feeling we might be working together again—son.''

''You taught me so much. This—''

''And you've managed to teach me a hell of a lot, too. How about it, Cap'n Trellyn?''

Melinda wanted to cry out loud in frustration as Roc continued to stand so stiffly. He was so proud.

Then she felt it. Felt the give within him, the massive release of tension. And he stretched out his hand to her father.

''Deal?'' Jonathan said softly.

''Deal,'' Roc agreed.

''Wow!'' Melinda cried.

She kissed her husband again, then her father, and then Bruce and Connie and Jinks.

And by then the *Crystal Lee* had come alongside them again, and it was agreed that Roc's boat was probably better equipped for the kind of celebration they had in mind for that evening. Jonathan's boat was left at anchor, and even gnarled old Jinks came aboard the *Crystal Lee*.

Within seconds the rest of the crew heard the news about the claim—no matter what Eric had done. Soon a bottle of champagne had been popped open, and everyone was kissing everyone.

Then Roc said with a determined purpose that he and Melinda were going to shower and change. The others nodded and lifted their glasses to them.

Melinda thought her father's eyes were sparkling, but she didn't really get a chance to see for sure. Roc was propelling her to his cabin. In a minute the door was closed behind them, and just seconds after that she found herself in his arms.

Feeling his kiss. The wild heat of his breath. The fire of his body.

"My God!" he whispered. "I was so scared. So damn scared. I thought I'd really lost you."

"You came for me!" she whispered. "Through sharks, through blood..."

He pulled away from her suddenly. "Does that mean you'll stay married to me?"

She drew in her breath swiftly and nodded, beautiful eyes on his. "As long as it means *you* don't intend to divorce *me,*" she said softly.

"Never," he promised. "Like I said before," he added huskily, "I've found my real treasure."

"Oh, Roc," she whispered as he swept her into his arms, carrying her to the bunk, "that really is beautiful."

He smiled, stretching her out then lying down beside her and tugging away the strap of her bathing suit so he could place a searing, sensual kiss on her shoulder.

"You are more precious than any treasure in the sea," he assured her. Then his lips found hers. When they broke away, he asked softly, "Forgive me?"

"Oh, God, yes!" she cried.

"Then I have everything I could ever want!" he told her.

She wound her arms around him. Felt his kiss again. His touch. Erotic, sweet...

He stripped away her suit, and she shivered, trembled, wanted him.

After all, they had life. And they had each other. But...

"Roc, we told my father we'd be right out—"

He laughed huskily, cobalt eyes touching hers. "Your father isn't expecting us any time soon."

"But the rest of the crew—"

"Well, I imagine they'll all think we're making mad, passionate love in my cabin."

"And—"

"And!" he said, placing a finger on her lips to still her words. "That's exactly what we're going to be doing."

He lifted his finger. She smiled slowly.

"Anything to say?" he asked her.

"Umm," she murmured.

"Well?"

"Let's get to the mad, passionate part!" she told him, winding her arms around him.

He proceeded to do so.

Epilogue

"**H**ow beautiful!" Melinda cried softly, looking out across the white-tipped waves.

It was a rough day; storm clouds were threatening. There weren't many people on the whale watch that had left from Plymouth Harbor that afternoon; the weather had steered them away. But it hadn't seemed so awful to Roc and Melinda.

It had taken them months to rescue the *Contessa*'s treasures from the sea, and they had been good months. Melinda would always be eternally grateful for them. Her father had worked with them hand in hand, and there had been a bond forged between them that could never be broken now.

She was happy. She had never thought she could be so happy.

Yet no matter how well work had gone, Roc had been determined that they were going to take a trip away for their fifth anniversary. He was determined to really celebrate the event—even if they had been apart for three of their married years.

He had decided they were going to do something different, so they had left their customary warm climate to spend a few weeks in a cool New England fall.

But they hadn't quite managed to leave the sea behind. Roc had suggested the whale watch, and since Melinda considered even the big humpbacks to be close relations to Hambone, she had readily agreed.

"Thar she blows!" someone called.

Everyone came rushing over to the rail to see the spectacular creature.

The humpback descended, and Roc turned his attention to Melinda. "Did you read Connie's letter yet?" he asked her suddenly.

She shook her head. This seemed like a good time, while they waited for another whale to surface. She drew the letter from her leather handbag and ripped it open. Roc studied her features.

"What?"

"Why—how could they!" Melinda exploded.

"What?" Roc repeated.

Melinda stared at him, eyes full of both anger and amusement.

"They eloped!"

"Connie and—"

"My father!"

"Well, we can hardly be shocked," Roc advised her. "There's definitely been something going on between those two for a long time now."

"I know that, but why would they elope…? I mean, we should have been there!"

"Your father isn't exactly a spring chicken," Roc said.

"But still, you'd think he'd want us there—oh!"

She had kept reading. Now she stared at Roc again.

"What?"

She started to giggle. "They, er, had to elope. Roc, I'm going to have a sibling!"

"Sibling?"

"They're having a baby—Connie's pregnant!"

Roc sat back and started to laugh. "Well, well."

Melinda stared thoughtfully at the letter. "Hmm. That makes Connie your stepmother-in-law."

"I suppose so."

"But now…my father will be our baby's grandfather, and

Connie will be a mother with a step-grandchild and I wonder what our—''

"Our what?" Roc demanded.

Melinda stared at him. Then she smiled slowly. "Our baby. We're, uh, we're having one, too. I didn't really discuss it with you, but then, I didn't really plan it." He was still staring at her. She sighed. "It's what happens when you make mad passionate love in a cabin."

He finally started to laugh. Then he said, "Really?" She nodded, and he swept her into his arms, cradled her chin in his hands and kissed her.

"There! Over there! Thar she blows gain!" someone called.

But neither of them paid the least bit of attention. Roc just kept kissing her.

And when his lips parted from hers, she whispered happily, "I wonder if it will be a boy or a girl."

He held her chin again and met her eyes. "It won't matter in the least. Because there's one thing I know it will be."

She arched a brow at him.

"A treasure," he said softly. And he smiled. "A treasure from the sea!"

She smiled again, then kissed him.

*   *   *   *   *

DREAMS AND SCHEMES

Merline Lovelace

One

Naked, wet and shivering, Kate stood framed in the open sliding glass door. Cool night air whispered against her bare back and combined with tentacles of fear to send goose bumps shimmering down her spine. For a long—seemingly endless—moment, she hovered there, one foot over the sill, the other just touching the wood deck behind her. Her eyes narrowed, trying to pierce the dim shadows of the bedroom. Her ears strained to catch an echo of the faint sounds that had made her halt so abruptly.

Another breeze hit her damp skin, causing Kate to clutch her towel tighter. The thin cotton barely covered her front from chest to hip, leaving the rest of her long body exposed to the cool New Mexico night air. She shivered again and tilted her head to one side, listening intently. The only sound she could hear over the pounding of her own heart was the hot tub bubbling on the deck behind her. When no other noise disturbed the summer night, she began to feel a little foolish standing there on one foot, like a tall, goose-pimply stork.

Taking a deep breath, Kate stepped into the dim bedroom and reached for the wall switch beside the door. Soft, warm light bathed the spacious room. Her gaze roamed the undisturbed serenity of a bed and accessories done in muted desert jewel tones of mauve and turquoise. She curled her bare toes into the thick carpet and felt her body relax with the familiar, luxurious sensation.

"You've been reading too many thrillers, Katey m'girl!" she told herself with a slow breath of relief.

Crossing the spacious bedroom, she headed for the wide, raised dais that formed the bathroom. A quick flip of a switch flooded the bath and dressing areas with cheerful light from the overhead spots. Depositing her wet towel in the wicker hamper, she pulled a fresh one from the basket beside the oval tub and attacked her goose bumps. The last of her tension faded with the warmth and light.

Tingling from the brisk rubdown, Kate slipped into a silk sleep shirt. A quick glance in the mirror confirmed that the hot tub had steamed her hair into a wild mass of auburn curls and melted her makeup to the merest hint of color. She ran a brush through her unruly hair without real expectation of subduing its stubborn resistance to any form of discipline. Grabbing a tissue, she wiped the smudged mascara from under her eyes. Her eyes were her best feature, she thought. Wide and clear and a deep violet-blue, they were framed by abundant lashes and a net of fine laugh lines at either corner. At least, Kate told herself that they were laugh lines. At thirty-one, she wasn't ready to admit they could be anything else.

Tossing aside the tissue, Kate wrinkled her nose at her reflection and flipped off the lights. She hummed her favorite tune from *Phantom of the Opera* as she headed for the living room and the work that awaited her. A few steps into the room she stopped, her breath catching in shock.

Her computer no longer sat on her desk. Kate stared at the empty space for a long, confused moment, then turned slowly to survey the large, high-ceilinged room. Stunned, she found a gaping blank space in the bookcase where her miniaturized stereo components once sat. When she saw the doors of the entertainment center hanging open, a frisson of fear darted down her spine. Both the TV and the VCR were gone, as was the collection of hand-carved kachina dolls that had graced the mantel above the adobe fireplace just a half hour ago. Her disbelieving eyes finished their sweep of the living room and fastened on the French doors leading to the enclosed side patio. Sheer, gauzy curtains stirred gently in the breeze beside the open doors.

Tucking her sleep shirt hastily into a pair of jeans, Kate ran to answer the doorbell. She'd called the police only moments ago and gave silent thanks for their swift response. Throwing open the wide front door, she gasped in surprise at the man who stood on the stoop.

He towered over her own five feet seven inches by a good half foot. In the dim porch light Kate made out a square jaw darkened with stubble, a thick, black mustache and eyes that studied her intently. A battered ball cap was perched on the back of his head and a T-shirt with Albuquerque Dukes emblazoned on the front stretched across what seemed like an acre and a half of chest.

Kate didn't take the time to absorb more. She stepped back, arm flexing to slam the heavy door shut.

"Ms. O'Sullivan?"

Her arm faltered in midswing.

"I'm here in response to your call."

The man lifted his hand to eye level, and for the first time Kate noticed the badge in his palm. She peered suspiciously at the metal shield. It appeared genuine, but then she'd never had any dealings with badges or shields before. This man certainly didn't look like any police officer she'd ever seen. Her gaze dropped from the shield to the picture ID right below it. There was no mistaking the shaggy mustache that identified him as Dan Kingman, Albuquerque Police Department.

"Sorry," she told him, stepping back. "I was expecting someone in uniform. Ah, a different uniform."

His lips quirked as he stepped inside. "I apologize for the less-than-professional attire. We were in the middle of our annual charity ball game with the Dukes when I got called out."

"You were pulled out of a ball game to answer my call?"

Kate asked, startled. "Isn't that above and beyond the call of duty?"

"Not exactly," Kingman replied, slipping his ID into the back pocket of his jeans. "One of my men wrapped his car around a tree during a high-speed chase in this area. I came to check on him. About the time they cut him out of his vehicle, a rash of reported break-in calls started coming over the net. We have two squad cars in the neighborhood now, taking reports. I was just down the hill when you called, so I decided to take this one myself. Mind if I do a walk-through?"

Kate shook her head and trailed behind him while he searched the house and outdoor areas with quick efficiency.

"Well, it looks like whoever came visiting is gone now. Suppose we sit down and you tell me exactly what happened."

Kate led the way back to the living room. "There's not much to tell. I got home from work, spent a half hour or so unwinding in the hot tub and walked in here to find my property missing."

He pulled a small notepad from his rear pocket, and Kate couldn't help wondering how he managed to fit anything, much less a badge and a notebook in those snug jeans. The glove-soft, skintight material was stretched taut over a pair of muscular thighs. *Very* muscular thighs.

"There were no signs of forced entry. Did you leave any doors unlocked?"

"The French doors were open to let in the air."

One dark brow arched over hazel eyes. They were an intriguing color, Kate noted, halfway between gray and green, with brown flecks in them. And at this moment those same eyes were regarding her with a faint air of disapproval.

"You mean you just left these living room doors wide open while you went to take a bath?"

"I took a hot tub, not a bath," she explained. "And I always leave the French doors open while I'm home."

Kingman frowned and glanced around the spacious living room. A blinking light next to the doors caught his attention. "Was the alarm system activated?"

"No. I don't use it."

"Why not?"

Kate felt herself stiffen slightly in her chair. She wasn't used to explaining her actions to anyone, especially not to men wearing ball caps with beer logos printed across the bill. She reminded herself that he was a police officer.

"I haven't had time to call the security folks out to rekey it since I rented this place."

"You should," he replied, still frowning. "It would provide some measure of protection for a woman living alone."

His tone was starting to raise her Irish temper. "How do you know I live alone?"

He shrugged. "You don't wear a wedding ring."

"Neither do you," she rejoined. "Does that mean you live alone?"

As soon as the tart words were out of her mouth, Kate regretted them. What did she care about this man's living arrangements?

"Most of the time," he replied solemnly, although amusement danced in his eyes. "Besides, I had a quick look through your bedroom and bathroom. I'm a police investigator, remember?"

"You could've fooled me," Kate muttered to herself.

"Seriously, Ms. O'Sullivan, you should be more careful. Don't fling open your door like you did to me tonight. And get that security system set. A woman your age, living alone, should exercise more caution."

Enough was enough. "Look, Sergeant...ah, Officer, let's leave my age out of this, shall we, and get on with the investigation."

One brow lifted at her crisp tone, then a corner of his disreputable mustache tugged up in a lazy grin. Kate stared, mesmerized by the effect. That the simple rearrangement of a few facial muscles could turn a collection of lean planes and angles into a devastating combination of white teeth, creased cheeks and glinting eyes astounded her.

"Sorry," he murmured. "Didn't mean to touch a nerve."

Kate drew in a deep breath. "No problem. For a moment there, you sounded just like my mother."

Kingman blinked, clearly surprised at being compared to anyone's mother.

"She reminds me on a regular and frequent basis of my age and single status," Kate drawled.

His grin widened. "Let me rephrase that last statement, then. An attractive young woman, living on her own, should take extra precautions. Like setting the alarm system."

"I'll consider it," Kate replied, her chin lifting. Robbery or no robbery, smile or no smile, she didn't like being lectured to.

Kingman studied her for a moment, then gave a slight shrug. "If you'll give me a list of your missing property, I'm done. There's not much to go on, but we'll do our best."

Flipping the notebook shut, the big man got to his feet. "You're sure you didn't see or hear anything?" he asked, moving toward the door.

Kate hesitated, remembering the indistinct sound that had frightened her earlier. "I thought I heard something when I got out of the hot tub. A sort of clicking sound. Nothing identifiable."

Kingman paused, one hand on the front door latch. "Look, I don't want to alarm you, but you live in a pricey neighborhood. It's a natural target. If you won't use the security system, I suggest you keep the French doors closed and locked when you're not in the immediate vicinity."

"I don't want to be a prisoner in my own home," Kate objected. "The main reason I rented this house was because of its spectacular view."

Kingman let out a long, impatient breath. "I'm not saying you have to barricade yourself inside. Just exercise a little caution. This isn't the first time this neighborhood's been hit. One of my men spoke at a neighborhood meeting last week. I take it you didn't attend?"

"No, Lieutenant...um, Detective. I'm only renting this place on a short-term lease. I'll be leaving Albuquerque in three more months. I don't have time to get involved in local issues."

Kingman's eyes narrowed, as if he wanted to say more—a lot

more—about her lack of involvement. Kate's chin tilted up another notch.

"You'll have to come down to the police department tomorrow and sign the official report," he said finally. "Ask for Detective Alvarado. He'll be handling the case. I'll give you his name and number."

He pulled a dog-eared card out of a leather case and scribbled across the back. "Here's my card. Call me if you think of anything else. It's 'Captain,' by the way."

Kate closed the door behind him with a mixture of relief and regret. The big man, for all his sexy smile, had rubbed her the wrong way. Still, as she stood in the foyer surveying the living room, she had to admit the house seemed suddenly empty without Kingman's solid presence filling it. Lifting the little card, she studied the bold print. "Captain Dan Kingman. Chief, Criminal Investigations, Albuquerque Police Department."

Card in hand, Kate ambled back into the living room. The soft, muted colors failed to give her the sense of tranquillity they usually did. She wasn't sure whether it was the aftereffects of having her privacy violated or the lingering aura of a certain police officer that disturbed the previously serene room. Whatever it was, she felt restless and edgy.

Tossing the card onto the coffee table, Kate crossed to the French doors to check them once again. Despite her brave words, the robbery had shaken her more than she cared to admit. The thought of someone, or possibly several someones, entering through those doors and invading her home with her in the hot tub, just a few yards away, sent a wave of goose bumps up her arms. She'd worked so hard to reach the point where she could afford some of the luxuries in life. Now she'd had her first taste of the penalties, as well as pleasures, that a beautiful home and fine possessions could bring.

With a determined shrug, she pushed the thought from her mind and headed for her briefcase. Even without her laptop computer, she had plenty of work to keep her busy and her mind off the robbery.

*   *   *

"You mean they came right into your house? While you were there?"

Swallowing a bite of flaky croissant, Kate nodded to the woman sitting opposite her at the small table. "I was in the hot tub. I thought I heard something when I got out, but convinced myself it was just my imagination."

"Jeez, you'd think this was New York or L.A. or something." Tricia Hansen leaned back in the cafeteria chair and held her coffee cup in both hands. "Are you okay? You should have called me last night. Something like that can be pretty traumatic."

"It was, although I have to admit I probably invited trouble by leaving the doors open. As the officer they sent to investigate reminded me, women who live alone—excuse me, women *my age* who live alone!—need to be more careful."

Tricia sputtered into her coffee cup. "I bet you appreciated that!" She toyed with her cup for a moment, then set it down, her expression sobering. "Do you think you should move out of that big house, Kate? You're all alone up there, with no neighbors within yelling distance."

"Oh, no," Kate groaned, "not you, too. I get that same lecture from my mother every time she calls."

"Well, in this instance she may be right."

Kate pushed a hand through her unruly hair. "I love that house, Trish. It's elegant and quiet and has a wonderful view. I was lucky to get it on a six-month lease. And you know I can't take time off to go house-hunting now. With only three more months left on the project, the pace is going to be frantic. Speaking of which," she added, rising, "we need to get back to the lab. I left the two new engineers alone on their consoles."

Trish looked wistfully at the remains of the croissant on Kate's plate and sighed as she pushed back her chair. "I don't know why I even come on these coffee breaks with you. All I do is sip black coffee while you stuff yourself. I wish I had your figure."

"Being so tall does have a few advantages," Kate agreed as

the two women strolled down the main corridor of the Phillips Laboratory computer center. "It takes a lot more to fill me up."

"And you don't even pretend to exercise," Trish complained, gesturing toward her own comfortably padded hips.

"I'm constitutionally opposed to strenuous physical activity," Kate declared, punching in the combination to a cipher lock. "Just the *idea* of sweating makes me sweat."

She pushed open a heavy door and passed into another world. Pausing on the threshold, Kate waited for her eyes to adjust to the fluorescent light flooding the vast open bay of the computer center. As her vision cleared, her ears picked up the subdued whir of half a dozen mainframes. A thrill ran up her spine—the same shiver of excitement Kate always felt around computers. There was so much power stored in those neat rows of innocuous-looking machines. Even the new supercomputer, standing by itself at the far end of the huge room, was no bigger than an average-size desk. Yet, that sleek, cream-colored box would be capable of thousands of calculations per second once she got it running.

And that particular box was her responsibility—a fifty-million-dollar machine, and she was the one who'd bring it online and integrate it with the lab's other supercomputers. This baby was a far cry from her first computer, a thirdhand one bought during her freshman year at college. She'd had to work extra shifts as a cocktail waitress to pay for that big, now antiquated, machine, but the late hours and lack of sleep had been worth it. Since the first moment she flipped on the power, she'd been hooked.

"All right, team, let's get to it. We've got to get this hummer online and start running the first test patterns."

"We're close, boss," one of the new engineers told her, laying the latest spreadsheets out on a wide worktable.

By the time the last of the crew left that evening, Kate was tired, but euphoric. They'd made more progress than she dared hope. She stuffed scattered papers and thick manuals into a bulging briefcase, grabbed a notebook computer and left the now-silent lab. Using a special access card to exit the front doors of the building, she headed for her car.

Driving the sleek little Audi down the main thoroughfare of Kirtland Air Force Base, Kate felt more cheerful than she had since the shock of the robbery the previous evening. Excitement bubbled in her veins like fine champagne. If her team held to the new schedule they'd worked out this afternoon, they'd finish the project ahead of schedule. That meant she'd be back in L.A. by the end of September with a big, fat bonus.

For the first time since she'd left her job at a high-powered Silicon Valley firm last year and struck out on her own, Kate knew success was within reach. After all those years of paying back student loans, of saving every penny to buy her mother a condominium, of working seven days a week on the toughest projects to gain experience, she was finally on her own and about to make a healthy profit. This was her first big contract as an independent consultant. If she did well, she'd have a secure entrée into the big-money world of supercomputers.

When she got home, Kate was too keyed-up even for the hot tub. She poured herself a celebratory glass of wine and wandered toward the wide doors leading to the patio. Her hand reached for the brass door handle, then hesitated.

With a quick shake of her head, she told herself not to be so timid. Pulling the French doors open, Kate caught her breath at the sight of the high Sandia peaks bathed in the last rays of the summer sun. She settled into an overstuffed rattan chair and watched the mountains turn a deep, glowing pink. Trish, an Albuquerque native, had told her *sandía* meant watermelon in Spanish. Early Spanish colonizers had named this range after witnessing these same spectacular sunsets. Kate sighed and sipped her drink in pure contentment as the pink peaks deepened to red, then to purple. Above them, a velvet-blue sky slowly darkened. Kate felt the quiet beauty of the night wash over her.

"Ouch, dammit!"

A loud shout and a sudden, furious barking on the other side of her patio wall shattered the evening calm. Kate nearly jumped out of her skin. Wine splashed all over her hand and a good part of her silk blouse.

"Hold still, you blasted mutt."

A series of wild howls accompanied the angry command.

Kate scrambled to her feet, toppling the chair behind her. She backed toward the French doors, trying desperately to recall if there was a poker beside the fireplace to use as a weapon. Before she could pull the doors closed, a hard pounding sounded on the wooden gate.

"Ms. O'Sullivan! Open up."

Kate stared at the gate.

"It's me. Dan Kingman. Open up, would you? Dammit, stop!"

Kate assumed the last command was directed toward the fierce growling, snapping sound coming from over the high wall.

"Look, I can see your lights. I know you're there. Open the gate before this animal has me for dinner."

Reluctantly, Kate headed back out on the now-dark patio and approached the gate. She recognized the captain's deep voice, but wasn't anxious to let in whatever it was he had with him. Pulling the bolt back, she opened the gate a crack, just enough to peer out at the dim figure bent almost double. He was holding a bucking, twisting, growling black shadow.

Kingman pushed the gate open with one hip and backed into the patio area, hauling his captive with him by the scruff of its neck. Kate's jaw sagged as she took in his uniform, or lack thereof. He wore another T-shirt, but this time it was tucked into the shortest, raggedest pair of cutoffs Kate had ever seen.

"Shut it, quick," he tossed at her over his shoulder.

Closing her mouth with a click, Kate shook her head. "No way! That thing sounds vicious. I don't want to pen it in with us."

"Shut the gate," Kingman snapped. "I can't hold him much longer. He's not vicious or he would have bitten me before now. He's just objecting to being held."

Kate blinked at his peremptory tone. Just whose patio was this, anyway? Kingman didn't look like he was about to let the

animal go until she complied, however. She slipped around him
and his vociferously protesting captive to close the gate.

When the captain released his grip, Kate jumped onto an ot-
toman while the dog ran around the patio in wild, panting circles.
Kingman might not have been bitten, but she wasn't taking any
chances.

After several mad circuits, the animal finally planted itself in
front of the gate and began to scratch at the wood with one paw,
howling all the while.

"For heaven's sake, let it out," Kate shouted.

Kingman moved to stand next to her shaky perch, his eyes
never leaving the dog. "No. He'll settle down," he yelled back.
"I think he's a stray."

"So why did you haul it in here?"

"What?"

"Why'd you bring him in here?"

Kingman shook his head and pointed to his ear. Exasperated,
Kate in turn gestured toward the French doors.

He nodded, then reached up and swept her into his arms. Too
astonished to protest, Kate felt his hard muscles bunch under her
back and legs as he carried her into the living room. He kicked
the door shut with one heel before he let her slide, half-indignant
and wholly flustered, from his arms.

"Whew, he sure can sound off." Kingman turned to peer out
the door.

Kate croaked out an unintelligible sound, then swallowed and
tried again. "Would you mind telling me what you were doing
outside my patio? And why did you haul that thing in here?"

Kingman turned, and for the second time in two nights Kate
found herself face-to-face with an endless expanse of chest. Tonight it was covered in navy cotton, with APD stitched in gold
letters over the pocket. Damp patches plastered the thin fabric
to his body. Kate swallowed as her fascinated gaze dropped from
his chest, past the cutoffs, and down legs covered with dark hair
and corded with muscles. His running shoes looked as if they'd
been left out in the rain for several weeks. Across the short
distance separating them, she could smell the faint tang of

healthy male sweat. She shook her head to dispel her sudden, overwhelming awareness of the man and tried to absorb his words.

"I was running in the open area along the mountains and decided to swing by to check on your patio gate. Just wanted to make sure it was locked." A rueful smile tugged at the thick brush of hair on his lip. "I got a little excited when I saw shadows moving in the scrub outside your patio wall and, uh, attacked. The hound resisted arrest."

Kate stared at him in confusion. "You came by to check my gate?"

"Thieves have been known to hit the same place in quick succession."

"So you came by to check my gate?" Kate repeated foolishly, still confused by his unexpected presence and the continual howls vibrating the glass planes of the French doors. She leaned her shoulders against the wall and struggled for a semblance of poise.

"Yeah, well, with you living alone, I thought it wouldn't hurt."

"Didn't we cover that subject last night?" she began, her eyes narrowing. "No, never mind! Look, Captain Kingman, I appreciate your concern. I really do. But—"

"We're just here to serve, ma'am," he interjected with a gleam in his eyes that disarmed Kate completely. She pushed her shoulders off the wall and edged away from him. Suddenly she felt the need for a little space, and a lot of air.

"There was no need for you to come by. Really, I learned a lesson last night. I'm more cautious now. A locksmith's coming tomorrow to change all the locks. And the security folks are coming out, as well, to show me how to use the alarm system."

"Good." He nodded. He started to say something else, only to be interrupted by a particularly loud, long yowl.

"Good grief," Kate exclaimed. "He sounds like he's auditioning for the Met!" Her lips curved in a reluctant smile as the howl gained in both volume and virtuosity. Her eyes met Kingman's in a moment of shared laughter.

"Why did you bring him in here, anyway? He probably wants to go home. Or meet his girlfriend or something."

"I'm pretty sure he's a stray. I could feel every one of his ribs while we were tussling out there, and his fur's all matted. He doesn't have on a collar, either."

Kate bent beside Kingman to peer through the glass. She could barely make out the deep shadow pacing back and forth by the gate.

"Well, we can't have him howling out there all night. You'll have to take him with you."

"I'm a good three-mile run from my car. I can't tug him that distance, resisting all the way." Kingman gave her a sidelong glance. "I suppose you could call the pound."

"*I* could call the pound? You call them! You captured him."

"Let me check him out again. Maybe I missed his collar under all that fur. Have you got anything to tempt him with?"

With the nasty suspicion that she was going to have a large—not to mention loud—uninvited guest unless she did some fast talking, Kate headed for the kitchen.

"Here, try this," she said, and offered Kingman a piece of meat.

Kingman took the hunk of steak and went back outside. He knelt, hand extended, with Kate peering cautiously over his shoulder. "Here, boy. Come here."

For long moments, the dog ignored them both and continued to pace back and forth by the gate. Finally, Kingman's soothing tones seemed to get his attention. That, or the scent of six-dollar-a-pound filet, Kate thought wryly. The dog stopped and eyed them both uncertainly. Kingman coaxed him with low, soft promises. The dog took one step forward, then another. He hesitated, then reached for the meat.

To Kate's surprise, he didn't snatch it away. Instead, he ate with a strange dignity, bit by bit, from Kingman's fingers.

"Good boy." Kingman stroked the dog's head, then felt his massive neck. "Nope, no collar. And his coat's a mess. Probably hasn't been combed in months. Here, feel him."

"No thanks. I'll take your word for it."

Kingman swiveled on his heels and looked up at her. "Look, why don't you keep him here tonight? He's not vicious, only hungry. See how he's calmed down? Feed him a little more and give him a blanket. I'll come back to get him as soon as I can make arrangements for him."

Kate groaned. She'd seen this coming. "No, I can't. I'm gone all day. I couldn't care for him."

"He's tough, he can take care of himself during the day." Kingman straightened and turned toward her. "Seriously, Ms. O'Sullivan, think about it. He'd be a good watchdog for you until the security system comes online. I'd feel better knowing you had protection tonight."

"Some protection," Kate retorted. "A thief would only have to toss a filet or two over the wall to get by him. Really, I can't keep him here."

"If he goes to the pound and isn't claimed in three days, they'll put him to sleep. Come on, lady, you don't want this old boy to be put down, do you?"

Kate bit her lip and glanced from Kingman's hazel eyes to a pair of soulful dark ones. She tried to protest once more, but knew before the words were even out of her mouth, they were only a token protest. She couldn't stand the thought of any animal being put to sleep.

A half hour later, as she wiped soap out of her eyes for the third time, she muttered something decidedly uncomplimentary about a certain police captain. From a mound of bubbles deep in her oval bathtub, a pink tongue darted out to take a swipe at her cheek.

"Ugh! Stop it, you dumb mutt. Just keep still. You're only going to be here a day or two, but at least you'll be clean when you leave. Now stop it!"

Two

Dan Kingman drove through the dark streets, thinking of the woman he'd just left. He chuckled as he remembered his last view of her, standing on the patio with both hands on her hips, enumerating all the reasons she couldn't keep the animal. He'd known she'd cave in, though. He'd seen the laughter in those incredible eyes at the dog's antics and guessed she wouldn't have the heart to toss the stray out on its ear.

His chuckle deepened when he thought of how she would've tossed *him* out if she'd known the real reason he'd decided to take his run in the Heights this evening. Somehow he suspected she wouldn't buy the fact that her sparkling eyes and long legs had interested him as much as whether or not she'd locked the gate. He wasn't quite sure he bought it himself.

Still, if the dog hadn't provided an excuse to barge in on her tonight, Dan knew he would've found some other reason to knock on her gate. He shifted on the worn leather seat, more than a little surprised at his sudden fascination with Kathleen O'Sullivan. At thirty-nine, he'd been around long enough to know first attractions rarely survived the light of morning. He'd also learned the hard way that he and stubbornly independent women didn't mix. His brief marriage had taught him that.

Yet Dan's first impression of Kathleen on the night of the robbery had teased at him throughout the day. Standing in the open door, silhouetted by the hallway lamps, she'd been a sight to spark any man's interest. Those long legs seemed to go on for miles, leading up to generously curving hips and small, high breasts. Her hair was a wild mass of red-brown waves, framing those remarkable violet eyes. So what if her nose was a little short and her chin tended to tilt at a determined angle? When she smiled, the sum of all her parts added up to one damned attractive female. And one very stubborn one, he reminded himself.

He tried without much success to push the image of the delectable Ms. O'Sullivan from his mind as he showered, then drove across town to a buddy's house. He decided that a night of poker and the companionship of his rowdy friends from the department was what he needed to ease the tightening in his lower body every time he remembered the husky timbre of her voice.

"Hiya, Chief. Sorry about the call last night."

Dan shot his assistant a disgusted look and settled into the creaking wooden chair behind his desk. "You sure have rotten timing, Peters. I had to throw in a full house."

The younger man shrugged, a smile on his lips. He knew from experience the captain's bark was worse than his bite...most of the time.

Dan waved him to a chair. "Let's go over what we have on last night's homicide. Then I want to review the status on the Sandia Heights break-ins. The mayor is giving me a real ration on that case."

"Just because he and most of his influential backers happen to live up in the Heights, the guy wants the case cracked like yesterday," the younger man commiserated.

"Politics is politics," Dan replied with a shrug.

The new mayor had campaigned on a platform of cleaning up crime and gang activities. So far he'd been less than pleased with the police progress on a number of cases. And very vocal about the Heights robberies.

An hour later, the two investigating officers assigned to the robbery case eased themselves into chairs in front of Dan's desk.

"Okay, troops, let's have it. Where are we on this?"

"We're close, Captain. The car in the chase belongs to a Dr. Henry. He was out of town yesterday and we couldn't get to him until this morning. Seems his son had the vehicle out the night of the break-ins. We brought the kid in for questioning. He's tough, but scared."

"Good. The juvenile division will know how to handle him. Keep on it. Let me know as soon as you find out anything."

Dan swiveled around in his chair when the two men left and stared out the window of his fourth-floor office. The morning sun was still hanging low behind the Bernallilo County Courthouse just across the street, leaving most of City Plaza bathed in rich violet shadows. Dan propped his feet up on the sill, studying the shifting patterns. He decided he was becoming very partial to that particular color, especially when it stared out at him from a pair of wide, sparkling eyes.

Giving in to a sudden impulse, he pulled the notepad out of his pocket and flipped through the crumpled pages until he found the phone number he was looking for. Settling the phone in his lap, he punched in the numbers.

"Phillips Lab, Scientific Computing Department," a crisp, young voice answered on the first ring.

"Ms. O'Sullivan, please. Tell her it's Captain Kingman, Albuquerque Police Department." Dan waited, his eyes on the gray wall opposite him, his mind on the woman he'd last seen trading doubtful glances with a large, scruffy hound.

"When are you coming to get the dog?" Her low, throaty voice interrupted his musing.

"Good morning to you, too, Ms. O'Sullivan."

After a short pause, she recovered. "Good morning, Captain. When do you intend to pick up your adopted son?"

"That's what I'm calling about. We had a little murder here

last night. Just your routine domestic squabble and drug-induced shooting. I'm afraid I'll be tied up for a while.''

''What! Look, Kingman, you have to do something about this mutt today. His singing is even worse than mine, and twice as loud. I think his vocal cords never passed puberty.''

Dan chuckled into the phone.

''It's not funny,'' Kate protested. She paused; then Dan heard her reluctant laugh come over the line. ''Well, at least I didn't think so when the clock radio clicked on at six this morning and your hound did a duet with Willie Nelson.''

Her laugh was like rich, dark chocolate. Dan felt a sudden tightening, low in his stomach. His feet slid to the floor. Hell, he'd thought he was long past the age of getting turned on by the sound of a woman's laugh. He better put some distance between himself and this woman—fast.

''Look, I'll need a few days to find someone to take him. I'll come after him as soon as I can, I promise.''

''Kingman—''

''I've got to go. The coroner's waiting outside. I'll call you.'' Dan hung up on her indignant protests.

He was still up to his ears in the homicides and an unraveling series of related drug cases when one of the young detectives knocked on his door the next afternoon.

''We got 'em, Captain.''

The man's excited voice pierced Dan's preoccupation with the reports spread out before him.

''Got who?''

''The boys who've been knocking off the homes in the Heights.''

''Tell me,'' Dan ordered, hiding his smile as he waved the man into his office. Sergeant Alvarado had just been promoted to detective a month ago. This was his first case with any high-level interest, and his eagerness to wrap it up showed.

''The kid driving the car wouldn't talk at first, but he finally gave us the names of the boys who were with him during their joyride the other night. We went visiting, and hit pay dirt at the second house. The kid wasn't home, but his mother took us out to the garage. Said she'd just found a stereo and video camera hidden under some boxes. She was afraid her son had gotten into trouble.''

"So Juvie confronted the kids with the evidence?''

"Yeah, had each one of them in individually. The youngest finally admitted to the break-ins.''

"What kind of evidence do you have, other than the one confession and the stereo?'' Dan asked quietly. Juvenile cases were tough. If the evidence wasn't airtight, the judge would throw the charges out in a heartbeat. Even when they had the case sewn up, juvenile offenders would get a break more often than not. Though he'd rather see a youngster get community service and a good scare than a record, Dan thought.

"You're not going to believe this, Captain. They actually videotaped their activities. Made a damn docudrama of every heist. We found the tapes with the stolen stereo in the garage. Only saw the first few minutes of one of the tapes, but it's dynamite.''

"Cocky little bastards, aren't they?'' Dan laughed and stood to shake the man's hand. "Good job, Alvarado. Give me a copy of the written report tomorrow so I can brief the mayor.''

Kate flopped into an overstuffed rattan patio chair with a tired groan. Taking an unwilling, loudly protesting animal to the vet for an exam was more work than she'd ever imagined. Throughout the ordeal, the hound had treated her to a series of hurt, reproachful looks. She'd tried to ignore his accusing eyes, telling herself the exam and shots were for his own good. At least now she knew he was healthy.

Kate watched the dog sniffing around the patio as if he hadn't seen it, much less watered it thoroughly, only an hour before. She sighed when he lifted his leg to drench a small piñon tree. He'd already drowned the yucca in the corner. She'd have to get a first-class landscaper out to redo the patio before she turned the house back to the owners. The dog finished his appointed rounds and wandered over to sit beside her. With a contented snuffle, he plunked his head in her lap and stared up at her.

"Don't give me any of those wide-eyed, innocent looks," Kate muttered.

Of its own accord, her hand reached out to rub the silky black head. She still couldn't believe how soft and fine his fur turned out to be after it had been washed—three times!—and clipped. The vet thought the mutt had some purebred Labrador retriever somewhere in his ancestry to account for his long body and silky ears. Kate shared a moment of unexpected companionship with the big hound before the shrill of the phone made them both jump.

"Ms. O'Sullivan, this is Detective Alvarado with the Albuquerque Police Department," said a voice when she picked up the receiver. "We think we've recovered some of your stolen property. Could you come downtown in the next day or so and identify the items?"

"Sure, Detective," Kate responded. "I took the afternoon off to take...uh, my dog to the vet. I can come down now, if it's convenient."

"Great. Please bring any lists of serial numbers or other identifying records you might have."

Kate hung up and strolled into the bedroom to change out of her jeans and T-shirt, the dog padding beside her.

"That was fast work, Enrico," Kate told him as she pulled on white linen slacks and a loose, silky tunic in her favorite shade of hot pink.

The dog grinned at her, his bushy tail thumping on the thick carpet. She fastened a wide leather belt low on her hips and slipped into a pair of matching sandals. Kate wondered briefly if she should take the dog along with her and leave him in a certain captain's office. No, Kingman might not be there, and then she'd have to make another drive home with Rico trying to convince her he was born a lapdog.

Late-afternoon heat shimmered above the pavement when Kate walked up the steps to the modern, adobe high rise that housed both the Bernalillo County Sheriff's Department and the Albuquerque Police Department. Following directions from the

officer on duty at the entrance, she made her way to the Burgla-
ries Branch on the fourth floor.

"Excuse me. I'm supposed to meet with Detective Alvarado.
My name is Kathleen O'Sullivan."

The young man at the littered reception desk glanced up. His
brows furrowed for a moment, then a slow smile spread across
his face.

"Yes, ma'am. You're here about the robberies in the Heights,
aren't you?"

"Yes, as a matter of fact. How did you know?"

"I, uh, saw the report."

Kate was surprised he would remember her particular case.
From the mounds of papers scattered across his desk waiting to
be filed, he must process hundreds of reports.

"Detective Alvarado is expecting you. His desk is the last one
on the right." The man waved Kate past the counter to a room
filled with long rows of modular desk units. His polite smile
broadened into something close to a smirk.

Puzzling over his strange behavior, Kate started down the corridor between the desks. The place vibrated with a low, incessant
hum. Phones rang, people talked in groups of two or three at
various desks and keyboards clattered at a constant rate. It
seemed to Kate some of the activity level died down as she
moved through the long room. More than one group broke off
their conversation and turned to stare at her. For a moment, she
wondered if she'd left the back buttons to her tunic undone or
something. She shrugged and stopped in front of the last desk.

"Detective Alvarado? I'm Kathleen O'Sullivan."

The young man jumped up and held out his hand. "Thanks
for coming down so quickly, Ms. O'Sullivan. Here, have a seat."

He shuffled through a stack of papers on his desk and pulled
out a sheet. "This is a list of property you reported stolen. Here's
a list, with accompanying pictures, of what we recovered. I need
you to scan it and mark any items you think may be yours. Then
we'll go down to the evidence storage area and tag them."

Kate took the lists and spread them out to review. "You do

good work, Detective. I'm surprised you solved this case so quickly.''

''We were lucky. Got some good leads and nailed all three of the teenagers involved. We've recovered almost everything from the ten houses in your neighborhood that they robbed.''

''Good heavens. I didn't know there were ten,'' Kate commented as she continued to scan the lists. She checked off what looked like her TV and VCR, matching the listed serial numbers with those on inventory she'd had the owners of the house fax to her. On the last page of the list, she found her laptop.

''Oh, great! I'm sure this is my computer. I was just about to buy another one. I can't be without one in my line of work.''

She frowned and flipped back through several pages. ''I don't see anything on the kachina collection.''

''They're on a separate list. Since the dolls don't have serial numbers, we did a special report and pictures on them.''

Alvarado spread out a colorful array of photos showing the brightly painted dolls in all their feathered glory. ''Good thing we got the tape, or we wouldn't have been able to ID them.''

''What tape?'' Kate asked absently as she reviewed the pictures. She didn't know much about Indian art, but these sure looked like the little wooden statues that had graced the mantel of her rented house.

''The videotape.'' When Kate gave him a blank look, the man's professional expression slipped slightly. He hesitated before continuing. ''The kids made a video of every place they broke into. Exterior and interior. It's made identifying the stolen property a lot easier.''

''Did they make one in my house?''

Alvarado's eyes slid away, as if he didn't want to discuss the tapes further. ''Well, yes. They did.''

Kate felt a tiny niggle of unease begin to curl in her stomach. ''They must've been in the house while I was in the hot tub. I thought I heard something when I got out. Surely they didn't—''

''Good afternoon, Ms. O'Sullivan.''

Kate jumped at the deep voice just behind her. She turned to see Dan Kingman, fully dressed for a change. Her mind barely registered the fact that he looked as good in black slacks and a lightweight summer sport coat as he had in cutoffs and T-shirts. She rose from her chair with an unsteady jerk.

Kate's nervousness about the tape turned to absolute, gut-wrenching certainty when she saw the amusement glinting in Kingman's eyes. She took a deep breath.

"Detective Alvarado just informed me that the boys who broke into my house that night made a video."

"As a matter of fact, they did."

"I'd like to have it, please."

"Sorry, ma'am, that's evidence. We can't release it until after the hearing."

Kate clenched her hands on her purse. "Is there...is there anything on that tape that... I mean, I don't like the idea of them taking pictures in my house. Especially since I was right there and didn't know it."

Kingman took her arm in a loose hold. "Why don't you come to my office? I think we need to talk about this."

As Kate traveled the length of the noisy room beside him, she felt herself to be the target of more interested, amused looks. Kingman barely shut the door of his office before she whirled, her words tumbling out.

"Just what's on that tape?"

"Sit down, Ms.—look, do you mind if I call you Kathleen? I think we're past the Ms. O'Sullivan stage."

"Kate," she said impatiently, her mind on the tape.

"What?"

"Call me Kate. Only my mother calls me Kathleen, and then just when she's about to deliver another lecture on the evils of spinsterhood." Kate dropped into a hard wooden chair. "About this tape, Captain..."

"Dan."

Kate ground her teeth. "Dan. Tell me about this tape. What's on it?"

"A scan of the house, inside and out, with a running commentary by one of the boys on what they would steal. Evidently the kid thinks he's a budding TV star."

She let out a little breath of relief.

"And a rather artistic series of shots of you in the hot tub."

Kate closed her eyes. She knew it! Those juvenile delinquents were in her house while she was sitting, blissfully ignorant, in the tub. She'd had a horrible premonition about this tape business as soon as Detective Alvarado refused to meet her eyes. Kate cringed inside. No wonder everyone in the room outside had stared when she walked by. Desperately, she tried to remember how much of herself she'd exposed in the tub. The water bubbled almost to her chin. Surely they couldn't have caught more than a few seconds when she climbed out and pulled that skimpy towel around her.

"I want that tape back, Captain." She managed to keep her voice low and steady, despite the embarrassment coursing through her.

Some of the teasing glint faded from Kingman's eyes. "I'm sorry. It's evidence. I can't give it to you."

Kate swallowed. "It's only evidence if I press charges. If I don't, you have no case and don't need evidence."

All traces of amusement left the face opposite her. Kingman leaned forward. "You've already filed a complaint."

"So I'll withdraw it."

"You can't do that, Kate. We have these kids dead-on. If they get away with this little stunt, who knows what they'll get into next."

"They robbed nine other houses. Use that evidence. You don't need mine." Embarrassment sharpened her voice to a curt, angry clip.

Kingman sat back and studied her for a long, silent moment. Kate refused to look away, although she still writhed inside at the thought of what must be on that tape. She blinked when he stood abruptly.

"Let's go get some dinner."

"What?"

"You shouldn't make hasty decisions while you're upset." Kingman held up his hand when she opened her mouth to protest. "You have every right to be upset. Your home was invaded, your privacy violated. You've had a shock and need something to settle your nerves. How about a margarita and a serving of the best enchiladas in town?''

Kate tilted her head to one side, surprised at his offer. One part of her mind still worried over the tape. The other part registered a desire to have dinner with this man—a desire so strong, it amazed her. Kingman's image had teased at her consciousness the past few days, from his disreputable mustache to the way his cutoffs had displayed a body that belonged in improbable TV ads for tummy flatteners or other exercise equipment. Before she had time to gather her scattered thoughts, Kingman reached down and took her arm.

"Come on, we'll sort this all out at the restaurant. I'm hungry."

A short time later Kate found herself crowded into a round booth beside the captain. She edged farther over on the smooth leather seat to give him more room and reached out a shaky hand for her frosted margarita glass.

"Are you okay?" His dark brows knit together in a frown.

"Fine." She took a large, salty gulp. "Why shouldn't I be? I mean, in the last few days I've been frightened half out of my mind. I've been robbed. I've been saddled with an animal who thinks he's Caruso reincarnated. And now I find out I'm the subject of an X-rated home video. What could possibly be upsetting me?"

Kate wiped a finger down the stem of her frosted glass and gave Kingman a wry glance. "Sounds like something out of *The Perils of Pauline,* doesn't it?"

He kept his face straight, but Kate could see amusement dancing in his expressive eyes. In fact, crowded so close to him in the little booth, Kate could see a lot more of Captain Dan Kingman than she could handle. She noted how his shoulders strained against the seams of his sport coat, how the strong column of his throat rose above a loosely knotted tie, how his hair held an almost indiscernible sprinkling of silver among its dark strands. She dropped her eyes and took another quick swallow of her drink.

"It's not really X-rated, you know," Kingman said gently. "More like R-plus."

"I take it you've seen it." Resignation threaded Kate's voice.

"I feel it's my duty to review the evidence in certain cases," he replied solemnly.

"Just how many other people have seen it?" she asked, afraid of the answer but needing to know.

"Only a handful—honest. But word of it spread pretty quickly around the department." He hesitated, then sent her a rueful glance. "I'm afraid you've become something of a celebrity."

Kate groaned and covered her face. She tried to resist when he reached out and pulled her hands down, but with little success. She was beginning to realize that resisting Captain Kingman in anything was next to impossible.

"Listen to me, Kate. I promise you, we won't show any part of the video that's offensive or embarrassing to you in court. We don't need to. But we need to use the part on the burglary."

"Why? You've got nine other tapes. Use them."

"I've worked with Judge Chavez for several years now. She's one of the best juvenile judges I've ever seen, but she's a real stickler. If there are any irregularities, any holes in the evidence, she'll throw our whole case out. I don't want to take that chance."

Kate looked up at him. His eyes were steady, with no trace of the teasing glints she'd seen before.

"Okay, okay," she grumbled. "If you *swear* the damn thing is edited."

The waiter's arrival with a tray of steaming plates cut short their conversation. Kate felt a fleeting regret when Dan's warm hands left hers, but it soon vanished in her enjoyment of the delicious, spicy food. The green chili sauce smothering the enchiladas brought tears to her eyes and made her empty the water glass twice, but she finished every bite. She still marveled at how much hotter New Mexican food was than the variety served in L.A.

With an easy deftness, Dan steered the conversation away from the burglary as they worked their way through dinner. Kate relaxed by imperceptible degrees and shared her impressions of Albuquerque. From there, talk turned to the trials and tribulations of living and working in L.A. Over coffee, she found herself giving him a brief description of her fledgling company.

"So you're a chief executive officer," he commented as he sent the hovering waiter off with a hefty tip and a big grin.

"CEO sounds like a more impressive title than it really is, in a small firm. I'm also marketing director, chief software engineer and head of the personnel department."

He slanted her a thoughtful glance as they walked out into the starry night.

"With all those additional responsibilities, do you think you're going to get this supercomputer all put together and spitting out scientific formulas in less than six months?"

"In less than three," she corrected, sliding into the passenger seat of his car. "I'm already halfway through the performance period of the contract."

"Will you make it?"

"Yes." The determined note in her voice gave way to a rueful laugh. "At least, I hope so. Phase Three depends on it."

The dark streets rolled by, bathed in velvety blue New Mexico twilight.

"Okay, I'll bite. What's Phase Three?"

"I made a schedule for myself when I got out of grad school." Holding up one hand, Kate ticked off each item as she recited it. "Phase One—pay back all my educational loans and settle my mother by twenty-five. Phase Two—enough financial independence to start my own company by thirty. Phase Three—a healthy profit by thirty-five. Phase Four, make the Fortune 500 list by forty."

"What about a personal life in this nice, neat little plan you've laid out? When do you phase in such things as marriage and a family?"

The cool note in his voice surprised Kate. She flicked him a quick glance, but couldn't make out his expression in the dim light.

"I've found you can't schedule or plan on such things as marriage," she replied, shrugging.

"No, you can't."

This time there was no mistaking the edge to his tone. She turned sideways to peer at him. Streetlights illuminated his face in intermittent flashes. It was a spare face, all planes and angles, in keeping with his finely honed athlete's body. Suddenly she was intensely curious about this man who rescued stray dogs and checked up on women living by themselves.

"Enough about me," she pronounced. "What about you? How did you get into the law-enforcement business?"

Although he disliked talking about himself, Dan welcomed the change in subject. Kate's blithe dismissal of marriage and a family had flicked a raw spot in him, one he'd thought long since healed. His wife hadn't wanted a family, either, hadn't even bothered to inform him when she terminated the pregnancy that she decided would interfere with her budding career as a dancer. By mutual consent, they'd terminated the marriage soon afterward.

"I did a stint in the marines," he replied a little stiffly, "then used the GI bill to go to law school."

Kate's gurgle of laughter brought his head around.

"I'm trying to picture you without that disreputable mustache."

"Try without any hair at all," he replied dryly, beguiled by her low, throaty laugh. He pushed the dim, distant memories into the past where they belonged and willed himself to relax.

"How did you get from law school to law enforcement?"

"I decided I didn't like the idea of helping bad guys weasel out of their just deserts because of some minor technicality. So I joined the police force."

Dan filled the rest of the short drive with outrageous anecdotes from his rookie days, as much to hear her low, musical laughter as to eat up the miles. Turning into the department's parking lot, he pulled up alongside her car and switched off the ignition. Sudden, blanketing silence wrapped them. Slewing sideways in his seat, Dan met her wide, luminous eyes and knew what would come next.

"Come here, Kate."

Before the words were out of his mouth, Dan knew he'd probably regret them. His every instinct told him he shouldn't take this woman in his arms. She was bright and ambitious and living according to a schedule that didn't appear to allow for the things he hungered for. He had enough complications in his life without a wide-eyed, long-legged redhead adding to them. Yet even as the arguments formed in his mind, he ignored them.

Slowly, deliberately, he slid his palm behind her neck and tugged her toward him. She leaned forward awkwardly, one elbow propped on the console between the bucket seats, her hands splayed against his chest. Her eyes gleamed in the glow of the streetlights before he lowered his head and blocked out the light altogether.

She tasted of salty margarita and something softer, something sweeter. Dan explored her lips with his tongue and, hiding in one corner of her mouth, found a tiny bead of honey from the sopapillas they'd consumed. Groaning, he deepened the kiss. She responded instinctively, leaning into him, opening her mouth under his hungry assault. When he finally raised his head, his breath rasped in his throat.

"I've been wanting to do that since the first moment I saw you." His admission was as reluctant as it was necessary.

"Me, too."

Her husky laugh sent a ripple of pleasure to every one of his extremities. His fingers tightened in her hair. His toes curled in his shoes. And he forced himself not to think about what was happening elsewhere. Leaning his forehead against hers, he drew in a deep breath.

"You taste good," he murmured.

"You, too," she whispered, lifting her face for another kiss.

Dan tangled his fingers in the soft mass of her hair, while his other hand slid slowly down to shape her hip. Her tongue began a sensual dance with his that left him wanting more. Much more. A hungry ache curled low in his belly.

When Dan leaned back, his breathing harsh in the quiet darkness, Kate felt a sense of loss that surprised her. She hadn't reached her advanced age without being in love once or twice, or at least without thinking she was. But she hadn't ever experienced so quickly such desire for anyone—not even her unlamented ex-fiancé.

She was still trying to sort out her confused feelings when Dan opened his door, then came around to hers.

"Come on, Kate. Let's get you home."

With a definite sense of regret, she slid out of his car and headed for her own. She could feel Dan's presence behind her as she fumbled with the keys. When the door opened, she turned back to the man looming behind her.

"Thanks for dinner," she told him softly.

"Thanks for *after* dinner." He smiled down at her.

She could see the stark whiteness of his teeth gleaming under that bushy mustache. Unconsciously, she licked her lips, remembering the way the soft, springy hairs had rubbed against her mouth.

Dan gave a little groan and took her in his arms. There was nothing gentle about his kiss this time. This time it was hard and hot and hungry. His tongue demanded entry, and she gave it willingly. He widened his stance, shifting Kate into the cradle of his thighs. She clung to him, off balance, feeling the hard evidence of his desire.

To her chagrin, it was Dan who lifted his head and drew in a deep, steadying breath.

"Any more of this and we won't make it out of the parking lot." His thumbs brushed her cheeks in tender feather-light strokes. "I'm too darned big to fit comfortably into the back seat of a car. And from what I've seen of that long, luscious body of yours, you wouldn't fit, either. But you better get home, before we put it to the test."

Kate gave a shaky laugh and had turned to slide into her car when his words penetrated her lingering pleasure. Slowly she faced him again.

"What do you mean, from what you've seen? Are you referring to that videotape?'' A tiny hurt formed deep in the pit of her stomach. ''Is that what this was all about, Dan? This big romantic scene?''

She frowned, the hurt spreading and changing to embarrassment when she thought of how she'd all but melted in his arms. First that damn tape, now her unabashed eagerness for his kisses. Kate refused to articulate, even to herself, what the man must think of her. She got into her car and started to slam the door.

Dan's strong hand held it open. He leaned down, trying to see her face in the dim light, but Kate kept her face turned away. She'd already exposed far too much to this man, literally and figuratively.

''Kate, listen to me. I kissed you because you're a lovely, desirable woman. It doesn't have anything to do with that tape.''

''Look, I really don't want to talk about this anymore. I've got to go.'' She shoved the key in the ignition and gunned the engine. Suddenly she needed to get away from this overwhelming, disturbing man.

''Dammit, you can't think I came on to you because of that tape. Kate, please, we need to talk about this.''

''No, we don't. What I need is to put this whole embarrassing episode out of my mind and my life. Let go of the door, Kingman.''

Kate breathed a sigh of relief when he stood back and let the door slam shut. She started to drive off, then braked to a quick stop. Pressing the button to open the window, she leaned out to yell back to him.

''And come get your dog!''

Three

"Dammit, Kate, don't hang up again. This is official business." Dan held his breath through the long pause that followed.

"I told you the last two times you called I don't want to see you again, Captain. Except when you come to pick up the hound."

Dan gripped the phone, hard. "Look, Kate, I know you're embarrassed about that damn tape, but you have to put it aside. We have a complication on the burglary case. I need to talk to you."

"So talk."

"It's too complex to handle over the phone. Can you come down to the office?"

"No, I'm busy."

Gritting his teeth, Dan swallowed his initial retort. When Ms. O'Sullivan got her Irish up, it stayed up.

"All right," he managed. "I'll come out to the base. What building are you in?"

Kate hung up before he'd even jotted down the building number. Dan restrained his own impulse to slam down the receiver. Detective Alvarado was sitting across the desk from him. He'd already witnessed Dan having to call Kate back after the two times she'd cut him off. No need to let the young sergeant know how much the stubborn woman got to him. Dan's chair groaned in protest as he leaned back to survey the man opposite him.

"Are you absolutely sure none of the other nine victims will take this on?"

Alvarado shook his head. "I've contacted each of them personally, Captain. Some I talked to twice, after I got the word from the juvenile caseworker. Ms. O'Sullivan is our last hope."

Dan shook his head and pulled the folder Alvarado had laid on his desk toward him.

"I would've called her myself," the detective continued, "but I thought you might have more influence with her since you...dealt with her when she was down here last week."

Dan glanced up to meet Alvarado's bland look. He knew darn well what thoughts were churning behind the man's impassive face. There weren't any secrets in the APD. The morning after his dinner with Kate, Dan's assistant had greeted him with a cup of coffee and the previous night's reports. He'd also mentioned that a couple of patrolmen going off-duty had seen a certain officer of the law putting the make on a tall, leggy redhead in the parking lot the evening before. The story was all over the department, his assistant mentioned casually. And the woman had already been ID'ed as the star of the videotape they'd all heard rumors about. Dan suspected the fact that the same woman had just hung up on him would make the rounds of the entire division within hours.

"I'll do my best to convince her. Now get out of here so I can study these profiles."

Dan spread the neat files out in front of him. He picked up the top one and studied the boy it documented. Only fifteen, a good student, son of a prominent University of New Mexico professor, residence in Sandia Heights.

The second suspect was sixteen, from a less privileged family in the valley. No father listed at home, mother worked nights, previous pickups for drug use and petty theft. A known gang member.

The third file was the one that held Dan's attention. Jason

Stone, eleven years old, parents dead. An older brother just out of the county detention center for armed robbery, busted parole—present whereabouts unknown. Jason had one previous pickup for running away from his foster home and roaming the streets late at night. The photo attached to the file showed a towheaded kid with wide, scared eyes. Dan folded the file, slipped it into his jacket pocket and headed out of his office.

Driving out to the base, he wondered how he'd break down the barrier Kate had erected between them. He also wondered why it was so darn important to him to do so. He'd thought about her all week, becoming irritated, then frustrated when she wouldn't take his calls. He told himself she was all wrong for him. She was too wrapped up in her job to have time for him, too eager to finish her project and head back to L.A. for anything to come of the sizzling attraction between them. But his pulse started to speed up as he passed through the sandstone front gate of Kirtland Air Force Base.

"Look at him, Kate. He's just a kid."

"I know, I know! But I just don't want to get involved."

"He's only eleven years old. This is the most serious trouble he's been in. If someone doesn't help him now, he could end up like his older brother, with a record of serious offenses."

"I can't, Dan. I'm embarrassed enough by this whole thing. I couldn't face this kid, knowing he spied on me like that." Kate paced the small office she'd commandeered for privacy.

Dan had to admire the picture she made, despite her agitation. In a calf-length skirt in a swirling pattern of greens and blues and a sapphire-colored shirt of some soft, slinky-looking material, she looked glowing and vibrant. She'd even tamed that mane of hers into a sleek braid that hung down between her shoulder blades.

"I'm sorry, I just can't," she repeated, turning to face him.

Dan studied her worried expression and tried again. "Judge Chavez is committed to this program. She believes that our community is too fragmented, too split into haves and have-nots. That people aren't talking to or getting involved with each other.

So she supports this community service program for first offenders in nonviolent cases. Instead of the juvenile detention center, the offender is given community service under the supervision of the victim. Assuming the victim agrees, of course."

"I can't say I think much of the program." Kate resumed her
pacing. "Whoever came up with this idea must never have been
on the receiving end of a crime."

Dan felt a tinge of red creeping up his cheeks but kept silent
while Kate continued.

"Besides, I just don't have time. My schedule on this project
is too tight. You'll have to find someone else."

"There isn't anyone else. The juvenile caseworker has covered the other two boys, but struck out on this one. Everyone's
either too busy or going on extended vacations or caring for an
elderly aunt. They don't have time to bother with a homeless
kid."

"Oh, no you don't!" Kate faced him, hands on hips. "Don't
try to lay a guilt trip on me. I'm the victim in this case, remember?"

Dan gave up. He'd learned in the marines when to fight and
when to beat a strategic retreat and regroup his forces. He slipped
the file back into his pocket, and leaned one hip against the desk.

"Okay, you can't do it. End of subject. Now let's talk about
us."

"I don't want to talk about us. There *is* no us to talk about.
I told you that last week."

"Yes, and every time I've tried to call you since."

"Well, stop calling," Kate tossed at him.

Dan eased off the desk and moved to stand beside her. "Are
you really so angry with me for one kiss?"

"Three kisses," she muttered, then flushed a dull red.

"Okay, three kisses. I know I don't have the world's greatest
technique, but I didn't think I was that bad."

His hangdog expression brought a smile to her lips. "Well,
I've had better—but not many," she amended hastily as his
brows drew together in a scowl.

"Do you still think I was so turned on by that video that I

couldn't wait to jump your bones?'' Dan asked, tackling the issue head-on.

Kate bit her lip and sighed. "No, not really. I guess my temper got the best of me and I overreacted. This whole situation has thrown me off balance. I...I was too embarrassed to face you again, after that damn tape and the way I responded in the car.''

Dan himself had had vivid dreams late at night about the way she'd responded.

"Why don't we get back on an even keel with dinner?'' he suggested. "Let me take you out tonight. I'll be on my best behavior, I promise. Any bone jumping will be strictly up to you.''

He could see reluctant laughter lighten her eyes.

"Come on, Kate. Even hot-tempered redheads have to eat.''

"No, I don't think it's a good idea,'' she responded after a moment. "I'll only be here a few more months. My schedule's just too tight for any socializing. I don't have time...neither one of us has time for any kind of relationship.''

Dan studied her determined chin. The contrast between the soft, smooth skin covering it and the firm bone beneath fascinated him.

"Not every relationship has to fit into a schedule, you know. Some just happen to develop, all on their own. Have dinner with me, Kate.''

Dan sucked in his breath as she took one corner of her lower lip between even, white teeth, totally unconscious of the provocative innocence of the gesture.

"All right,'' she finally agreed. The reluctance in her voice made him smile.

"It'll have to be late. Around eight-thirty or nine. I have a city council meeting this evening.''

"That's better for me, anyway. I'll be here late, as well.'' She hesitated, chewing on her lip once more. "Look, why don't you just come up to my place. Neither of us will feel like going out that late. I'll put some lasagna in the oven.''

"Deal! See you tonight.''

* * *

Kate was smiling when she punched in the cipher code and strolled into the lab after escorting Dan out. Seeing him face-to-face had helped eliminate most of the lingering embarrassment from their last encounter.

Trish met her, clipboard in hand and a smug grin on her face. "So that's the mysterious Captain Kingman who's been calling here all week, the one you've been palming off with excuses. Not bad, Kate. Not bad at all. I sure wouldn't have put him off." Trish wriggled her eyebrows in an exaggerated leer.

Kate laughed and led the way back to their worktable. "Captain Kingman can be a bit overpowering at times. But I've decided I can take him in small doses."

"Well, however you take him, take him! He looks like a keeper."

"I wouldn't know a keeper if I saw one, Trish," Kate told her, only half joking. "The men in my life have been noticeably short-term."

Trish nodded sympathetically. The two women had shared a little of their pasts over the months they'd worked together. When Kate first hired her for this project, Trish confided afterward how desperate she'd been for work. Her husband had just left her stranded, with car and house payments to make and three kids in school. In this era of layoffs and defense cutbacks, she'd had a hard time finding immediate employment, even with her computer skills.

Her situation had struck a chord with Kate. Her own father had taken off when she was still a child. Kate and her mother had worked hard all their lives to support themselves. Holding down two jobs throughout college and then putting everything she had into her career, Kate hadn't had much time for dating. The few men she'd gone out with hadn't appreciated taking a back seat to her determined career goals, and they soon drifted away. The one man she thought she loved had betrayed her, much as Trish's husband had.

She'd met Charles at a conference on advanced concepts in software development. He worked for a rival Silicon Valley firm, although at a lower management level than Kate. At first he was attracted by her dedication to the business. Then he professed to be captivated by her spirit and warmth. Surprised that such a charming man was so interested in her, Kate soon tumbled into love and a full-blown affair. When Charles gave her a small diamond ring, Kate's mother was as ecstatic as the bride-to-be herself.

It was one of the shortest engagements on record, lasting less than a week. Her mother hadn't even finished calling all her friends with the happy news that her only daughter was *finally* engaged, when Kate discovered her fiancé had somehow neglected to mention the fact he already had a wife. Oh, his wife didn't understand him, of course. She had no appreciation of the stress of this cutthroat business, not like Kate did. Charles swore he'd planned all along to get a divorce. Too hurt and angry to listen to his pathetic pleas, Kate had given him back the ring and refused to see him again. She could laugh about it now, but it had hurt then. Not as much as she'd thought it would, but enough to make her even more determined to carve an independent life for herself. She threw herself totally into her career, then into her fledgling business.

Pushing the unpleasant memories away, Kate leaned over the table next to Trish. Long, computer-generated runs felt smooth and slick under her fingers.

"What have we got here?"

"The first test patterns." Trish traced the wavering patterns with a green felt tip pen. "Unit One is running the test perfectly."

"Great!" Kate exclaimed, her excitement building as she examined the new estimates to completion. "We should have the first unit finished tomorrow."

"Tonight, if we keep at it. Both engineers working the programming are willing to stay all night, if necessary. My mother's got my kids, so I can stay as long as you need me."

Kate nibbled on the tip of her pen. Her first impulse was to call Dan and cancel their impromptu date. Getting this first unit online was a critical deliverable in her contract with the air force. If this went well, she'd get the first big installment of her fee. It was all she needed to pay off her small business loan. Future payments of her fee would be pure profit, after operating expenses. And she was ahead of schedule to completion. Tantalizing visions of the future danced in her mind.

"Do you want me to tell the guys to stay, Kate?"

She blinked and focused on Trish, waiting patiently beside her at the worktable. The delicious visions faded.

"No. Tell them to knock off early. We're in good shape and there's no need for us to kill ourselves. I'd rather have everyone fresh and rested tomorrow so we do this first unit right."

As she drove home later through the summer evening, Kate refused to admit, even to herself, how much a reluctance to cancel her date with Dan played in her decision to send the team home. It was true she'd get a better product from a rested staff. In her heart, though, she knew that wasn't the real reason. A shiver of anticipation raised the fine hairs on her arms as she thought of spending the evening with the complex, fascinating man that was Dan.

For some reason, she couldn't sort out her confused feelings about him. A part of her still cringed whenever she thought of the uninhibited way she'd responded to his kisses, like some teenager with hyperactive hormones. At the same time, she had to admit he intrigued her. And attracted her. And *dis*tracted her when she should have been concentrating on work. Even Charles hadn't generated such a welter of conflicting emotions.

That last thought surprised her. After she'd given Charles back his ring, she'd vowed not to get involved with another man until she had achieved her self-imposed goals. Kate frowned, wondering once again just why she'd agreed to dinner. Every instinct told her this man could complicate her life. He was too smooth, too forceful, too damn attractive. She shouldn't have agreed to see him again, she thought. Well, at least she could send the dog home with him tonight. Kate's frown deepened when she realized the idea didn't please as much as it should have.

"Mmm, something smells good." Dan sniffed the air when Kate opened the door.

"My mother's own recipe. She makes pretty good lasagna for second-generation Irish." Kate smiled as she stood aside to let him in.

"No, that's not what I smell."

Dan stepped inside and tugged her into his arms. He bent down to nuzzle his face in her hair. "Just what I thought— gardenias." He leaned back with a smug expression.

Kate laughed. "Some investigator you make, Captain Kingman. It's plain old shampoo and a spritz of Chanel No. 5." She pushed out of his arms and closed the door.

Dan grinned and followed her into the kitchen. "Did you have trouble getting away?"

"Actually, I took off an hour early and treated myself to a good soak in the hot tub."

"I may have to revise my opinion of those contraptions if they give you such a healthy glow. You look— Watch it, mutt!"

Dan nearly tripped over a black, squirming body that wrapped itself around his knees. "Good Lord, is this the same hound I left with you?"

"One and the same."

Kate paused at the built-in bar to watch while Dan fondled the dog's eager head. Even in the subdued living room lighting, she could see traces of fatigue fanning out from his eyes. He wore a dark summer suit, the well-cut lines adding a touch of sophistication to his tall frame. For the first time, Kate could envision him as an attorney. But the shaggy mustache and loosened tie made him all-too-human—and attractive—in Kate's eyes.

"Rough meeting?" she asked.

He nodded absently, absorbed in tugging the dog's silky ears. "The city council is up in arms about the increase in gang-related drug cases. Statistically, we're below average for a city our size, but the trend isn't good."

Dan sat back on the couch, eased his long legs out in front of him and lifted one hand to rub the back of his neck.

"How about a drink?" Kate asked to cover the unexpected pang of concern that shot through her. She was surprised at how much it bothered her that Dan had a tough job, one that put dark shadows under his eyes. She mixed the drink he requested and poured herself a glass of wine.

She watched him unobtrusively throughout their meal of crisp, green salad and savory lasagna. He'd removed his coat and tie and the small revolver he wore at his waist. He looked more relaxed as he kept up his end of their light conversation, which ranged from music to books to leisure activities. His tastes in literature were much more eclectic than hers, but they shared a common passion for suspense. Dan made her laugh with his highly embellished, totally improbable plot for the mystery novel he was going to write someday.

They lingered at the table, empty plates pushed aside. As she sipped her coffee, Kate found herself growing more and more aware of the man opposite her. He made the airy, high-ceilinged dining room shrink until she could see only him. Her eyes dropped to his hand, resting casually on the table. He had strong, blunt fingers. Heat crept across Kate's cheeks as she remembered how incredibly erotic those fingers felt against her cheek and hip on that to-be-forgotten night. Hastily she lifted her gaze to his face.

The lines of fatigue around his hazel eyes brought a new wave of concern. When he rubbed his neck once more, she rose abruptly.

"Come with me."

"What?"

"Come on. I've got the cure for what ails you."

Dan got to his feet slowly, a wicked grin lifting one corner of his mustache.

"Not that," Kate told him, laughing. "There, on the deck. A good soak will relax those muscles."

"No, thanks. I'm not into the Southern California hot-tub scene."

Kate grinned at the unconscious sneer in his voice. "Talk about reverse snobbery! The tub has a very therapeutic value, you know."

"I can think of a lot better ways to relax," Dan told her, reaching out to pull her against his chest.

A spark of heat flared in Kate's stomach at the feel of his hard flesh under her fingertips. He was so solid, so warm and welcoming. She resisted the impulse to lay her head on his chest and looked up instead, a question in her eyes.

"I know, Kate, I know. I'm not sure about this, either. But if I don't kiss you again soon, I'm going to regret it."

"Dan, about that night, in your car...the tape..."

"If you even think about, let alone mention that damn tape again, I swear I'll run you in." He bent down to nuzzle his face in her hair once more. "Ah, I love this mop of yours."

Kate felt something inside of her give a little lurch. Her limited experience with Charles hadn't prepared her for the way her breath caught in her throat when Dan held her. Or for the way her heart seemed to beat double time when she touched him. A tiny voice far back in her mind warned her that she was about to take a dangerous step, that giving in to these swamping sensations would create complications in her life she wasn't prepared for. She lifted her head to stare at him, her lower lip caught between her teeth.

Dan smiled down at her. "Don't worry about it so much, sweetheart."

Kate could see the amusement and some strange, indefinable emotion in his eyes.

"We'll just take it as it comes," he growled softly.

When he lowered his head and covered her mouth with his, Kate stopped worrying. She also stopped breathing. His tongue began to run over her lips, first the upper and then the lower, in soft, sensuous strokes. Kate stood it as long as she could, then opened her mouth to taste him fully. The bristles on his chin rasped against her, sending an erotic, tactile message of raw maleness. This was crazy, she thought, while she could still think at all. Just the feel of Dan's whiskers shouldn't make her stomach clench in hot desire. But it did, and then some!

She barely noticed when he shifted his stance. His hands no longer supported her. They roamed at will up and down her rib cage, then caught the silk of her blouse, half lifting it and baring her skin to the cooled air. When one hand moved around to cover her breast, she started.

"Don't you want me to do this?" Dan breathed into her ear as his palm rested, hot and heavy, on the thin lace of her bra. Kate felt her nipples hardening.

"Hmm, I guess you do," he teased, his breath moist in her ear. His hand resumed its stroking and kneading. She felt his thumb circle the hard tip, tease it, rub it. When he bent his head suddenly and covered the aching nipple with his mouth, Kate gasped. A sweet, burning sensation radiated from her breast. Her stomach clenched as the fire turned to hot, molten lava.

"Wait...Dan, wait," she whispered to the dark head bent over her. He straightened, looking down with a quiet question in his eyes.

"I...you...this is too fast! I'm confused. I can't think when you do that."

"That's the whole idea." He grinned, running the backs of two fingers down her cheek. "I want you confused. I want you as hungry as I am. Hell, woman, I just want you. But we'll slow it down until you make up your mind."

With a quick stoop, he lifted her in his arms and carried her back into the living room. He settled them both in a corner of the couch, holding her across his lap with one arm while he pushed the dog off the couch with the other.

"Go find your own female," he told the grinning mutt. "This one's taken."

"He thinks you want to play," Kate told him, nestling deeper in his arms.

"I do. But not with him. Outta here, mutt."

"Go away, Rico," Kate instructed.

Dan paused with his lips only inches from hers. "Rico?"

"After Enrico Caruso," Kate breathed, distracted by the face hovering above her. She could hardly remember her own name, let alone the dog's.

"He loves opera," she gasped, around the tiny, stinging nips Dan was giving her lower lip.

"And country and western."

Dan turned his attention to her upper lip.

"And anything else that happens to be on the radio."

Kate thought she heard a low chuckle before he filled her mouth with a deep, hungry kiss. When she surfaced for air long minutes—or maybe hours—later, she leaned back in his arms. Dan slowly lowered her onto the smooth, cool fabric of the couch, then leaned over her.

"Still confused, Kate?"

Kate looked up at the dark head above hers. "Yes," she whispered. "More than ever. But it's the most wonderful confusion I've ever felt." She wrapped both arms around his neck and drew him down.

He didn't hesitate to take her up on her invitation. One of his hard thighs wedged between hers, rubbing against her center, sending shafts of pure pleasure rippling through her whole body. She took a couple of quick breaths, then turned her hungry mouth back to his.

Her doubts melted under the onslaught of his mouth and hands. She'd never experienced the desire this man was rousing in her with his touch, with his dark, delicious taste. This time it was Dan who pulled back, gulping.

"Much more of this and it'll be very painful to stop."

Kate looked up at the harsh face just inches above her own. Her lids felt heavy with desire. She took a corner of her lip between her teeth, then felt an overpowering urge to bite his. "So don't stop," she whispered.

"Are you sure?"

"Yes."

"No worries about the tape, no angry recriminations?"

"No."

"No feelings of being taken advantage of, no—"

"Look, do you want to do this or don't you?" Kate asked, exasperated. She would have struggled up if the man wasn't sprawled on top of her, weighing her down.

"Yes, ma'am, I surely do." Dan laughed at her indignant face, then covered her mouth again. His sure fingers removed her clothes and his own shirt before he had to get up and haul the pesky, inquisitive dog into the bedroom. Kate lay still, watching him through half-closed eyes. He looked like an ad for a runner's magazine. Sleek muscles roped his arms and shoulders, and his broad back tapered down to a narrow waist. He moved with a lithe, casual grace that belied his height.

Returning, he stretched out beside her and curled her into his arms. One hand held her cradled, the other pushed down the lacy fabric of her bra and stroked her nipple with a teasing touch. He played with her breasts, testing their shape, tantalizing their sensitive peaks.

Kate felt the feather-light touch in parts of her body she never realized were connected to her breast before. And when he bent to take one taut bud in his mouth, she gasped, arching under him.

A red tinge crept up his cheeks and his breathing quickened. Shifting her on the narrow couch, Dan pulled her body beneath his. He nudged her legs apart with one knee. His hand slid between her legs, cupping her mound, then stroking the tight, hot bud it protected. Kate bit down on her lower lip, hard, as moistness gathered at her core.

"Are you protected?"

His low, rasped question barely penetrated Kate's utter absorption in the sensations his hand was producing. She looked up at him blankly for a moment, then shook her head.

He swore, low and succinctly and crushed her against his chest. "Me, neither."

Hot, searing disappointment flooded Kate's veins, warring with a perverse pleasure that he didn't carry an emergency supply of condoms. Somehow the thought that he hadn't planned to go this far helped her bring her whirling senses under control.

"You're mashing me to a pulp," she murmured against his chest when he seemed disinclined to move. His arms loosened, and she sucked in a quick breath. "And you've probably given that dog a complex. He's not used to being shut up. If there are any wet spots on the rug, you've got clean-up duty."

Dan shifted and rolled to a sitting position. Taking her hand, he pulled her up beside him. One hand brushed the tangled hair back from her face.

"I'm sorry about this, Kate. I won't be so unprepared next time."

Embarrassed, Kate could only shake her head.

"Oh, yes, there'll be a next time."

His low promise sent shivers down her spine. A loud, ear-shattering howl prevented her from having to respond, which was fortunate because she didn't know quite what to say to the utter certainty in his eyes. Dan shook his head and went to release the indignant prisoner.

Kate used the few moments respite to pull on her blouse. She'd just slipped the last button into its loop when an ecstatic Rico came bounding out of the bedroom. Knowing it was useless, she didn't try to hold him off. Instead, she wrapped her arms around his thick neck and absorbed the force of his greeting against her body.

"Are you sure you want me to take him away?"

Kate held the wiggling dog in a firm grip as she looked up to find Dan watching them both. Her breath caught at the sight of him. He leaned casually against one wall, arms crossed over his chest, pants slung low on his hips. His hair was rumpled and standing up in spikes. She felt a deep, primal urge to go to him and smooth it down.

The intensity of the feeling startled her. To cover her confusion, she buried her face in Rico's silky fur. The dog's squirming reminded her she had yet to answer his question.

"Where would you take him?"

"Well, I could keep him at my place until I find someone to give him a home. But I have a second-floor apartment, with only a small balcony. No place for him to go during the day."

Kate buried her face in the soft, silky fur. "I guess you better leave him here until you find someone. Just make sure you do though," she warned.

Dan grinned and came back into the living room to finish dressing. "Yes, ma'am. I'll give it my top priority."

"Sure you will. After your murders and drug heists and bank

robberies. I have a feeling he's going to be with me for the duration." Kate propped her chin on Rico's convenient head and watched Dan pull on his shirt. She felt a definite sense of regret when the now wrinkled cotton covered his torso.

"Speaking of robberies," Dan said as he buckled his belt, "the hearing on your case is next week."

"So?"

"So you'll have to be there."

"Me? Why? I gave you my statement. You've got the evidence—which *you promised* to edit."

He held up his hands, palms out. "It's done, it's done."

He came and sat beside her on the couch. Kate and Rico found themselves scooted aside to make room for him. Both of them arched under his hand to be stroked, first her neck, then the dog's ears.

"The judge wants the victims there. Detective Alvarado will call you with the time."

Kate swiveled out from under his hand. "I still don't understand why I have to be there. I didn't see anything. It's not like I can identify the kids. I can't add anything that's not already in the sworn statement."

"So tell it to the judge," Dan mocked her gently. Before she could protest further, he slid his hand around her neck and pulled her to him. He rested his forehead against hers and rubbed noses.

"Thanks for dinner, Kate," he whispered.

"Thanks for *after* dinner," she whispered back, laughing.

Four

Kate shifted uncomfortably on the hard wooden bench. She tried not to stare at the three boys with their respective parents scattered along the long hallway outside the hearing room, but her gaze returned to them time and again. The youngest in particular drew her attention. He sat on a bench down the hall, sandy-haired, with a half frightened, half defiant expression that hadn't changed in the hour they'd been waiting. Sitting next to him was a small, dark-haired woman—his foster mother according to Detective Alvarado. An irritated frown marred her face, as if the whole proceeding constituted a personal annoyance.

Just looking at the youngsters made Kate nervous. The thought of them spying on her still raised goose bumps. She avoided the first boy's eyes when he was called into the hearing room, but couldn't help noticing his chastened, apologetic air. His father and the lawyer who entered the room with him must have told him to show the proper remorse, Kate decided.

Evidently the judge didn't buy his act. The boy looked shaken when he and his escorts came out of the hearing room some time later. Detective Alvarado was right behind them, taking advantage of the break in the proceedings to slip outside for a stretch. Recognizing Kate, he strolled over to stand beside her.

''Well, that's one kid who won't have much time to get into trouble for the next six months.'' He nodded to the group leaving the juvenile courthouse. ''The judge gave him a blistering lecture and a hundred hours of community service.''

''What kind of service?'' Kate asked.

''One of the victims is a doctor who volunteers Saturday mornings at a free clinic. The kid will perform janitorial duty at the clinic under the doc's supervision.''

Alvarado broke off as the bailiff called the next boy and his sponsor, a tough-looking air force colonel with a rack of ribbons on his chest.

''If the colonel can't straighten that kid up, no one can.'' Alvarado chuckled as he got to his feet and headed back into the courtroom.

Kate shifted again and crossed her legs, trying to find a comfortable position on the hard seat. A sharp movement down the hall caught her attention.

The dark-haired woman had the young boy's arm in a tight grip and was shaking him. Defiance edged out the fright that had darkened his eyes. From the whiteness of the woman's knuckles, Kate knew the hold must hurt, yet the boy refused to either answer her angry whisper or look at her.

''Hello, Red.''

Startled, Kate glanced up to find Dan beside her. She'd been so absorbed in the small drama, she hadn't even heard his approach. A welcoming smile spread across her face. They hadn't seen much of each other in the past few days—just shared one hurried dinner, followed by a distinctly unhurried kiss before Dan was called away. Kate felt her heart speed up just looking at him.

Dan slouched down on the bench next to her, tiredness written in the deep lines fanning from his eyes.

''How's it going?'' he asked.

''Okay, I guess. Detective Alvarado told me the first boy got a tongue-lashing and one hundred hours of community service. The second boy's in there now.''

Dan whistled softly. ''That'll keep him on the straight and

narrow for some time to come. Did Alvarado mention that the oldest boy confessed that he was the one who took the video-tapes?''

Kate shook her head.

''It came out in the formal statements. I thought you might want to know only one of them stayed in your house to tape you. The other two got scared when they saw you in the tub and ran out. The oldest boy hid behind the bedroom door and used a zoom lens.''

Even as the familiar wash of embarrassment swept over her, Kate felt some of her tension ease. Somehow, she was relieved to know only one of them had seen her. Involuntarily, her eyes flickered back to the youngest, sandy-haired boy. She started to comment to Dan about the interplay she'd seen earlier between the boy and his foster mother, when the hearing room doors opened once more.

She stood while the small party exited, then waited with Dan until the young boy and his foster mother entered. Kate followed in their wake and settled herself on a wooden chair in the paneled hearing room. Other than the dozen or so witness chairs, the room held only a small table where the boy, his mother and the public defender sat, a worktable for the clerk and court stenographer, and a wide, polished oak desk for the judge. Behind the desk sat a neat, petite woman in a dark business suit. A marble nameplate on the desk identified her as Judge Julia Chavez.

To Kate's surprise, only one other person entered when Dan and she did. Frowning, she turned to Dan.

''Where are the others?'' she whispered. ''The other victims?''

Dan gave her a puzzled glance, but had no chance to reply.

The bailiff called the hearing into session in a singsong, ritualistic cadence and the proceedings began. Detective Alvarado and the other officers gave their statements; then the public defender assigned to the case pleaded the boy's side. There was no denying the evidence, of course, especially with the tapes, so the main argument for leniency was the boy's age and previous clean record.

Judge Chavez tried to encourage Jason to speak for himself, but the boy gave only clipped, curt responses. No matter how she phrased the question, his only answer to why he joined the older boys in their lawlessness was a shrug and an "I dunno." The one time she elicited a real response was when she asked if he stole for drug money. The boy's blue eyes flashed and he looked straight at her.

"I don't do drugs."

"Then why were you stealing, Jason?" the judge asked once more.

The boy hunched his shoulder and looked down at the floor. Judge Chavez threw a questioning look at the dark-haired woman beside him.

"He just did it for the thrill. He's always bored and giving me a hard time at home."

"Aren't there any school or sport activities you're interested in?" the judge asked, trying to reach the towheaded boy. When he just shrugged, she frowned and looked to the foster mother again.

"I got two other foster kids, plus my own," she responded with a touch of belligerence. "I don't have time to keep them all occupied every minute of the day."

Judge Chavez sat back in her chair and studied the boy for a long moment. She pushed a pair of glasses up higher on her nose to peer through a sheaf of papers. With another frown she turned to the juvenile officer.

"I don't see anyone named to act as this boy's sponsor for community service."

"No, ma'am," the young woman responded. "We weren't able to identify anyone."

"Did you tell them the alternative is the Juvenile Detention Center?"

Kate's stomach clenched at the stark fear that settled on the boy's face for a brief instant.

"Yes, ma'am."

"Are any of the other victims present?"

"Yes, ma'am. Two."

Kate started to simmer. Where the heck were all the others? Feeling as if she'd been trapped into this hearing, she forced herself to concentrate on the ongoing exchange.

The judge suspended the actual proceedings to delve into the issue of sponsorship. The other victim, an executive with a defense-related electronics firm, was questioned first. Judge Chavez's frown grew, and the boy's defiant look hardened, as the man pleaded an imminent overseas trip as an excuse.

"Ms. O'Sullivan?"

Kate held up her hand to indicate her presence.

"I see you're self-employed. Is the nature of your business such that you could find time to participate in this program?"

"No, Judge. I own a small consulting firm that specializes in the integration of computer systems. My hours are long and fluctuate from day to day according to the demands of the job." Kate's eyes flickered to the boy once more.

"I'm willing to work with you on the number of hours and days for Jason, given his age."

Kate swallowed, starting to feel guilty at her own excuses. She tried to remind herself that she was the victim, but somehow that assurance didn't help when she glanced over at the boy again. "I'll only be here a few more months. I'm on a short-term contract at Kirtland Air Force Base."

"No reason why you can't learn more about our city in those few months as you work with this child. Tell me what kind of outside interests you have."

"None, really. My life revolves around work."

"Thanks a lot," Dan murmured sotto voce.

"Are you interested in sports? Running, by any chance?"

"No, ma'am. I consider any form of strenuous exercise a pointless waste of good calories."

The judge smiled. "The reason that I ask is that our annual Duke City Marathon is coming up in September. My husband's chairing the volunteer-coordinating committee. Just last night he was complaining about the thousands of tasks that have to be done. We can use your help, and Jason's."

Kate opened her mouth to protest, then clamped it shut when she saw a desperate hope flare in the boy's eyes.

"Yes, ma'am," she murmured, accepting defeat with what grace she could muster.

"Good." The judge nodded briskly. Her dark eyes slid to Dan. "I saw you talking to Captain Kingman earlier. Are you two acquainted?"

Surprised, Kate nodded. "Yes, we are."

"Great." The other woman beamed. "Since you're a visitor to town and may not know the ropes, get Captain Kingman to explain the sponsorship program to you. He can give you some ideas on how to work with Jason. After all, this whole community-service program was his idea in the first place. He built it from scratch."

Kate swiveled in her seat, her eyes narrowing as they leveled a glare at the big man next to her. The suspicion that she'd been set up flared into certainty. She started to tell him just what she thought of such underhanded tricks when the judge reopened the formal hearing. Seething, Kate heard her assign Jason fifty hours of service, then close the proceedings. At her signal, Dan went forward to speak with her. Kate found herself facing Jason and his foster mother across the clerk's small table. The busy man passed her a stack of papers.

"Here's the phone number where you can reach Jason at home to schedule your appointments. A caseworker will contact you in the next few days to discuss procedures and reporting. Wait until you hear from her or him before you schedule your first session with Jason. And here's a pamphlet explaining the program."

Kate barely heard the clerk's voice. Despite her simmering anger at Dan, her eyes kept straying to the thin young boy opposite her. After giving her one quick look, he turned away. When the clerk finished, Kate hesitated, then held out her hand to the boy.

"I guess we're partners now, Jason. At least for the next few months. I'll call you next week."

The boy's mother had to poke him before he responded at all. "Yeah."

Great, Kate thought as she walked down the hall of the juvenile courthouse toward the front doors. Just great! She'd come to Albuquerque determined to concentrate on this contract, collect her fee, then head back to L.A. Now her life was complicated by a mutt who rattled her windowpanes every time she turned on the stereo and a juvenile delinquent whose idea of fun was probably knocking off small convenience stores.

Kate pushed the heavy doors open. A driving summer rain hit her in the face and did nothing to improve her mood.

"Kate, wait a minute."

Head down, hurrying through the rain, she ignored the deep voice.

"Wait up."

She had almost reached the haven of her car when Dan caught her arm. She turned, wet, straggling hair slithering against her cheeks.

"I don't want to talk to you right now, Dan."

"What?"

"You know darn well I don't have time to get involved in this community-service program. Why did you set me up?"

"Hey, hold on. I didn't set you up."

"Oh, no? Then where were the other six or seven victims today?"

"How the hell should I know? This is Alvarado's case. Except for one particular victim, I haven't been taking much of a personal interest in it."

"Hah!" Kate jerked her arm loose.

"This is ridiculous," Dan muttered. "Why are we standing in the pouring rain arguing? Come on back to my office and let me dry you off."

"No, thanks." Kate backed away from him, her feet almost slipping out from under her on the wet sidewalk.

Dan caught her as she teetered. "What's going on here, Kate? Why are you pulling away from me?"

"Look, I'm feeling slightly overwhelmed right now with all

the new distractions in my life. I've got to sort things out. Just back off, okay?''

Dan's eyes narrowed. ''I'm not sure I like being classified as a 'distraction.' ''

''Well, it's the best I can do right now.'' Kate pushed a heavy mass of wet hair off her forehead. ''I've got to get back to work. I'll see you later.''

''Yes, ma'am, you will,'' Dan muttered, his jaw tight.

It was still raining when Kate left work late that night. Her clothes felt clammy against her skin in the evening air, although Trish had done her best to help dry them out. She'd whisked Kate into the ladies' room and stripped her down to her underwear. Draping the skirt over one hand dryer and blouse over another, Trish perched on a sink in between, punching the two dryers alternately until most of the moisture was gone. Still, her linen skirt would never be the same, Kate thought as she smoothed the wrinkled fabric.

She shivered as she drove through the rain and darkness, and reached down to switch off the air conditioner. Opening her window a crack, she breathed in the soft, drizzly night air.

Albuquerque's climate continued to surprise her. The days were hot, with heat waves shimmering off the asphalt in clear, iridescent curtains, but it was usually a dry, bearable heat. Not like the suffocating, smog-laden air of L.A. The nights were wonderful, filled with velvety blackness and a breathtaking array of stars so bright and close, Kate was often tempted to reach up and touch them.

Tonight, the rain gave the air a sharp, clean edge. As she rounded a corner and drove up the steep hill leading to her house, the lights of the city filled the rearview mirror. They glittered like yellow diamonds in the rain.

Suddenly, a flashing red light blazed in the mirror, obscuring the city view. Instinctively, Kate glanced down at the speedometer. Oh, no! All she needed to cap off her day was a speeding ticket. Biting back a muttered curse, she drove the last few yards to her house and pulled into the wide driveway. The car drew up behind her, light flashing. Kate fumbled in her purse for her license. She was still rummaging in her leather bag when a sharp rap sounded against her window. She pushed the button to lower the window and saw Dan's dark face above her. Irritated relief filled her.

"That wasn't funny, Kingman. You almost made my heart stop with that red light."

"You were going a good ten miles over the speed limit," he told her mildly, leaning one arm against the roof of the Audi. "You ought to be glad it's me and not the neighborhood patrol."

"So what are you going to do, give me a ticket?"

"Nope, just a warning. And a good talking to. And a kiss, if you've gotten over this morning's spurt of temper."

"And if I haven't?"

"I'll probably kiss you anyway." He straightened, pushing himself away from the car. "Drive on into the garage. I'll follow you."

Kate sighed, watching him head back through the drizzle to his own car. During the long afternoon, she'd worked through her anger over getting involved with man, boy and dog. She was her own woman, after all. If she hadn't wanted to take on the responsibilities of the boy, she should have said so. It wasn't fair to take it out on Dan. Not for the first time, she wondered what it was about this man that aroused such reactions in her. In the brief time she'd known him, she'd run the gamut from irritation to surprise to amusement to blazing passion.

She led the way in through the kitchen, tossed her briefcase on the kitchen counter, and headed for the living room. Flipping on the patio lights, she could see Rico on top of his doghouse, watching the French doors with ears perked and tail wagging furiously.

"Smart dog," she muttered, letting him in. "I pay a hundred dollars for a custom-built house, guaranteed to keep you warm and dry, and you don't even have the sense to get in it, out of the rain."

He pressed a wet, sloppy welcome against her hand, then ran to greet Dan. Hunkering down, the man knuckled the squirming dog's ears. Kate watched, a smile tugging at her lips, as two males dripped all over her mauve carpet. When Dan looked up, flashing her a quick grin over Rico's dark head, she forgot all about the carpet. He looked tired, and wet, and incredibly good to her, puddles and all.

She padded past them both and brought a couple of thick, fluffy towels from the bathroom.

"Here. Dry yourself and your buddy off while I change. Then I'll make some coffee."

Kate quickly shed her wrinkled clothes, then slipped into worn jeans and a loose, butternut-yellow T-shirt. She was back in the kitchen, with its glowing tile counters and oven set in a recessed adobe arch, within minutes. Grinding fresh beans, she arranged a tray with thick ceramic mugs and leftover pound cake while the coffee perked.

Dan settled himself on the living room floor, his back resting against the sturdy couch and the towel beneath him. Rico plopped down companionably beside him, filled with unadulterated pleasure at having his two favorite humans home. Handing Dan a mug, Kate settled into a corner of the couch. He smiled his thanks, took a long swallow, then twisted his face into a disgusted grimace.

"What is this?" he asked, staring down into the mug.

"Decaf. Viennese cinnamon decaf, to be specific."

"Ugh. I thought you were making coffee."

"Don't push your luck, fella. You're lucky you got served anything at all after that little stunt with the flashing light."

"I had to get your attention somehow. You can be one stubborn female at times." Dan set his mug down and angled his shoulders to look up at her. "I didn't set you up this morning, you know."

"Why didn't you tell me this whole community-service program is your baby?" Kate asked, resisting the urge to run her fingers through the thick, black hair so close to her knee.

"Would it have made a difference if I had?"

"Yes. No. Oh, I don't know." She leaned her head against the sofa back.

"I didn't want you to become a sponsor because I helped put the program together. Taking on the responsibility for a child has to be a voluntary act, an act of love."

Kate raised her head, her attention snagged by the flatness in his voice. When he didn't volunteer anything further, she gave a small shrug.

"I couldn't let him go to the detention center. He looked so young and scared, despite his bravado."

"That's why I think there's hope for him. He's still smart enough to be scared."

She eyed him thoughtfully. "You really want this one to make it, don't you? Do you get a commission on every save?"

Dan's mustache lifted in a rueful smile. "In a way. The more of these kids we turn around now, the fewer we'll have stabbing old ladies in the street for drug money a few years from now."

Kate narrowed her eyes, studying his face just below her, intriguing in its sharp planes and shadows. "There's more to it than that, isn't there?" she said quietly. "Why are you so personally involved?"

As if weighing how much of himself he wanted to reveal, Dan spoke slowly, almost hesitantly. "Remember I told you I had a stint in the marines?"

Kate nodded.

"I had a choice—either the marines or jail. Neither alternative was particularly attractive. At seventeen, I had my own gang and was just on the edge of a brilliant street career. Luckily, my first gunnery sergeant took one look and told me he'd either beat or run the cockiness out of me."

Dan smiled to himself, his eyes on Rico's slumbering, snoring body. "I opted for running and ended up representing the marines at the interservice trials for the Olympics. I got beat out by an army grunt, to my platoon's everlasting disgust."

Kate kept still, not wanting to disturb this moment of quiet sharing. Dan lifted his head to look at her.

"The point is, that Gunny cared enough to spend some time with me. He kicked me in the rear, rode me unmercifully and gave me a reason to feel proud of myself. He even got me into a GED program so I could finish high school and college in the marines. I used my GI bill for law school after I got out.

"I could see myself in that kid, Kate. Jason needs someone to help him, just like I did."

Kate shifted uncomfortably. "I never said he didn't. But I'm not sure I'm the right one to help him. I don't know anything about boys, Dan. Or girls, either, for that matter. I'm an only child and stayed at my grandmother's after school while my mother worked to support us both. I've never been to basketball games or...or camp...or cruised the malls. My whole world since puberty has been computers."

Dan laughed and shifted the dog's head off his lap. "Yes, I've been meaning to do something about that." He pushed himself off the floor and turned to grin down at her.

"No, I'm serious. I—"

"Come here, Kate." With one sure tug he had her off the couch and into his arms.

Kate put up her hands, holding herself stiff in his arms. "Dan, listen to me. Maybe we're going too fast. I wasn't kidding this morning when I said I was feeling overwhelmed by all the changes in my life lately."

Dan buried his face in her hair. "I'm feeling a bit over-whelmed, too," he murmured against its thickness. "What do you suggest we do about it?"

"We *should* stop right here and you *should* go home," Kate whispered.

"But?"

"But it's raining, and you feel good. Real good." With a sigh, Kate slid her arms up around his neck. She lifted her mouth for his kiss, then pulled back abruptly. "Are you prepared this time?"

"More than you'll ever know," he murmured, shifting so that his rock-hard member pressed against her stomach. Kate felt a flash of sensation deep in her belly. Her mouth dropped in sheer surprise. She'd never felt anything like the instant heat Dan gen-erated in her.

He took quick advantage of her opened mouth, bending to

cover it with his own. His lips were hard and hot and demanding, and the need that had built between them exploded. Kate groaned, wrapping her arms more tightly around his neck and straining against his body. Her breasts flattened against his chest, the nipples stiffening as she rubbed back and forth. Dan's arms tightened, pressing her waist and hips into even more intimate contact.

When she moaned and would have sagged down on the couch, Dan caught her up in his arms.

"Oh, no, Katey mine. No couches or back seats for us. I want you spread out beneath me, with every single inch of that luscious body available."

Dan carried her into the bedroom, whispering dark, hot promises of what he planned to do, inch by inch. By the time he laid her on the thick spread, Kate was in a fever of anticipation. Her blood pounded in her ears, in her heart—in places she'd never even realized had blood vessels. Dan straightened and began to undress. Before he'd kicked off his slacks, Kate had shimmied out of her jeans and had reached for the hem of her T-shirt.

His hands stopped hers. "I'll take it from here, sweetheart."

Dan joined her in the wide bed, keeping most of his weight propped on one arm, a heavy leg thrown across hers. Every nerve in Kate's body screamed at him to hurry, but he took his time. With agonizing slowness, he edged up the hem of her shirt. His fingers brushed the swell of her breasts. Finally, he slipped the shirt over her head. His hand shaped her breast in its lacy cup, kneading it gently.

"Mmm, you're beautiful, Kate."

Kate was well aware that she'd been far more liberally endowed with brains than mammary muscle, but his husky words made her feel feminine and incredibly desirable. She arched and her nipple pushed against his hand, demanding attention. Dan obliged, sliding the bra down so that he could take her in his mouth. His rough tongue sent sharp shivers of fire darting throughout her body. After interminable moments, he shifted his attention to her other breast.

Dan's heavy leg slid between her thighs and pried them apart.

Impatiently, Kate tugged his head up and explored his mouth with hers while his hand began a slow, deliberate descent from her aching breasts, down her belly. It closed over her mound, encasing her in hard warmth. With incredible sureness, he stroked her, letting the fabric of her panties add to the friction he generated. One finger slipped past the lace trim to press against her core, then slid inside to test her wetness.

Kate arched as he found her center. His hand began an ancient rhythm, heightening her already spiraling sensations. His tongue picked up the rhythm and thrust into her mouth with hungry strokes. His weight was fully atop her now, pressing her down into the spread, holding her immobile while he readied her flowering body. Kate moaned under his assault and pressed against him, rubbing her breasts back and forth against the wiry hair on his chest. She moved her legs, trying to pull his lower body into hers. He resisted, his hand and his mouth working their fiery magic. When Kate thought she'd scream for wanting him, he finally kneed her legs farther apart and thrust into her welcoming wetness.

Bracing himself on both arms, Dan buried his fists in her hair and slanted his mouth over hers. Kate's last thought, before his hands and his hips and his mouth took her beyond thinking, was that this was better—much better—than hot-tubbing.

Five

Kate awakened the next morning to the shrill ring of the phone. Struggling out from under a mound of covers, she found herself trapped by the deadweight of Dan's leg across her thighs. Adding to that immovable impediment was Rico's heavy black head, grinning at her from the foot of the bed.

"Good grief, dog! When did you decide to join us? Get off the bed. Go on." Kate pushed herself up and reached for the phone. Rico wriggled his body a few more inches up the rumpled covers.

"Get out of the bed!" she ordered in exasperation, then gave a flustered hello into the phone.

A heavy silence was her only answer. Kate frowned and leaned back against the padded headboard. "Hello?"

She was about to hang up when she heard her name.

"Kathleen Brigit O'Sullivan! Just who's in bed with you?"

"Oh, hello, Mother." Hunching one shoulder to cradle the phone, she pushed her tangled hair out of her eyes with one hand and the dog off the bed with the other.

"Never mind the 'Hello, Mother'! Who's there with you?"

Kate hesitated, trying to come up with an answer acceptable to her staunchly old-fashioned, Catholic mother. Fortunately,

Rico saved her at the last moment. He gave a loud, enthusiastic woof, then jumped over her restraining hand. Kate prayed her mother didn't hear Dan's startled grunt when the dog landed square on his middle.

"Kate, you don't have that dog in bed with you, do you?". Her mother's shocked voice came crackling over the line.

"Not by choice. Why are you calling so early, Mother?"

Another long silence filled the phone. "It's almost ten. Are you all right, Kate?"

"Yes, yes I am. Honestly."

"You never stay in bed past seven, even on weekends. It's one of your least lovable traits, darling."

"Thanks, Mother. Uh, is there a special reason for this call or is it just a social chat?"

Kate felt the mountain beside her begin to stir and decided she'd better hurry the conversation. She wasn't ready to explain Dan to her inquisitive mother. Especially not with him lying next to her naked. Eyeing the large, hairy leg that pushed its way out from under the covers, she vaguely heard her mother's worried voice.

"Are you sure you're all right? You're not sick, are you?"

"No, really, I'm not. Why?"

"Didn't you hear what I just said. Charles called."

"That's nice," she breathed. Another hairy leg snaked out. Kate clutched frantically at the covers as Dan's big hands began to push them down, away from his face—and her chest. She struggled to keep a firm grip on the sheet. It was a few moments before she realized there was total silence at the other end of the line again.

"Ah, Charles called?" she asked, holding on to the sheet with all her strength.

"Yes, you remember Charles. Your fiancé. The one who left you at the altar."

"Not quite at the altar, Mother. We didn't make it that far before he happened to remember he already had a wife." She tried to lower her voice, but to her dismay Dan's dark head turned on the rumpled pillow. His eyes were wide-awake, his black brows raised in interest.

"Look, this really isn't a good time to chat. The—um, the darn dog's being a pest. Why don't I call you back later this afternoon?"

"No, you can't. I've got bingo this afternoon. I just wanted to tell you that Charles called to ask for your address and phone number. He has business in Albuquerque in the next couple of weeks and said he wanted to call you. Said it was important."

"That's nice," Kate muttered again inanely. She tried to push Dan's dark head from her lap where it had suddenly taken up residence. He rolled his head on her belly to give her a wicked grin.

"Yes, very nice."

"Shh," she hissed, hand over the mouthpiece. "This is my mother."

"But I thought you said it was all over between you." Her mother's voice held confusion and just a hint of exasperation. "That you didn't want to see him again. Ever. I wasn't sure I should give him your number."

"What? Oh, sure." Kate barely got out the words. Her breath was caught in her throat. Dan had pulled the sheet out of her clenched fist and was doing things to the bare skin of her stomach she was sure were illegal. "Look, I'll call you tonight, okay? I, ah, really do have to see to the dog."

"The mutt's fine," Dan murmured against her belly when the receiver clattered down a few moments later. "But I could use some attention."

"Dan!" Kate skittered sideways to the edge of the bed. "It's almost ten. Don't you have some bank robbery or something to go solve?"

She finally got one foot planted on the floor and managed to wriggle out of his arms. He rolled over, taking the covers with him, to stand beside her.

"Nope." He grinned as he slid his palm around her neck. "All's quiet on the Albuquerque front or my beeper would have been pinging like crazy. Besides, I threatened my assistant with demotion to patrolman third-class if he bothered me with anything less than a major disaster last night.''

''It's morning, Dan,'' Kate breathed, trying not to blush at what his hands were doing to her in the bright light of day. ''I've got to shower and get to work.''

''On Saturday?'' His dark, stubbly chin rasped against her cheek.

''Especially on Saturday.''

Kate eased out of his arms once more and reached for her crumpled T-shirt lying halfway between the bed and the bathroom. It barely covered her fanny, but she felt much better when she pulled it on. She tried not to stare as Dan reached for his own clothes. Maybe there was something to this exercise business after all, Kate thought. Wide shoulders with muscles that rippled in the morning light caught her fascinated gaze. Lean, white buttocks contrasted sharply with the hair-covered columns of his legs as he turned to step into his shorts.

Visions of how those legs had wrapped around her in the dark floated through her mind. Kate gulped and headed for the shower. Her hands trembled as she adjusted the water from warm to cool.

Resting against the slick tiles, Kate let the water wash over her heated body. Memories of the night filled her consciousness, flashing scenes of incredible tenderness and wild passion behind her closed eyes. She clutched her shampoo bottle in a tight hand and held her face up to the water.

What in the world had she gotten into? She'd only known this big, complex man for a few weeks and already she was beginning to crave both his company and his very skilled lovemaking. She swallowed, feeling a flush heat her body even under the cool spray. Was that all it was, just sex? She smiled to herself. No, there was no way she would label what they had shared as ''just'' sex. There was nothing ''just'' about it.

But what was it, then? Kate asked herself again, lathering her hair into a pile of rich bubbles. And where could it—whatever ''it'' was—go? After all these years of struggling, she was finally her own boss and on her way up. She had her future planned almost to the day for the next few years. Where and how would Dan fit into her scheme? Assuming he wanted to, Kate told herself with a slight shock. Dan hadn't given any indication he was interested in anything more than a physical relationship. Kate's lingering pleasure from the night before began to ebb, and a distinct wariness edged its way into her consciousness.

By the time she'd finished her shower and dressed, unease and doubt had nibbled away the last of her pleasure. She walked into the kitchen to find Dan sitting at the counter, grimacing into his coffee mug.

"I'm going to have to get you some decent coffee. I need something stronger than this stuff to get me going in the mornings."

Kate walked around the counter to pour herself a cup. Cradling it in both hands, she leaned back against the stove and surveyed the man sitting so calmly across from her. "Do you plan to spend many mornings here?"

Dan raised his brows. "As many as I can."

Kate took a quick sip. The hot, rich coffee gave her courage. "We need to talk about that. I told you last night I thought this was all going too fast."

"So you did," Dan agreed, a smile cutting through the dark stubble of his chin and cheeks. "And then the pace picked up even more."

Kate felt heat rising in her face. "Maybe we both let ourselves get a bit carried away."

"Oh, no—*a lot* carried away." Dan levered himself off the stool and crossed the kitchen to stand in front of her. "And it was very nice, too, thank you very much."

He reached out and twisted a strand of wet, red silky hair around his finger. Kate looked up to find a rueful smile lighting his gray eyes.

"Don't look so worried, sweetheart. I'm not planning to move in this weekend. I know I can be a little overpowering at times. I'll give you some space, if that's what you want."

She took her lower lip between her teeth. "Yes. At least, I think that's what I want."

"Fine." Dan turned and headed for the door to the garage. "Call me and let me know when your first appointment is with Jason. I'll go with you." The door closed gently behind him.

Kate's jaw dropped. A shaft of pure feminine pique shot through her. She'd expected an argument. Or at least a token protest, for heaven's sake. After what they'd just shared, she didn't think he would just...just leave! She stood rooted to the spot, staring at the door, until the dog plopped himself down on her foot to get her attention.

Dan drove through the bright, sunny morning, his fists tight on the steering wheel. He wasn't as calm as he'd pretended with Kate. It'd taken all his professional cool to stroll out, leaving her there looking so delectable in her canary-yellow shirt and shiny auburn hair that he wanted to... A wide grin spread across his face as he thought of all the things he wanted to do to Kate. He'd done many of them last night. And early this morning. But a few definitely bore repeating.

He shifted uncomfortably in the car seat as his body hardened. Good grief, he'd thought he'd need a hot shower, a long sleep and a thick steak before he'd be ready for his next meeting with Kate. Yet every one of his instincts was urging him to turn his car around, head back up the hill and lose himself in her soft body again and again.

The thought that maybe Kate was right about needing some time to cool off flashed in his mind. He pulled the thought into his consciousness, turned it around, dissected it.

No, he didn't need to cool down. What he needed was Kate. He felt the certainty growing in him with every turn of the car's wheels. The woman he'd just left aroused and intrigued him. She was a mass of contradictions—warm and loving one minute, stubborn and in a temper the next. He never quite knew what to expect of her, and the uncertainty was slowly driving him crazy.

He squinted into the bright sunlight as he compared Kate to his ex-wife. He knew with instinctive certainty that this long-legged redhead had worked her way deeper into his being in the short time he'd known her than his wife had in the three years they'd been married. He'd had enough liaisons in the years since his divorce to know that what he was feeling for Kate was special, unique, completely outside his previous experience. Something to be explored slowly and savored.

Dan frowned as another frustration overlaid the physical one that was making him so uncomfortable. How long was left on that contract of hers? He tried to remember when Kate said she'd be done and heading back for L.A. A couple of months at most. And he just promised to back off, to give her space. Great tactics, he told himself disgustedly. The marines would never have taken Iwo Jima with him laying out the battle plan. He wheeled the car into his parking space, knowing this was going to be one of the longest periods of his life. He'd promised her that he'd wait for her call, and he would. But he wouldn't like the waiting one bit.

By noon the following Friday, Dan was close to breaking his promise. Very close. He'd reached for the phone half a dozen times in the past week. Once he'd even punched in Kate's number at work, but hung up before it rang. He cursed himself once again for his tactical blunder in letting her have her space. As stubborn as she was, she might think that just because he'd allowed her a little breathing room she was rid of him completely. Dan scowled at the phone one more time, then tried to focus on the reports spread out in front of him.

He was elbow-deep in files when the phone rang.

"Kingman," he growled into the receiver, his eyes and mind still on the intricate white-collar fraud report in front of him.

"Hello, Dan. It's Kate."

A surging sense of relief spread through him, even as excitement began to tingle in his veins. The woman's voice over the phone was enough to put him in a sweat. Dan shook his head, realizing he had it bad.

"I'm supposed to pick Jason up tomorrow morning at eight. Do you still want to join us?"

"Yes, but I can't make it at eight. Where will you be?"

"We're going down to Dr. Chavez's offices. He's got all the material on the marathon there and says he can use some help."

She gave him the address in a distant tone. Dan jotted it down, frowning at the constraint in her voice. "We were supposed to use this time to cool off, not go into a deep freeze. What's the matter?"

Kate sighed. "I've had a rough few days. We've encountered some problems getting all the units online."

Dan could hear the strain in her husky voice. "What kind of problems?"

"I don't know," she told him, half laughing, half rueful. "If I did, I could fix them."

"And here I was hoping you were going to say you had a rotten week because you missed me."

Dan cursed himself for his bluntness when a long silence stretched out over the phone. He was searching for something smooth to say when she finally answered.

"I did, a lot."

"Good. Me, too. *A lot.*"

Kate laughed softly. Regret threaded her voice when she spoke. "I'm sorry, Dan, I really can't talk now. We should've had this last unit up two days ago. We're going to keep at it as late as we can tonight. I've got to get this last one running so we can start the integration programming next week."

"Okay, I won't keep you. See you tomorrow."

Dan hung up and stared at the phone thoughtfully, wondering what this hitch would do to her schedule. He knew how much Kate was counting on finishing this job early. She'd mentioned a bonus, a pretty hefty one as he recalled. Well, there wasn't much he could do to help her with this problem, whatever it was. He knew about as much about computers as Rico did.

Kate hung up the phone and looked at it thoughtfully. She was astounded at how just hearing Dan's voice sent shivers of desire down her neck. All week long he'd intruded into her thoughts: during work, during the night, whenever she took a sip of her special cinnamon coffee.

The time away from him hadn't helped at all. Instead of clarifying her own feelings, she was more confused than ever. Kate knew she wanted him with a carnal passion that amazed her. In all her thirty-one years, she'd never felt such intense physical desire. Just thinking of the way his hands and lips had explored her body was enough to make her blush a bright red. Once Trish even noticed her flush and asked if she was feeling all right. Mumbling some incoherent answer, Kate had buried her face and her decidedly lascivious thoughts in a stack of computer manuals.

Adding to her stress was the fact that they'd fallen behind schedule on the project. It was only by a few days, but enough to jeopardize the bonus for early completion. For some unexplained reason, the seventh and eighth sequential memory units failed to integrate with the first six. Until they had all nine subunits installed and integrated, the supercomputer was just a box of brightly colored parts of no use to anyone.

Kate rubbed her forehead and went over to the small cluster of engineers hunched around a worktable.

"Okay, let's go over the integration programming scheme one more time," she said with determined enthusiasm.

The next morning, Dan arrived at the medical center a little after ten. He could see at a glance that the problems at work had kept Kate up late. Lines of strain bracketed her eyes and faint blue shadows darkened the skin under them. But even tired and grouchy, she looked good enough to eat. She had on a pair of cutoff jeans that hugged her hips and made Dan break out in a light sweat. Over them she wore a bright red Stanford T-shirt. The color looked stunning on her. It brought out the deep mahogany sheen of her hair and creamy whiteness of her skin. Dan stirred uncomfortably and forced himself to concentrate on the interaction between woman and boy.

Neither one looked particularly happy to be there. Maybe it was dealing with Jason that was causing the stress in Kate's features, Dan thought. He stood in the open doorway and watched the two of them for a few moments. Kate was bent over a long table, sorting through stacks of haphazardly piled papers. Jason stood on the opposite side of the table, idly shuffling one hand through the piles of forms. His face had a sullen, closed look.

"Here, Jason, I'll show you. We have to sort the different forms by category—for the full marathon, the half marathon and the five-kilometer fun run. Then, when the applications come in, race officials can send out just the information each runner needs."

"This is stupid." The boy pushed at the papers. A stack tee-tered precariously, then slid to the floor.

Dan watched Kate bite her lip in an obvious effort to hold back her temper. "Please, Jason, I'm not exactly thrilled to be spending my morning playing file clerk, either. Let's just dig in and get it done." She bent to pick up the papers and saw Dan standing in the doorway.

"Good, another sacrificial victim. Come on in and help us sort through this mess."

Dan smiled as he strolled into the spacious, brightly lit room. "Hello, Jason. I'm Dan Kingman."

The boy eyed Dan's hand for a long minute. With a show of reluctance, he put out his own.

"What's the drill?" Dan asked, eyeing the littered table.

Kate dumped the pile of papers from the floor back onto the table. "The printers just delivered the various forms for this year's race. Dr. Chavez volunteered his committee to help sort through them and put together information packages for each of the various runs."

"So where's the committee?" Dan asked, pulling a stack toward him.

"They start getting together regularly in a couple of weeks. Jason and I are the advance guard, so to speak. We're going to put together the prototype packages." Kate gave the boy a tentative smile, which he ignored.

Dan watched a flush creep up her cheeks. She and Jason were definitely off to a rocky start.

"What do I do?"

Kate grinned at Dan in relief. "Why don't you start with the blue stack, the ones for the full marathon? We ought to be able to make a good dent in those."

She stood, frowning down at the papers in her hand. "You know, all this could easily be computerized."

"So put it on a computer," Dan told her as he pulled a chair over beside Jason. "Here, you take this little pile and I'll take the big one."

The boy gave an involuntary grin when Dan pushed a towering stack toward him and pulled one about three sheets high in front of himself. Kate snorted.

"Great! At that rate we'll be here till midnight."

"Paperwork was never my strong suit," Dan told her, eyes twinkling. "Come on, kid, get to it. I've got the worst craving for an extralarge pepperoni pizza. Slave driver O'Sullivan here probably won't let either of us out for food until we get through this stuff."

"What did I tell you?" Dan asked Jason in a loud whisper two hours later.

Kate looked at the accusing looks on the two male faces opposite her and relented. "Okay, okay, we'll go eat. Here, pile the stacks neatly in this box. Anyone who gets so much as one sheet out of order will answer to me."

When the last of the papers were stored away, she picked up a small box she'd set aside. In response to Dan's inquiring glance, she told him she wanted to take some of the forms home.

"I think I can come up with a simple program to enter the race data with an optical scanner. It would make correlating all the related items, like entrance fees, runners' categories and such, so much easier."

"For someone who professes to hate exercise, you're sure getting into this race business," Dan commented.

"I hate inefficiency even more," Kate responded as the three of them walked out of the spacious medical complex into an afternoon filled with bright blue skies and shimmering sunshine. The temperature hovered around ninety degrees, but the dry heat felt invigorating after the coolness of the medical center. Brilliant pink oleander bushes bordering the entrance added a bright splash of color to the summer day.

"Albuquerque at its finest," Dan commented, holding his face up to the sun. "Bet you don't have many days like this in L.A."

Kate arched her stiff neck and leaned back to study the brilliant, cloudless sky with tired eyes. "No, not many."

Dan gave her a thoughtful look, then reached over to take the box out of her hand. "I'll put this in your car, then we'll take mine."

"What time do you have to be back, Jason?" he asked when he returned and opened the doors to his nondescript official car to let the trapped, stifling air out.

The boy shrugged.

"I told Mrs. Grant, his foster mother, I'd bring him home after lunch. No specific time," Kate volunteered.

Dan turned to the boy, standing silent beside them. "Do you have anything planned for the afternoon?"

Jason squinted up, his blue eyes doubtful. "No, nothing special," he finally replied.

"Good. Come on, we'll call Mrs. Grant from the car."

Jason hung back, obviously reluctant to enter the police car. Although it was unmarked, the crackling radios and litter of official paraphernalia in the front seat made it undeniably an official vehicle. Dan knew the boy was remembering the last time he'd ridden in a police car, on his way to the detention center.

"You sit in back, Kate," Dan suggested casually. "I need Jason up front so he can order the pizza. Do you know how to work a portable phone, kid?"

"Sure," the boy said.

"Come on then, let's go. A man my size can only go so long without sustenance."

Kate slid into the back seat, sucking in her breath when her thighs encountered the hot leather, while Jason settled in the front. Handing the boy the phone, Dan told him to call his foster mother first for permission.

"Now call Information for the number to the pizzeria on Coors Road."

"Isn't that on the other side of town?" Kate asked.

"Yes, it is. Across the Rio Grande."

"Why in the world would we order from someplace so far away?"

Dan winked at Jason, still holding the phone in his hand. "So they can deliver a couple pizzas to Petroglyph Park. We're going to have a picnic, then go exploring."

Six

They arrived at the small national park nestled in the shadow of five volcanic peaks just minutes before the pizza delivery van drove up. Dan paid for the pizzas, handed one to Jason and a carton of soft drinks to Kate, then led the way to picnic tables set among a stand of Russian olive trees. Settling in the shade of the silver-green, feathery branches, they spent the next half hour enjoying the warm sun, cold drinks and spicy pizza. Few tourists had braved the afternoon heat, leaving the trio wrapped in a quiet world of their own.

The high mesa shimmered in the sunlight, while far to the east, Albuquerque sprawled in a somnolent haze. Dan slouched comfortably on the hard wooden bench. He felt infinitely better—he had a full stomach, and the woman he was coming to think of as his own sat next to him. Moreover, he could see that the lines of strain had faded from around Kate's eyes.

"Thanks, Dan." She smiled at him. "I needed some fresh air and good food." She glanced over at Jason.

"Yeah, thanks," the boy mumbled around a large chunk of crust.

"Finish up, troops," Dan ordered. "We've got this whole park to explore."

Both woman and boy groaned in protest.

"Do we have to?" Kate asked. "It'll take too much energy to climb those rocks in this heat."

"Who wants to look at a bunch of silly rocks?" Jason muttered.

"I do. You do, too—both of you. You just don't realize it yet. Come on, eat up." Dan gave Jason the last slice and carried the trash to a handy container.

He led them, still protesting, to the entrance. The Park Service ranger on duty handed them a brochure, then Dan herded them onto the walking trail. It led up a low hill toward a mound of twisted black rock.

"Here, read it to us, Kate. We don't want to miss any of the details."

Dan smiled to himself when he intercepted the resigned look Kate flashed at Jason, and the boy's answering half smile. Given the right circumstances, they just might find some way to communicate yet.

His silent satisfaction grew as he watched the two of them clamber over the rocks to peer at the prehistoric figures carved on the black surfaces. At one point, Jason scrambled up a steep incline, then reached a hand back down to help Kate up. Together they explored a perpendicular wall with delicate carving traced across its surface. Kate's deep auburn curls brushed Jason's sandy mop as their heads bent over the rock. The boy ran a finger over the surprisingly detailed, flowing lines of a horse. A man figure ran beside the horse, holding its mane.

"This is fascinating," Kate breathed. "Look, Jason, they almost seem to be moving in the sunlight." She read from the brochure. "'This figure is thought to be one of the finest examples of prehistoric Anazasi rock art. Both horse and man are drawn in representational style and capture the essence of movement and grace.'"

Jason responded with a low murmur, although Dan could see his eyes drawn to the graceful figure.

Dan followed behind leisurely as they explored the rest of the small park. Kate exclaimed over abstract bird figures, running

horses and masks of exotic gods. According to the brochure Kate
read faithfully, there were an estimated fifteen hundred figures
carved into the black basalt rock of the volcanic escarpment.
Most were relics of the prehistoric Indians who had camped
there, but many were left by Spanish invaders centuries later.

The park was almost closing by the time Dan led them out
and back to the car. Kate filled the long drive back to the medical
center with more tidbits from the brochure.

"I'd never even heard of petroglyphs before," she finally said,
lowering the crumpled paper.

"Now you're an expert," Dan teased. "They're scattered all
over this part of the country. You need to take the time to explore
more while you're here. You and Jason."

"Mmm," Kate murmured, while Jason stared out the window.

When he drove into the medical center parking lot and pulled
up beside her car, Dan instructed Jason to wait a moment. He
joined Kate outside the car and put a firm hand under her chin
to tilt her face to the sunlight.

"Much better."

"Better than what?" Her violet eyes smiled up at him.

"You look much better with a touch of sun on your face and
the lines gone from your eyes. Go on home, Kate. Indulge yourself in that hot tub contraption of yours, then get some rest. I'll
take Jason home." Dan bent to brush her lips.

When he pulled back, his heart leapt at the sudden frustration
that darkened her eyes. At least, he thought it was frustration.
That sure as hell was what he was feeling. Maybe this period of
"space" was worth it, he thought. If it put that disgruntled,
unsatisfied look in her eyes, if it made her realize how right they
were together, it certainly was worth it. Dan just hoped he would
survive long enough for Kate to recognize what she was feeling.
He'd never thought of himself as particularly aggressive sexu-
ally, but this self-imposed abstinence was starting to make him
think in terms of carrying his woman off, much as the prehistoric
men of the rock carvings probably had.

For a moment, he was tempted to follow her home and relieve
their shared frustration. Kate's eyes told him she wouldn't object.

But he held back, his arms falling lightly from her shoulders. He'd sworn to give her time, and he would. She'd tell him when she was ready. He just hoped she was ready damn soon. This nobility crap was for the birds.

Dan waited until her car pulled out of the parking lot before he rejoined Jason. The boy was quiet as they drove toward the southwestern sector of town, his eyes fixed on the passing view.

"You know, you should give Kate a chance. She's okay, once you get to know her."

Jason turned to look at him. A sneer settled over his face, making it look oddly old and cynical. "Looks like you've gotten to know her pretty well."

"Can it, kid," Dan told him mildly. "All you have to do is meet her halfway. Use this time to get to know new people, enjoy some new experiences. Believe me, there's a lot more to the world than the gang you were running with."

"Yeah, sure." Jason turned back to the window.

Dan didn't push it. He knew from long experience the chances of breaking through to the boy were fifty-fifty at best. They had about as many failures as successes in this sponsorship program. It would be tough to reach the boy with just a few hours a week spent outside his normal environment unless Jason opened up to it. And the boy wasn't sending out any signals that he wanted change just yet. Dan could only hope that Kate found some way to capture his interest in the next couple of months.

The kid was worth saving. Dan had discerned intelligence and an adolescent defiance in his blue eyes that reminded him all too much of himself at that age. Jason was street smart, cocky, yet hungry, all at the same time. If they could just feed that hunger, just spark something that interested him. If anyone could, Kate could, Dan thought. She threw herself heart and soul into a project once committed to it.

Dan grinned as he thought of the plush doghouse sitting in solitary splendor in her once-green patio garden. And the box of papers Kate was taking home so she could computerize the marathon details. And the way she had given herself so passionately to his hungry mouth and seeking hands. No, the woman didn't do anything halfway.

Dan glanced over at the still, silent Jason. If anyone could reach the boy, Dan was convinced Kate could.

"I just can't get through to him, Trish."

Tricia nodded absently, her eyes on Kate's plate. "You've only had a couple sessions with the boy so far. Give it time."

"I don't have much time. Only a few hours each weekend."

"Well, you can't expect miracles in just a few weeks. The kid hasn't had a home or family to care for him in years, from what you've told me. You're going to have to work to win his confidence."

The small blonde broke off to shake her head in unabashed admiration as Kate lifted another heaping forkful. "You know, you're the first woman I've ever seen finish off a half of a Travis special."

Kate grinned as she demolished the last of a heaping mound of enchiladas covered with crisp, golden french fries. This was Kate's first visit to the K&I Diner and her first taste of their house specialty, named after the truck driver who invented it. It wouldn't be the last.

"Most men who come here can't even eat a half order. That's why they have a quarter- and eighth-Travis's on the menu," Trish commented, her envious eyes on Kate's plate.

All around them the small, crowded restaurant hummed with the sound of hungry people and the air was filled with a tangy aroma of crisp french fries and spicy enchilada sauce. Kate and Trish had stood in line for over twenty minutes before they'd secured a table. The diner was as popular with the military and civilian personnel from nearby Kirtland Air Force Base as with the locals.

"You shouldn't have brought me to a truck stop if you didn't want me to eat like a truck driver," Kate grinned. "I would never have believed this unlikely combination could be so delicious. I'll have to bring Dan and Jason back here. They could put away a full order each."

Kate frowned as she wiped up the last bit of sauce with a fork full of now-soggy french fries.

"I don't know what I'm going to do with Jason. We've had two sessions together now and he hasn't spoken more than twenty words to me, at most. The first session wasn't so bad, because Dan was there, but the last time was awful. He was bored and all I did was pick at him. I'm really dreading our session tomorrow."

She looked at Trish hopefully. "Any advice? Your son is just a few years older than Jason."

The blonde shook her head. "No, not really. Eleven is a tough age. Sort of in-between. At that stage they're too old for children's toys and too young to be preoccupied with dating and the opposite sex. I think sports like soccer or baseball and electronic games are about all my son was interested in at that age."

Kate sighed. "Jason's different. He doesn't want to participate in any team activities. I suggested the programs at the Y, but he shot that down the first day."

"Sorry I can't help you, Kate," the younger woman said. "Enough about this kid, though. I want to hear how it's going with the incredible hunk."

Kate smiled at the irrepressible blonde. Trish had prodded her to go after Dan ever since she'd glimpsed him that one time he'd come to the lab.

"Okay, I guess."

"You *guess?* Don't you know?"

Kate looked down at her clean plate. "No, not really." She sighed. "He's trying to give me the room I said I wanted, but the man's about as subtle as a pit bull. He's more than ready to take our...relationship further. He's waiting—not very patiently—for me to make up my mind."

"You're nuts," Trish said decisively. "You know you like the guy. Go for it!"

"For what? I'll be leaving in a few months. And the project is starting to heat up. I just can't afford to get too involved, emotionally or timewise."

"Believe me, for someone like Dan, I'd find both the time and the emotion."

Kate laughed and grabbed the check. "You would. Come on, back to work."

Much as she tried to keep her mind on the complicated flow plans before her, Kate found herself thinking more about her conversation with Trish than about mainframes that afternoon. She finally gave up and headed home, hoping a good soaking in the hot tub might help her unwind.

Relaxing in the warm, bubbling water, with Rico stretched out blissfully beside the tub, Kate tried to understand just what it was about Dan that disturbed her so much. During the infrequent times they were together these last weeks, she enjoyed his irreverent company as much as she relished his skilled lovemaking. What there was of it. The man had taken her at her word and didn't push her. He teased her and took her to out-of-the-way restaurants and kissed her until she was breathless with longing, then left her.

Perversely, Kate had come to resent his restraint. She didn't like this confused, unsatisfied, unsettled state, even if it was of her own making. Her irritation rose, and the hot tub failed to work its usual magic on her. Darn the man, anyway.

She dried herself off, pulled on a thigh-length, silky sleep shirt and settled into her wide platform bed. Her frustration only increased as she thought of how big and empty the bed seemed now, and how small and crowded and wonderfully warm it had seemed when Dan had taken up more than his fair share of it.

She snuggled into the covers, recognizing that this uncertain state had gone on long enough. She wanted Dan, pure and simple. Tomorrow night she'd tell him so.

Kate was still restless and edgy when she picked up Jason the following morning. He trudged down the short walk from his foster parent's weather-beaten house. His usual sullen expression made the lines of his young face appear set and hard. Kate sighed, then pinned a welcoming smile on her lips.

"Hi, Jason. All set for our meeting with the race officials?"

"Yeah."

"I've got the model program all ready to demo. It took a few late nights to design, but it's pretty slick, if I do say so myself. I even rented an optical scanner to show how they can enter the data as it's received from the applications, then correlate it to the other files, like expenses and finish times, and such."

"Big deal."

Kate's jaw clenched. She wheeled the car through the light Saturday-morning traffic toward the medical center and tried to remember Dan's conviction that Jason was worth the effort.

"It's designed to run on little notebook computers. We can enter all the advance information as we receive it. Then the other volunteers can take the computers right down to the finish lines on the day of the race to punch in times. They'll get instant feedback in each category and can even print out the certified results for each runner, if they want to."

Despite her work schedule and growing preoccupation with a certain officer of the law, Kate was getting more and more excited about the marathon. Now just a little over a month away, the pace of preparatory activities had gone from hectic to frenetic. With an expected record turnout, this year's race promised to be the biggest and most elaborate in its ten-year history.

"Just think what a madhouse it will be, with five-thousand-plus runners in all different categories crossing the finish in waves." She glanced at Jason to see if he felt any of the infectious excitement.

The boy didn't even bother to reply. He kept his head turned away from Kate to stare out the window. Kate gave up. They finished the short ride in silence.

Kate's program was a hit with the committee of volunteers who'd come together to manage the big event. She set up her laptop computer and ran through several sample entries, to their rave reviews. In addition to a database that pulled together all the race information, a simple graphics program printed out fancy certificates for all participants, as well as thank-you letters to the hundreds of volunteers.

"Are you sure you don't want to move to Albuquerque permanently, Ms. O'Sullivan?'' Dr. Chavez beamed at her after the demo. ''In just a couple weeks, you've done more for the marathon than I've been able to do all year. The race director will love this program. I've told him what you were working on and he wants to meet with you himself, at your convenience.''

''Anytime.'' Kate laughed. ''I have to admit, I'm starting to get as excited as the rest of you about this race.''

''Well, we sure appreciate your work. Come into the other office. I'll show you the bookkeeping files used last year so you can adapt them to the computer.''

''Sure.'' Kate turned to the boy standing to one side. ''Jason, why don't you put the folding chairs away and start opening the envelopes with the first applications. We'll test-input a few of them when I get back.''

She spent nearly an hour with Dr. Chavez, trying to sort through last year's finances. The volunteer who'd managed the books was a professional accountant and used a sophisticated program much different from the one she employed in her own small business. By the time she'd run through it and wandered back into the reception area, Kate had a more thorough grounding in the race finances than she'd ever wanted. She stopped abruptly when she saw Jason seated at the long table, punching the keyboard of her laptop with busy fingers.

''What are you doing?''

The boy slipped quickly out of the chair. Kate went over to scan the small screen.

''Oh, no,'' she groaned. ''You've erased the templates. And I was in such a rush I didn't back up the last couple.''

''So?'' The boy's low, defiant tone almost shredded Kate's volatile temper. She counted to ten under her breath before she turned to the boy.

''So I put a lot of hours into this program, hours I didn't have to spare.'' Her eyes widened as a horrible thought struck her. ''Did you do that on purpose?'' she asked, her voice raising. ''Did you deliberately try to destroy the templates?''

''No!''

''Really?''

"Yeah. I don't care about your stupid program."

"Well, what were you doing fooling around with it? Answer me!"

"I don't have to. I'm sick of you telling me what to do." Jason's own anger surfaced. He kicked a box out of his way and headed for the door. "I'm sick of this stupid race. I'm getting out of here."

"Oh, no, you're not." Kate planted herself in front of the door. Boy and woman glared at each other for a long moment. Kate took a long breath and reminded herself that she was supposed to be the adult here.

"Look, Jason, I'm sorry I snapped at you. Really. Can we try again? Please?"

Some of the mutinous expression left the boy's face, but he remained standing stiff and still before her.

"What were you doing on the computer?" she asked in a milder tone.

"I was just seeing how it worked." Jason's lower lip stuck out, but at least he raised his head to look at her. "I've never tried one of these little jobbies before."

Kate almost missed the significance of his words. Her eyes narrowed as they studied the freckled face before her. "Have you tried other kinds of computers?"

Jason shrugged. "Some. We have a few old ones at school that I mess around on. Some company donated them. Half of them don't even work. But we're supposed to get some new ones this year."

"What do you do on them?" she asked, genuinely curious now.

The boy shrugged again. "I use the typing tutor and play a few word games. And a Magic Quest game. I'm pretty good at that."

"I've got a game like that on my computer. It's pretty tough, though. Do you want to try it after we finish cleaning up here and get some lunch?"

"I guess so."

It wasn't much, Kate told herself grimly as they straightened the office and gathered their belongings. But maybe, just maybe, it was a start.

Seven

Later that afternoon, Dan rang Kate's doorbell three times before she answered.

"Hi, beautiful." He bent to kiss her—a hard hungry kiss that left him aching and Kate panting. "Were you in your tub or something?"

"Hmm?" Kate leaned back in the circle of his strong arms to smile up at him.

"What took you so long to get to the door?" He put her gently out of his arms.

"I was being attacked by the evil sorcerer. I had to zap him with my magic cudgel to get away." She waved toward Jason, hunched over her computer, tapping on the keyboard with two flying fingers. The boy called out to her, never taking his eyes from the small, greenish screen.

"Kate, look! I figured out that if you take the mirror from the wall you can reflect the spell right back onto the bad guy. He'll destroy himself. Oh, hi, Dan."

"Hi, yourself, kid." Dan turned back to Kate, brows raised.

"Jason is a near genius at foiling dark knights and wicked sorcerers. He's faster on the keyboard with two fingers than I am with ten. And much more bloodthirsty,'' she added, laughing at Jason's low, exultant yell.

''Yes! Got him! Took his head right off with the sword of light.''

Despite Dan's vociferous protests, he soon found himself taking Kate's seat beside the boy. She hung over his shoulder and tried to help. He grinned when Kate and Jason both laughed, then groaned every time his clumsy fingers hit the wrong key. After sending them all to the darkest dungeons for the third time, he was banished to the couch and the baseball game on TV.

Dan was more than content to relax on the comfy sofa with Rico sprawled across his lap in blissful companionship. He kept a lazy eye on the TV, but Kate's burnished hair and Jason's excited shouts captured his attention more than the players' lackluster performance. His gut tightened slowly as he surveyed the jean-clad woman, sitting with her back to him and her head bent close to Jason's. Her fluffy pink top followed the long curve of her back and flared over the swelling hips. A vivid memory of planting kisses all along those hips and back flashed through his mind. Dan took a hasty swallow of his beer and shifted on the couch. Suddenly he couldn't seem to find a comfortable position. Rico lifted his head when his pillow moved for the fifth time in as many minutes and sent Dan a reproachful look.

''Sorry, boy,'' Dan told him quietly. His gaze went back to Kate.

Just how much space did one woman need, anyway? He'd been more patient than he ever believed he could be with anyone, especially a feisty, hot-tempered female who fired his blood with her laughter and his imagination with her long-limbed body.

At first, his restraint had made him feel almost virtuous, like some medieval knight waiting for his lady to bestow her favors. That feeling faded completely the day of their visit to Petroglyph Park. When he'd put Kate, all soft and pliant, out of his arms and seen frustration deepen her eyes to a bluish purple, he knew he wasn't cut out for the role of noble knight. All this week his own frustration had grown. Hot, edgy, irritable, mounting frustration. Enough was enough.

He was more of a cowboy than a knight, Dan decided. And not one of the good guys in a white hat, either. He'd be damned if he was going to be content with lifting his woman gently to the saddle and riding off into the sunset. Kate would be lucky if she made it to dusk before he threw her across his shoulder and carried her off to his bed. And if she brought up any more objections or mentioned her blasted schedule once more, he might just handcuff her to the damn bed frame. His groin tightened as he planned the evening to come. The ball game drew to a tepid finish, the dark sorcerer was finally vanquished and Dan's patience ran out.

"Come on, you two. It's after four. Let's get some hamburgers, then take Jason home." He pushed a protesting Rico out of his lap and rose.

"That's the first time he's even said goodbye," Kate mused, watching Jason make his way toward the battered screen door of his house.

"I was amazed to find you two actually talking to each other this afternoon," Dan commented as he backed the car out of the driveway.

"Well, it was touch and go for a while. I lost my cool with him this morning and we had a little shouting match. I'm afraid I'm not very good with kids."

Dan reached over to take her hand. "You're doing fine. Just give him some time and attention. That's what he needs most."

"You have such natural instincts with him," Kate mused, twining her fingers in his. "He responds to you so well. Didn't you want children of your own?"

He lifted his shoulders in a slight shrug. "I did. My ex-wife didn't."

Kate glanced from his impassive face to the hand holding hers. His fingers had tightened imperceptibly, unconsciously. She felt their painful bite, and a corresponding pain clutched at her heart. Dan had never known a family's love, as a child or as a man.

Kate was quiet for the rest of the trip. She roused only when he pulled into an unfamiliar parking lot.

"My place," he responded to her unspoken question.

Nodding, she followed him up the stairs. A smile spread across her face as she surveyed this man's kingdom. It reflected his personality. Two large, comfortable sofas in soft leather faced each other with a large glass coffee table between them. Books, some open and laid facedown, some stacked haphazardly, littered the coffee table and spilled over onto the end tables. Shelves filled with more books and an expensive-looking stereo system stretched the length of one wall. At the far end of the living room, sliding glass doors led to a small balcony with a view across the valley to the west mesa. Kate could see the five volcanoes sketched across the far horizon in slowly darkening purple majesty.

Dan went into the small kitchenette, to return a few minutes later with a beer for him, a glass of wine for her. He grinned in response to her appreciative sip.

"I figure I can invest in some good wine if you'll invest in some decent coffee. I like it strong and black in the mornings."

Kate looked at him over the rim of her glass as he settled himself beside her on the couch. She took another sip and savored the sharp, fruity tang while she considered his words.

"Do you think it's time for me to start making you coffee in the mornings?" she asked him slowly.

"Nope." Dan smiled. "I'll make it. You may not be ready, Kate, but I am. More than ready. I can't play the gentleman anymore and leave you at your doorstep with a chaste kiss while you try to find a way to fit me into your nice, neat, well-planned world. I'll just fit you into mine, instead."

He set his beer down on the coffee table and reached for her glass. Kate watched his hands move from the drinks to her arms. He pulled her against his chest and settled his chin on top of her head. He felt so good—so strong and solid and good. She wrapped her arms around his ribs and fit herself against him.

"That's better. You need to relax more. You worry too much."

"I can't help it," Kate murmured, nestling her cheek against his warmth. "I have to know where I'm going, try to anticipate and plan for what's coming next."

"I'll tell you where you're going." His voice rumbled against her ear. "You're going into my bedroom. And there's no way you can plan for what's coming next."

When Dan lifted her in his arms and headed down the dim hallway, Kate smiled to herself. Funny that they both decided to end their self-imposed restraint at the same time. After her long, sleepless night, filled with chaotic, yearning thoughts of Dan, she still hadn't resolved just where this relationship was going. But Kate had finally acknowledged, deep in her heart, that wherever it went, she hoped they would be together.

Still, when he laid her on his bed she bit her lip as she looked up at the face hovering over her. She sensed a new determination in him and felt the faint flutter of walls closing in on her.

"Don't worry so." Dan's fingers worked at the zipper of her jeans. "You don't have to have a preplanned milestone chart for everything in your life. Just lie back and enjoy it."

Kate gave a shaky laugh when Dan wiggled his eyebrows and gave her an exaggerated, lecherous grin. Her last conscious thought, before his hands and mouth went to work on her, was that she'd do just that—enjoy it.

And she did. Dan stretched every stroke and every kiss to their limit. He lingered over her breasts and belly and the insides of her thighs until she felt tiny, rippling sensations over every square inch of her body. When she brought a hand down to give him back stroke for stroke, he raised it over her head, capturing both her wrists in one big fist.

"Oh, no, Katey mine. I don't want you doing any work of any kind tonight. Tonight, I'm going to show you that *not* being in control can have its own rewards."

Kate squirmed under him, half aroused, half embarrassed at the pleasure her own helplessness gave her. Dan didn't even release her hands to remove her loose top. He just pushed it up until his free hand and his mouth had access to her aching nipples. In the same manner, he dragged her jeans and panties down until he could free one of her legs, then left the clothes tangled around the other. Kate gasped when his knee pushed itself between hers and forced them apart, leaving her open and vulnerable.

Even when he fumbled with the zipper on his own jeans, he held her. When he used his teeth and one hand on the foil packet he pulled out of his pocket, he held her.

"This might take a little practice," he muttered when he dropped the package on her chest for the second time.

"Dan, for heaven's sakes, let me loose. Let me touch you."

"Nope. This is my fantasy. I kinda like being the one with the black hat, after all."

"What in the world are you talking about?" she asked breathlessly. His hand had finished its business and was now buried in the curls between her widespread legs.

"Never mind."

He bent his head to her breast. Kate felt the sharp edge of his teeth against her engorged nipple the same moment he slid his fingers into her core. Her body arched, pulling against his restraining hand and the heavy leg thrown over hers. She couldn't escape him. He filled every one of her senses. She felt the rasp of his mustache against the tender skin of her breast. She breathed in the scent of him, dark and musky and all male.

When he thrust into her, Kate thought she would explode. Dan wouldn't allow her even that release. He pulled out slowly, letting her feel every ridge and rock-hard inch. He held himself just outside her until her rioting senses stopped whirling. Then he thrust in again, so hard and deep she almost screamed in wild pleasure. Her hips bucked against his and he moved against her, fast and hard.

Kate's consciousness narrowed, her senses sharpened. Dan released her wrists to cradle her head, holding her steady for his kiss. Her hands finally free, Kate clutched the sleek sinews that flexed with every thrust. She panted, straining against him, clenching and unclenching her muscles around his shaft. A rushing tide of heat began at her core, spread slowly, then moved with gathering momentum up her body. Groaning far back in her throat, Kate climaxed in a blinding rush of sensation.

Vaguely, Kate heard Dan give a low, savage moan. He stiffened, holding himself rigid while she rode the waves of pleasure. When the world stopped spinning, she opened her eyes to find him watching her intently.

"That was almost worth it," he told her with grim satisfaction.

Kate swallowed, feeling a rawness in her throat. "What? What was worth what?"

"Seeing you explode in my arms is almost worth the weeks we've wasted. You've just run out of space, woman."

Before Kate could gather her disordered thoughts enough for a coherent response, Dan began to move again. Slowly at first, then with gathering force.

Dan left on Tuesday for a conference in California, something to do with the migration of gangs from the West Coast. Kate felt his absence more with each passing day. Memories of their nights together would crop up at the most embarrassing moments—like when one of her engineers brought up the milestone chart for the first series test pattern for the integrated system. Kate stared at the computer screen with unseeing eyes. She could hear Dan's deep voice telling her that life didn't have to be laid out in precise, measured increments just before he made her forget where she was, much less where she was going.

"With luck, we can run the first pattern this weekend."

She blinked up at the engineer hovering over her shoulder. "Oh...great, Rich."

She shook away the last of her preoccupation and bent over the screen. "We just might make up for the days we lost trying to work out the bugs in that faulty unit."

She felt a familiar excitement course through her as she went back to her own workstation and called up the timelines. While she waited for the program to come up, she glanced at the calendar hanging on the wall of her workstation. They could just do it. With luck and a lot of late nights, they could still finish a week ahead of schedule, just enough to qualify for the bonus. It would mean working day and night for the next few weeks. This was the most critical phase of the whole integration effort.

Kate knew taking down the lab's other supercomputer was a significant undertaking with global ramifications. Phillips Lab was one of four existing nodes for air force scientific research, heavily involved in the space program. When she first started the contract, an earnest young air force major had gone into excruciating detail on the lab's role in space research. Even keeping to an unclassified level of detail, he'd lost Kate after the first five minutes. All she knew was that if she delayed his super-computing time beyond the period scheduled for it to be down, the fate of the world would be in jeopardy.

Her adrenaline was still pumping when she left late that night. It wasn't until she was halfway home that she remembered she was supposed to pick up Jason the next morning. No, she wasn't picking him up this time. His foster mother was going to drop him off at the medical center because she had some appointment, Kate recalled. It was after midnight now. Too late to call and cancel. She'd have to try to catch them before they left in the morning.

She smiled as she drove through the darkness, feeling a sense of forward movement, of definable progress. Jason was at least talking to her, the job was going well and Dan...well, Dan was filling her mind and her nights more and more. She'd been both surprised and a little alarmed by how much she missed him this past week. She let herself into the house and fell asleep thinking of various ways to welcome him home.

Exhausted, she slept through the alarm the following morning. It was after eight when she woke to see the sunlight streaming through the skylights in her bedroom. Kate yelped and scrambled up, dislodging a snoring Rico from his nest at the foot of the bed. She rushed through her shower and pulled on a pair of slacks and a light jersey top. She hated being late. It threw off her schedule for the whole day and made her feel as though she never quite caught up. While she waited impatiently for the coffee to perk, she punched Jason's home number into the phone. Getting no answer, she tried the number at the outer office of the medical center. The phone rang half a dozen times before she heard a hesitant hello.

"Jason? I'm sorry I didn't catch you before you left your house. Look, I've got to go in to work for a little while this morning. Can you keep busy until I get there?"

"Yeah, I guess so."

"There should be a stack of new race-entry applications. Why don't you open and sort through them? I'll be there as soon as I can, okay?"

"Okay."

"Is Dr. Chavez there yet? Can you put him on the line?"

She spoke to him and explained that she had to work and that she'd be there as soon as she could. He agreed to check on Jason occasionally. It would only be for a few hours, she told herself as she rushed out to the garage.

Kate kept one harried eye on the clock throughout the long, frantic morning. The first test pattern bombed and they had to restart it. Around noon, she called Jason again. He sounded bored and irritable when he finally picked up the phone.

"I can't get away after all, Jason. Do you think your foster mother could come get you?"

She frowned at the brief silence that filled the phone. Her conscience pricked her. Despite the urgency of the work, she could halt the test program and slip out for the hour it would take to drive across town and back.

"I'll get a ride."

Kate felt a guilty stab of relief at Jason's concurrence. "The center's only a few miles from your house. I'll call Mrs. Grant. If she can't come for you, I will."

Sue Grant was less than enthusiastic about gathering up her other children to go get Jason. Kate wished she hadn't even called, but the other woman snapped that she'd go and cut the connection. Kate hung up, biting her lower lip, and tried to shrug off her nagging guilt. She'd make it up to the boy, she promised. Next week they'd do something special. She turned back to her console to lose herself in the test pattern once again.

* * *

"Where is she?"

Kate jumped at the deep, angry voice slicing through the quiet of the lab. She looked up to find Trish holding open the heavy doors, Dan looming just beyond her.

The two men sitting beside her scooted back their wheeled chairs when she jumped up and headed for the entrance.

"Dan! I thought you weren't coming back until tomorrow. What are you doing here?"

Kate's wide, welcoming smile faltered at the rigid set to his face. His black brows were drawn together in a dark slash across his forehead.

"Come out here."

Kate stared, totally confused by his harsh tone and cold look. She'd never seen him angry before, but there was no mistaking the fury in his eyes. She walked out into the corridor and pulled the heavy door shut on Trish's interested gaze.

"Come on." Dan didn't wait for the door to close behind her before he took her arm in a hard grip. He turned and headed down the dim corridor, pulling her behind him.

"Hey, wait a minute. Dan, stop!" Kate stumbled, trying to keep up with his rapid stride. She jerked her arm free, almost as angry as she was confused now. "Just what do you think you're doing?"

She almost tripped over her own feet when Dan whirled to face her. "I'm taking you to the hospital. So you can visit your charge."

Kate backed away from the icy rage shimmering in his eyes. "What...what charge?" she whispered. "Oh, God, you don't mean Jason?"

"Right the first time, lady," Dan told her, his voice as cold and as hard as his eyes.

"What happened? Is he all right?"

"No."

The stark word hit Kate like a fist in the stomach. She lifted a trembling hand to her lips.

"He's in intensive care."

"Intensive care?" Kate's voice cracked.

"Yeah. I guess he got a little bored waiting for you at the medical center and took off on his own. The police have been looking for him ever since Mrs. Grant reported him missing late this evening. They just found him an hour ago."

Dan took her arm again. "In an alley. Unconscious."

Eight

Kate never knew the hours between midnight and dawn could stretch so endlessly. Nor had she realized how many violent emotions could wrack a person at one time. She stood in front of the window of the lounge in St. Joseph's Hospital, arms wrapped tight around her chest. Her unseeing eyes gazed at the few city lights still glowing in the empty hours before sunrise.

Dan's credentials had gained her a brief visit with Jason. The few minutes she'd spent staring down at his still body had helped neither him nor her. The boy was still unconscious, with a severe concussion. He looked so young and helpless in the wide bed, with tubes and IVs snaking from his body. A vicious bruise discolored one cheek and he had grotesque circles around both his eyes. Thick bandages covered one side of his head, where a "blunt instrument" had slammed up against his skull. They still weren't quite sure what had caused the injury. Neither the patrolmen nor the paramedics had found anything in the alley that looked like a weapon.

The lights outside the window blurred as tears filled her eyes. Emotions roiled through her—guilt, fear, a nagging sense of failure, desperate hope that Jason would recover. When she tried to focus on one feeling, another would rise up to swamp her. She couldn't ever remember being so confused, or so helpless.

For the first time in her adult life she found herself questioning her values. Since her very first afterschool job, she'd believed that hard work and a little talent would get her everything she wanted: financial security, a nice home, challenging work. And maybe a family someday, when she'd met all her other goals. Now she faced the bitter fact that she'd put so much emphasis on her job, on getting ahead, on sticking to her damned schedule, that it could have cost a child's life.

With wrenching uncertainty, Kate wondered if she would ever have children. How could any parent bear the pain of seeing their child lying so pale and still, stretched out in a wide hospital bed? Her stomach clenched again.

"Here, Kate, have some coffee."

She took the cup Dan offered and blinked back incipient tears, unable to speak through the tight constriction of her throat. Although his anger at her had dissipated, Kate still had difficulty facing him.

"And a couple of sweet rolls from the vending machine."

She shook her head, not trusting her voice.

"Go ahead. You need the energy. This could be a long night."

"I'm not hungry," she managed to whisper.

"Well, I am," Dan replied, tearing open the cellophane wrapper. "I didn't have anything on the plane tonight."

Kate frowned, remembering what she'd forgotten in her fear and panic over Jason. "Why did you come back early? I thought you had a meeting with some other police officials tomorrow, after the convention."

"I worked it in earlier." Dan gave her a long, slow look from under half-lowered lids. "I wanted to get home, to you."

Thick waves of guilt washed over her when she remembered how she'd been looking forward with delicious anticipation to welcoming him back. She'd even bought a sexy little teddy, with ribbons that conveniently tied at the shoulder. She'd imagined in excruciating detail just how he'd untie the ribbons. Those frivolous, silly plans seemed obscene against the stark reality of

Jason lying in a hospital bed. She swallowed fiercely, forcing tears back.

"Why didn't you call when you got in?" she asked.

"I did. There was no answer at your place, so I figured you were at work. I decided to stop by my office on the way home from the airport. Detective Alvarado heard about Jason and told me."

Dan took a sip of his coffee before continuing. "I got to the trauma center just after they brought him in. When he was stabilized and moved to ICU, I came for you."

Kate groaned, leaning her head back against the wall. "I'll never forgive myself for leaving him alone this morning, never!"

He looked at her steadily, sympathy in his eyes. "That's something you'll have to work through for yourself, Kate. I can't help you. I can only be here for you."

Dan's quiet words dropped like stones in the echoing well of her heart. Kate wanted to look away again, to avoid his steady, level look, but she wouldn't allow herself that small act of cowardice.

"Tell me what happened. Jason was fine when I talked to him at noon, and his foster mother was on her way to pick him up."

"He called her back to say he had a ride home and he'd see her later. She didn't start to get nervous until late afternoon. She finally notified the police early this evening."

"I wish she'd called me. I could have gone to look for him."

"She did. Several times. She only had your home phone number."

Dan's voice held no accusation, but Kate flinched. She took a deep breath, pushing her guilt down. Remorse and recriminations would come later, when she could berate herself in private. Right now she needed to focus on Jason.

"Do you have any idea who might have hurt him or why?"

Dan shook his head. "No. We'll have to wait and see what he says."

"My God, he's only a boy. Who could hurt a child like that?" Kate cried.

"There aren't any children on the street. Only losers and a

few who think they've won. I can name a hundred hurting souls who might try to relieve their pain by inflicting it on others.''

Kate stared at the man opposite her, hearing echoes of his own childhood in his quiet words. The minutes ticked away slowly as they sat, surrounded by the heavy stillness that descends just before dawn. A few yards away, medical personnel worked and talked in low voices at the ICU control station. Orderlies moved along the dimmed hallways, pushing rubber-wheeled carts.

Faint red streaks were just piercing the darkness of the night when the physician on duty came to look for Dan. Kate watched, shoulders hunched with tension, while the two men conferred quietly. She breathed a ragged sob at Dan's tired but relieved smile as he came back to her.

''Jason's going to be okay. He woke up for a few moments and knew his name, understood where he was. The doctor's confident he hasn't suffered any permanent damage.''

Kate bit her lip to hold back her tears. She nodded when he told her quietly it was time to go home. They walked out of the hospital into the graying half-light of morning and headed for Dan's car.

''What will happen to him now?'' Kate asked, her eyes on the slowly lightening street outside the window. In the window's reflection, she saw Dan give her a long look. Slowly she turned to face him.

''The Grants have washed their hands of him. Mrs. Grant told the caseworker tonight he was too much trouble and she wouldn't have him back in her home. She has other foster children to worry about.''

Kate felt a knife twist in her chest. Not only had she abandoned the boy, but as a result of her actions, he'd lost the only home he had.

''So where will he go, once he gets out of the hospital?''

''His caseworker will try to line up a new foster home and convince the judge to allow another placement.'' Dan glanced over at her. Even in the dim light, Kate could see the doubt and regret in his eyes.

"It'll be tough finding a family who'll want to take him in, with his record of running away and the break-ins. I'm afraid Jason's facing the county home."

"No! We can't just give up on him so easily."

Dan's brows raised slightly and he slanted her another, deliberate look.

Kate flushed. "*I* can't give up on him. I made a mistake and I'm not about to let Jason suffer for it for the rest of his life."

A surge of determination swept through her, blunting the sharp edges of pain.

"What do you think you can do?"

"I...I don't know yet," Kate admitted. "I'll have to talk to the caseworker. And to Jason, when he's able."

That would be the hardest part, Kate knew. But she had to try. She couldn't just shrug her shoulders and walk off, leaving the boy to face the consequences of her negligence.

She was still weighing her limited options when Dan brought her back to the lab to get her car, then followed her home. The golden dawn backlit the mountains behind her house as she swung into her driveway. Dan stopped her with a gentle hand on her arm when she would have led the way into the house.

"'Night, Kate." Dan leaned down to brush her lips lightly.

"Aren't you coming in?"

"No, I'm tired." He ran his knuckle down her cheek in soft, gentle strokes. "We both need some rest."

Kate bit her lip. What she needed was the feel of Dan's arms around her and his deep, soothing voice telling her everything would be all right. But everything was not all right, she reminded herself, and he looked even more exhausted than she felt. She nodded slowly.

"When will I see you?"

Dan smiled, the lines at the corners of his eyes crinkling. "Later. Get some sleep." He turned her around, gave her rear a gentle shove and pushed her toward Rico's ecstatic, wiggling body.

Kate closed the door and knelt down to take the grinning, slurping dog into her arms. Not for the first time, she understood why some people filled their homes and their lives with pets. Those eccentric old maids with all their cats and dogs weren't so dotty after all, she realized. Rico's warm, wet, uncritical love was incredibly soothing to her lacerated soul. She fell asleep, the dog draped across her feet at the bottom of the bed, just as the sun cleared the first mountain peak.

The next few days were as emotionally trying as she'd feared. She only saw Dan once, but he was distracted and only had time for a quick sandwich in a crowded coffee shop. She made two trips downtown to see Jason's caseworker, who was having little luck finding another foster home. At least the doctor was cheerful, assuring her the boy had suffered no permanent damage and predicting his complete recovery within a week.

She went daily to see Jason in the room he shared with two other boys. He shrugged off her halting apologies and kept his bruised face turned to the window during most of her visits, giving no sign that he was pleased or that he even cared whether she came to see him. He wouldn't talk about what happened— not to her or to Dan or to his caseworker. He'd hardly talk at all.

Kate refused to give up. She ignored his closed expression and drew up a chair beside his bed to fill him in on the growing numbers of race entrants, Rico's latest antics and even, in desperation, her mother's frequent calls to inquire about his progress.

Nothing seemed to penetrate, however, until she stopped by after work one night. As she was getting out of her car, her eyes fell on the little laptop computer in the passenger seat. Thoughtfully, she eyed the gray plastic case. It worked once, it might work again, she thought grimly.

She plunked the computer down on the tray beside Jason's bed and plugged it in. After some coaxing, she got him and the other boys in the room into a bloodthirsty quest to retrieve an abducted galactic princess. For the first time, Jason's battered face lost some of its tightness as he became immersed in the game.

"Here, keep this with you," Kate told him at the end of visiting hours. She closed the case and stored the little computer in the stand beside his bed.

"Aren't you afraid it'll get stolen?" Jason asked, with unconscious irony.

"No," Kate told him, smiling. "And I expect you to have Princess Tessala back and the whole crew off on the next level of adventure when I come tomorrow."

"You don't have to come every day." Jason picked at the blue cord cover, not meeting her eyes.

"Do you want me to?"

The boy shrugged, head still bent.

"Then I'll come," Kate told him. She gathered her purse and headed for the door. "'Night, Jason."

"'Night, Kate."

She almost missed his muttered goodbye. She turned back, but the boy was already settled down under the covers, his shoulder hunched away from her. Kate stood for a moment in the door, staring at the pitifully small mound he made in the wide bed. Her jaw clenched. She'd be damned if she would allow the bureaucracy to send this boy to an institution. She fumbled in her purse for her calling card and headed for a phone.

Three days later Dan sat beside an agitated Kate in the cavernous, upstairs airport lounge. He watched her fidget with her purse strap while a throng of arriving and departing travelers flowed around them.

"Are you sure you can handle this, Kate?"

"No, I'm not sure, but I'm going to give it one helluva try."

Dan felt his heart lurch. This was the Kate he loved, this fierce, determined creature. In the last couple days he'd worked through his disappointment in her for leaving Jason alone, just as she had worked through her own guilt and bleak despair. Everyone made mistakes. He'd certainly made his share. But Kate was going to do something about hers. She'd detailed her plan in a breathless phone call only this morning, asking—no demanding his support.

With characteristic stubbornness, she'd bullied Judge Chavez into a special hearing this afternoon, in just a few hours. Now she waited with unconcealed impatience for the next piece to fall in place. Dan bit back a grin, wondering if she'd programmed the whole damn scheme, complete with milestones and color-coded objectives, into her computer.

"I hope the plane isn't late," she said, worrying. "The judge wasn't too thrilled with making a special trip in this afternoon."

She stood and began to pace back and forth, in short, restless steps. "Are you sure Detective Alvarado will get Jason there?"

"Yes, I'm sure."

"I just hope the caseworker gets the time of the hearing right. I left two messages on her recorder."

"She'll be there."

"Dr. Henderson assured me he could slip out for—"

Dan reached out a lazy hand and pulled her down beside him. "The doc will be there. Calm down, Kate. You're making me nervous with all that pacing."

When she smiled at him, Dan felt a tight knot begin to unravel in his gut. He hadn't seen her smile in days, nor had he realized how much he'd missed it.

"If that's nervous, I'd hate to see you relaxed. You'd probably slide to the floor in one huge, boneless blob."

"I'm saving my energy for—"

"There she is!"

Kate jumped up and ran toward a group of passengers just passing through the control point. Dan watched her throw her arms around a small, high-cheeked woman whose fading red hair still bore traces of her daughter's bright mahogany. The two women hugged and kissed and stood chattering while waves of passengers eddied around them. Dan waited patiently until Kate clutched her mother's arm and tugged her over to him. The older woman lifted one brow as she took his measure, then dismissed his courteous "Mrs. O'Sullivan" with a wave of her hand.

"Call me Mary Catherine. We might as well start as we mean to go on. From what my Kathleen *hasn't* told me in her calls these last few weeks, I'd bet my grandmother's prayer book you're well beyond the formal stage by now.''

Dan laughed at Kate's smothered groan. ''Good enough, Mary Catherine. And you're right, we're well beyond formal. We've passed downright informal, in fact.''

''Oh, for Pete's sake, come on, you two. You can discuss the precise stage of our...relationship later.'' Kate herded them both toward the escalator. ''We have to claim mother's luggage and get her some lunch before the hearing.''

Dan dutifully retrieved Mary Catherine's bags, then settled the women in the airport's lavish restaurant.

''I really appreciate your coming so quickly, Mother.'' Kate barely got the words out around a mouth full of warm sopapilla slathered in honey. Dan handed her another napkin as she licked the sticky goo off her fingers.

''It's not as if I had other, unbreakable commitments, dear.'' Mary Catherine picked up one corner of the huge, puffed pastry and stared at it doubtfully.

''Go ahead, they're wonderful,'' Kate told her, swallowing the last chewy chunk. She reached for her glass of ice tea, then stopped, a slight frown marring the line of her brow. ''I thought you were busy with your volunteer work and church activities. And at the senior center.''

The older woman shrugged, taking tentative bites of the sopapilla.

Kate's frown deepened. ''You're living in one of the best-run retirement centers in California. They pride themselves on all their activities, from golf to chess tournaments to Jazzercise.''

Mary Catherine gave up on the dough square and set it carefully on her half-full plate. ''Those are just time fillers, darling. Not quite like working full-time and cooking and keeping my own house.''

The older woman's eyes, so like her daughter's in color, twinkled as she turned to Dan. ''Kate bought me this beautiful condominium and insisted I retire when she got her first promotion. I tried to get her to spend the bonus on herself, but she had her list of 'to-do's' all laid out and I was at the top of the list.''

Dan laughed. "I'm familiar with your daughter's determination to proceed according to plan. She's got a master schedule for the next twenty years."

"And I'll bet you're throwing her schemes all out of kilter, aren't you?"

Mary Catherine grinned at Dan, and they both turned to the subject of their conversation, sitting between them in frowning silence. Dan could see confusion, and a hint of hurt, clouding Kate's expressive eyes.

"I thought you were happy there, Mother. I...I thought you'd be thrilled to leave your twenty-hour days behind and enjoy life a little."

"I am, darling, I am." Her mother reached over to pat her hand. "But it's good to be needed. It's good to have *you* need me again. That's why I was so quick to jump on a plane when you called. Now tell me about this boy, Jason."

Dan watched Kate struggle to throw off the doubt still lingering on her face. He sat back, only half listening while she recounted the boy's history. Obviously, her mother's comments bothered her. Dan wondered if she was beginning to realize that even the best-laid plans were fallible. That not everyone lived their life according to a preplanned agenda.

Less than an hour later, they walked up the steps to the county courthouse. Dan stayed in the background when they entered the judge's chambers, where the informal hearing would be held. While waiting for the judge's arrival, Kate introduced her mother to Jason and his caseworker. Dan could see the doubt and fear and a pitiful hope in the boy's blue eyes as he looked up at the two women. They all rose as Judge Chavez entered.

"Ms. O'Sullivan, you've petitioned the court for temporary custody of Jason Stone. Do you really understand the magnitude of the responsibility you're requesting?"

Kate stood and met the judge's hard look with a characteristic tilt to her chin. "Probably not. I've not been responsible for anyone but myself for years, until I agreed to sponsor Jason. And I didn't do a very good job at that."

She took a deep breath. "Judge Chavez, I know you don't have much reason to trust me after I let Jason down, but I assure you it won't happen again. I want to rectify my mistake."

"I hope you're not toying with a child's life just to assuage some misplaced sense of guilt, Ms. O'Sullivan."

Kate stiffened at the sharp tone. "No, ma'am. I'm not using Jason to excuse my negligence. But since my actions did contribute directly to his problems, I want to help solve them."

"Temporary custody won't solve his difficulties."

"It will buy him some time to recover completely and be placed in another, hopefully more supportive, foster home."

"What makes you think you're qualified to see to a child's needs?" Julia Chavez pushed her glasses up on her nose and leaned forward, her gaze sharp and stern.

"I'm not. But my mother flew in from California this morning and will stay with us for the duration. She's more than qualified, as I can personally attest."

Mary Catherine O'Sullivan stood beside her daughter. Viewing them from behind, Dan saw identical stiff spines and an almost palpable aura of determination radiating from them both.

Judge Chavez studied them both for a long moment, then turned to the boy.

"What about you, Jason? I saw from your caseworker's report you still won't tell us what happened to cause your hospitalization. What assurance do I have that you won't abuse Ms. O'Sullivan's hospitality or run away again?"

Jason swallowed. "I won't."

"How can I believe that? You ran away from the Grants, twice."

The boy's face paled, making his fading bruises stand out in stark relief. He struggled for words, but could only manage, "I won't."

"Will you tell us what happened? Who hurt you?"

Kate bit her lip so hard she tasted the faint, metallic tincture of blood. With determined obstinacy, Jason had refused to discuss the incident. She was afraid the judge would hold his stubborn silence against him.

"Please, Judge Chavez, the doctor has submitted a private opinion on Jason's injuries." Kate leaned forward in her eagerness. "He thinks—"

"I've read the report, Ms. O'Sullivan."

Dan lifted one hand to stroke his mustache. He'd talked with Judge Chavez himself earlier, voicing his own opinion of what might have happened. He and the doctor believed the boy had somehow run afoul of his old gang. The hematoma was severe, but not as severe as if he'd been attacked by an adult intending serious harm.

"The juvenile probation officer has also submitted a report," Kate offered.

The woman behind the broad wooden desk gave a faint smile at Kate's determined persistence. "I've read that, also, Ms. O'Sullivan." She sat back in her high leather chair and surveyed the assembled group.

"Obviously, you're all sincere in wanting to help Jason." She leveled a steady look at Kate, still standing beside her mother. "My head tells me you don't really grasp the difficulties associated with taking a child into your home, but my heart says you've already learned one very valuable lesson the hard way. Children demand time and attention. Can you spare time from your work and your other interests?"

Julia Chavez's dry tone and bland glance at Dan weren't lost on anyone in the room. Mary Catherine's brows rose as she looked at her daughter's flushed face, and Dan knew they'd have some explaining to do later.

"Yes, ma'am," Kate managed through stiff lips.

"All right," the judge said briskly, coming to a decision. "I'll ask Welfare to expedite your background check and psychological profile. Assuming the reports are positive, you'll have temporary custody for sixty days. You'll report to the caseworker weekly, and continue your community-service program."

Kate hurried over to Jason as the judge rose and gathered her papers. From the back of the room, Dan watched as she held out her hand and, after a moment's hesitation, Jason slipped his into hers.

Julia Chavez turned back. "Incidentally, my husband tells me you and Jason have done yeoman work on the race. He couldn't have managed without you both."

Kate and Jason shared a wide smile. Dan strolled forward, took Mary Catherine's arm and escorted her across the room. "Come on, troops. I think this calls for a celebration. How about hot dogs and hamburgers at your place?"

"Some celebration," Kate laughed.

"I like hot dogs," Jason volunteered shyly. "With chili."

"And onions," Mary Catherine added, taking his other hand.

"Dripping with mustard and relish." Dan smacked his lips.

"Yech!" Kate looked at the circle of grinning faces and relented. "All right, all right, hot dogs it is. If there are any left. Rico likes them, too, you know." With that parting shot, she led the way home.

"You cook a mean chili dog, woman."

Kate sighed contentedly and snuggled down into Dan's arms as best she could on the rattan patio lounge. Although roomy and comfortably padded, it wasn't made for two people, let alone two generously sized people.

"They were pretty good, weren't they? Not that I can claim full credit."

In fact, she'd barely been allowed in the kitchen. Dan had decided to instruct a still-shy Jason in the fine art of grilling hot dogs over the Jenn-Air. Kate and her mother had been relegated to onion chopping and chili-cooking duty. Kate had stepped in to save the last half-dozen wieners after Dan "accidentally" dropped two to the ever-alert Rico and Jason had burnt his to blackened cinders. Just the way he liked them, he solemnly declared.

Kate turned her head on Dan's shoulder, listening to the faint call of coyotes sounding a distant counterpoint to the soft, lilting sounds of Mary Catherine's favorite tape of Irish ballads. They'd taken Jason back to the hospital. He'd move in with Kate within the next few days, according to Judge Chavez. Her mother had excused herself for the night, claiming a need to unpack. Kate and Dan had retired to the patio for the first private moment in days. If being poked in the back every few minutes by a large, wet nose could be called private, Kate amended, pushing Rico away once more. She propped herself up on one arm to survey the complacent male beside her.

"I almost cried when Jason smiled at me tonight. Did you see him wince? It hurt his bruised face just to smile."

"It'll take time for him to recover from his hurts, both inside and out. Don't expect too much, Kate." Dan tightened his arms, drawing her close. "Don't do too much, either. For Jason, I mean."

"Why not? He deserves some care and attention. I owe it to him."

Dan curled a finger under Kate's chin, tilting her head up until she could see the moonlight tinting his eyes to silvery gray.

"You'll only hurt him more if you get too close to him. This is a temporary arrangement, remember? Don't spoil or lavish too much love on a boy who'll be going to another foster home when you leave. If he's lucky."

Kate sighed and nodded. "I know you're right, but I hate this uncertainty about Jason's future. I'm going to make sure he's happily settled before I leave."

Her voice trailed off. The thought of her leaving hung between them, like a shadow. Hesitantly, Kate looked up at Dan's face. The moonlight highlighted its lean planes and angles and glinted in his eyes.

Kate knew now she loved that face, and the man that went with it. Although she wasn't sure when in the past weeks she'd fallen for him. Maybe it was when he'd fed her and Jason pizza in the sun-drenched park. Or when he'd tumbled her into bed with laughing eagerness. But when he'd taken her hand that night at the hospital and shared her pain and fear for Jason, he'd become part of her somehow.

Slowly, her eyes drinking in the stark lines of his face, Kate lifted one finger to trace the line of his chin, then test the thick softness of his mustache. Her finger brushed back and forth gently, tentatively, only to still in startled surprise.

The high, pure tones of a tenor drifted out across the still air, filling the night with the hauntingly beautiful strains of "Danny Boy."

Kate's finger left Dan's mustache to trail slowly down his throat. She stroked the strong column, feeling his pulse beating sure and steady. Lowering her head, she placed her lips against the pulse, drinking in his blood's rhythm. She opened her lips and licked the warm skin, savoring his taste.

Above her, Dan gave a low groan and tightened his arms. The rattan creaked ominously as he pulled her up until her lips brushed his own.

"'Oh, Danny boy, I love you so.'" Kate's breathless whisper kept time with the tenor.

He pulled back, studying her face as if trying to decide whether she meant it.

"Kate, I—"

Whatever he was about to say was lost when a loud, mournful howl suddenly filled the night air. Both Dan and Kate jumped, nearly rolling off the lounge as Rico joined in the chorus.

Under her splayed fingertips, Kate felt the laughter rumbling in Dan's chest.

"I love you, too," he managed between chuckles.

Kate sat up, her soft, languorous mood dissolving. "Could you say that again, without laughing?"

A particularly loud, distinctly unmelodic yowl rent the air.

"No," Dan gasped. Shoulders shaking, he pushed himself off the lounge and pulled Kate to her feet. Rico's enthusiastic refrain drowned out Kate's indignant protest.

While dog and tenor soared to a dramatic finale, Dan kissed her, long and hard and thoroughly.

When he lifted his head, Kate saw with satisfaction that at least the blasted man wasn't laughing anymore. His eyes blazed with a hunger that matched her own.

"Dan, we need to…"

"Yes, Kate, we need to. But not tonight, with your mother just arrived."

"We need to talk," she ground out.

"I know, sweetheart. And we will. But not now. Not when you've got your contract hanging over you and your mother to settle and Jason to care for. And Rico to quiet."

Laughter welled up in his chest once more as the dog joined in a new ballad with unrestrained gusto.

Nine

If the pace of Kate's life was hectic before, it soon became positively whirlwind. Or maybe chaotic was the more correct description, she amended, racing to work weeks later. Impatiently, she wove through what the locals considered rush hour, but Southern Californians would deem practically deserted streets.

School had started and Kate would get up early, fix breakfast, take Jason to his old school across town, then dash to work. Mary Catherine would pick him up in the afternoons and fix dinner for them all, Dan included, whenever he or Kate weren't working late, which was more often than not.

Twice, Kate had met with Jason's caseworker, who was still trying to place the boy. Once the woman had taken him to an interview, and brought him back quiet and sullen. It seemed the prospective foster parents had been turned off by Jason's record of running away and his less-than-cooperative attitude.

Kate sighed and pulled into her parking space, hurrying across the lot to the lab. Time was running out. There were only two more weeks left on her contract, three more on the lease for the house. She had to get Jason settled and sort out her relationship with Dan. And to think she'd come to Albuquerque just a few short months ago, completely unencumbered, minus boy and mother and dog and...

"We've done it, Kate!"

Trish's excited yell greeted her as she walked into the computer center. "The last data base is up and running!"

With a surge of excitement, Kate leaned over Trish's shoulder to scan the previous night's results. They'd taken the lab's last major mainframe down the night before to migrate its data base. Sure enough, the program had run smoothly, without a single glitch. This was it, Kate thought, the last major milestone.

"We're two days ahead of schedule!" one of the engineers exclaimed.

"Let's get these runs done," Kate smiled. "As soon as we certify the results and get them reviewed by the air force, there's a big bonus in this for everyone. The rest of the work is just cleanup."

The entire team hustled for the rest of the day. In the midst of their frenetic activity, Trish called Kate to the phone.

"Kate O'Sullivan speaking."

"Katie, it's Jessica. I just got word. We're in the final round of bidders on the UCLA project!"

Kate drew in a sharp breath as she listened to her part-time office manager/secretary/personal assistant babble on. The thought of leaving Albuquerque to begin her next project should have thrown Kate into a fever of anticipation. Instead she felt an incipient panic. Events were moving too fast on the job and not fast enough in her personal life. The only time she and Dan had been together lately was when they could snatch a few hours between appointments and work and the demands of her family.

A flush stained Kate's face as she thought of their rare times together. It was amazing what that man could cram into such short periods. His lovemaking got more adventurous with every stolen moment. Kate banished the vivid images before her blush melted her makeup, mumbled a response to her assistant, and went back to work.

As a reward for their efforts, Kate sent everyone home early that afternoon. Heading for her car sometime later, Kate felt a curious sense of freedom. Where before she'd always lived for her work, now she was glad they were over the hump. The long days and nights were behind them. Now she could devote some time to herself and Jason. And to Dan!

When Kate arrived home, the house was deserted. Dan had taken Jason to a ball game and Mary Catherine was indulging her passion for bingo at one of the Indian pueblos with another aficionado she'd met at the supermarket. Only Rico remained to greet her. He padded alongside while she stripped off her clothes and headed for the hot tub, his big body stretching out in blissful slumber on the wooden deck.

To her surprise, the tub failed to work its soothing magic. Kate stirred restlessly in the warm, bubbling water, fingers tapping the slick fiberglass rim. What was the matter with her? A few months ago, she would have enjoyed the peace and serenity of the night. She would've relaxed, wine in hand, eyes on the soft evening sky, congratulating herself on being able to afford such quiet, soothing luxury. Now the house seemed too still, the luxury too sterile. Kate laid her head back against the rim, finally recognizing the problem. She was lonely.

Disgruntled, Kate climbed out of the tub and dried off. She might as well get some work done, since she couldn't seem to relax. Flipping on her computer, she forced herself to work on the UCLA proposal.

She was still at the laptop when Mary Catherine let herself in some time later. With a welcome smile, Kate turned off the computer and went to greet her mother.

"Any luck?"

"No." The older woman plopped herself down on the sofa in disgust and lifted one leg, then the other, onto the magazine-strewn coffee table. "I was only two spaces away from a thousand-dollar jackpot, too."

"Hang in there, Mother," Kate said encouragingly. She joined her mother on the couch, propping her bare feet up companionably beside Mary Catherine's sneakered ones.

"Remember when you used to get excited about winning five-dollar jackpots? Father Shaw always complained you had the devil's own luck. Maybe you'll get lucky here, too, before you leave.''

Mary Catherine laughed and rested her head on the back of the sofa. "I remember. Those little jackpots were real bonanzas to us then, weren't they? I think I bought your school shoes one entire year with my bingo winnings.''

Kate reached over and took her mother's hand. "You know, I never heard you complain once about how hard those times were.''

"What good would it have done to complain?" Her mother smiled. "Besides, I had you to love, and your grandmother helped as much as she could.''

Kate laid her head back beside her mother's and stared at the ceiling thoughtfully. "It took me a long time to forgive my father for running off and leaving you to care for both of us alone.''

The older woman turned, her hair rustling against the soft fabric of the couch. "Are you sure you forgave him?''

"Yes—at least I think so. Why?''

"You work so hard, Kate. You haven't taken time in your life for anything except school and work. It's as if financial success has been your only joy in life.''

"I saw what marrying young and being left to raise a child by yourself did to you, Mother. Is it so wrong to want a little financial independence? To not have to depend on any man? On anyone but myself?''

"No, of course it's not wrong. But there are more important things in life than money. I'd hoped you discovered that when you and Charles became engaged.''

Kate grimaced up at the ceiling. "Charles cared even more for financial security than I did. He wanted to make sure wife number two was making plenty before he ditched wife number one.''

"Well, you're better off without him," Mary Catherine declared. "Now, this one, this Dan, is a different story.''

Mary Catherine straightened and a determined look filled her eyes.

"You need to hold on to this one.''

"I think so, too," Kate agreed softy. "But we can't seem to get around to resolving the future."

"That's because you're enjoying the present too much! Instead of using every hour you can steal away to jump in the sack, go see a priest."

"Mother!" Kate's laughing protest didn't faze Mary Catherine.

"Don't 'Mother' me, girl! I'd be more worried if you *weren't* enjoying a man like that."

Kate sputtered with laughter while her mother returned to her favorite theme. "You're thirty-one. It's long past time you were married. I want to be a grandmother!"

"Gimme a break, Mom. There's a slight matter of juggling our careers and finding some time to work things out. Besides, he hasn't asked me."

"Well, work on him."

"I'm working, I'm working," Kate protested.

Her loving mother snorted in exasperation. "Kathleen Brigit O'Sullivan, you're not the woman I think you are if you can't get a proposal out of a man who's as nuts about you as that man is."

Dan and Jason arrived home from the ball game just as the sun dipped toward the mountain peaks. They decided to work off the pent-up energy from the game in a quick run while Kate and Mary Catherine ordered pizza.

Kate smiled as they walked out on the patio, Jason in the baggy sweats she'd bought him, Dan in the disreputable cutoffs he now kept at her house. While Kate had been so wrapped up in her work, Dan had invited Jason to join him on his evening runs whenever his own work schedule would follow. To Kate's surprise, Jason had agreed. She supposed it was some kind of male bonding thing. Whatever it was, they'd fallen into a routine, jogging along the popular dirt trail that wound along the base of the mountains, an ecstatic Rico bounding ahead.

"Sure you don't want to join us?" Dan asked, one hand lifting up to brush her cheek.

"No way." Kate laughed. "Huffing and puffing and sweating along a dirt trail is not my idea of fun. I can think of a lot better things to do to my body."

"Mmm, so can I," he murmured low, for her ears only.

Kate shooed him off. "Go run. When you get back we'll have pizza. And then we need to talk."

Dan's brows rose at her determined tone.

"We finished the supercomputer integration today. The rest is just cleanup."

A satisfied gleam leapt into his eyes and he took a quick step toward her. Jason's shy voice halted him.

"That's great, Kate. Did you get the bonus?"

"Yep." She smiled. "The pizza's on me tonight. Go run, you two, and work up an appetite."

Dan drew sharp, clean air into his lungs as he set an easy pace beside Jason. The boy was running smoothly, his baggy sweats flattened against thin legs. Rico was in dog heaven, stopping frequently to sniff at interesting piles along the popular path, then charging wildly to catch up.

Dan kept his eye on his two charges, but his mind was on the talk he and Kate would have tonight. He hadn't wanted to put any more pressure on her during these past hectic weeks. She had enough strain with trying to reach Jason and working through the last, critical phase of her project. Now that she was in the home stretch at work, much of the pressure she'd been under was gone. Although Jason wasn't set yet, the caseworker had called yesterday to tell them she had a good prospect. Now was the time for Dan to make his move.

Dan dodged a delicate tumbleweed drifting across the path, thinking about Kate's success on the project, remembering her timetable. Her business was off and running. The next job had something to do with a new astronomy lab at UCLA and a batch of scientific computers. Could he ask her to give up, or at least modify, her dream for him? Could he alter the frantic pace of his job for her? Damn straight, he could.

Absently, he watched Rico's joyous pursuit of a scurrying

mouse. Strange how dynamic personal relationships could be. A few weeks ago, he'd been content just to break through Kate's preoccupied focus on work and discover the sensual, passionate woman behind the computer. Now, passion wasn't enough. Now, he wanted commitment. And companionship. And love—not just sex. He wanted a future with Kate, one they'd build together. One that didn't include eighteen-hour days, seven days a week for him and six-month absences for her.

His instincts told him that's what Kate wanted, as well. He just wasn't quite sure she knew it yet. That uncertainty had held him back, kept him from asking outright for a commitment. Dan grimaced at his own gutlessness, and at the realization that his hesitancy these past weeks stemmed as much from his failed first marriage as from any nobility on his part. He didn't have a good track record at combining careers and dreams and the business of everyday life. He wanted Kate to achieve her goals, to satisfy her drive to succeed before he made his move. He wanted her to realize that he could provide her with as much pleasure in life as Phase Four or Five ever would.

But time was running out. They needed to sit down and discuss their future—calmly, rationally. He knew Kate loved him. Now he'd just have to show her that marriage was the logical next step in their relationship.

That's it, he told himself. He'd keep his zipper zipped and his mind clear. Before the night was over, he'd convince Kate they could share their dreams and their lives.

Pleased with his calm determination, Dan herded his two charges back toward the house. The sun was just sinking behind the mesa to the west, and darkness would make it difficult to run on the rock and tumbleweed-strewn path.

"Come on, guys, let's go in. The pizza's probably here. I can smell the pepperoni already."

If the pizza had arrived, they couldn't smell it when they entered the house. When Dan came through the dark kitchen, he noted the absence of any aroma, pepperoni or otherwise. Frowning, he headed for the softly lit living room. He expected to find

Kate and Mary Catherine relaxing on the couch. Instead, he found Kate straining against the hold of a muscular, dark-shirted man.

Every fighting instinct, honed by years on the streets and in the marines, kicked into overdrive. In the space of a heartbeat, Dan noted the open French doors behind the twisting pair, scanned the man from head to toe for any signs of a weapon and attacked. He launched himself across the room, Rico snarling furiously at his side.

"What the—ummph!"

"Dan!"

"Grrrrrr…"

Kate's startled cry mingled with the man's grunt of pain and Rico's ferocious snarls. Dan felt a savage satisfaction when his fist connected with a midsection for the second time and the assailant went down. Planting one foot on either side of the man's body, Dan grabbed a handful of the dark shirt and pulled the intruder two feet off the carpet. He raised his fist to strike again.

All hell broke loose around him. Even to a man trained in riot-control procedures, the ensuing pandemonium was startling.

"Dan, no! Wait!"

"Heavens above, what's going on?"

"Are you crazy?"

Kate grabbed frantically at his upraised arm just as Mary Catherine came running from the back of the house. He could barely hear their shouts over Rico's furious barking. His hand tightened when the man below him scrambled backward, trying to break his hold. With a grunt, Dan heaved him to his feet.

Hauling him over to the wall, he pushed the man's face and hands up against it. He used one foot to spread his legs and ran a hand down his body to search for weapons. Rico danced around them both excitedly, his ear-splitting barks bouncing off the walls. Satisfied that the man was unarmed, Dan backed away and let him turn slowly to face the room.

"Rico, shut up!" Kate grabbed the dog's collar with one hand to haul him back.

"What's happening?" A confused, scared-looking Jason hovered at the edge of the living room.

"That's what I'd like to know," Mary Catherine exclaimed over the dog's excited barking. She put a protective arm around the boy, hauling him close against her.

"It's all a mis—" Kate began.

"Who the hell do you think—" the man sputtered.

"Be quiet!"

Everyone in the room jumped at Dan's harsh command. Satisfied he had their attention, he moderated both his tone and the direction of his command. "Here, boy. Sit!"

"Thank heavens," Kate gasped when the barking finally stopped. She took Dan's arm again and tried to pull him away. He stepped back a few paces but kept his eyes on the man who, very prudently, remained against the wall.

"Are you okay, Kate?"

"Yes." She gulped. "Dan—"

"You sure?"

"Yes!"

He flashed her a quick look. He saw relief, exasperation and the beginnings of amusement in her eyes, but no fear.

Frowning, he turned back to the man still splayed against the wall. For the first time he noticed that the dark shirt was a well-tailored, designer edition. The blond head above the shirt was just as well tended, with a tan that deepened his angry blue eyes. His hair somehow managed to look stylish even after the manhandling.

"Who the hell are you?" Dan snapped.

"I'm Kate's fiancé. Who the hell are you?"

Dan stepped back and surveyed the man through narrowed eyes.

"I'm her lover," he drawled. "And the man she's going to marry."

A stunned silence descended over the room, to be broken long moments later by Mary Catherine's delighted chuckle.

"You did it, Kate!"

Ten

Kate barely heard her mother's gleeful exclamation. Her stunned gaze locked on the two men before her, still eyeing each other with a bristling male animosity that was totally outside her field of experience.

"What is this, Kate?" Charles accused angrily. "You didn't mention any 'lover' in our little discussion a few minutes ago."

"You…you didn't give me much of a chance to mention anything."

Kate's eyes strayed to Dan, standing with arms folded, watching her from hooded eyes. When Charles pushed himself from the wall, she forced her attention back to her indignant fiancé. Ex-fiancé!

"Well, you sure didn't waste much time in Albuquerque," he said with a sneer. "And after all I went through to start divorce proceedings! I thought you'd wait for me, Kate."

"I guess you thought wrong, pal." Dan unfolded his arms.

"Why don't you just butt out?"

Kate swallowed as the two men squared off at each other again, fists clenched. Rico's warning growl sounded a low, ominous tattoo, raising the hairs on her neck. Hastily, she moved between them.

"Charles, please, you'd better go. I'll...I'll call you tomorrow, at the hotel."

"Like hell you will!"

Kate blinked at Dan's snarl. Somehow, this business of being fought over by two attractive men wasn't living up to all her youthful romantic fantasies. It was unsettling. Downright uncomfortable, in fact. Kate's own temper began to rise. She took a firm grip on her composure, ignored Dan's thunderous scowl and hustled Charles out of the living room toward the front door.

"I'll call you," she told him, pushing him out into the night. With a sigh of relief, she leaned back against the door. Ruefully, she surveyed the ring of faces watching her with varying degrees of motherly glee, childish bewilderment and pure, unadulterated male possessiveness.

"We need to discuss your visitor," Dan growled, breaking the silence.

"I'd rather discuss your announcement," Kate told him sweetly.

"Me, too!" Mary Catherine added. Her wide grin turned to outright laughter as both Kate and Dan swung toward her. Consternation was plainly written on his face, an outright plea on hers. "But I guess I can wait until later to hear all the details. Come on, Jason. Let's wait for our pizza in the kitchen."

Kate waited until the kitchen door swung shut behind them before moving to the still, silent Dan. She stopped a few paces away, trying to read the expression in his glittering eyes. To her surprise, and relief, it was one of rueful laughter.

Dan reached out and pulled her into his arms. She felt an answering smile spread across her face as she leaned back in the strong circle of his embrace. Her breath caught as his hazel eyes turned smoky with desire and an indefinable emotion that made her heart thump painfully.

"I think someone mentioned something about marriage?" she prompted.

Dan grinned down at her. "Seems there are a number of men around here tonight with marriage on their minds. You want to fill me in on this Charles character?"

"Not really. He's history."

"He doesn't seem to realize that," Dan said dryly.

"Well, I was trying to make it clear when you, uh, flattened him."

Dan tightened his arms, narrowing the space between them. "I have this thing about seeing my woman in another man's arms. Old-fashioned, I admit, but now you know."

Kate slid her hands up his chest to curl them around his neck. Her hips settled intimately against the cradle of his thighs, discovering the rampant, insistent desire under the thin fabric of his cutoffs.

"Now I know," she whispered.

"What do you say we skip the pizza? I find I'm hungry for something else entirely."

"So when is the wedding? And where?" Mary Catherine perched on a rawhide stool and surveyed her daughter across the wide expanse of the kitchen counter. "Here, or in L.A.? Kathleen, are you listening to me?"

Kate looked up from the oranges she was feeding into the electric juicer. Noticing her mother's impatient glare, she turned the machine off. "Sorry, Mother, I didn't hear you."

"You've been off in la-la land since you got out of bed this morning! You promised a few details when you breezed out of here last night, young lady."

"We didn't quite get around to specifics," Kate told her with a sheepish grin.

"Well, of all the…!" Mary Catherine shook her head. "Don't you know you have to strike while the iron—not to mention the man—is hot?"

Kate burst out laughing at the total disgust on her mother's face. "I had enough trouble explaining Charles and soothing Dan's ruffled feathers to pin him down to the exact hour."

"Considering the fact that you didn't get back here until almost dawn, I think you could have settled the time, the place and the entire guest list," her mother rejoined tartly.

"We will," Kate promised.

"It's not like you have months to plan all this, you know." Mary Catherine's voice was almost grumpy. "Your lease is up in a couple of weeks, you've still got Jason to settle and you're spending every free moment lately on this darn marathon."

Kate sighed. "I know, I know. I've been thinking about Dan and me for weeks. Yet now that we've actually made the commitment, I can't seem to focus on details."

"And this is the woman who has her life all laid out in five-year increments! You better get with it, girl. The two of you have some major decisions to work out."

"The big decisions are the easiest," Kate said confidently, pouring them each a glass of juice.

"Oh? Like where you're going to live? And what you'll do about your business?"

"I can work out of Albuquerque as easily as L.A., so the business is no problem. And there are plenty of nice houses available here in this neighborhood. I called an agent on a couple of them."

"What does Dan say about your business?"

"We haven't actually discussed it, but he's supportive of my career goals."

Mary Catherine frowned. "A home and how you operate your business are major decisions, Kate. I think you and Dan should sit down and sort through them together."

"We will," she promised again, still too wrapped up in the delicious thought of marriage to Dan to worry about the details.

Her mother gave her daughter one last, exasperated look and climbed down off the stool. "You will let me know when you finally decide on a date, I hope!"

"You'll be the first, I promise." Kate laughed. "Now let's go get dressed and then unglue Jason from his keyboard. I promised to have us all down at the race center by noon to help with the last-minute registrations. Wear something comfortable."

The race headquarters was a scene of cheerful, controlled chaos on this day before the big event. Kate set Jason and Mary Catherine to work sorting through the hundreds of last-minute applications. She herself joined a rank of volunteer hackers who were busily inputting data into the donated computers set up for the occasion. Eager participants and harried officials hustled around stacks of boxes, racks of bright vests to be worn by road guides and piles of T-shirts. The shirts came in every size from toddler to extra-extra large, and all proclaimed this year's Duke City Marathon the best yet.

Kate was showing a new volunteer how to use the scanner when Jason's caseworker called to ask if she could slip away for a few moments. Leaving Jason and Mary Catherine surrounded by a busy, laughing crowd of kids and indulgent parents, she headed downtown. During the short drive through the deserted streets, Kate was torn by conflicting emotions. She hoped that Mrs. Harris had found a good foster home for Jason, yet felt a confused reluctance to let him go. Somehow, the idea of sending Jason to someone else's home held less and less appeal.

"Thanks for coming in, Kate," the young woman greeted her. "I know you've been busy with the marathon, but we don't have much time left to work out a solution for Jason."

"No problem," Kate assured her, taking a seat in the small, neat office. In the weeks they'd worked together, Kate had grown to respect and admire Elizabeth Harris. A young mother and dedicated social worker, Liz put her heart and soul into her work. She took a personal interest in every one of her cases. She knew almost as well as Kate how Jason was doing in school, what his favorite computer game was and how his fears and insecurities had turned him into a quiet, contained, solemn youngster.

"I think I've found the perfect home." Liz pulled a thick folder toward her and opened it to scan an ink-filled form. "The Kents came down and applied for foster-parent status a few days ago. The psychological test results just came back, as well as the background checks. They're all good."

Liz sorted through the papers and pulled out the profile she'd compiled on the prospective foster parents. Most of the information was confidential, of course, but she could tell Kate enough to reassure her Jason would be going to a good home.

"The Kents are a middle-aged couple with three children of

their own. Their youngest son just started high school and they want to share their home and their love with a child who needs help. I talked to all of their children. The boy in high school is outgoing and well adjusted, no reported problems of any kind. There's also a daughter at UNM and another married daughter in town with two children of her own. The whole family has a very positive focus. They're just the kind of family to give Jason the long-term stability he needs in these critical years.''

Kate listened to Liz's account with a sinking feeling in her stomach. She'd wanted desperately to settle Jason in just such a stable environment. So why did the thought make her insides churn?

''I hate to spring this on you on such short notice, but would it be possible for Jason to meet with them this afternoon? I visited them yesterday and discussed his background. They're interested, but are leaving for a long-planned vacation on Sunday. If I'm going to wrap this up in the next couple weeks, I'll have to start the paperwork while they're gone.''

Kate swallowed the lump in her throat. ''Sure, we can make it. What time, and where?''

It was a quiet, subdued trio that met Dan for dinner at their favorite Mexican restaurant that evening.

''What's with everyone?'' Dan asked, sliding into the booth beside Kate. ''Why so glum? Did your computer program bomb and you lost a couple thousand marathoners?''

Kate mustered a thin smile and told him about the prospective foster home in a determined, cheerful voice. ''The Kents are really nice, Dan. Mother and I only stayed for a few minutes of the interview, but we could see they liked Jason. They have a big home, so he would have a room of his own, and...and their son has a collection of computer games that made us both drool, right, Jason?''

The boy looked up from the soda he'd been stirring with a straw. The closed, sullen look that had almost disappeared from his eyes in the past few weeks was back. ''Yeah, I guess so.''

The meal passed uncomfortably. Kate tried to project a positive attitude, with Mary Catherine's help. Jason kept his eyes down. Dan observed them all calmly.

He slipped a hand around Kate's wrist when they drove up to her house, holding her in her seat. "We're going for a drive, Mary Catherine. We'll see you and Jason later."

"We won't wait up for you," Kate's knowing mother replied.

Kate didn't even try to make conversation as they drove through the deepening twilight. She hunched in her seat and nibbled at one fingernail nervously. Dan shot her an assessing look, but didn't say anything until they pulled into the parking lot of his apartment complex. He led her inside, then settled them both in one of the large leather sofas. His strong arms rested lightly on her waist and his broad shoulder was just the right height for her to lean her head against. Relaxing in his arms, she watched through the sliding glass doors as the flaming colors of sunset began to deepen far across the mesa.

"Okay, let's have it." His deep voice finally broke the stillness of the gathering night.

Kate sighed. "Oh, Dan, I can't believe how confused I am about all this. I thought I'd be so happy to find a family like the Kents for Jason, but…" Her voice trailed off. She didn't quite understand herself what the *but* meant.

"I tried to warn you not to get too close to him, honey."

"I know, I know. It's not that we're even that close, really. I mean, he rarely talks to me and we're not totally comfortable with each other all the time. Maybe it's just that I've gotten used to him," she said in a small voice.

Dan shifted her weight and pulled her closer. Kate could feel his warmth under her, infinitely soothing and reassuring.

"Don't sell yourself short. You've done a good job with the boy, and you're more than just 'used to' each other."

"It's just that we didn't have much time. I think I could have reached him, given a few more months." She watched the sun slip down behind Mount Taylor in a blaze of red and gold.

"I…I even thought about *us* adopting him," she said hesitantly, her eyes still on the far peak.

When Dan made no comment, she turned in his arms to face

him. She could barely make out his features in the last, lingering light. "I've been thinking about it for days. I mean, we'll be living here. I'll move my business headquarters from L.A. We could get a house with room for Jason and Mary Catherine, when she wanted to visit."

Her voice picked up speed as the ideas which had been simmering in the back of her mind tumbled out. "There are a number of homes for sale up where I'm renting now. I went to look at one just a few streets down. It has lots of room for us and Jason—and even Rico. With an established home, we wouldn't have any trouble adopting Jason, or at least extending the custody arrangement. You've certainly got enough standing with Judge Chavez to swing it."

Her excitement faltered a bit at Dan's continuing silence. Realizing the whole scheme was a surprise to him, she rushed on. "It will work out fine. Honestly, Dan. Jason's a good kid, really. And I owe him. He's still not completely recovered psychologically from that beating. The visit to the Kents this afternoon upset him, I could see it. He needs—"

Kate broke off as Dan stood suddenly and set her on her feet. He walked across the room to turn on a lamp. The light cast a golden glow over the room. It also highlighted the stark, rigid planes of Dan's face.

"Is that why you're marrying me?" he asked, his voice low and taut.

"What?"

"To give Jason a home? To lift this guilt trip you've been on ever since he was hurt?"

Shocked, Kate gaped at him. "Dan, surely...you can't think I..." She stuttered in confusion. The fierce glare in his eyes deepened to a steady silvery flame.

"You've got it all worked out, haven't you? Kid, home, business. And a convenient marriage that ties it all together. Did you enter it all into your little computer and weigh the variables?"

"I thought you liked Jason," Kate got out, helpless in the face of his obvious anger.

"I do," he growled. "You know I do."

Kate felt her confusion growing to overwhelming proportions. "Then why does the idea of adopting him upset you so much? I know it's tough starting a marriage with a ready-made family, but lots of people do these days."

Dan strode forward, taking her arms in an iron grip. "Listen to me, Kate, and listen good. *Liking* is not a good enough reason to take a child into your home permanently. You have to take him into your heart. And *liking* sure as hell isn't a good enough reason to get married."

A searing shaft of hurt lanced through Kate. "What do you mean?" she whispered.

"I mean maybe we ought to think this through a little more. I love you, more than I'd ever dreamed it was possible to love anyone. But I'll be damned if I'm going to be just another neat phase in the new plans you've laid out for yourself. I want a say in decisions that affect our life, Kate. We'll shape our future together, or not at all."

Kate felt panic start to rise. "Dan, I'm sorry. I should have talked to you about these ideas and plans."

"You sure should have, lady. We should've talked about a lot of things." He gave an exasperated sigh and loosened his grip.

"It's just that there hasn't been any time!" Kate cried. "With this race hanging over us, and your responsibilities and mine, and—"

"I know, I know." Dan turned away and ran a hand through his hair. Kate watched, her heart in her throat. She couldn't be losing this man, she thought desperately. He'd become the center of her existence, the focal point of all her plans. Crossing the small space between them, she tugged gently on his arm.

"I love you, Daniel Kingman. With my whole heart and soul. I'm sorry if I've let my schemes and plans run away with me. They don't mean anything without you. Please, please, let me try again."

The last of the anger in Dan's eyes faded. He stared down at her for a long, quiet minute, then took her in his arms. He rested his chin on her head and they clung to each other in the stillness.

"Damn straight, we'll try again," he finally told her in a low, level voice. "I'm as much at fault as anyone in this. I haven't wanted to waste the few hours we've had alone together with talk. We haven't taken the time to sort things out in a measured way."

A surge of wild relief washed through Kate. Her arms tightened around his waist, and she nuzzled her cheek into the warm, scented hollow of his neck. The familiar tang of his aftershave and taste of his skin filled her, infinitely arousing and incredibly reassuring. Her arms slid up around his neck, pulling him even closer to her lips and darting tongue. Unconsciously, she rubbed her breasts against the hard planes of his chest.

His breath sounded harsh and ragged in her ear. "Dammit, Kate. That's what I mean! I can't think when you do that."

"That's the whole point, fella," she whispered.

Dan groaned and picked her up in his arms. "We *will* sit down and straighten out a few details of our lives...later."

They talked very little that night. In fact, Kate barely got home in time to wake Mary Catherine and Jason to get them ready for the start of the marathon.

Eleven

The day of the big race dawned bright and clear, with a cloudless blue sky and sharp-etched sunshine that only New Mexico could produce. A little before seven, Kate loaded Jason in running gear, Mary Catherine in a neon green volunteer T-shirt, and a grinning Rico with a rakish red handkerchief around his neck into the Audi.

Throughout the drive to the race center she tried to recapture the excitement she'd felt previously for the marathon. Still shaken from her near fight with Dan and confused about her reaction to the thought of Jason leaving, it was hard to do. The boy was as quiet as she was. Kate guessed he was thinking of the visit to the Kents, but by tacit agreement no one mentioned it.

The frenetic level of last-minute activity at the center soon caught them all up. They worked until nearly nine—even Rico, who provided impromptu baby-sitting services for the young children of several volunteers—then joined the caravan of vehicles that made its way to the finish line on Fourth Avenue. Kate had done all she could with the prerace data entry. Now her assignment was to oversee the ranks of volunteers at the finish point who would input the times as the runners came across. There were the three different race events to record: the full twenty-six mile marathon, which Dan was participating in; a half marathon; and a five-kilometer fun run that Jason entered.

They made their way from the underground parking lot reserved for race officials and volunteers to the finish area. It was a scene of teeming color and noisy, bustling activity. Police cars with flashing lights kept the echoing downtown streets clear of traffic. Spectators spread blankets and lawn chairs on sidewalks while race officials and volunteers hurried back and forth setting up relief stations. Street vendors were already hawking everything from Sno-Kones to breakfast burritos. Kate knew that the scene at the starting line some miles away had to be just as chaotic, with the added presence of more than three hundred runners warming up for the full marathon. It would be even worse as thousands of half marathoners converged later, and then the fun runners.

A loudspeaker set on the roof of a TV van kept them informed as the runners gathered at the starting line. Kate cheered with everyone else when the sound of the gunshot signaling the start boomed over the speakers, then listened with half an ear to the race's progress. It would be another three hours before the first runner crossed the finish line, and she had plenty to keep her occupied until then.

With Jason busy setting up tables and Mary Catherine helping out in the Gatorade brigade, Kate devoted herself to organizing the bank of laptop computers that would record the events. She panicked momentarily when she discovered that the small, borrowed generator would provide only a three-hour supply of power. Luckily, half of the volunteers had brought back-up battery packs for their machines. Kate had a spare in the car, and she'd have to retrieve it as soon as there was a slack in the preparations.

The loudspeakers crackled as they blared out the news that the first runner passed the halfway point. The crowd at the finish line began to grow. One of the volunteer hackers crashed his hard disk and worked feverishly with Kate's determined assistance to get it back up. Even Jason helped, rerunning the operating software on Kate's machine to transfer to the reconstructed hard disk. While they were reloading the race program, they heard the excited announcer relate that a local favorite had taken the lead at the twenty-mile point. It wasn't Dan, but then he hadn't hoped to do more than finish respectably in this race. Tension began to grip the crowd as more and more people strained to see down the empty stretch. Tall buildings on either side of the city street echoed the almost palpable waves of excitement. Kate's own tension level peaked at about the same moment her computer screen flickered, then dimmed to an unreadable gray.

"Oh, no!"

"What?" Jason's blue eyes swung toward her.

"My battery's running down, and I forgot to get my back-up power pack from the car!"

"Can't you borrow one?"

"No, they're all in use," she groaned. "I can't believe it! After all the work we put into this blasted program, we won't even be able to help run it!"

"I'll go get the back-up," Jason volunteered.

"No, it'll take too long. You'll miss all the excitement. I'll go."

"The first runner's still a couple miles out. I can run to the car and be back before he crosses the line."

"Well..."

"I'll go, Kate. You'd never make it in time. You're, um, not exactly in shape, you know."

Kate's breath caught at the mischievous grin that spread across his face. It was so like the grin of a normal, happy eleven-year-old, and so unexpected on Jason's usually solemn face, that pain sliced through her. This was the way he should always look. This was the way she wanted him to look! Swallowing the sudden ache, she summoned up a cheeky, answering grin.

"I'm going to ignore that last remark," she replied, tossing him the keys to her car. "Move it, kid!"

When the first red lights of the advance convoy appeared, Jason still hadn't returned. The crowd surged to its feet. Far off in the distance came the muted roar of shouting and applause. Frowning, Kate scanned the edges of the band of volunteers. She spotted Mary Catherine and Rico and hurried over to them.

"Have you seen Jason? He went to get my power pack from the car and isn't back yet."

Her mother shook her head just as an armada of police cars, ambulances and TV vans turned onto Fourth and began heading toward them.

"Kate, they're coming!" One of the volunteers at the computer bank waved frantically.

Chewing on her lower lip, Kate ran back to the row of seated hackers. A quick glance told her they were as ready as they'd ever be to record the results. But even if they weren't, she couldn't worry about it now. Now she had to find Jason.

Asking her mother to tell Dan she'd gone looking for Jason, Kate edged her way out of the crowd and headed for the garage a few blocks away. Her sneakered feet slapped against the pavement, strangely loud in the deserted streets as she left the tumult of the race behind. Puffing, she ran down two flights of steps to the dim, subterranean level where she'd left her car.

The unease that had been curling in her belly with each step sharpened as her calls for Jason went unanswered in the cavernous depths. It turned to outright alarm when she dashed around the end of the row where her car was parked. The Audi's trunk gaped open and her power pack lay on the concrete a few feet away.

"Jason! Jason, where are you?"

Fighting down a swamping fear, she scooped up the power pack by its strap and slammed down the trunk. For an endless moment she stood leaning on the fender, her blood hammering in her ears, her throat constricted.

She shouted for him again, panic adding a hint of shrillness to her voice.

"Kate!"

The thin, muffled cry was cut off almost immediately, but it was enough to send Kate running for the far end of the garage. She rounded a pickup truck and skidded to a halt, her eyes searching the dim area frantically. At the sound of a thud and a keening cry her head whipped around. To her right, in the dark shadows of a corner stall, two figures bent over Jason. One figure drew his foot back even as she watched and swung it toward the boy in a vicious arc.

Without stopping to think, Kate yelled at the top of her lungs and ran toward them. She swung the only weapon she had in a wild loop over her head. The power pack only weighed about six pounds, but it was better than nothing.

Both men turned in startled surprise at her ferocious charge. The one closest to Kate flung up an arm as she brought the power pack down at his head with all her strength. It hit his forearm with a solid thud. The rifle crack of splitting bone sounded a second before his scream of pain. He doubled over and sank to his knees, his arm cradled against his chest.

"Hey!" The second man jumped back, out of the circle of the whirling pack.

Wild anger made Kate reckless. She stepped over Jason's still-prone body and swung again.

"Kate, no!"

"You stupid bitch."

Jason's cry and the man's shouted curse rang in her ears. The man—no, Kate could see now he wasn't a man, but a lean, wiry teenager—ducked. And came up with a long, vicious-looking knife in his hand.

Kate dragged air and fear in equal parts into her lungs. She backed away from the gleaming blade, stooping to haul Jason up and into her arms.

"Stay right where you are, lady. I ain't never used this knife on a woman before, but I got a real urge to right now."

Half crouching, he edged around her to his fallen comrade. Kate's fear turned to sick dread as she saw the sweat glistening on his face and the nervous way he tossed the knife from hand to hand. Under his thin T-shirt, his stomach muscles twitched uncontrollably. She'd never seen a drug user before, but it was obvious this kid was high on something and she didn't think it had anything to do with the excitement from the race.

"Danny! Danny, you okay?"

"She broke my arm," the other boy moaned, rolling on the floor in pain.

The teen holding the knife turned back to her, his face twisted in an ugly sneer.

"You're gonna pay for that, bitch."

"No, Pete, leave her alone!"

Kate stared down, astounded, as Jason pushed himself out of her arms and took two shaky steps toward the other boy.

"Jason, do you know these guys? Are they your...your gang?"

The older boy laughed, and the sound sent goose bumps shivering down Kate's arms.

Jason sent her a wide, scared look over his shoulder. "No, Kate..." he started.

"You sniveling little wimp," the older boy spat. "You were happy enough to be part of my gang before."

"I wasn't, Pete! I never wanted to be part of this."

"Is that why you turned us in to the cops? Your own damn brother?"

"No! No! I didn't!"

Neither of them appeared to hear Kate's swift, indrawn breath. They formed a macabre tableau in the dim light: a menacing, crouching figure with an obscene knife in his hands; a thin, frightened boy in white running shorts; and Kate, the power pack still dangling from her fingers.

"The police have been harassing our gang for weeks, ever since you went to live with this broad. I done some checking, Jase. She's shacking up with a cop and you're in with them, right in the middle."

"No, I never said anything, Pete. Honest!"

"I thought the beating we gave you would teach you something. Instead you sicced the cops on us. You need another lesson, Jase. Her, too!''

The knife flashed as he swung it in a wide arc, moving toward them slowly on the balls of his feet. Kate's fingers tightened on the strap, and she pushed Jason behind her.

''Leave him alone,'' she ground out. ''He never said a word about any of you. Believe me, I would've remembered if Jason happened to mention that it was his own brother who sent him to the hospital.''

The vitriolic scorn in her voice stopped him. For a breathless moment, Kate thought she might have shamed him into letting them go. But then the other boy groaned, a long, ragged sob of pain that sliced through the still air.

Pete stiffened, and his eyes took on a wild, feral glaze that told Kate he was going to lunge.

She shoved Jason away from her and swung the pack.

''Run, Jason!'' she screamed.

''No, Pete!''

''Get back, Kate!''

Dan's frantic shout crashed into her consciousness at the same instant a savage growl sounded right behind her left ear. She whirled and took a glancing blow from a flying black body as it sailed through the air and landed with a slam against Pete's chest. Fear ripped through her, until she saw the hand gripping the knife caught in Rico's snarling mouth.

Heavy footfalls pounded the concrete behind her.

''Hold him, Rico,'' Dan shouted.

Rico was more than happy to oblige. The knife clattered to the pavement, and the screaming boy went down under the onslaught of a hundred pounds of snarling, twisting beast.

''Are you okay? Kate! Jason! Are you okay?''

Other footsteps sounded as a couple of uniformed officers ran up, but Kate barely noticed them. She and Jason were wrapped in Dan's hard, sweat-slicked embrace. His arm crushed her ribs, the pin holding the race number to his tank top bit into her cheek, and Kate had never felt anything so wonderful in her entire life.

* * *

By the time the last of the squad cars drove away and Dan had bundled Kate and her family into the Audi, she'd almost stopped shaking. And by the time they pulled into her garage and piled out of the car, she was able to make her own, if unsteady, way into the house.

While Mary Catherine and Dan went into the kitchen to get them all much-needed sustenance, she sank down on the couch and let the last of the fear drain from her body.

"Thanks, Kate."

Jason's thin, hesitant form hovered beside the couch, his face pale and his blue eyes staring from a face that looked much too old for a child. Kate's throat tightened once more, this time with a need to cry so sharp, it took every ounce of her depleted strength to hold it back. She lifted trembling hands to the boy.

With a muffled sob, he flung himself into her arms. Her own tears began to flow, washing runnels down her cheeks as she clutched his body to hers. They rocked against each other, bonded by shared fear, by relief and by something else, something Kate struggled to understand. When Jason finally lifted his head, she met his tear-washed look with one of her own. At that moment, she knew what that other something was.

"I love him, Dan."

Her low voice was barely audible above the bubbling of the hot tub. It was late, well after midnight. An exhausted Jason had finally fallen into bed, Mary Catherine was sound asleep and even Rico was absent from his usual post beside them. Sated from the feast of steak and chili Mary Catherine had fed him in honor of his hero status, the dog slept blissfully beside Jason's bed. Only Dan and Kate were awake, and she'd managed at last to coax him into the hot tub to soak away the residue of tension.

Dan leaned against one of the backrests, his legs splayed out in front of him. Kate lay with her back against his chest, her arms resting on the forearms wrapped around her waist, her head lolling comfortably on his shoulder. A bright, full moon hung over the mountains and bathed the deck, making it seem as if they floated in a pool of liquid, bubbling silver.

"When his own brother pulled that knife on us today, my heart stopped. I would have strangled the bastard with my bare hands before I let him hurt Jason again."

She floated against Dan, feeling the smooth satin of his skin beneath her bare thighs and buttocks. "He's been hurt so much already, Dan. I knew then that if...when...we got away, I couldn't let him go."

Holding her breath, Kate waited for him to say something. Bubbles broke against the water's surface in an iridescent foam. Far off in the distance, a lone coyote called to its mate. Finally, after what seemed like an eternity, Dan shifted slightly on his seat and turned her in his arms. The hazy silver of his eyes gleamed richer and more luminous than moonlight on the water.

"So we won't let him go," he said.

Kate searched his eyes. "Do you really mean it? I know you had doubts about taking Jason in. Are you sure you—"

"I never had any doubts about Jason," he interrupted gently. "But I had doubts about why you wanted him. Guilt is no substitute for love. I learned a long time ago you can't force that love."

"Oh, Dan..."

His lips cut off her tremulous cry. Kate flung her arms around his neck and slithered her wet body up his until she returned his kiss with all her pent-up emotion.

"Good Lord." Dan's chest heaved under her when he broke off contact some moments later. "If this damn contraption wasn't already heating me past the safe point, that kiss would have done it! No, wait!"

He took her hips in a firm hold and pushed her back down his long, wet torso. Anchoring her legs with one of his, Dan held her immobile.

"Wait a minute, Kate, before I disintegrate on the spot." He dragged in several deep breaths, which he realized instantly was a mistake. His chest hair tickled Kate's already-aroused nipples and turned them into hard, aching buds.

"Sorry, Captain Kingman. I'm afraid I can't wait," she breathed, while her hands and her mouth and her hips went to work.

Just before the stars exploded all around him, Dan admitted that maybe there was something to this hot tub business after all.

Epilogue

Kate thought her heart would burst with pride as she waited to walk through the rows of guests toward the two figures waiting for her in the gazebo. They stood side by side in matching gray cutaways, one tall, dark and indescribably handsome, the other small, sandy-haired and beaming with excitement. Rich organ music filled the square, rolling off the surrounding adobe buildings in sonorous waves.

A light breeze lifted her short veil, giving her a clearer picture of the colorful crowd filling the square. Half the guests wore police uniforms, the other half sported everything from dark jeans and cowboy hats to bright silks and flowered dresses. Kate was amazed at the number of guests. With less than a week to arrange everything, she hadn't expected this big a turnout. Both she and Mary Catherine had protested the short notice during a lively dinner discussion the day after the marathon.

Dan had told them calmly he wasn't going to take a chance on any more stray fiancés or lost brothers showing up. He wanted the thing sewed up as soon as possible. He'd already asked Judge Chavez to perform the ceremony the following Saturday in the plaza of Old Town. Kate couldn't have come up with a more romantic setting for a wedding. Her objections melted away.

With the enthusiastic help of Trish and Mary Catherine's bingo buddies, Kate had managed to pull it off. Invitations were printed and distributed within two days. Dan took charge of outfitting himself and Jason. Trish arranged the reception, then accompanied Kate and Mary Catherine on a wild shopping expedition.

The shopping trip was extravagantly successful. Kate found a lustrous satin gown studded with seed pearls along its low, rounded neckline and bell-shaped short sleeves. It hugged her long body to the hips, then fell in swirling folds of glistening white to the floor. A short train swept behind her as she walked. The gown's stunning simplicity was in inverse proportion to its cost, but Kate knew every penny was well spent when she started down the aisle on Dr. Chavez's arm.

Dan came down the few steps in front of the gazebo to take her hand. Her gaze fastened on his magnificent figure and smiling eyes. He stood with one foot resting on the first step, his outstretched hand holding hers. The arch above him trailed garlands of white roses, baby's breath and fluttering white satin ribbons. Against the white background, his dark hair and rakish mustache caught both her breath and her eyes.

She smiled, radiant with love and joy. Dan's hand tightened around hers and one corner of his mouth lifted in a lopsided grin that made her heart ache. Together, they ascended the few steps to where Trish, Jason and a beaming Judge Chavez waited for them.

"You're a beautiful bride, Mrs. Kingman."

Dan's deep, dark voice shivered across her senses. Kate stirred sleepily. When his hand slid under the light covering to stroke her breast, she moaned.

"Is that passion or sleep?"

"Both," she groaned, rolling over onto her back.

Dan leaned on one elbow, head in his hand, looking down at her. In the dim light of the one candle still fluttering in its crystal holder, Kate saw desire flowing in his eyes like molten silver.

His free hand rested lightly on her breast, the fingers just brushing against its tip.

As if it had a will of its own, her own hand slipped out from under the covers to slide along his chest. Dark, curly hair trapped her fingers. Beneath them, his heart beat an increasingly erratic rhythm.

"I don't know if I have the energy left for this," she said, half laughing, half serious.

"What?" He scowled down at her ferociously. "Already reneging on your vows to love and cherish?"

"I've cherished you twice tonight. If you want this marriage to last longer than twenty-four hours, you'll have to let me recharge my batteries."

Her batteries started recharging on their own when his hand left her breast to trail down across the soft flesh of her belly. His callused fingers rasped against her skin, raising delightful shivers from her neck to her knees. She nearly moaned again when they buried themselves in the tangled curls between her legs. Her head fell back on the pillow in lazy passion. Her breath came in shallow gasps.

To her surprise, his fingers ceased their magic and Dan rolled out of bed. Kate propped herself up on both elbows to watch him stroll across the room. Utterly confused, she waited while he rooted through the small gym bag he'd brought with him on their weekend honeymoon. She'd teased him about bringing so little, only to be reminded that honeymooners didn't need any clothes anyway.

"Here." He tossed a little package onto the bed. "I was going to save this for our fiftieth anniversary, when we're old and gray and need something to stimulate our senses. But I think I'll make it a wedding present, instead."

"What is this?" Kate eyed the plain, brown paper wrapping dubiously. She wasn't the kind for kinky sex aids, and didn't think Dan was, either.

"Open it."

Kate chewed at one corner of her lower lip.

"Trust me, Katey mine. It's art. Beautiful, sensuous, wonderful art." His laughing eyes encouraged her.

Frowning, she slid a finger under the edge of the wrapping. The brown paper fell away, leaving a plain, unmarked videocassette in her hand. She gave him a puzzled, questioning look.

He took the cassette and slipped it into the VCR. Their luxurious suite came equipped with TVs and every other modern amenity in each of its four rooms.

Nervously, Kate watched gray lines flash across the screen in dizzying horizontal patterns. Gradually, they settled, then cleared entirely. Kate gasped as the familiar dimensions of her bedroom slowly took on definition. The camera swept the room once, twice, then came back to the open sliding glass doors just beyond her bed. As if an unseen hand were operating a zoom lens, the area beyond the doors grew. Dark patterns resolved into separate, distinct shapes. The eye of the camera adjusted, and one of the objects became a round hot tub! Clearly visible above the rim of the tub was a profile of her head, shoulders and the swell of her breasts.

"Dan Kingman! I don't believe you had the nerve to bring this on our honeymoon." Kate's voice sputtered with choked laughter. She tore her embarrassed gaze from the flickering screen to find her husband grinning down at her.

"I never go anywhere without it," he told her simply.

Embarrassed, exasperated, enthralled, Kate pulled him down beside her. The tape ran on, then ran out. Flickering shadows danced over the two oblivious figures on the wide, rumpled bed.

Dan arched above Kate, his powerful body poised. She lay panting under him, her arms wrapped tight around the strong column of his neck.

"The real thing is so much better than the tape," Dan murmured, before he lost the power of speech altogether.

*   *   *   *   *

WHAT THIS
PASSION MEANS

Ann Major

In loving memory
of Dr. David Allen Major, a real hero,
and to his wife, Mabel K. Major.

One

———

Kate Andrews tensed as she stepped out of the cabin onto the deck of her shrimp boat. She stretched her slim frame, which was encased in skintight worn jeans and a sleeveless ribbed T-shirt that had long ago become her uniform. Then she relaxed and let the quiet sounds of the early morning wash over her. Soaring gulls cried against a lavender sky. There was the hum of a distant outboard being cranked. She heard the splash of a fish jumping nearby.

The sun peeped over the horizon and set the billowing cumulus clouds that hovered over the water on fire. There wasn't a single ripple on the mirrorlike surface of the gilded water.

It was a beautiful day. A helluva day to wake up broke after only managing to get an hour's sleep on a hard cot. *Another still, hot day like yesterday,* Kate thought dispiritedly as she stepped over a net and poured fresh ice into an ice chest filled with the shrimp she and her crew had caught the previous night.

It was a typical June morning in Key West. A muscle in her shoulder ached, and she set the bag of ice down and stared at the flag hanging limply against the flagpole on the pier.

It would have been a perfect day for diving. For treasure hunting. But would she ever be able to go again? Or was she finished like everyone said she was?

Her eyes took in the sorry state of her boat, *Bright Star*—the rusted fittings, peeling paint and torn nets. There was no money left to spend on chasing a dream. The investors who'd backed her father were too skeptical to finance an untried woman in her search.

Briefly her tired mind flicked to her father's lifelong dream that had inevitably become hers as well, finding the *Marta Isabella,* the Golden Galleon as it had come to be called. The ship had disappeared without a trace in a terrible hurricane in the Caribbean three centuries earlier with no survivors to tell her tale and scarcely a clue as to where she had gone down. Even the incredibly lucky seventeenth-century hunter, William Phipps, the English "wracker" had failed to find her.

For more than a decade, Kate and her father had ransacked the archives of London and Madrid for clues. Her father was certain that the wreck lay at the foot of a reef in the shape of a question mark southwest of the Florida Keys. Jake had gleaned that clue from a letter written by a Spanish captain a year after the *Marta Isabella* had gone down. When the captain had been blown off course, he'd spied a wreck buried in a forest of coral and theorized that she could be the *Marta Isabella.*

For years, Jake Andrews had taken Kate up in a borrowed plane, with Kate leaning out the door as far as her seat belt would let her so she could search for such a reef. Shortly before his death, Jake had found what he'd believed to be the reef south of the Florida Keys. He'd taken Kate with him on what neither of them realized would be his last voyage aboard *Bright Star.* They'd navigated for hours through a treacherous forest of vertical coral pillars rising from the bottom of the sea to within eight or ten feet of the surface. One mistake, and the hull of *Bright Star* would have been ripped open.

Then, at the southern tip of the reef, they'd dropped anchor and dived. Two days later, they'd found a few gold coins sprinkled in the coarse sand, but no cannon or ballast rock, the sure indicators that a wreck lay buried beneath. They'd believed the ship was nearby, but they'd never had time to prove it.

The tension and excitement of the search had been too much for Jake. He'd had his first heart attack on board, and they'd returned to Key West immediately. But it had not been soon enough.

"Hello there, Kate Andrews," a suntanned captain yelled from the shrimp boat chugging into the marina, interrupting her reverie. A stream of noisy gulls followed in the wake of the boat, and the scent of diesel mingled with the odor of fresh shrimp.

Kate waved back, but not too jauntily because, much as she liked Don Taylor, she didn't want to encourage him. Sometimes when they went out together, he drank a few too many beers, and not long ago he'd asked her again to marry him. Just the thought of being a shrimper's wife and shrimping for the rest of her life made her feel slightly nauseated. Still, Don would probably catch her in a weak moment some day when the loneliness and the worry got to be too much for her, when the longing to be part of a family—even if the man wasn't really the right man—overpowered her fierce desire to remain independent.

Suddenly she felt too tired to sell shrimp to tourists after staying up all night catching them, but she had no choice. She would just have to push herself, she thought as she sat down on a stool by the ice chest. If Pedro and Juan could do it, she could, too. Besides, the money from the sale of the shrimp was all she had to pay them with. The payment on *Bright Star*'s note was due in a week, and she'd skipped the last payment. She'd already gone to her banker and begged him to extend her loan, but he'd informed her she was already overextended. He'd advised her to sell out to Rex Reynolds while she still had something to sell and while Reynolds was still fool enough to buy. At the mention of Rex's name, Kate had stormed out of the bank, but not in time to avoid a parting shot from Mr. Thomas: "Sometimes you're just as stubborn as your father, girl. You've got more pride than sense."

That was true when it came to selling all her dreams to that rogue Rex Reynolds. After what Rex had done to her father and herself ten years ago, Rex was the last person she wanted to turn to for help.

But he was the only person left.

Oh, why had her father had to die ten months ago and leave her all alone? She'd never been afraid until then. Somehow, together, they'd been able to manage. Now it was as if she was running scared all the time. Her tiny inheritance was gone. No matter how she'd pleaded, her father's investors wouldn't advance her a dime to go after the *Marta Isabella*. Now, there was always this terrible empty feeling gnawing at her in the pit of her stomach. But she couldn't let anyone know. As she'd done for years, she presented a tough exterior to the world.

She was proud Kate Andrews, the girl who'd tried to be the son Jake Andrews had so desperately wanted and failed to have. She rarely wore dresses or high heels. Instead, she wore boots and jeans and loose cotton work shirts when she wasn't in a faded bathing suit and her diving gear. She seldom wore makeup or perfume and almost never curled her waist-length black hair. Every summer she let the sun darken her skin to a honey gold. She worked as hard as any man, but there was a touch of feminine defiance in everything she did.

She was not beautiful, but she was not exactly plain, either. There was something about her that made men notice her when she was in one of her softer moods. That was almost never these days. Hers was a delicately featured, narrow face. Beneath the slender bridge of her nose, her full, sensuous mouth was too large. Though she would never have consciously admitted to such feminine vanity, she rarely wore lipstick, because she did not want to call attention to her mouth, which she considered her worst feature. Her white teeth were slightly crooked. Her one redeeming asset was her eyes.

From her long-dead mother, Kate had inherited gorgeous harem eyes. Enormous jewel-green eyes fringed by bristly black lashes. Slanting eyes that sparkled and bewitched when she was happy and blazed when she was angry. They alone saved her from mere ordinariness. They alone betrayed a vital inner spirit she would have preferred to keep hidden. They held a man. They fascinated. And she was completely unconscious of their power.

The blood-red sun had emerged in all its glory and was now squatting low on the horizon. It was going to be a beautiful day, but the scarlet magnificence only heightened Kate's feelings of doom.

She was broke. Flat broke. It was time she stopped dreaming and did something about the harsh reality of her situation. She had to go after that treasure, not only because she desperately needed the money, but because she wanted people to remember her father's name with respect. Even before Jake's death, there had been those who had laughed at him behind his back for pauperizing himself chasing what they considered a foolish fantasy.

Kate would have to get the money for the hunt and salvage operation from somewhere. And she would have to be very careful when she tried to borrow the money she needed. The last thing she wanted to do was to alert treasure-seeking sharks of her intentions. It wouldn't be smart to confide either her real reasons for needing money or the location of the *Marta Isabella.*

She got up from her rickety stool, and wiped her smelly hands against her jeans. She wasn't going to sell shrimp, after all. It would take more money than she'd earn by doing that to pay her bills. She was going to take a shower and put on clean clothes and go into town.

It was time she faced a hard fact. There was only one person she could turn to, and that was the man she hated more than any other: Rex Reynolds. At the mere thought of going to Rex, a cold chill swept her.

Rex was known for driving hard bargains. He'd built his business on brute work and guts. But he owed her something, didn't he? Jake had taught Rex everything he knew about diving techniques and sunken treasure, as well as the mysteries and dangers of the sea itself. Rex had taken that knowledge and turned it into an empire. Rex had harvested a fortune in treasure and artifacts from sunken wrecks off Caribbean reefs. He owned a fleet of boats. He took thousands of tourists annually on diving trips to explore wrecks. He had a string of dive shops all across the country and put together diving trips everywhere in the world. He was a skilled promoter, making movies of his explorations, writing books that all seemed to become instant bestsellers and giving lectures. Because of his charismatic manner, he was the darling of the press. "An innovative marine archaeologist," some journalist had written about him. That was a laugh. Rex Reynolds was a high-school dropout.

But a damned successful one! If Kate were to be fair, even she would acknowledge that Rex was probably better educated than most college graduates. Her father had forced her to go to college. Rex, who had a brilliant mind and an incessant thirst for knowledge, had never had the opportunity. But even without a college degree, he'd invented several air pumps that divers now used routinely. In the past ten years, oil companies had hired him to probe the ocean floor for oil, and he'd done so successfully. But Rex owed everything he was to her father. When Jake had found him unconscious by the side of a Florida highway, Rex was running from his past. Jake had given him a chance, hired Rex on as crew and carefully taught him every skill he had.

How had Rex repaid Jake? By ruthlessly stealing his only daughter's heart and virginity and then callously jilting her and leaving Jake when Jake needed him most, because a better opportunity presented itself. From there, he'd gone straight to the top, while Jake and she had remained on the bottom.

Once, when no one else would loan Jake money, he'd gone to Rex and borrowed a small sum. Rex had demanded that Jake pay him back with interest. Repaying the money had been a constant worry to Jake, and perhaps it had even hastened his death.

Oh, Kate hated Rex Reynolds, all right, for more reasons than she cared to name, but most of all for the way he'd changed her from a soft young girl into a lonely woman. If she was afraid to be feminine, whose brutal rejection had made her feel that she was a failure at being a woman?

Yes, Rex owed her, and it was high time she demanded that he pay.

Kate was aware of him even before she saw him.

From the other side of the glossy mahogany door came that husky drawl Kate remembered so well, that velvet, male sound she dreaded more than anything.

Her stomach twisted into a painful knot. Why couldn't she forget the special, tender way his deep voice had always murmured her name in a honey-toned caress?

"Well, show her in, Nancy. It's bad manners to keep an old friend waiting."

Friend! Rex Reynolds was hardly a friend, Kate thought in fury. And as for manners, he hadn't any.

Nevertheless, Kate clasped her clammy fingers together and rose as the pretty red-haired secretary hurried out and ushered her into Rex's vast office.

Kate's footsteps were soundless on the plush brown carpet. There was only the sound of the soft whir of the air conditioner. She glanced around quickly, feeling as stiff and unnatural as the glassy-eyed Marlin displayed on Rex's wall.

Rex's back was to Kate. Deliberately so, in all probability. He was muttering something impatiently into the phone.

"All right, Susan," he whispered. "Whatever you say. Tonight. Seven o'clock."

Did he want Kate to know he was talking to a woman? And why should this knowledge set her on edge? She ground her nails into her clenched palm. She couldn't care less who he dated!

Kate tried not to listen. She forced herself to stare out the floor-to-ceiling windows that overlooked Key West's marina. In the distance she saw the kraals, or pens, where the sea turtles were kept. Nearer, on the sidewalk across the street, a conch vendor hawked the stack of great pink shells in front of his umbrella.

It was impossible to ignore Rex. Impossible not to stare wordlessly. The emotion he evoked was too powerful, too all-consuming.

His shoulders were as broad and heavily muscled as she remembered. Unbidden came the memory of the hard tanned body concealed beneath his perfectly tailored navy suit. She fought against a vision of his sleek dark muscular chest divided down the middle by a thick matting of sunbleached hair. Once she'd traced every contour so lovingly.

His golden hair was still thick and lush and uncombed. How well she remembered its softness when she'd threaded her fingers lovingly though it.

Damn him! Why did he have to be so rugged? So handsome? And so heartless? Kate hated him because she wasn't as indifferent as she wanted to be.

Rex hung up and swiveled in his black leather chair to face her. He rocked back and stared at her hard. His mesmerizing gaze held hers long after she wanted to look away. His intense blue eyes pierced through to the very marrow of her soul. Despite his elegant office and his elegant clothes, the man was every bit as tough and as masculine as she remembered. A shudder swept her from the top of her glossy black hair to the tip of her scuffed white heels.

Why couldn't she stop looking at him? She hated herself for being drawn to those tanned features—the wide forehead, the thick dark brows over those incredibly blue eyes, the carved cheeks and jaw, harsher now than she remembered, the sensual mouth, the long nose that would have been classically straight if he hadn't broken it once. His face was leaner and harder than it had been in youth but was somehow more attractive, despite her disturbing knowledge that those good looks masked a ruthless nature.

She caught her breath on a little rush of pain. When she swayed forward, as if she were overcome by his male beauty, she had to grip the edge of the chair in front of Rex's desk to steady herself.

"Hello, Kate. Long time no see." Blue eyes skimmed her

body with an intensity that made her feel she was standing before him naked. "Too long."

A hot rapid pulse had begun to pound in her throat.

Suddenly she was conscious that her faded yellow sundress was hardly the latest fashion and was just as conscious of how revealingly it clung to her every curve. She almost wished that she had curled her hair and put on powder and lipstick just to show him that she wasn't totally unattractive. Not that it mattered to him, judging from the way he was devouring her with those bedroom eyes of his.

"Not long enough," she cried in desperation, whirling away from him before she remembered it hardly served her purpose to lash out at him. She had to be contrite and humble, but how could she be when it was such torment being here with him?

He flashed her that white, white smile of his that was so devastating against his swarthy face. His eyes gleamed as he watched her struggle with her emotions. He was enjoying himself at her expense. "Still as charming as I remember," he retaliated silkily. "All bark but...a helluva bite, as well—" he hesitated, knowingly "—if my memory of that last night we were together serves me correctly."

She flushed with shame, but her eyes blazed dagger-points of fire. He was referring to something no gentleman would ever have referred to, their last night in bed. He'd held her against his hard warm body and whispered in her ear that she was his little wildcat after she'd accidentally bitten him a trifle too enthusiastically. Not that he'd seemed to mind, then.

Odd that after so many women he still remembered.

Aloud, she hissed, "That's exactly the sort of low-down, gutter remark I expected from you."

"Oh, really? So you still hate me?"

"Yes." The one word was a frozen whisper.

He stood up, and though she was tall, he towered over her. "And so ferociously, too? But then you do everything ferociously, don't you, Kate? It's in your loving as well as in your hating."

He knew too much. She should never have come.

Blazing green eyes were his only answer.

"If looks could kill..." he mused derisively.

You wouldn't live an hour, she thought.

"But you came to me, anyway." His voice was casual, and she didn't notice that he balled his hands into hard fists before sliding them into the pockets of his navy slacks.

"Only because I had to."

"I wondered how long it would take you to get around to me," he said with an arrogant self-assurance that infuriated Kate.

"You were the very last person on my list."

"Maybe I should have been the first."

"Why?"

"Because I'm the only one foolish enough to consider helping you."

"You mean you're at least willing to listen?" She gasped in disbelief, realizing she'd hardly taken any pains to ingratiate herself.

"Yes."

This was going more easily than she'd imagined it would. Maybe she'd been wrong all these years, thinking him a mean, heartless bastard. Maybe he was actually sorry for what he'd done.

"Why, thank you, Rex," she said almost softly.

"Nothing like the thought of money to warm a woman's heart," came his low, cynical drawl.

His remark snapped her out of the brief illusion that his character might have improved over the years, and she glared at him. Then she quickly reminded herself that at least he hadn't turned her down without hearing her out.

"Now tell me what you want," he said.

She hadn't meant to come to the point quite so bluntly, but under the circumstances she saw no way to avoid doing so. "I need three months' worth of operating expenses..." She began to calculate her costs: her loan payments, fuel, wages and maintenance on the boat. She reeled off a stream of figures and came up with a total.

"What do you want all that money for when you hate shrimping?"

"Oh, I..." It would never do to tell him how close she thought she was to finding the Golden Galleon. "At least it's an outdoor job," she hedged.

His eyes were fathomless, and just for a moment she wondered how much he knew or guessed. She tried not to think about the fact that he was a dangerous man to lie to.

"Wouldn't you be better off if you gave up *Bright Star*?" he asked carefully. "Jake's dead. You could go back to teaching school."

"The only reason I got that teaching degree was because it meant so much to Jake."

"And what would be wrong with starting to act like a woman for a change? Maybe marry some nice guy. Have kids. You wanted all those things once."

"That was a long time ago," she said bitterly.

"You've grown hard, Kate. I've often wondered why."

"Take a good look in the mirror, Rex Reynolds, and you'll have your answer." Oh, why had she admitted that he'd meant that much to her? Childishly she didn't want him to know how he'd hurt her by his rejection of her love.

"You can't mean...that I'm somehow responsible." He was staring at her oddly.

As he came closer, she backed away. "Of course not!" she snapped too hastily, wishing he'd stop studying her so intently.

"I walked out on you for your own good."

Sure. She just stared back at him.

"I would have hurt you more if I'd stayed."

"We'll never know, will we?" She tried to make her voice light and indifferent, but the cracked sounds that came out failed miserably. "Look, we could talk over old times for hours. Have you made up your mind about the money or not?"

"All right," he said at length, still with an expression of puzzlement on his dark face. "Let's get down to business. If I give you the money, how do you intend to repay me?"

She hadn't the slightest intention of telling him that she might have discovered the *Marta Isabella* and that she was going to use his money to go after the treasure. After the sale of a few artifacts, her father's old investors would be standing in line to help her. No! Rex Reynolds was the last man on earth she would confide in. He'd only beat her there and take the treasure for himself. "I guess you could draw up a note, and I'll start paying on it in a month or two," she said evasively.

"With what—your good intentions? You're operating a losing business. Every month, you're digging yourself into a deeper hole."

"I could give you a second lien on *Bright Star*."

He came toward her, and she caught the tangy scent of his aftershave. She'd run out of room, and couldn't escape him. Sunlight glinted in his bright gold hair.

"Now what would I want with an interest in another boat, especially one that's already mortgaged to the hilt?" He moved even closer, his gaze raking her in slow, male appraisal. "Surely you have something else you could offer in the way of collateral."

"But I don't."

"Oh, yes you do." His eyes continued to sear her in that predatory way of his that made her so uncomfortable. "You have something I want very badly."

He reached out, and she felt the rasping brush of his fingertips lifting the shining thickness of her hair. She felt the feather-light touch in every pore of her body before she jumped quickly to one side. She raised her nose haughtily and pretended to stare past him out the window.

"Don't play with me, Rex Reynolds. Either give me the money, or tell me no."

"It seems you and I have some unfinished business."

"What are you talking about?"

"You think I jilted you because I didn't want you anymore. That's not true. The only reason I walked out on you was that your dad told me he didn't want a bum like me fooling around with his daughter. He was determined for you to get that college degree. He wanted a better man and a better life for you. For your information, that hurt like hell, but I left because I owed Jake too much not to.''

''That's a lie! Jake would never—''

''He damn sure did!''

''You stirred up Jake's men against him and then you left him right in the middle of that salvage operation when Jake needed you and his crew the most.''

''Kate, Jake asked me to pull that stunt so you'd think the worst of me. That way you'd get over me in a hurry. Which you damn sure did!''

''I don't want to hear another word!''

Kate couldn't bear the way Rex was trying to blame a dead man for what he'd done himself. With a little cry, she bolted for the door. Rex leaped forward and grabbed her arm, hauling her slender frame against his work-toughened body. A muscular navy-clad thigh insinuated itself between her legs as she was arched against him.

Never had she been more piercingly aware of a man's body against her own. She felt the heat of him, the hardness of his muscles. Every feminine nerve ending screamed in primitive awareness of him, and he knew it. She felt her heart pounding, but it was no faster than the racing rhythm of his own.

''Not so fast,'' he growled. ''I'll give you the money, but the collateral I want is you.''

''What?'' Beneath her dark suntan, her face went bloodless.

With his thumb and forefinger, he lifted her chin so that he could see into her eyes. 'I've never forgotten you, Kate Andrews.''

''I never forgot you, either. But if you're smart, you'll realize that's the furthest thing from a compliment.''

He only grinned that slashing white grin that made him so handsome. ''Coming from you, I'll take it as a compliment, anyway. I kind of like the thought that I was unforgettable,'' he said in a low, sexy voice that sent a shiver through her. Louder, he went on, ''After Jake let me know he didn't think I was good enough for you, I held a grudge against the two of you for quite a while, but I'm over all that now. I want another chance—to be your friend.''

''You can't buy friendship, Rex Reynolds.''

''Someone impractical must have pounded that platitude into your hard little head. For your information, usually I can. When I can't, there are other experiences I can buy from a woman that are sometimes even more interesting than their friendship.''

''You're rude, coarse. I won't waste my time enumerating your character faults.''

''How generous of you!'' He grinned at her unrepentantly.

She struggled to free herself, but his hard fingers were like iron manacles.

''I don't know what you've got, Kate. You're not even pretty. You're too skinny, and you never wear anything but those unflattering rags. You don't try to be soft or feminine. But leaving you behind was the hardest damn thing I ever had to do. Maybe it's because you have more guts than any woman I've ever known. Who else would have dived in after me and saved me from a shark attack on that first dive when I lost my nerve? And then there was that time I stayed down too long and got caught in that wreck and ran out of air. You shared yours with me until Jake came down and cut me loose. And since Jake's death, you've fought harder to keep your head above water than any woman ought to ever have to fight. I want you back as my friend, and now that Jake's no longer around to object, I intend to have you.''

How dare he insult her by saying she wasn't pretty or feminine and then debase her with such an offer? He said he wanted friendship. What he really meant was sex! Why, he was treating her as though she were no better than a prostitute.

''I won't sleep with you no matter how much of your hateful money you dangle in front of me.'' Her quivering chin belied the sharp challenge of her attack.

''Wait a minute!'' he murmured ever so softly, tilting her face so that her lips were mere inches from his. ''Now it's your mind that's in the gutter.''

Her gaze traced the sensual outline of his mouth with horrifying avidity. Why was she remembering how those lips had once claimed hers? So vivid was the memory that she could almost taste him, could almost feel the sharp edge of his teeth against her soft lips, almost feel the hard pressure of his lips claiming hers, almost feel his tongue entering and exploring the depths of her mouth. The strange little thrill in the pit of her stomach had nothing to do with anger. "I'd like to know who dragged it down there," she whispered, her cheeks flooding with color.

"Not me," he mocked innocently. "I never said anything about going to bed with you, at least, not right now. Sorry to disappoint you, honey, but I just want to be friends."

His eyes lingered on the pouting shape of her puckered mouth. "Even though you look like you're dying to be kissed, I don't think you're really ready. I like my women soft and womanly. Up till now you've been about as friendly as a prickly old sea urchin and about as kissable."

Dying to be kissed! She unpursed her lips in stupefied shock. How had they gotten into such a damning pose? Disappoint her! He liked his women soft and womanly! The urge to murder was very strong. But why had the mere thought of him wanting her in that other way make her skin tingle feverishly even while she loathed him for it?

"The answer's no," she replied huffily. "No! You and I can never be friends!"

"I'll give you a week to change your mind," he said agreeably, "if you really want the money, that is."

If...

"What about the Sue who you were talking to on the phone when I came in? How would she take to our friendship?"

"Eavesdropper," he taunted. "And it's Susan. I'll stop dating her and be true to you."

"True?" Kate snorted. "You don't even know the definition of that word."

"But won't it be fun teaching me?" His look was suddenly very male and very suggestive.

Kate felt a rush of hot confusion. "I thought we were only going to be friends."

"That's where we'll start until—"

"Until?"

"Until I turn you into the kind of woman I want," he said with maddening insolence as he let his gaze drift downward to her firm young breasts, which were rising and falling against her sundress in fury.

"I have no intention of changing for you," she countered breathlessly.

"Maybe not, but you will." His eyes seemed to burn right through the yellow cotton. To her horror, she felt her nipples peak against the thin material and prayed silently he wouldn't notice. But, of course, he did. She could tell by that insolent quirk of triumph at the corner of his mouth. He was deliberately letting her know that he found her body appealing, no matter how she tried to camouflage her natural female endowments.

"Want to make a bet, Rex?"

"I already did, the minute I agreed to give you the money you want."

"You can't do anything just to be nice, can you?"

"Why should I? I'm a businessman. I like to be repaid for anything I give, and with you, I'm looking forward to enjoying the repayment of my loan far more than usual."

Relentlessly he held her gaze. His hand molded itself to the curve of her neck, his long fingers sliding into the silky thickness of her black hair. His other hand lifted her chin with his thumb. There was possessiveness in his touch, and something else, something indefinable and yet all powerful. It held her frozen in his arms.

She felt her cheeks getting hot. "Things may not turn out the way you think, Rex Reynolds."

"Maybe not. But I'm playing for keeps. Winner take all. And you're the grand prize."

Two

Kate turned on the hose and began to spray down the decks of *Bright Star*. A week had passed since her humiliating interview with Rex, and though she longed to take him up on his offer, she hadn't been able to swallow her pride and go back and tell him. Not that she really had a choice. Only this morning *Bright Star*'s engine had started making a funny burping sound that wasn't funny at all. Kate knew she wasn't going to be able to put off having it checked. She'd barely managed to scrape enough money together to pay her note or Pedro and Juan. She was just getting by. There was no money left for the smallest crisis, like unforeseen engine problems.

"Hi there, Kate," came the deep, male tones of a certain, softly modulated Southern drawl that she'd recognize anywhere.

She pivoted and nearly stumbled over a tangle of black hose. She caught herself in the nick of time.

Rex was standing on the edge of the pier in a shower of sunlight. His blue eyes were bright with mockery. With his legs thrust widely apart, his stance was that of some arrogant, golden god.

"Hello, Rex," she mumbled, aware of how good he looked, while she herself was a wreck. He was dressed in tight, pressed jeans that molded his thighs like denim skin and a white knit shirt that was very becoming against the darkness of his tan. She hadn't had a chance to shower and change clothes, since she'd worked all night. Gray little half-moons beneath her eyes betrayed how tired she was from too much work and stress, and she probably smelled like shrimp.

She sprayed the cabin more viciously, forgetting in her agitation that the glass window was broken.

"Cuidado, gringa," Juan yelped from inside.

"Your mood doesn't seem to have improved in the week since I last saw you," Rex said with a throaty chuckle. "Sorry I wasn't more comfort."

If he didn't look out she would spray him, and it wouldn't be an accident! "My mood was fine till you happened by," she replied stonily. "And the last thing I want from you is comfort."

He chuckled. "At least you're honest. The rest of the women in my life are after my money, too, only they try to pretend it's really me they care about." His voice was soft, but there was a vibrant note in it. "I think I actually prefer the direct approach. Or is it just that I prefer you?"

The warmth in his eyes stirred all sorts of fires.

She shook her hair back from her face and fought to achieve a calm she did not feel. Oh, why had the good Lord given such a devil such gorgeous, perfectly sculpted male features and a beautiful voice and body to go along with them? Why couldn't Rex have been fat or short? Or anything other than the devastating male that he was?

"It certainly doesn't matter to me who you prefer," she retorted archly, inwardly battling the warm tide of excitement his obvious interest in her evoked.

"Then did you find someone else to help you?" he asked with what sounded like genuine concern.

"No."

"So things are just as bad as ever?" His voice was very quiet.

"Worse. The engine—" She bit back the end of her sentence. She shot him a look of pure dislike, hating him because he was so rich and so superior. She didn't want his pity. If only she didn't need his money!

He read every emotion that was scrawled on her tired young face. Her despair as well as her fiercely stubborn pride.

She was startled when, instead of mocking her and acting superior, he said in that same quiet, kindly tone, "I'll bet you could use some breakfast, Kate."

"Just look at me."

He grinned. "If you insist."

His bold eyes raked her in a way that made her breathless. She had the feeling that his gaze stripped away the damp shirt and saw only the lacy, transparent bra beneath that cupped her breasts. His eyes were hot and familiar. Her own emotions grew treacherous.

"Don't look at me like that!" she muttered furiously.

"You're the one who asked me to," he replied ever so innocently.

"I meant that I'm not dressed for breakfast, you idiot," she rasped.

Those dancing, blue eyes continued to regard her disheveled appearance with amused, male approval. "You look cute in wet T-shirts. Too cute. But I'm sure you know that."

She flushed crimson, but she wasn't as displeased as she tried to pretend.

"All right, I'll give you time to run home and change," he replied easily. "Look, I've got to go over a few problems I'm having with the new captain I hired for *Wanderer.* When I'm through, I'll pick you up at your apartment. It'll probably be in an hour or so. Think you can be ready by then?" When she only glared at him, his voice thickened huskily. "For God's sake, Kate, just this once don't say no!"

She breathed in sharply, the intensity of his request affecting her more than she wanted it to. Why did she nod meekly, almost gratefully? Why did her heartbeat accelerate at the prospect of going out with him, even if it was only for breakfast, when she should have bitten his head off and sent him packing?

He took her silence for acquiescence.

He grinned again, his tanned face awash with relief. "Good! I'll see you in an hour."

Then he was gone.

She stared after him, her stomach constricting, but that was only a hunger pain, she thought irritably as she turned off the water. It couldn't be the beginning of that old, all-consuming need he'd once aroused in her. He made her nervous. That was all.

She was over Rex.

She had to be.

By the time Kate got home, she had to hurry to get her hair up in hot rollers and herself into a soothing hot shower. Putting on her best green dress, a frilly, feminine thing she hadn't worn in years, she felt different in some new and unfathomable way that didn't bear close analysis.

Was it a crime for a girl to dress up?

When she took her hair down it fell in soft black waves over her shoulders. After she finished putting on her makeup, she gazed critically at her reflection in the little cracked mirror over her lavatory. She really didn't look all that different, except that the eyeshadow emphasized the seductive shape of her slanting eyes, and the green dress brought out their color. Lipstick made her full lips lush and moist. She started to put on more color, and then she stopped herself. After all, she was only going out with Rex Reynolds, and she hated him, didn't she?

She'd been waiting for Rex outside for about ten minutes in the deep shade of the porch, balancing herself precariously on the gingerbread railing, when he drove up in his pale blue Cadillac. She'd gone outside because she hadn't wanted him to come in and see how plain her three little rooms were. It would just give him something else to feel superior about.

As soon as she saw him, she raced down the sidewalk so he wouldn't get out and get a closer view of the shabby apartment house. He probably wouldn't see it as a quaint, charming historical dwelling the way she did, a house typical of old-time, romantic Key West.

Rex leaned across the front seat and opened the door, and she slid into the leather interior. The car was new and luxurious. Cool air was blasting from the air conditioner. There was the faint lilt of soothing music from the radio, but she scarcely noticed anything about the car. The minute she was inside, she was aware only of Rex, of his immense, male size, his clean scent.

She felt strange, unlike herself, and yet excited. She stared straight ahead, but she felt the disturbing heat of his eyes upon her. In the rearview mirror she caught the flash of his smile. It seemed he liked the change in her.

If he dared laugh at her because she'd curled her hair and put on a flattering dress, she would stomp back inside and slam the door in his face.

He seemed to sense her mood, but that didn't make him stop his slow, sensual appraisal.

"Well, are we going or not?" she snapped haughtily. "I don't have all day. I'm a working girl."

"Neither do I," he replied with a chuckle. "I'm a working boy."

She glanced at him furtively. What she saw heightened her impression of him as a primitive male, mature, powerful and latently dangerous. His was a body laced with corded muscles. "You're hardly a boy," she gasped.

He chuckled again, and she flushed, furious at herself for having uttered such a stupid, revealing remark.

"It's about time you admitted you noticed me as a man," he replied huskily.

Oh, she'd noticed.

He didn't take his eyes off her. They ran the length of her supple, perfectly conditioned body. His gaze seemed to burn through the thin material of her dress like the most intimate caress.

"What's the matter?" she demanded.

"Oh, nothing's the matter. On the contrary, I like what I see. You're not a girl anymore, either, Kate. You're all woman."

To that, she said nothing.

"Do you have to sit as far from me as you can get?" he

murmured. Before she could protest, a bronzed arm curved around her shoulder and pulled her closer until her left thigh was aligned against his. Even such casual contact with his hard, muscled body seemed too intimate somehow. But she knew better than to make an issue of resisting him.

He smiled down at her, and she knew he probably realized the upheaval being this near him was creating in her. Her legs felt boneless. Her heart was fluttering crazily.

Oh, what was she doing? Why had she come?

"That's better, isn't it?" he asked softly. "Much better. There's nothing to be afraid of, Kate. Not from me."

He kissed her gently on her brow. His lips were warm, his breath a velvet caress that made a faint tingling sensation against her skin.

Oh, he was wrong! Wrong! Wrong!

She didn't dare say another word. She just sat there, feeling very unsure and self-conscious, until at last he started the car, breaking the silent, unbearable tension between them.

Rex took her to a very expensive restaurant, and an unctuous waiter seated them at the best table in the dining room, with a wonderful view of the water. Though Kate felt wary and unsure, some part of her enjoyed being wrapped in luxury and treated like royalty for a change. Usually she was fighting to survive. When she tried to order something inexpensive, Rex insisted on ordering the largest breakfast on the menu for her. She hated the fact that he probably sensed she was starving from having worked all night.

When her steak and eggs and biscuits arrived, she had to force herself to eat slowly and daintily. Rex did most of the talking, staying on safe, neutral topics for much of the time.

At last he said, "I was sorry when I heard about Jake, Kate, but there didn't seem to be any way I could tell you how I felt at the time."

She remembered seeing Rex at the funeral and snubbing him when he'd come up to her and offered to help her in any way that he could. She'd told herself at the time that he really hadn't been sincere.

"No, I guess there wasn't," she admitted guiltily. "I was so completely wrapped up in my grief that I wasn't aware of anyone else's."

"I guess it hasn't been easy for you since then. Why don't you tell me about it, Kate?"

Kate wasn't used to confiding her problems in others, but Rex's eyes seemed so kind as they met hers that she suddenly found herself pouring out everything that had happened to her in the long dark months since her father's death. She'd never managed the financial end of their operation before, so she'd made mistakes, spending too much when she should have been more conservative. She told Rex about the unforeseen repairs to *Bright Star* and that she'd had to pay all the bills for Juan when he'd broken his arm. There were taxes she hadn't anticipated having to pay. But most of all, she told him about her feelings of aloneness.

By the time she finished, she was leaning toward him, and his hand had closed comfortingly around hers. For the moment, she'd forgotten her animosity toward Rex. She was vaguely conscious of how wonderful it was to be able to share personal things with someone who seemed to care.

"Poor darling," he said softly. "I know what it is to be poor and have it rough. I was a lot poorer than you can possibly imagine. I think those old memories are what drive me so hard." His fingers tightened around hers, and then he brought her hand to his lips, kissing the back ever so gently before he released it. There was a haunted look in his eyes that she hadn't seen in years.

For a time, they lapsed into silence. He watched her eat, and he seemed to enjoy the way she didn't leave a single edible morsel on her plate, not even the sprig of parsley.

Without thinking, she blurted out, "That might have been the best meal I've ever eaten, Rex. Thank you."

He threw back his golden head and laughed. "Maybe you were just hungry."

"It was really very sweet of you to bring me here. I'm sure

you have better things to do than to sit here listening to my troubles.''

''There's nothing I like better than being sweet—to you.'' His hand closed over hers again and she began to tremble.

She stiffened, remembering once more that he was the last person she should trust and confide in. ''I think we'd better go, Rex.'' Carefully she pulled her hand free of his.

His expression darkened with the old cynicism she hated. ''All right,'' he muttered tightly as she averted her eyes.

Later, when they were back in his Cadillac, he said, ''So what have you decided, Kate? Are you going to take me up on my offer or not?'' There was something almost ominous in his low tone, but she failed to notice it.

She was feeling full and replete. It was impossible to be properly mad at a man who'd just been so nice and fed her such a splendid breakfast.

''I really have no choice,'' she said. ''Either I borrow the money from you or I go bankrupt.''

''There's one condition I haven't told you about,'' he said in a cool, level voice.

''What do you mean?'' she asked guardedly.

''If I give you the money, your shrimping days are over.''

''What?''

''You'll be the sole owner of *Bright Star,* and, though I intend to keep a close eye on her operation myself, you can manage her. But from now on, Juan and Pedro do the shrimping while you stay onshore. There'll be no more nights when you work all night out on that boat with them. And I want to know of every expedition that you plan for *Bright Star.* That boat won't go anywhere without my permission.''

''You have to be joking!'' A tiny hammer of tension had begun to pound against her temples.

''I've never been more serious in my life. You're a woman, and I won't have you working yourself to the bone at a man's job the way you do. Not as long as it's my money you're using.''

''You don't have the right to tell me what to do.''

"If you take my money, we're going to put my rights in writing."

"Oh, I wish I'd never come to you, never confided in you."

"Nobody's forcing you to take my money, Kate," Rex said quietly.

"But if I take it, I'll be a slave, taking orders from you."

"That's your interpretation, not mine." His voice softened. "I told you I wanted to be your friend, Kate. Ever since Jake died, there's been no one to look after you properly, and you're doing a damn poor job. You're wearing yourself too thin, driving yourself too hard."

"You don't care what happens to me!"

"I do care," he replied levelly, meeting her infuriated glance. "You're too stubborn and proud to see things the way they are. You're a woman, Kate, and it's about time you started acting like one."

"You just want to take away my independence because it threatens your macho image."

A wry smile crooked his mouth. "Only you could come up with a gem like that."

"It's the truth."

"On the contrary, I'm not threatened by anything about you. My feelings are quite different. I want to protect you."

"I don't need your protection," she murmured tightly.

"You need a lot of things you won't admit you need."

Inside she was blazing with anger. With saccharine sweetness she asked, "Like what?"

"Like this, honey."

Even before he leaned across the seat and slid his arms around her shoulders, she sensed his intention. A warm fire burned in his eyes. He was looking at her as if he could barely keep his hands off her, as if he were fighting a losing battle to conquer some smoldering desire. She should know. She was fighting the same battle.

When she drew back, frightened, it was already too late.

"I thought all you wanted was my friendship," she whispered shakily.

"That was before you dressed up especially for me. I told you I liked my women soft and feminine. Today you made yourself that way for me."

"I did not."

"We'll never know. The truth is you want me every bit as much as I want you."

He let his hands drift down over her tanned shoulders with deliberate slowness. Kate could not stop herself from trembling as he gently pulled her body closer until it was pressed intimately against his.

"I hate you," she managed shakily. "I've hated you for years."

"Maybe. Maybe not. But you want me. Of that, I'm sure. All I have to do to prove my point is kiss you."

"No."

"Oh, yes," he murmured, his low voice a caress that ran the length of her spine.

She expected him to assault her mouth. Instead, his broad hands lifted the heavy weight of her black hair, and he gently caressed her bare neck with his lips. His kiss was butterfly-soft, but the shock of it make her shudder. She felt wrapped in warmth and tenderness, and this lovely gesture on his part was even more threatening than violence from him would have been.

"Oh, Kate, I thought you'd never get around to coming to me for help," he groaned. "It was hell, watching you go to every other man in town first. Hell...waiting."

What did he mean? What did it matter?

Tiny shivers of pulsing fire darted through her, shattering her flimsy defenses, and she fought to stifle the strangled moan of desire that escaped in a little tremor through her half-opened lips. Kate wanted to push him away, but his hands on her waist and neck forced her head toward his descending lips. The instant his mouth touched hers, her mind erased all memory of every other man and every other kiss since the last one Rex had bestowed upon her ten years ago.

It was as if there had never been anyone but him.

All her nerves and senses came vibrantly alive, and she

glowed under the devouring heat of his kiss. Its warmth melted away her reservations, and a languorous passion that had long been dormant stole through her. She had wanted this, ached for this, for too long. He had only to touch her to prove to her she was his.

Her arms curved around his neck, and she returned the slow-burning fire of his kiss, opening her mouth to let his tongue enter and probe the honey-warm moist sweetness of her. Her fingers combed the unruly silken waves of his hair. She was flooded with a thousand romantic memories.

Once he'd kissed her on a deserted, moonlit beach as the waves crashed over their bodies. Once they'd gone swimming together in crystal azure waters off a deserted island. Once the intensity of their youthful passion had held them in thrall.

"Rex," she said unsteadily, knowing she should force him to stop, that she should get out of the car and run, that she should never, never have anything to do with him again.

Wisely he silenced her once more with a kiss that poured the passion in his body into hers. With every fiber of her being, she was conscious of him, of his hot lips on hers, of his fingers stroking her body everywhere, of the hard, male shape of him against her own softer curves.

His hand slid under the neckline of her ruffled dress, touching bare skin, setting her flesh feverishly on fire. At the indescribable rapture of that possessing hand, she sucked in her breath. Slowly his fingertips slid beneath her lacy bra, his fingers circling her breast, kneading her nipple into a taut, aching button.

She strangled back a gasping moan as his lips covered hers once again.

He forced her backward into the leather cushions. His hands were molding her hips and thighs, fitting her to every hard contour of his body. A primitive need ached through her, a savage, throbbing need to know the wondrous fulfillment of his love-making once again.

One kiss, and she'd gone up in flames.

But she was still determined to fight it and him and herself.

She opened her eyes dazedly, struggling against the deliciously languorous feelings that enveloped her. "We'd better stop," she murmured in a low drowsy tone as she floated back into awareness from the nirvana of her golden sensual haze.

To her amazement, he pulled his mouth from hers and loosened his grip, though he continued to cradle her trembling body in his strong arms. "You're damned right we'd better," he muttered thickly, his voice muffled in the softness of her hair. "While we still can. Remind me not to kiss you again unless we're alone. Somewhere private."

"This was a mistake. I promise you it'll never happen again, Rex," Kate said in shaken embarrassment.

"And I promise you that it will."

"We mustn't, Rex."

"Oh, but we must. Look at me, Kate," Rex commanded softly in the same deep, resonant tone.

She met his eyes with a mixture of emotions: shyness, desire, embarrassment and confusion.

"Don't you remember how it was with us, Kate? There was always something special, something that was impossible to fight."

He'd managed to fight it. Hadn't he left her?

"Rex, please," she begged aloud. "It only hurts to remember."

"Maybe it doesn't have to hurt anymore, Kate. There's nothing to stop us from finding each other again."

She looked into his eyes. They were intense, and he seemed so earnest and sincere. But there had been too many years since the terrible hurt he had inflicted, too many years since that ancient pain had hardened into hatred. There was the barrier of his overwhelming success in life, as well. Most of all she was afraid that all he wanted was another brief torrid affair like they'd had together so long ago.

"I can't go back, Rex," she said pleadingly. "Please don't think this means I can. I couldn't ever trust you again. We're not the same people anymore. You've grown beyond me. We want different things now."

"We still want each other."

"Lust," she whispered with a weak little smile. "That's all it is."

"You make it sound so deliciously wicked." He reached out and touched her hair. Then he clasped her tightly, burying his face once more in the thick inky waves of her hair. "Forgive me, Kate. I never meant to hurt you when I left," he murmured in an odd, tortured voice. "I swear it. I never even knew I had. Jake said all you felt for me was a childish crush. I had so many problems of my own at the time that I never even considered yours. You went away to college. I thought you were happy. You dated all those college guys."

While I longed for you and was too proud to show it, she thought silently.

Aloud she said, "You were married for a while. To Carla, that girl from your hometown."

His blue eyes narrowed. "Not even for a year." A bitter edge had come into his voice. "We were talking about you," he said. "Kate, it's only been in the last few years that I began to wonder if you were really happy. You never married. You were always so distant. It was as if you'd wrapped yourself up in a shell and were hiding from everyone in the world. Still, it never crossed my mind until a week ago that I might have really hurt you. Even then I wasn't sure."

Her voice was muffled. "But you did hurt me, Rex, and I don't think I can ever get over it. I'm not sure I want to."

Her eyes held his, rejecting him. Splayed fingers pushed against his muscular chest with all their might.

She felt him tense. "You're sure, Kate?"

"Very sure. You're the last man on earth I want to have a personal relationship with."

There was a sudden unnatural stillness about him. For a long moment, his eyes steadily examined her face.

"All right, Kate." Slowly he pulled away from her and started the engine. He drove her back to her apartment in silence.

As he braked beside the curb, he said, "I'll be out of town for a couple of weeks, but the money's still yours if you want it. I'll leave a contract and a check for you with my secretary. You can pick it up anytime.''

She nodded silently. When she got out of the car, she didn't even bid him goodbye.

So it's finished, she thought as she watched him drive away. *At last.*

It was what she wanted.

But, oh, why was the pain in her heart even worse than it had been when she'd lost him ten years before?

Three

───

Rex strode into his office and set his cup of coffee down on his desk beside the stacks of papers that had accumulated in the two weeks he'd been out of town. The minute he saw the thick brown envelope on top of the clutter his secretary had heaped on his desk, adrenaline began to pump through his arteries. The information from the Archives of the Indies in Spain, the largest repository in the world of Spanish colonial records, had finally arrived.

Even after all these years, Rex still felt the same rush of excitement as when he'd been young and had begun to research the first wreck he'd gone after. What was it about the quest for treasure that brought this quickening in his blood?

With a letter opener, he slashed into the envelope. Two rolls of microfilm spilled onto the glossy surface of his desk, as well as several typewritten pages in Spanish from the graduate student Rex had hired eight months ago to research the *Marta Isabella,* the Golden Galleon. Rex doubted there would be much to go on.

He'd learned through experience that researching shipwrecks was an extremely difficult and frustrating undertaking. Through the centuries, many historical documents had been destroyed in fires, wars and floods. Thousands that had survived had never been cataloged. Volumes were still stacked in unopened bundles, collecting dust and being chewed up by rats in ancient buildings owned by libraries and museums in Europe. Nevertheless Rex had graduate students in London, Madrid and Seville working on the project.

What would Kate say when she found out he had decided to go after the wreck that had eluded Jake for more than a decade? Everyone had laughed at Jake for exhausting his resources searching for the galleon. Everyone except Rex. Rex had always believed in Jake, and Rex had believed that the *Marta Isabella* could be found. The question was, who would find her? Up till now, the only reason Rex hadn't gone after her himself was his respect for the man who'd taught him everything he knew. Well, Jake was dead, and Rex could see no reason now why he shouldn't go after that treasure.

Carefully Rex replaced the materials in the heavy envelope. He would have to pay Skip Kendrick, his friend who was a National Park Service historian and an authority on old Spanish documents, to translate the information for him.

Rex was about to replace the envelope on the pile of papers when he saw the legal documents Kate had signed in order to borrow money from him.

He picked up the stack of papers and glanced through them, his eyes zeroing in on the sloping letters of her careful, feminine signature right above his own black scrawl. Then he slammed the papers back down on his desk. The envelope from the Archives to the Indies fell onto the carpet.

He gulped a swig of coffee, and it burned all the way down his throat.

What was he going to do about Kate? He'd learned from Bill, his right-hand man, that she'd broken the contract she'd signed in just about every way imaginable. She went shrimping whenever it pleased her. There was even a rumor that she was outfitting *Bright Star* for a diving expedition. With his money! Without accounting for a single expenditure! She was deliberately making a fool out of him.

This morning he'd been down to the docks to have it out with her and learned that she'd taken *Bright Star* out shortly before dawn and she hadn't bothered to inform anyone where she was going. Worse still, she hadn't taken Juan or Pedro along, which meant she was totally alone. Someone had seen her loading tanks and scuba gear onto the boat all by herself. He'd ordered Bill to look for her.

What in the hell was she up to? Didn't she realize that a woman had no business at sea by herself? Anything could happen. *Bright Star* was hardly the most seaworthy vessel afloat. There were boats in the Gulf of Mexico filled with desperate illegal aliens. There were dope runners who were equally desperate. And no one but a fool went diving alone.

Damn the green-eyed witch, but she'd gotten to him! For the past two weeks, Rex had thought of her constantly.

He wanted her. He had wanted her for years, but his pride and the ancient promise he'd made to Jake had stood in the way. For ten years, Rex had worked to prove that he was as good or better as any man Jake would have preferred for his precious daughter. For ten years, he'd endured the way Kate had always cut him dead every time she saw him on the street, the way she acted as if she was some queen and he wasn't good enough to kiss her shoes. Who did she think she was? Then, when Jake had died and Rex had offered to help her after the funeral service, she'd just turned haughtily away from him, without saying anything.

Even when she'd come to him and asked him to help her a couple of weeks ago, she'd tried to make him feel as if he'd wronged her. It had come as a terrible shock to him to discover that she'd been hurt when he'd left her. Not that he believed her. The scars from his youth were too deep to permit him to really accept that. He believed that secretly she'd always looked down upon him ever since Jake had found him on the side of the highway, beaten nearly to death, and brought him home that night long ago. Despite Rex's success, he'd never been able to erase the memory of being poor and despised, and Kate was part of that memory.

Wearily Rex rubbed his brow with his hand, as if to push away the haunting memories, but they kept coming. As if it were yesterday, he remembered his stark terror and his humiliation the night Jake found him.

Rex had only been in his early twenties then, but he'd been in the worst jam of his life. That was saying a lot, considering the rough way he'd grown up.

Three guys were holding him down in the back seat of a speeding car. His lip was split where one of them had slugged him earlier. His temple throbbed, and it felt as if every one of his ribs was broken where they'd kicked him when they'd over-powered him and had had him on the ground.

He was vaguely aware of tires whirring on rain-slick asphalt and of the windshield washers jerking back and forth, back and forth, savagely slashing water out of the way. The stale humid air inside the confines of the car made him feel claustrophobic. There was the stench of liquor, sweat and his own blood, and the excited, youthful yells of his captors. There was pain so sharp that it left him breathless, paralyzing every other sense. But most of all there was fear. He could taste it every time he swallowed and smell it every time he drew a breath. It was suffocating him, devouring him, leaving no room for any other emotion.

The other guys were enraged because Carla Jones had quit dating one of them to date Rex, and they didn't consider a Reynolds fit company for her. An hour before, they'd caught Rex walking Carla home after a movie, and they'd begun following them, taunting Carla and then Rex. Having little choice in the matter, Rex had tried to defend Carla, but there had been too many of them. They'd forced him to the ground. Carla had run for help, but before she'd returned the boys had thrown Rex into their car and driven off.

Suddenly one of the boys opened the car door, and a cold torrent of wind and rain blasted inside. The car careened wildly.

"End of the line for you, Reynolds," Luther whispered with an evil chuckle.

Rex stared silently at Luther's blotchy face and tangled red hair and knew it would do no good to plead mercy.

"And if you know what's good for you, turkey, you won't

come back, either," Luther growled. "Next time, we won't be so friendly. Carla was my girl before you came along."

"Lucky Carla," Rex whispered derisively.

Luther didn't hear him. "You're as bad as your no-good mother, Reynolds. Don't you know when you're out of your class? Hell, you're nothing but a bastard."

Rex forced a grin that looked more like a sneer. Though it cost him a great deal, he made his voice louder. "With me, it was an accident of birth. In your case, Luther, you've made the grade all by yourself." Rex had heard a line something like that in a movie once.

Luther's freckled face contorted with rage. "I'm gonna kill the son—"

A fist slammed into Rex's jaw. Suddenly he felt himself being shoved out of the car. He hit concrete hard and rolled. Rocks ripped through his clothes and bit into his skin.

The next thing Rex knew, he was lying beside the road with the rain drenching him, in too much pain to even try to stand and seek help. Cars kept whizzing by, sometimes close enough so that gravel and flecks of mud bombarded him like pellets. After what seemed an eternity, he blacked out.

He returned to consciousness reluctantly, semidelirious from pain and fever, with his wet icy clothes stuck to his body. He was vaguely aware of the strangeness of his surroundings, of the softness of a bed instead of the hard gravel shoulder of a road, of the cleanliness and the pleasant sensation of security and quietness. There was only the sound of hushed voices instead of the roar of highway traffic.

"You must've taken leave of your senses, Dad, to bring him home. He's probably drunk or worse."

"There's no smell of liquor on him."

"Look how filthy he is. Why, it wouldn't surprise me if he tried to kill us."

"It'd surprise me mightily, Kate. For all that he's tall, the boy's as thin as a rail. He hardly looks strong enough to hurt a fly, girl. And as for being filthy, you wouldn't look so great if someone threw you out on a rainy night. What should I have done, left him out there to die?''

"You should have taken him to a hospital."

"What for? His pulse is strong. He doesn't seem to have any broken bones. He's young. He'll be okay."

"You're just afraid that maybe he's running from the law. You'll never get over the way you were framed for that crime you didn't commit when you were a teenager. Dad, that was a one-in-a-million mistake. The police aren't like that now."

'I know all I want to know about cops, Kate, and more.''

Days later—or was it only hours?—Rex awakened again in a blur of agony. Through half-shuttered eyes, he saw the flash of a blade coming toward his face in the dimly lit room as a scrawny-looking boy leaned hesitantly toward his throat. Operating on reflexes, Rex summoned his last remnant of strength. Coiling, he lunged for the scissors, dragging the boy to the bed and pinning him beneath his body.

Pulsating waves of pain splintered through Rex's battered body, and it was all he could manage to lie on top of the squirming boy and breathe in great gulps of air. When the boy tried to cry out, Rex covered his mouth. Then the brat bit into one of his fingers. Rex, who was used to abuse, merely tightened his grip.

"You little savage! Do that again, kid, and I swear I'll hurt you. Do you understand?'' Rex warned in a rough voice.

The boy, who really looked scared now, nodded.

After the kid lay still for a couple of minutes, as if afraid that any careless movement might provoke Rex to further violence, Rex decided he was properly cowed.

"I'll take my hand off your mouth if you won't yell,'' Rex whispered at last. "Can I trust you?''

The kid nodded again, and Rex slowly removed his hand.

The boy's eyes were enormous, great almond-shaped, green orbs. Beautiful eyes. Too beautiful to belong to this thin brown-faced boy. Fleetingly, Rex remembered the lure of Carla Jones's ice-blue eyes. Carla was a beauty with her red hair and pale eyes, but her eyes didn't even begin to compare with this kid's.

"Little boy, you've got nasty habits for a half-grown kid. You shouldn't have snuck up on me like that with scissors. What did you think? That I was too weak to stop you?" Rex chuckled hollowly. "That I'd just lie there and let you stick me?"

Rex brought the scissors menacingly toward the boy's face, deliberately wanting to terrorize him as he'd just been terrorized himself, and it was satisfying, the way the huge green eyes grew even bigger. Rex could feel him trembling as he seemed to shrink into the mattress.

Rex savored a brief moment of power. It was a pleasant sensation after what he'd been through.

At last the boy found his voice, which sounded little better than some swamp creature's croak. "I—I wasn't going to hurt you, mister."

"Sure. You were just sneaking up on me like that with a pair of scissors to be friendly."

"I—I was scared of you. That's why I was moving so slowly. I was going to cut your wet clothes off and put some more dry blankets on you. My dad found you unconscious on the side of the road tonight and brought you home. Honest, I was only trying to help you. And you're wrong about something else, too."

"What's that?"

"I'm not a boy. And you're as heavy as lead. If you're not going to hurt me, why don't you get off me so I can breathe?"

The kid had certainly recovered his nerve in a hell of a hurry. Wrong! *Her* nerve.

"You're not a boy?" Unconsciously Rex's voice had gentled as had his rough hold on her body. If there was one thing he knew, it was how to touch a woman.

Rex gaped at her in shock as she shook her head. For the first time, she smiled, and her tentative smile transformed her features from plainness to beauty. Rex dropped the scissors onto the bedside table. He realized his hand lay against her breast. He pulled it back as if he'd touched fire, but not before he'd become too keenly aware of the full, ripe flesh beneath his fingers. She was a girl, all right.

Then it happened. One minute she was a boy out to kill him,

and the next, she was a woman pressed beneath his body in a bed. He felt the way her soft contours pleasantly molded his shape. The slight scent of lavender soap emanated from her young form. A shaft of fire pierced every male cell in his body.

"How old are you, girl?"

"Seventeen," she whispered.

"You don't look a day over twelve, except for—" When his eyes ran over her body, her face grew still.

How could he have lain like this with her even for a second and not have felt the fullness of her breasts, the silkiness of her skin? Because of his pain and his fear that he was about to be murdered, he answered silently.

The pain came back in waves, but he resisted losing consciousness again. She was trying to cringe away from him. He liked the fact that she was small and delicate.

But she wasn't his type. He didn't go for boyish girls. Rex Reynolds went for girls with ample curves, girls who dolled themselves up with every sort of artifice. He liked eyeliner and cinched-in waists and high heels. He liked fluttery eyelashes and coyness.

But she was his type. Despite his pain, just her nearness made every one of his muscles harden. She'd been kind to him, and how was he treating her?

Suddenly Rex remembered the humiliation of his circumstances. All his life, people had said he was no good because of his mother. And whatever Dolly Reynolds had or hadn't been, he was her flesh and blood, and Rex had loved her.

From his first day in school, he'd heard the other children whisper about Dolly behind his back. He'd gotten into lots of fights as a result of that, and after a while he'd gotten a reputation of his own for wildness.

This girl was no different from the rest of them. If she knew about his past, she would despise him the way everyone else always had. He wanted her to like him, but because he wanted it so much, he lashed out at her to prove he didn't. Acting tough when he felt vulnerable was an old habit of his.

"Why in the hell would a girl cut all her hair off and dress like a boy, too?" he demanded. "A girl ought to act like a girl."

Then he began to shiver, the icy wetness of his clothes penetrating his weakened state at last.

"Maybe you're not so tough after all," she taunted softly. "Maybe you're just sick and cold and hurt. And why don't you get off me—" She turned beet red, and that made her cuter than ever somehow.

"Maybe..." He rolled away. He was faint with agony.

"Lie still," she murmured, "so I can help you." She was about to pick up the scissors again when his hand snaked out and grabbed her wrist.

"Maybe I don't want your help," he growled. "And I thought I'd convinced you that scissors make me nervous."

"Oh, you convinced me," she said faintly, "but I have a job to do."

"Undressing me?" he jeered nastily.

Again, her innocent face turned bright red and a heady sense of power swept him at her obvious embarrassment. In spite of his pain, the strange desire to torment her persisted. That wasn't the way he usually acted around girls, but then this was hardly his usual kind of girl.

"What's the matter, girl? Why don't you get on with it?" He unbuttoned the first button of his shirt, and she looked even more embarrassed. "Why don't you go ahead? I'll let you take my clothes off. I don't care if you remove every stitch. It might even be fun."

The girl's eyes widened with shock and anger at his jeering words, but he preferred her fury to her condescension or pity.

"Why, you ungrateful wretch!" she said. "If it weren't for my father bringing you home, you might be dead. He did that out of kindness, and I was trying to help you out of kindness, too. You're crazy if you think I'd get a thrill out of undressing some dirty—"

Her words hit a nerve. He yanked her toward him until she was almost lying on top of him. With a groan, he rolled on his side, trapping her against his body. "Oh, really?" he snarled. "You think you're better than me, I suppose?"

Her face was tellingly white.

"I can see it in your eyes," he muttered. "You think I'm trash."

"I—I shouldn't have said that. I never meant—"

"Well, I'm not trash. I'm not a criminal, either. Do you understand? And I don't want help from anybody who thinks I am." His mouth curled with dislike. "I'd rather die than have some plain do-gooder like you take care of me."

"Then maybe you will, 'cause now I'm not going to help you. And...and I wish those people that tried to kill you had beaten you to death. I bet you had it coming."

"Did it ever occur to you that if you have murder in your heart, you're not so perfect yourself, little girl?"

She said something then, something meant to goad him past the fragile limits of his patience, but he didn't hear her. Vivid green eyes blurred in a swirl of blackness and piercing pain. He felt himself reaching out to her, calling her, but the cruel black tide sucked him under.

He was scarcely aware of her hand closing with infinite tenderness over the one he stretched toward her, of his pulling her closer. He pressed her into the length of his pain-ravaged body and clung to her as though she represented his salvation, all the while begging her not to leave him to die alone.

Months later, she'd confessed that she'd stayed with him that night, cradling him in her arms when he groaned deliriously, bathing his feverish body with cool cloths, lying next to him when he managed to sleep in fitful spurts.

The next time he came to, sunshine was beaming against brown cotton draperies and casting blazing rectangles of light against a paneled wall. Every muscle and joint felt sore and throbbingly alive. His wet clothes were gone, and the layers of blankets that smothered him felt hot and scratchy. He was about to push them aside when something cold and wet dabbed his lip—something that stung like hell when it seeped into a dry cracked place on his mouth and tasted even worse.

"Ouch!"

He opened his eyes, and there she was, the girl with the close-cropped hair and jewel-green eyes.

"I thought I told you I didn't want your help," he muttered grouchily.

"So I don't always do as I'm told."

Somehow, during the night, she had gained the upper hand.

She was sitting on the bed, hovering over him. In her jeans and green plaid shirt she looked very small and dainty. Her breasts pushed against the faded green cotton. He liked the way she looked. Too much.

"Aren't you scared to be in here with me all alone?" he mocked.

"No." Her answer was calm, but the pulse in her throat had speeded up.

He lowered his eyes so that his gaze wandered over her body. "Don't you know what I might do to you?"

He was aware of a little gasp on her part, but she managed a tart, "You're pretty banged up. I imagine I could get away from you if I had to. I'd just punch you in one of your bruises."

"Oh, you would?"

"Yes, I would. And I know where they all are."

"You must have had a busy night, inspecting me," he murmured suggestively.

She pretended not to understand. "Besides," she said crisply, "I don't think I have anything to worry about. Last night you called me a plain do-gooder. You made it very clear that you don't like me."

"Maybe you look better to me in the morning. I like to eat little girls for breakfast."

She did look better, and despite his pain, she aroused a tightness deep in his belly, as well as a quick heating of his blood that made him feel on fire. "For a skinny girl, you're not all that bad. If you let her hair grow out and put on a little lipstick, you might even be pretty."

His eyes met hers, but she looked away quickly. No matter

how she tried to conceal it, he was aware of how nervous she was in his presence.

"You're definitely feeling better this morning," she retorted in that brisk, no-nonsense tone of hers. It was obvious that she was ignoring his backhanded compliments, but from the way her white teeth were biting into her bottom lip, he suspected the effort was taking all her willpower.

"What makes you say that?" he asked.

"The way you've started picking on me again."

She was looking down at the bottle of medicine she was holding in her hands instead of looking at him. Her thick lashes lay like black fans against cheeks that were darkly flushed.

It was enchanting the way she blushed so easily. "I'm not picking on you," he said almost gently.

"You're definitely not Prince Charming."

"No, I guess not," he replied crossly, remembering anew all his deficiencies. She probably had a very low opinion of him, and he wasn't doing much to improve it.

The wool blankets were making him itch everywhere. Didn't she have any sheets?

"What happened to my clothes?" he demanded, determined to embarrass her. Just why it was so much fun to make her turn red and stammer, he didn't know.

Kate jumped, as if his voice had bitten her. "They're over there in the garbage can," she said, attempting a casual tone that did little to conceal her agitation. "I'm afraid they've been cut to ribbons."

"Who took them off?" he asked pointedly.

Her expression froze. A falling feather could have been heard.

"W-what difference does it make?" she asked at last, blushing again.

"A big difference—to me."

"I did," she whispered. "While you were asleep, I cut them off of you."

"All of them? Even my blue jeans?"

Her eyelashes were fluttering above her scarlet cheeks, and she was twisting the end of his blanket in her fingers.

"Why do the details matter?" she pleaded wretchedly.

"They just do," he replied in a low, quiet voice. He found her shyness irresistible.

"I covered you with a blanket. I didn't look at you, if that's what you're worried about."

He grinned. "Oh, I wasn't worried about it. I sort of like the idea of you undressing me. How do you know where my bruises are if you didn't sneak a little peek?" He punctuated this last with a knowing chuckle.

Slim fingers just kept twisting brown wool. She finally looked up, her eyes shooting violent green fire at him. She was lovely in her own special way.

"You're disgusting, you know that? Have you ever tried being nice to somebody? Maybe then you wouldn't get yourself all smashed up. I snipped along the sides of your jeans. I wouldn't have done it except I didn't want to wake Jake when I was already awake. You were so cold that you were shaking. I was just trying to help you. I—I didn't do it for any of the reasons you're implying."

She met his eyes again, this time beseechingly, and he felt an inexplicable rush of tenderness for her. There was something fragile and defenseless about her. She was obviously innocent. Beautifully so. Suddenly he experienced an emotion he'd never felt before. He wanted to keep her that way. He wanted to protect her. Even from himself.

"When you're better," she began, desperate to change the subject from herself to him, "where will you be going? Do you have a home to go back to? A family?"

"No, I don't have anywhere or anyone." Bitterly he imagined that Carla was probably secretly relieved he was gone so that she could get over her shameful attraction to a Reynolds.

"How terrible," Kate murmured, the genuine concern in her voice touching him.

"I'm afraid you're stuck with me, at least for a while, even if I'm not Prince Charming."

At that she smiled. Without knowing she did so, she took his large callused hand in hers. "So who needs Prince Charming?

A skinny do-gooder like me wouldn't know how to act around him. I guess I'll just have to get used to being picked on.''

''Oh, you're not skinny everywhere.'' His eyes raked the area where green plaid stretched tightly over her swollen breasts. ''And you're sort of an unwilling do-gooder, at best.'' Something low and intimate had come into his voice, something he himself was at a loss to understand.

Suddenly she grew aware of the long bronzed fingers intertwined with hers, and she began to blush furiously at her own boldness and perhaps at the pleasure she found in his touch. But when she attempted to free herself, he wouldn't release her. Instead he turned the tiny hand over in his much broader palm.

His gaze met hers. She was offering him something that he'd never had from a woman before. There was kindness, sympathy and friendship in her eyes. Never before had he wanted these things from a woman. He'd only wanted sex.

But with Kate it was different from the first moment, and it always would be.

Her gentleness was soothing and lessened the pain of the bitter feelings he had always known. Suddenly he knew that he needed her sweetness and kindness more desperately than he'd ever needed anything. He craved them. He had to have them, or he would be lost forever.

''Kiss me,'' he begged hoarsely.

She hesitated. Then to his astonishment, she did, but it wasn't the kind of kiss he had in mind.

He'd fallen asleep as her lips had innocently brushed his brow.

The telephone began to ring, jerking Rex back to the present. His secretary answered it in the outer officer. He lifted his cup of coffee to his lips and then rejected the cold bitter stuff.

Hell, yes, he wanted Kate. Somehow, during their year together all those years ago, she'd made herself a part of him. He'd always wanted her, even though after their affair, all she'd ever done was make him miserable. Now all she wanted was to use him.

Well, maybe it was time she learned that using him was going to come at a price. He'd warned her, hadn't he?

The phone rang again, and this time his secretary buzzed him. Rex picked it up.

"Boss, our spotter plane just called in the coordinates for the Andrews trawler."

"Give them to me, Bill."

"She's anchored just off Purple Key, that little deserted island where Jake Andrews salvaged *La Reina Hermosa* eleven years ago."

"I know where it is." Rex had never liked the place, but it had always been a favorite of Kate's. It was remote and strewn with shoals. There always seemed to be an overabundance of sharks in the area. Not that they would deter Kate. "Thanks, Bill."

What in the hell was she doing there?

Four

A plume of black fumes hovered over the stern of *Recess* as the huge outboard engine roared irritably. Rex untied a dock line and was about to cast it off when Susan Peerson walked toward him, her sleek golden body clad in tight-fitting white slacks and blouse.

"Hi, Rex. You haven't called me lately, you mean ole devil." Her voice caressed the word *devil* as though it were *darling.*

Rex hated being chased, even by beautiful women. Today he hated it even more than he usually did because Kate had put him in such a foul humor by thwarting his authority. "I've been out of town," he replied curtly.

"I missed you."

"That's hard to believe," he said cynically. "From what I hear, you've got quite a few men on the string."

"Not men like you."

He caught the look in her eye and said nothing. He threw off another line.

"Got room for one more, Rex? You haven't taken me out on *Recess* in simply ages."

He hesitated, but only briefly. Why not? At least Susan wanted to be with him. "Sure, Susan." Extending his brown hand, he helped her aboard.

"I hope we're going somewhere isolated and remote," she teased coquettishly.

"Oh, we are." She didn't catch the note of irony in his hard voice as he left her to throw off the other dock lines. He knew she wouldn't be happy when she realized he was going after Kate.

As soon as they were out of the marina, Rex pushed the throttle down, and the yacht almost flew toward Purple Key. Susan went below to keep her hair from blowing. *Recess* cut a frothy white wake as she sped across the blue crystalline surface of the water at a speed of more than forty knots.

In less than half an hour, Rex saw the deserted white beaches of Purple Key, as well as the emerald crown of pines that grew on the deserted island. He slowed down and turned on his depth finder. The shoals and reefs got nasty near the key.

"Susan, come on up and get on the bow. I need you to keep a lookout for anything we might hit."

"Aye, aye, *capitán,*" Susan quipped playfully in a mock Cuban accent. She emerged from the cabin in a miniscule black bikini that revealed almost every asset of her well-endowed golden body.

"What's that supposed to be? Three postage stamps?"

"Last time we were together, you said you liked it," she cooed.

"Last time, I wasn't trying to keep from tearing the hull of my boat out on a piece of coral. If you don't want us to wind up being dinner for the sharks, go back below. I'm afraid you'll only distract me," he growled. For some reason, he found her blatant sexiness irritating rather than arousing. Bringing Susan along had definitely been a mistake.

"Okay, okay." She was clearly miffed that he was concentrating on navigating instead of on her. Sulkily she disappeared below.

Rex slowed *Recess* to less than two knots. Fortunately the sea was a tranquil blue green rippled occasionally by a slight breeze.

The water was like glass, and Rex could see the bottom forty feet below. Around him, peaks of coral reef glinted white and gold in the sunlight as they thrust up to the surface.

When *Recess* came around the curve of the island, Rex saw *Bright Star* nodding serenely at her anchorage. But what was that contraption on her stern?

Sure enough, Bill was right. While Rex had been gone, Kate had reinstalled *Bright Star*'s mailbox, a machine that was also called a blaster or duster, a type of salvage equipment used to funnel the prop wash toward the bottom in a swirling tornado of water to rapidly excavate holes in the ocean floor. Now why had she done that if she intended to keep shrimping?

Because she didn't intend to shrimp. She'd borrowed his money for some other purpose, and he had a sneaking suspicion he knew exactly what it was. A tight ball of fury began to build inside Rex.

Rex brought his boat up beside the other vessel. Several tanks of compressed air littered *Bright Star*'s deck, but there was no sign of Kate. She was either in the cabin or down in the water by herself.

Rex put his engine in neutral and went forward to drop his anchor. Only after he'd made sure it was holding did he turn off the motor.

What he saw next brought a cold chill to the pit of his stomach. Several fins were lazily circling *Bright Star*. Sharks! And they seemed more aggressive than usual.

"Kate!" Rex called in alarm. Had she gone down alone? Was she—

The thought of her down there in trouble and all by herself was more than he could endure. He went wild inside.

It was impossible to swallow the hard lump of fear that rose in his throat.

"Kate!" he yelled again.

At last, Kate's black head popped out of the cabin. Long-lashed green eyes grew bright and startled when she met his grim gaze. An unmistakable expression of pain and anger passed over her face before she jerked her gaze from his.

"Hello, there, Rex. While you're passing by, why don't you just pull up anchor and keep on passing? This is my anchorage."

"Because I wasn't passing by. And thanks for the welcome," he muttered through gritted teeth. "It's even warmer than I expected."

Relief that she was alive brought a surge of fierce, terrible fury. It made him even angrier that just the sight of her made him as hungry as a sex-starved kid. Had it only been a few weeks since he'd seen her? It felt like forever.

Kate was wearing a tan swimsuit that glistened with dripping water. The umber shade of her suit matched so exactly the color of her tanned skin that at first Rex thought she was wearing nothing. She seemed like a naked goddess—an ebony-haired Venus risen from the depths of an aquamarine sea.

He caught his breath sharply at the sheer deliciousness of that sleek brown body revealed in such a tantalizing way. She seemed clothed only by the black wet shining waves of her hair that cascaded over her shoulders.

She'd been swimming—with the sharks. Naturally! His anger hit him again full force.

Jake had taught her to be fearless when it came to sharks. All professional divers eventually got used to them, and Kate had been with them all her life. Jake, however, had done more than merely grow accustomed to sharks while he worked around them. Because Jake could sell any movie with sharks and a human in it for twenty-five dollars a foot, he'd actually sold a lot of underwater films of himself or his daredevil daughter doing ridiculous things with them, like swimming up to them and hitting them on the nose with a hammer.

What other girl would go down when a fin was visible on the surface? Not *girl*, Rex amended in silent anger, *woman*.

The raging fire searing his veins was not entirely due to his fury. His gaze moved insolently down her body, touching on her large high breasts, her slim waist, the delicate curve of her narrow hips. Then his eyes slid down the tanned length of her legs.

"You have no business being out here alone. Don't you know it's dangerous?" Rex began heatedly.

"I needed to be alone, Rex," she said quietly. "Sometimes I come here to think about Jake."

The sadness in her voice caught at his heart. Then he remembered. This place had always been special to her. He fought against the sudden softening he felt toward her.

"Were you diving?" he demanded in a savage undertone.

"Only for a few minutes."

"With all those sharks?"

"There weren't so many when I went down, and you know I'm not afraid of sharks like you are, you big sissy. I've dived around them all my life. They won't bother you if you don't bother them. They're probably just as afraid of us as we are of them."

"That's what you always say."

"It's the truth."

"Well, have you ever seen so many fins circling around?"

"No."

"Does it really seem prudent to go in when you do?"

"I wasn't worried about being prudent."

"Obviously."

Susan chose that moment to re-emerge in her half-naked state with two opened beers from the ice chest. At the sight of Susan, the expression of pain on Kate's face intensified.

"What are you doing here, anyway, Rex?" Kate asked.

"I came after you." Rex took one of the beers from Susan.

"Why?" Kate returned defensively, glancing toward Susan. "It's obvious you're not looking for female companionship, and even if you are, I don't want to be part of a collection."

His gaze narrowed, slicing over Kate's pale face. "You signed an agreement stating *Bright Star* doesn't leave the dock without my knowledge."

"That contract was unfair, Rex."

"Nevertheless, your signature's on that document."

"I thought you were out of town. Otherwise, I would have told you," she hedged.

"Sure."

"Well, if you don't believe me—"

"I don't. You've been out shrimping twice, too."

"That was because Juan was sick. You weren't here, so I couldn't ask your permission."

"Either you're going to live up to our agreement, or you're going to repay my money, plus interest."

"So what do you want me to do now?"

"I want you to pull up your anchor and head back to Key West."

She glared at him. "Or?"

"Or you can return the money you owe me. And I'll collect that collateral you put up as security."

As his predatory male gaze drifted over her curves, her eyes rounded with sudden fear. Just as he'd intended, she'd caught his meaning, but she recovered herself almost immediately.

She scowled at Rex with even more hatred than before. "You win, Rex. But then I don't really have a choice, do I?"

He couldn't stop looking at her. Her beauty tantalized him despite his rage. As she moved away from him with feline grace, her ebony hair swung over her shoulders like spilled skeins of glossy black silk. But he wasn't watching her hair, he was watching the undulating slither of her slim hips and the graceful loveliness of her long legs. She probably planned every voluptuous move.

She went forward, and leaning over the bow in an inviting pose that made him feel hot all over, she began to pull up the anchor. After pulling in about twenty feet of line, she couldn't pull in any more no matter how hard she tugged.

"It's stuck," she yelled.

"What?"

"My anchor must be caught on a coral ledge or something. I'm going to have to go back down."

"No!"

"If you think I'm going to leave my anchor—"

"Damn right, you're going to leave it! Cut the line!"

She began to put on her weight belt. Then her flippers.

"Kate!" he screamed.

Ignoring him, she grabbed her mask and tank. Then she picked up her shark pricker, a hand spear without prongs or barbs on the end of it.

While he watched in horror, she waved breezily in his direction and then jumped in. All the sharks followed her down.

"She's crazy," Susan murmured in awe, watching the trail of bubbles disappear.

"She damn sure is," Rex muttered furiously as he went below and grabbed his diving gear. He stripped out of his shirt and put on his mask and tank.

"Well, since you're so determined to play hero, Rex," Susan said sulkily, "I'm going below. The humidity's making my hair fall."

Rex scarcely heard Susan. He was staring fixedly at the blue-green water. Even though Kate's bubbles were still coming up fine, Rex's stomach was a hard knot of fear as he dived in after her.

With her shark pricker in one hand, Kate was striking any sharks that dared to venture too close while with her other hand she tried to free the anchor's fluke, which had hooked on a ledge of coral.

At a depth of forty feet, sunlight turned the water a hazy blue. Kate looked like a naked blue ghost performing some mystic ritual as she paused at her work just long enough to pantomime instructions that Rex should leave her alone and surface.

He swam toward her all the faster. Just as Rex reached her, the ledge broke loose, and he managed to grab Kate and pull her and the anchor free.

In an explosion of bubbles, Rex dragged her, kicking and fighting, all the way up to the surface. At least twenty sharks started coming at them as they began to swim for *Bright Star,* which was about thirty feet away. Rex pushed Kate toward the boat while he defended her from the rear. Removing his tank, he hit any sharks that came too close on the nose. Every time he hit one, it turned and swam away, but more kept coming.

Two sharks came up and nudged his leg, and he just managed to jerk his leg away in the nick of time. Kate had reached the ladder and was climbing on board. He was right behind her, but the sharks were darting toward him faster than ever. He felt one brush his thigh, and he twisted away.

When Rex got to the boat and began to pull himself up, the biggest shark of all rushed toward his feet and legs. Rex was too exhausted to defend himself. His weight belt and heavy gear kept him from climbing up the ladder. He tried to remove the belt, but the end of it had gone through a loop. When he jerked on it, it tightened into a knot. The open-mouthed giant was almost on him. Kate screamed and then leaned down and jabbed the monster in the nose with her spear.

Then she took Rex's tank from him and lifted it into the boat. When he finally pulled himself on board, he towered over her like a dark angry god. His well-muscled chest was heaving. He ripped off his flippers and his mask.

For a long minute he glared at her in wordless rage.

Her green eyes blazed mutinously.

"You little fool! Why did you deliberately dive in there with them?" he began.

"Because I wanted my anchor."

"You nearly got me killed."

"That's entirely your own fault. No one invited you down there. In fact, if you hadn't made me so mad by ordering me not to, I might never had gone after it myself. I just wanted to show you—"

"That's the stubbornest, stupidest answer anyone ever gave me," he yelled.

"Look, if divers waited till there was nothing in the water but sea horses, they wouldn't swim anywhere but in swimming pools."

"Your logic stinks," he said in a voice gritty with anger.

"I've never been afraid of sharks before."

"Do you still hold to your line that they won't bother you if you don't bother them? They just bothered the hell out of me!"

"And you were pretty brave—for a big sissy. Thank you, Rex."

"Kate!"

Her eyes grew enormous as she realized how furious he was,

but she'd never lacked courage in the face of danger. And she didn't now.

"Don't look so mad, Rex. So, I admit that maybe today you had a point. Maybe I've changed my mind about sharks. So, just this once, you were right. Okay? They were pretty scary when they ganged up like that. I just hope this one bad experience won't make me into as big a sissy as you."

"That's the last smart remark I intend to take from you, Kate Andrews. It's time you learned who's calling the shots." He moved toward her.

Too late, she realized she'd pushed him too far. She tried to back away, but he clamped his fingers around her forearm in a viselike grip. With brutal pressure, he jerked her forward so that her face was close to his. She was forced to look into the harsh blue glitter of his eyes.

"Take your hands off me, you—"

Violent, raw emotion claimed him. She felt it in the ominous vibration of his soft voice. "I'm calling in my note," he whispered. "I want my money." There was hunger as well as rage in his eyes. "And my collateral."

"Well, you'll never get it."

"The hell you say."

Shooting pain flamed from her imprisoned arm as Rex hardened the pressure of his grip and drew her closer. Despite the pain, Kate fought desperately to escape the steel trap of his fingers. Her bones felt as if they were being ground together, but some animal wildness made it impossible for her to submit. She kicked and clawed, preferring self-destruction to being owned by him.

"You're going to pay back everything you owe and more, my sharp-clawed little cat," he mocked cruelly. "Starting now."

"Don't you dare touch me," she cried.

"Did you really think you could have it all your own way, Kate? That you could take my money, lie to me and then make a fool of me by going against our contract? Well, maybe it's time you learned that nobody plays Rex Reynolds for a fool and gets away with it. Not even you, Kate Andrews."

His other hand closed around the back of her neck and lifted her face to receive his descending mouth. She fought to evade him, but he was too strong, and he overpowered her easily. An instant later, he met her soft lips in a kiss of savage possession. His mouth was hard and hot as he took what he wanted from her trembling lips. She felt his teeth against her tongue. She tasted the saltiness that clung to his mouth.

He kissed her over and over again, long, hot kisses that conquered all resistance. His hands moved over her body as if she belonged to him.

"You said all you wanted was my friendship." She choked out the words.

"I lied," he said softly, baring his teeth at her in what was more a sneer than a smile. "If you could lie to me about your reasons for wanting to borrow my money, why shouldn't I lie to you about mine for giving it to you? Yes, Kate, I want much more than friendship now. And I intend to have it." There was intensifying passion as well as a warning in his drawling voice.

He was about to lower his lips to Kate's once again, but Susan chose that moment to emerge from the cabin where she'd been protecting her hair and began blasting away at *Recess*'s horn.

"What in the hell!" Rex muttered furiously.

"Sounds like your girlfriend's jealous. I think you've taken on more women than even you can handle, lover boy," Kate jeered softly in triumph as he let her go. "If she wants you, she can have you."

The horn kept tooting.

"And apparently she does. There's no accounting for a woman's taste, now is there?" Kate smiled up at him nastily.

A muscle jumped convulsively in his jaw. Cold blue eyes roamed insolently over her body, lingering on her tensed nipples.

"Nor for a man's taste," he finished cuttingly. "This isn't over, you know. It's only just begun."

Her dark face went white.

Five

Kate flew about her tiny apartment, grabbing clothes from drawers and throwing them toward the open suitcase on her bed. She had to get away. At least for a few days.

Why did Rex have to come back to town so soon? She'd known he'd give her a hard time. Even though she'd never intended to pay any attention to those ridiculous demands he'd put in that contract, she should have realized he'd make her stick to them.

Oh, she should have known better than to ever have had anything to do with him. Maybe he was rich now, but he hadn't really changed. Deep inside he was still that poor, embittered young man, determined to take his revenge against life from anyone unlucky enough to fall into his clutches. Why—

A loud banging commenced at her front door, and her frantic thought was never completed. A glass paperweight began to bounce across her desk. She raced to catch it before it fell.

What was that madman out there trying to do, shake the house down? Surely in a minute he would stop and go away. Or maybe she'd get lucky, and he'd bruise his knuckles and have to stop.

But he didn't. The knocking grew even louder.

Oh, dear, there was no way she could ignore thunder like that.

Gossipy Mrs. Benson would be rushing downstairs in no time if she did.

With her heart beating fiercely, Kate went to the door and looked through the peephole.

Her eyes slid down over the thatch of golden hair, the masculine splendor of the dark face, the wide shoulders and broad chest, now clothed in a spotless white shirt. Rex. He looked so cold and angry that she felt sick.

She opened the door an inch, but it was still held by a chain.

"I see you're expecting me," he drawled silkily.

Through the tiny opening, she saw the flash of his white grin and his unsmiling blue eyes.

"You'd better let me in, Kate."

Something in his voice convinced her she'd better. Trembling fingers fumbled with the chain, releasing it, though she didn't open the door any farther. He leaned forward and began pushing it open. Though she was pushing against it, he opened it easily and strode inside as if he owned the place.

"Do come in," she said sarcastically.

He merely smiled, his fingertips lightly brushing hers as he removed the paperweight from her shaking fingers and set it on a low table.

Kate started visibly at Rex's casual touch, the slight contact making her skin feel tingly.

"I'll feel safer if you aren't armed," he said.

She wouldn't have felt safe if she'd had a bear club.

"Make yourself at home," she said coolly.

"Oh, I intend to. Especially if my hostess continues to be so accommodating." The tone of his husky voice made the last word nastily suggestive.

His blue eyes danced over her with a mocking gleam that left her breathless, and she realized how dangerous it was for her to be alone with him even when she was mad at him. Despite her anger, a soft warmth was spreading through every tight muscle in her body.

Quivering with renewed misgivings, Kate stared up into

the beautiful masculine face beneath that unruly shower of golden hair.

He towered over her, his hands jammed into his pockets. He dominated the tiny room with his fierce male presence. But if she didn't know better, she might have thought he was as ill at ease as she was.

His gaze took in her fearful face, as well as the untidiness of her sparsely furnished apartment. She was aware of the stained place in the ceiling where rain had leaked in last winter. Her desk was littered with bills and papers. Magazines were stacked on the bright quilt that concealed the shabbiness of her gray sofa.

"Nice place," he murmured dryly.

"Don't be condescending," she hissed.

"I wasn't. It's not lavish, but it's got a cozy feel. And that, Kate, is something all the money in the world can't buy. You've made this place into a home."

There was a hot light in his eyes that she didn't trust. "You didn't come here to discuss my apartment," she said stiffly.

"No."

"Why are you here?"

"You know why."

"No, I don't."

He prowled about the room restlessly like a predator exploring new territory. As he went toward her desk, she suddenly remembered that the night before she'd been studying the charts on which she'd marked the spot she believed the *Marta Isabella* was located. At all costs she had to keep him from seeing them.

Swiftly she moved between him and her desk to block his view. For a moment he looked beyond her. Then he studied her in quiet, puzzled interest.

"Rex, you didn't tell me why you came over tonight," she persisted.

"I thought I made it clear this afternoon what I wanted from you." The intensity of his blue eyes seared her.

"This is the twentieth century, Rex. Surely you don't plan to force me."

"Force won't be necessary." The words were soft, but they sounded brutal to Kate.

"That's a horrible thing for you to say to me," she rasped indignantly.

"But true." He smiled. His knowing glance held hers.

Kate felt panic rise within her at his words. "The last time you took me out, you promised me you'd leave me alone."

"And I did, damn it." His low voice roughened. "For two weeks. And I would have held to that if you hadn't betrayed every legal promise you made to me. You shouldn't have lied to me, Kate, if you wanted me to keep my word to you."

"I won't anymore, Rex. I promise I'll—"

"It's too late for more false promises, Kate."

Kate shook her head, wide-eyed. "No, Rex."

"Maybe it's time you started saying yes to me for a change," he murmured.

She turned toward him, her expression deliberately cool and disdainful. "So you're determined to exact your pound of flesh?"

He chuckled. Lazily he let his eyes drift over the slim length of her body. "One hundred and twenty pounds—roughly."

"One hundred and fif—" She caught herself, but not in time.

"Close." He dazzled her with another grin.

For a numbed moment she could only stare at him. "Why?"

"Hell, I don't know why any more than you do. I want you, Kate."

"And what you want, you take?"

He smiled faintly. "In this case, yes." His voice now held a hard edge.

"Why can't you just forget me?"

His face darkened. For the first time, she realized the effort it must have cost him to play it light since he'd come inside.

"Damn it, Kate, do you think I haven't tried?" he exploded as he spun away from her. He clenched his fists and pounded them once, only once, against the wall before he managed to regain control.

Kate shuddered at the intensity of the sheer raw violence consuming him, and for a moment she was too upset to worry about what Mrs. Benson might be thinking.

"You've haunted me for ten years, girl. Hell, yes, I tried to forget you, but I couldn't." His blue eyes slashed her mercilessly. "Do you know what it's like to want someone so bad that it hurts and to have her act as if she despises you?"

Kate swallowed. Oh, yes. She knew.

Some treacherous part of her was secretly thrilled that once again he was claiming he found her as unforgettable as she'd found him. Not that she really believed him. He'd walked out on her, hadn't he? She was sure he'd lied about what he'd said about Jake.

"It can't be true," Kate said in a helpless whisper.

"But it is," Rex replied roughly, his anger still not completely controlled. "There hasn't been a day or a night that I haven't thought of you, that I haven't remembered the way your green eyes could dazzle me after we made love, the way your long slim body fitted mine so perfectly, the way your hair felt like silk when I wound it in my fingers, the way you blushed all the time, the way you defied me at every turn. No one is like you, Kate. No one. And you knew just how susceptible I was, didn't you? That's why you came to me for money."

"That isn't true, Rex. I thought you owed me something for what you did to me."

"Owed you something. Hell, yes, I owed you something. My life. My soul. You gave me the chance to become the man I am. You could have asked me for anything, Kate, and I would have given it to you. But all you wanted was my money. So you took my money, and then you lied to me. I couldn't stand your twisting me around as if you still thought I was nothing. I grew up with that, Kate, and it's the one thing I can't endure now, not even from you."

She turned crimson in shame as she realized how he'd misinterpreted everything she'd done. Was what he'd said true? She could sense his agony and anger, and yet her own hurt got in the way of her trusting him. Besides, she couldn't forget that he'd stuck his nose into her business on the pretext that he was helping her and then had tried to boss her around. Why, only this afternoon he'd come out to her anchorage and humiliated her in front of his girlfriend. How could Kate reverse her opinion of him instantly? He probably sensed how susceptible she was to him. He was just enough of a rat to play on her vulnerable emotions.

If only she knew whether he was telling the truth.

She didn't know what to say. What to do.

The tremulous silence lengthened between them.

Her mind whirled. She wanted to run. Then she looked into his eyes, and she felt herself drowning in those warm blue depths. His anger was gone. There was hunger now, but there was infinite tenderness, as well. She didn't move a muscle as he came closer.

Reaching out, he caught her shoulders and pulled her into his arms. When she felt the warmth of his hands on her cool skin, she couldn't suppress the shivers that raced through her. She clenched her teeth as she fought the sensations his touch aroused in her. But it was no use.

"Let me go," she pleaded softly, even as her body melted into his.

How could she react to him instantly in such a complete and humiliating manner? She only hoped that he couldn't feel the way her breasts seemed to swell against the muscular contours of his hard chest or the way her nipples hardened until they pressed against her thin cotton blouse like tiny buds.

Her breath came unevenly. She felt his heat. She trembled beneath the pressure of his hands. He had always known how to touch her, how to hold her.

"Don't you think it's time we stopped fighting each other long enough to discover what this passion means?" he whispered huskily as his mouth descended toward hers.

"But I don't want to know," she protested weakly.

"You don't have any choice." His eyes smoldered, making her burn with the same heat that consumed him.

Her lips opened, but he muffled her words with his mouth. His hard kiss annihilated every feeling except her volcanic need for him. Her anger and fear and distrust of him dissolved. She'd wanted him so long, and she'd fought the wanting of him for just as long.

Every female nerve ending in her body reveled in the fierceness of his building desire for her. She wanted his strength and wildness; she wanted to feel his powerful body on hers.

Sensual longing flamed under the skilled persuasion of Rex's mouth. His tongue was inside her mouth, tasting her, exploring her. A glowing heat spread through her veins. She'd thought she had forgotten how it had been between them, but she'd been wrong. His kiss brought back the past with all its scorching passion and intensity. Her heart throbbed with its old ache. She felt herself surrendering to her old love. There was no way she could any longer deny to herself how he stirred her.

Into this flaming paradise of her aroused senses, a lazy voice drawled, "I thought for sure you'd slap me." He chuckled. "Instead you turned to fire in my arms."

Green eyes fluttered and then opened with a startled expression. Slowly the awful words seeped into her conscious mind.

Why, why the conceited devil was laughing at her, laughing because it had been so easy to overpower her and make her his. Shame and fury blotted out desire.

She *would* slap him, too. She drew back her hand and would have struck him with all her might, but he seized her wrist inches before it made contact with his cheek.

She ground her teeth and lunged toward him, but he merely ducked.

"No, my little wildcat, you're not going to hit me. Not tonight." He merely laughed as she struggled all the more furiously. "You're going to make love to me."

Her body writhed against his, and his grin broadened.

"I am not," she snarled.

"Darling," he murmured hoarsely before he began to kiss her again with such wild violence that she felt faint and so deliciously dizzy that she was soon clinging to him more tightly than before. Even her toes turned traitor and curled.

His tongue invaded her mouth, and she met it with the tip of her own. Her hands curved around his neck to twine the curling tendrils of gold through her fingers with mindless need. She wanted to touch him, to know every part of him.

At last, his mouth left hers to trace a hot path along her cheek to her earlobe. When he began to nibble lightly on the edge of her lobe, she felt the exquisite shock wave of sensation in every part of her body. Then his mouth slid to her throat, kissing the mad drumbeat that pulsated against his hard mouth. At last, he stopped, resting against her for a moment, his harsh, uneven breaths hot against the skin of her throat. She could feel the depth of his passion in the light trembling that shook his hands as he crushed her against him.

Suddenly she felt triumph, too. He was just as much under her power as she was under his.

Then his mouth sought hers again, and his hard kiss robbed her of every emotion other than the spiraling passion that she knew could no longer be denied.

Wrapped in breathless expectation as well as in the Cadillac's plush luxury, they were speeding along palm-lined boulevards and past softly glowing night lamps towards Rex's home. Silvery reflections shone in the gutter wetness.

Rock music throbbed from the radio, the sound of it as breathlessly wild and primitive as the emotions of the man and woman in the car.

"Being so afraid of Mrs. Benson that you wouldn't let me make love to you at your apartment is ridiculous, you know," Rex murmured, coiling a silken black strand of shampoo-sweet hair through his tense fingers.

Kate's head was resting lightly upon his shoulder. She looked up at him through the thick fringe of her lashes, her shining gaze so loving that he couldn't resist taking his eyes from the road just for a moment to return the look.

The air between them sizzled like an electric current. His need was a red-hot whirlwind that gripped every muscle in his body. The invitation in her gaze was so blatant and wanton that he wanted to take her then and there.

His eyes darkened to a midnight blue, and his arm tightened around her. He felt the quickening of his pulse. The intensity of his excitement was so fierce that it almost hurt.

Kate had no idea that the effects of their recent lovemaking were still visible on her upturned face. She had no idea that her lush, satiny lips were half-open and sensually swollen from his hard kisses or that her black hair was spread in silken disarray over the blue leather of the seat or that her green eyes were still aglow with rapturous hunger. The soft air of surrender about her mesmerized him.

"Watch the road," she whispered. "You're on the wrong side of the street and there's a car coming."

"Damn."

A horn blasted furiously, and Rex swerved in the nick of time.

It took all his control to keep his gaze from the tempting lure of her beautiful face. He had wanted her like this, soft and yielding and radiant with anticipation. He had wanted her for years. Now that he had her, his wanting had become a savage pain searing his lower body, hardening him, making him ache with a suppressed but all-consuming need. His every nerve pulsed in awareness of her.

His fingers tightened around the wheel, but it took all his effort to concentrate on his driving. The scent of lavender invaded his senses. He could feel the light pressure of her palm resting on his thigh. The slender outline of every single finger burned through the thick denim to his skin. She was touching him, intimately tracing a corded muscle, leaving a trail of tingling fire. He could feel her breath every time it fanned his throat.

She was gentle and soft. She was woman.

His woman.

When she squeezed his leg, he almost died. He pulled the car over with a groan.

Brakes squealed, but neither of them heard the noise. A tire bumped the curb.

He grabbed her and pulled her against himself, her heavy breasts pushing against the wall of his chest. She was trembling, and he could feel her hunger, as hot and terrible as his own. He rained kisses onto her hair. His fingers clutched her tightly, pressing her closer and closer. He was probably hurting her, but she didn't seem to care. It was as if he wanted to pull her completely inside himself. God, did she have any idea of what she was doing to him? It was as if he'd never had a woman. As if he couldn't wait.

"Stop teasing me, you little vixen," he pleaded thickly, "or we're never going to make it to my house."

She traced the length of his muscled thigh with her wayward fingertip again, and a hot tremor swept him.

"I thought you liked it when I teased you," she whispered.

He shuddered, and his hand closed over hers, stopping the exquisite torture of those caressing fingers.

"Oh, I like it," he muttered raggedly. "Too much. But then you know that."

She giggled. "Maybe I like to flex my power over you."

"Maybe it's time I flexed mine over you."

He was starved for her, and she was pushing him too far. His arms circled her in a steel band and crushed her into his body. Arched roughly against the long length of his male hardness, she let him kiss her long and deeply. When he touched her breasts, she wrenched her mouth away. "We've got to stop, Rex."

"So, you know that now, too," he muttered against her lips in a thick, hoarse voice that didn't sound like his at all.

With a muffled groan, Rex released her and pushed her away from him.

He raked his fingers through his hair, but it only fell over his forehead as untidily as ever. "Kate, if you touch me again, anywhere, I swear I won't be able to stop."

Wisely she moved even farther away from him, but her presence drew him like a magnet. He could smell her. He could still taste her. He wanted to touch her, to take her. But he had to make himself wait. He bit the inside of his bottom lip until it was raw with pain, until the bitter flavor of his own blood washed away the tantalizing taste of her.

He sat there for a minute, gripping the steering wheel, the

wild jungle beat of the music mocking the wildness inside of him.

He was dying. Never had he felt more piercingly alive.

Across the darkness that separated them came the sweet, gentle sound of her voice. "Rex," she whispered.

"Don't even talk to me," he growled, the mere sound of her making his savage longing more terrible than ever.

Hurt, she clamped her lips together.

At last he pulled the car back onto the road. The music throbbed, but the silence between the man and the woman was still thick and violently charged with sensual tension.

The road seemed as endless as the night, as endless as his fierce wanting.

Six

Rex parked in front of an immense white house circled by verandas. Beside the house, a flamboyant flame tree spread its branches, shadowing the wide paved driveway. There were other trees, indistinguishable in the moonlit darkness, a thick stand of tropical jungle and tangled undergrowth. A wind was blowing through them with a great rushing sound.

As Rex helped Kate from the car, she heard the murmur of the Atlantic. She caught the scent of jasmine and honeysuckle, the tangy fragrance of salt air.

Rex's warm, brown fingers were upon Kate's bare shoulder in that proprietary fashion she found disturbing.

"Oh, Rex, it's all so beautiful," she gasped.

When he ran a callused fingertip along her throat, she jumped.

"Then you like it." He was inordinately pleased.

Her eyes were shining. "I love it."

"Could you ever love the man who owns it?"

Kate's startled eyes flew to his. A warm flush of pleasure ran through her, a terrifying longing that was astonishing in its intensity.

His dark face was unreadable.

Was he teasing her? Playing with her? Suddenly she wanted to run, but she was trapped in his hard arms.

He felt her tension, her terror. He misread the wildness in her eyes.

"I shouldn't have asked you that," he replied coldly.

"No, you shouldn't have," she managed in a tight, choked voice that betrayed her utter misery that he thought love between them so impossible.

"Just because we're attracted to each other..." he began.

"Doesn't have to mean anything," she finished wretchedly.

"Kate, I want you. You want me. That has to be enough."

It would never be enough! Not for her.

She shot him a brilliant smile. "Sounds great," she lied. Would nights like this be all she ever had of him? Would she be left with more memories that could only break her heart? She fought valiantly to conceal her pain.

A brown fingertip tilted her chin, and she was forced to look straight at him. He had the oddest expression on his face, as if everything she'd said had baffled him.

"You don't want to like me," he said, "do you?"

What could she say? Afraid to look at him, she only stared mutely into the darkness.

"But you do, more than you bargained for. Well, I damn sure have feelings for you I never bargained for, either. And maybe I don't like having them any more than you do."

A sob of pain clogged her throat.

Before she could say anything, he swept her into his arms and kissed her roughly, his hard mouth more brutal than it had ever been before. It was as if he wanted to possess her completely. As if he wanted to burn his maleness into her soul and drive out all her resistance toward him.

He held her so close that she could feel the blistering warmth of his hard-muscled belly burning through the layers of fabric that separated their skin. Above the tangy fragrance of his after-shave, she caught the musky scent that was his alone.

As suddenly as he'd kissed her, he let her go and, without saying another word, took her hand in his and led her to the house. Instead of taking her inside as she'd expected, he deliberately led her around to the back of the house onto one of the terraces overlooking the glimmering ocean.

Moonlight sifted into the garden beneath them, lighting a palm frond, a clump of frangipani, a trail of purple bougainvillea cascading over a low pink wall. In the distance, waves lapped against the crescent beach.

For a moment they stood together, his arms still about her shoulders and waist as they admired the beauty of the night. Suddenly she was filled with tremulous fear, and when she shivered, he pulled her even closer.

"Cold?" Never before had he spoken to her so gently.

She felt on fire. She didn't dare answer, but he seemed to understand. He was being so sweet that she wondered if she'd only imagined his anger before.

"I'll bet it's been lonely for you since Jake died," he said at last, smoothing a stray tendril from her forehead.

"It's been terrible," she admitted.

"But you're too proud to ever show it," he continued, "being who you are." The finger traced the soft edge of her hairline, the curve of her cheek, her throat. "You shouldn't be so afraid of your feelings, Kate. You should stop running away from yourself, stop trying to pretend you're anything other than what you are—a very beautiful and emotional woman." Again his tone was uncharacteristically gentle, just as his touch was.

Through the years, all she'd considered was his success. Now something in his eyes told her he was well acquainted with loneliness.

"I suppose everyone is a little bit lonely," she admitted, "but I like being independent. I don't want anyone in my life. Especially not a man."

"Maybe you need someone more than you think," he said quietly. "That day you came to me for money, I thought I saw a shimmer of loneliness in your eyes. It was as if you had some hidden need that you were determined to hide by acting angry and defiant."

"Well, you were wrong."

Oh, if only he were.

"I just want you to know that I'm here, Kate, to be your friend if you ever need one. I don't want you just for sex. And I know all about loneliness."

He was being kind, and he sounded almost...almost vulnerable.

She didn't know what to say, but it no longer mattered. His blond head was descending, and she knew that this time he would not stay his passion for her.

Then his mouth was on hers in a hard and demanding kiss. For an instant she tensed, then she bent her head back and let him kiss her. He crushed her body against his, and she was kissing him as hungrily as he kissed her, her lips trembling and opening to accept the invasion of his tongue. They tasted each other, drank each other. She knew that very soon she would find the completeness in his arms that she ached for.

He was the first man she'd ever known and the only one who would ever matter.

"You're quite something when you finally get around to being friendly," he murmured.

It didn't matter what he said, how he teased her. Wanting to have his lips on hers again, she kissed him a second time. Her fingers moved beneath his shirt, seeking to caress his skin.

He pulled his shirt from the waistband of his pants and led her fingertips beneath the cotton to caress his hard warmth. As her hands glided up she felt the prickly matting of blond hair that covered his chest. She heard the harsh sound of Rex's breath as he adjusted her body to his. Her own breathing was just as ragged.

"Oh, Rex," she murmured, "why does it have to be you?" The words were muttered shudderingly against his lips as she clung to him as if she would never let him go.

"I'm here, I guess," came his cynical reply. "You wanted my money and I wanted you."

His mouth devoured hers. His hands slid inside her blouse and cupped her breasts, touching the firm, satiny mounds until the nipples hardened in his palms. Her entire being quickened under his expert titillation. He kissed her throat, licked the tip of her earlobe as he had in the car. He stroked her, molding her body to his. Every sensation he evoked was so exquisitely delicious that she moaned helplessly.

He pulled away and grabbed her hand.

"Don't stop," she pleaded.

"Oh, I'm not stopping," he muttered thickly, pausing to bury his lips in her hair tenderly one last time. She felt him shudder. "Not for long, anyway."

Then he was leading her swiftly across the terrace. They were running eagerly down the stairs, beneath the palms, toward the little bathhouse lost in the deepest shadows of the garden.

Rex pulled Kate inside and locked the door. The darkened room had the stale scent of a place that had been shut up too long, and Rex opened two windows so that they could hear the sound of the sea and smell the perfume of the flowers.

They looked at each other, the mystery of the unknown and the forbidden fanning the flames of their desire.

"Are you sure you want this?" he asked hoarsely, warningly.

"Very sure," she breathed.

He chuckled. "Week before last, you hated my guts. I suppose it's a woman's prerogative to change her mind."

Kate's thoughts were a blur as Rex reached for her, putting his arm around her waist and turning her to him. He kissed the curve of her jaw, beneath her ear, moving his mouth slowly until their lips found each other.

There was ownership in his hard kiss, the unconscious mastery of a man who had finally found his mate. In the wild, primitive explosion that shook them, every barrier that had separated them dissolved. They were a man and a woman who'd been incomplete until this moment. Never again would they fall back into their old comfortable habits.

In an instant he had unbuttoned her blouse and pushed it down her arms so that it slid carelessly against her body to the floor.

She laughed softly, recklessly. Her black hair spilled over her shoulders.

She was a goddess with rose-petal-soft silken skin. Green eyes beckoned him, promising.

He began to remove her jeans and panties, her only remaining garments. As he peeled them away from her waist, his mouth traced a burning line of light kisses from her navel over the luminous skin downward to the cluster of dark curls that trembled at the bold invasion of his lips and tongue.

Kate tried to draw away, but he held her against his mouth, exploring her until she was quivering with new pulsing sensations, until her fingers clenched his black hair and dug into his scalp. She didn't want to pull away.

At last he stopped. A flood of crimson swept over her face as his gaze ranged upward, savoring the length of her rich, opulent loveliness. She had never let a man kiss her there before, not even him. She had never imagined she could react in such an uninhibited way.

She felt abandonment as well as a primeval thirst for him.

He stood up slowly. One brown hand was unknotting his tie. His magnetic eyes never left hers.

As if in a dream, Kate heard herself say, "Let me."

Then she was boldly undressing him. She loosened his tie and pulled the dangling ends down the front of his shirt. Slowly, sensuously she undressed him, exploring his body with eager, caressing fingertips.

At last he was naked. And beautiful. A great bronzed monolith of a man, uncompromisingly male and completely aroused.

She gazed at his tough, muscular body in wonder. "Why, I'd forgotten how lovely you were," she whispered in awe.

"Lovely?" He grinned at her choice of words. "What exactly did you have in mind?"

She reached out and touched him. He groaned as her fingers circled him. "You'll do," she just managed to say on a breathless note before he lifted her in his arms and carried her to the bed.

He was on top of her, his powerful body seeking hers with a greedy, all-consuming passion. He forced her legs apart. As desperate as he, she eagerly guided him to her.

He thrust inside her, and she clung to him, her need as urgent as his. His mouth captured hers again, and he kissed her fiercely. Again and again he plunged inside her, and she arched upward, welcoming him, crying out, whimpering.

Then she could stand it no longer. Suddenly she was spiraling in a blaze or glory as he thrust into her one last time, even harder than before.

Afterward, they lay in the silent darkness, their bodies coiled in a tight embrace, their minds far apart.

Never had Kate indulged in casual sex, and she wasn't now. No matter what Rex said to the contrary, she doubted that she meant much more to him than a sexual challenge. As soon as he satisfied his appetite for her, he would move on to another woman. Why did he have to be the only man for her?

Not that she was sorry about tonight. It had been too wonderful. Remorse would come later, after he left her again.

"You were even better than I remembered," he drawled softly. "For a girl who's afraid to be a woman, you're great in bed."

That was exactly the sort of remark she should have expected from him. Kate managed tightly, "Am I supposed to take that as a compliment?"

He caught the hurt note in her gentle voice.

"I wouldn't have put it like that if I thought you'd mind. For a girl who thinks she's tough, you have a funny way of wanting to be prim and proper and romantic when it comes to talking about sex. I kind of like that in you." His hand ran the length of her thigh. "I want to do it again," he whispered huskily.

Suddenly so did she.

"This time I want to do everything," he said, biting her neck ever so gently.

She wondered what he meant by "everything."

And he taught her.

It was long, hot and wild. It was all she had ever dreamed of and more. He knew more about her body than she did, and he revealed her to herself. In the last moment of complete release her pleasure was so sharp, so overwhelming that it frightened her.

She had always thought she was too tough and independent to want a man to tell her what to do. But Rex made her revel in his fierce, male possession of her. He was changing her more swiftly than she'd ever imagined possible.

Later, when he rolled away from her and lay on his back, he stared thoughtfully at the ceiling and said nothing.

Kate felt completed, at peace and warmly aglow. And yet in doubt. She wondered what he felt, what he thought, but she was too shy to ask him. Though he lay beside her, an endless gulf seemed to separate them.

How could she be shy after all they had done together? But she was. It made her sad to think that soon he would probably walk out of her life without ever looking back.

They were quiet for a long time. In the darkness she studied him. He had a long scar across his muscular chest and another on his shoulder. Other than that, he was perfectly made. He was strong, but he could be incredibly gentle.

She traced the path of the scar across his chest with the palm of her hand. "I don't know what to say."

He reached out and touched her cheek. "You don't have to say anything. Only tell me this. Are you sorry about tonight?"

"No."

"I'll understand if you want things back the way they were before."

"I like them fine the way they are."

"Then it was good for you, too?"

"Egotist. Do you have to hear me say it?" she asked, smiling. He grinned. "Of course."

"Very, very good," she whispered, blowing a hot kiss into his ear. "But then you already knew that."

They lapsed into silence once again, but this time it was different. She could tell that there was something on his mind, something he didn't quite know how to put into words.

His hand caressed her breast. "Kate, we have to talk, and I think it's pretty important. Maybe I should wait until later, but then again, maybe we should go on and get everything out in the open. I don't feel comfortable with all these secrets between us, not after what we've shared tonight."

"What secrets, Rex?"

"Isn't it about time you leveled with me about your real reasons for borrowing money from me? You don't suppose it would be too much to ask why you reinstalled your mailbox on *Bright Star*?"

She went rigid beside him, the most terrible premonition seeping into her consciousness. He had just made love to her, and now it was back to business as usual. His fingertips burned the tip of her nipple, but the poetry was over. Once more there was only harsh reality.

"You're planning to go after the *Marta Isabella,* aren't you, Kate?" he whispered, his voice ominously soft.

Kate tensed warily. Her pulse began to pound with the heart-thumping fear a trapped animal feels just before the predator closes in for the kill.

Seven

"You're planning to go after the *Marta Isabella*, aren't you, Kate?" Rex persisted.

"How did you—" Kate reddened with guilt and pushed the leaden weight of his hand away from her breast. "Of course not, Rex."

A silver bar of moonlight intensified the paleness of her face and the wild brilliance of her eyes.

He watched her for a long moment, a faint grimness hardening his chiseled features as he read her panic. He smiled cynically to himself as if he'd made up his mind about something. "Well, that's good," he said at last, his voice carefully casual, "and since you aren't, I guess it won't bother you to learn that I've decided to go after her myself."

The gently drawled words hit her like a bombshell. He laughed softly as she tried to jump out of bed. Effortlessly he pulled her back. Even in her fury, she was aware of the hot naked length of him. His flesh burned into hers. The curling hairs on his body prickled her sensitive skin as he held her close.

"What are you so mad about if you were telling the truth, Kate darling?" he whispered, his mouth mere inches above hers.

"The *Marta Isabella* was Jake's dream," she sputtered.

"Jake's dead."

"You have no right, Rex."

"Wrong again. Why shouldn't I? If I don't, it's only a matter of time until someone else does."

"Because—"

She tried to get up, but his right hand closed around her wrist and held her fast. Again she was conscious of the way the lower half of her body was firmly shaped against his, of the way her hips fitted so snugly into the accepting cradle of his. His slightest movement made their bodies rub intimately together, reminding her that only moments before she'd given herself to him utterly.

She froze. All her old hatred of him came flooding back into her heart, but as much as she despised him, she despised herself even more. What had she expected? A knight in shining armor? She knew him—what he'd been as well as what he was now. She remembered the night Jake found him, how dirty and poor Rex had been then. He'd had a hard life, and as a result he'd become a hard man.

He misinterpreted her anger for disgust, and the line of his jaw tightened dangerously.

"If you don't mind," she said coldly, "I'll get up and get dressed and call a taxi to take me home."

"But I mind," he taunted. His white teeth gleamed, and his bold eyes jeered at her. "I can see the distrust in your eyes. You think I'm being ruthless and unfair. You're sorry you went to bed with me."

She swelled with indignation and shame and tried to yank her wrist free. "I'd be crazy if I were proud of my behavior," she lashed out, wanting to hurt him.

His fingers bit roughly into her flesh. "Just this once, why don't you be honest with me, Kate? You wanted to use my money to go after the *Marta Isabella* yourself, didn't you?" His fierce blue eyes held hers.

"Oh, all right!" she snapped. "So I wanted to go after her myself. So that's why I came to you for money. It was something I had to do for Jake!"

"You came to me because you already know where she is. You found her on that last trip Jake made, didn't you?"

"How—"

"I've heard a few rumors, Kate. Juan got drunk one night this past winter and did a little talking in a bar with some of my men. Then you came to me for money. I knew you didn't want to shrimp, so I figured maybe the rumors were true. I was sure of it when I saw your mailbox back on *Bright Star*. You would never go to that expense if you didn't know where the wreck was. Then tonight at your apartment I saw the chart where you'd marked the location with the letters *M.I.* What else could they stand for but the *Marta Isabella*?"

Paralyzed with fear, Kate could only stare numbly into his dark face. At last she found her voice. "And naturally, you memorized the coordinates, you low-down snake."

"Naturally."

"And since you cleverly have me tied up by that horrible contract you made me sign, legally you have the right to keep *Bright Star* at her dock while you go after her yourself."

"I suppose I could do that."

He let a hand trail over the curve of her neck possessively, and despite her anger, she shivered. "Rex, don't you feel any guilt for the way you've used me?"

His fingertips played with a long silken tail of black hair. His eyes, which had been fixed on that ebony length moved to stare at her face. "Do you really think you're such a paragon of virtue yourself? What were you trying to do to me, Kate darling? You took my money under false pretenses."

"That was different."

A corner of his handsomely cut mouth lifted with insolent amusement. "Because it was you doing it?"

"The last thing I need from you is a lecture on morality," she muttered indignantly. "You gave me money, tied me up in legal knots, forced me into your bed, while all the time you were just planning to use me to go after something that rightfully belongs to me. Oh, there isn't a word bad enough to do justice to describing you!"

"Thank the lord for that small mercy! And as for forcing you into my bed…"

He drew her even tighter against his body, and pulled himself on top of her. The hard feel of his naked flesh rocked her senses, and she gasped. The musky smell of him enveloped her. The warmth of his breath fell against her lips. He lowered his mouth to the throbbing beat at the base of her throat and gently nuzzled it with his tongue. He could almost taste her excitement.

"Why is your heart going crazy?" he murmured.

It made her furious that she could feel anything for him other than dislike. With a little cry of rage, she pushed at his chest, but he was too heavy and too strong. She pounded his shoulders with her tiny balled fists, but it was no use. He felt as tough and invincible as a sun-warmed granite wall.

Kate twisted, but he held her with gentle firmness. She felt his powerful, muscular legs brush against hers, and she realized that he wanted her again.

"Why do we always end up fighting when she would be loving?" he murmured.

Her blood raced in feverish response to his arousal. There was an intensity in his dark face as he stared into the blaze of her eyes that softened her and made her feel vulnerable.

Quickly she averted her gaze. Why was it that even when she was angry, she was not immune to his golden, sun-bronzed handsomeness? He had only to touch her, to look at her, and he captured her soul.

Rex sought her trembling lips, kissing her with soul-destroying intensity, filling her mouth with his thrusting tongue, slowly, lingeringly, conquering what little will she had left to fight him. All too soon she was aching for him. When he finished kissing her, he laughed softly, pleased at her response.

"You deserve to be shot," she said, but her faint, breathless voice lacked conviction.

"For what—arousing you? You arouse me, too."

His skilled hands glided down her throat, running lightly between her breasts to trace the smooth curve of her stomach. Then he cupped her full breasts and lowered his mouth to tease and warm each pouting nipple until it peaked.

Within seconds a dizzying weakness spread through her limbs. Her hands wound around his neck, and she pulled him closer.

"Somehow, I think you'd be that last person on earth who'd pull the trigger," he mocked gently.

"Just hand me a gun," she murmured. "And let me do the world a favor." She traced the line of his jaw lovingly, belying her words.

"Kate, don't you know that I wouldn't hurt you for anything?"

His voice was gentle and sincere, and that hurt more than anything. His golden head lay pressed into the lush curve of her breast.

"You're such a liar," she managed in a low, throbbing voice.

"If you'd quit dreaming up insults and listen to me for once, you might learn something," he said impatiently, lifting his head.

"Like what? I've learned everything I want to about you and your dishonorable intentions, inside the bedroom and out of it."

"Then you haven't learned a damn thing!" He stopped himself. His face went dark with suppressed fury as he struggled to curb his anger. "Look, Kate," he managed at last in a more controlled tone, "you have it all wrong. I don't want to go after the treasure alone. I'll make you a partner. If you're right about the location, I'll give you a five percent finder's fee. If the ship's manifest is anywhere near accurate, that could make you a millionaire."

"And you'll take ninety-five percent."

"No, I couldn't afford to risk that much myself. I'll bring in other investors. I'll put up my own capital, too, of course. Your five percent will be free and clear, and you won't have to pay a cent in operating expenses. A wreck like the *Marta Isabella* could take years to properly excavate. You know that it costs thousands of dollars a week to pay divers, operate boats, deal with the state and the feds. There may be legal battles."

Strangely, his logic made her mad all over again. Her teeth clenched in pure rage.

"Kate, there's no way you could afford that. Plus you wouldn't be able to salvage her properly. You'd be forced to go after her treasure without taking proper time to research the wreck and protect the artifacts. You know how expensive it is to dehydrate and preserve damaged artifacts properly. Surely you don't want them all lost—"

"No." It was no more than a reluctant whisper. She didn't really believe him. But he was smart. He knew exactly what to say. How to win her over. She couldn't let herself trust him.

"If we work together, we'll be able to make a contribution to marine archaeology instead of just destroying the shipwreck site in an indiscriminate search for gold and treasure."

"I can see you've got it all thought out."

"As a matter of fact, I do. Is that a crime?"

"I'm not sure."

"Is it so hard for you to believe in me?"

"Impossible." Oh, she wanted to hurt him, as he'd hurt her. She had to put some emotional distance between them. And she knew his most vulnerable spot. "Remember, I know what you were before you got to be rich and famous, Rex, and you weren't anything much back then. Less than nothing. Well, you haven't changed. I could never trust a person with your background. Never! And I'm ashamed of myself because I slept with you. I don't want to be partners with you."

When he paled, his mouth thinning into a tight line, his blue eyes growing bleak, she knew that her blow was right on target.

"Then we won't be partners," he snarled. "I'll take it all for myself!"

"That's exactly what you intended from the first!"

"And I'll sleep with you anytime I want to. Only from now on there won't be any pretense of tenderness when I do."

"That's all it was before—pretense. I'd rather die than have you touch me again."

"We'll see."

"You're despicable, insufferable!" she cried in rage, her eyes ablaze.

"Is that so?" Rex's lips curled in an unfriendly smile.

"You intend to do as you please with no regard for my feelings."

"Oh, I intend to please you, too. That's not so hard, you know."

Kate uttered an infuriated cry and tried to fling herself away from him. He caught her hands in one swift movement, his grip seemingly casual but cruelly tight, and wrenched her back into his arms.

Her cheeks brightened in shameful awareness of his body. His hands burned into her hips, inflaming her with desire despite her anger. Her traitorous emotions humiliated her even more than he did.

"I hate you, Rex," she cried out. "If I could erase every trace of you from the earth, I would." Her eyes glittered hotly with contempt.

There was tense silence, save for the rasping of her own breath.

His jaw tightened in anger and frustration as he strangled a curse. He had been fair to her. Even gentle. He'd tried everything he knew to win her over, and she had treated him like dirt because she couldn't forget what he'd once been. He'd given her money when she'd needed it, tried to stop her from overworking herself. There were hundreds of wrecks he could go after, but he'd chosen the *Marta Isabella* because it had special meaning to her. He remembered the way she'd so coldly scorned him at Jake's funeral and made him feel like dirt.

Wild, ungovernable emotion drove him past the limits of his control. He gripped her upper arms and jerked her against his chest, the granite strength of his arms imprisoning her. "Erase this if you can."

His mouth fell on hers with devastating fury, crushing her stiff lips to his, forcing them to open. He pressed his tongue insolently into her mouth, touching her tongue deliberately with his. He felt the rounded sweetness of her breasts flattened against his chest, the long length of her slim legs tangled with his. He felt the quivering of her mouth, the tentative beginnings of her response to him, the first stirrings of the fire he knew she felt for him. He wanted to take her and make her know that no matter what she said, she belonged to him.

The stupid, little fool, didn't she know that he loved her? That he'd always loved her? That he always would.

He buried his face against her throat, holding her hard to him so that she could feel the heat in him, burning him. His desire set a torch to her body, igniting her passion.

He felt her whimper with unwanted longing. Her arms came up and curved around his neck, her nails digging into his shoulders. Her tongue met and tasted his. Her body moved convulsively beneath his.

"None of this...matters anymore," she whispered in agonized surrender. "I'm yours, Rex."

He shuddered, his feelings for her more intense than they'd ever been before as he drew her closer in the soft, tropical swirl of darkness. Outside, there was the rustle of the palm fronds against the windowpanes, the thunder of the ocean.

Without even knowing that he did so, Rex relaxed his grip on her arms, and her lips descended from his mouth down the brown column of his throat to explore his body. She was whispering incoherent things that he couldn't hear. Her passionate love words made tiny shivers against his skin.

Nothing existed but this woman, her feverish lips moving over his body, evoking feelings he'd never felt before. Her long black hair swept his belly as her head moved lower. He felt her tongue touch his thigh, her lips kissing him through bristly hair, and a bolt of sensation went through him.

At last she took him in her mouth, kissing him so tenderly and so lovingly. He knew a wild thrill such as he had never known. It was madness, ecstasy, torment, the most piercingly erotic excitement.

If she didn't stop, he would explode. He groaned, and very gently he pushed the black silken head away.

"Rex," she murmured through kiss-dampened lips. Her emerald eyes fluttered open and lifted to his, her eyelids heavy with languorous passion, and he gazed tenderly upon her beautiful radiant features for a moment.

But just for a moment.

Wild for her, he pulled her into his arms, aligning their bodies. Moist and warm, her body flowered open to accept him. Her arms wound around his neck and her lips were trembling as they met his. He pressed his mouth onto hers, their kiss deepening.

Her bare skin caressed his. She was soft and yielding womanly flesh.

He slowly stroked her warm body, rubbing the tips of her nipples softly between his fingers, caressing the silky inner flesh of her legs. Her breath came irregularly, quivering with mounting sensual sensations.

His kisses deepened, and he was lost in the velvety, sea-scented darkness which was soft and warm and all enveloping.

He wanted to tell her that he loved her, that he would never want another woman, but something held him back. That night she was an unbridled wanton in his arms, returning his passion hopelessly, mindlessly, as they brought each other to new heights of pleasure. Finally he experienced a feeling of fulfillment and blazing emotion beyond his wildest memories of rapture. He lay beside her, completely satiated and contented.

They fell asleep wrapped in each others arms, their limbs intimately tangled, the warmth of her breath falling against his throat.

She was his, he thought contentedly. At last.

But he was wrong.

The next morning when he awoke she was gone.

Eight

A brilliant sun hung low in the late-afternoon sky. Weaving between cars with daredevil, split-second timing, Kate pedaled her ten-speed down Duval toward Mallory Square. She was a pretty, graceful sight in her red shorts and white knit shirt that fit snugly over the slim curves of her body. Though she was too immersed in her own thoughts to notice the attention she was getting, the flash of tanned legs caught every male eye. There were frequent honks and enthusiastic wolf whistles.

She leaned over the handlebars, squinting despite her over-sized sunglasses. Her black hair was pulled back in a ponytail, and it flew behind her in the wind.

As she sped by, she scarcely saw the blur of old white wooden houses with their slim columns, wide verandas and gingerbread molding that gave the subtropical island a New England flavor. She was too used to the sight of them.

Crumbling concrete buildings and sleazy bars were mixed in with the old mansions—squalor in the midst of history. Hippie types with bare feet and dirty hair lolled about street corners. She whizzed by a ragged brown-faced boy with a bright gold earring in one ear, and he called after her in Spanish.

When Duval dead-ended, she jumped lightly from her bike

while it was still rolling and parked it, locking it to a bike stand. She was hot suddenly from the heat and humidity, from the long ride. She could feel the warmth of her hair against her shoulders. Her clothes stuck to her skin. She'd pedaled as if a thousand demons were after her.

Only one was: Rex.

Not that he'd actually done anything lately. She'd scarcely seen him since the night she'd run out of the bathhouse. Still, she couldn't stop herself from dwelling on him constantly, and she'd taken quite a few long bicycle rides lately just to work off her frustration.

During the day, she carried on constant silent arguments in her head with him. In these little daydreams she always rewrote the reality of what had occurred between them. She always came out the victor, using clever wit to flail him unmercifully for having used her so callously.

When she slept, he filled her dreams. And they weren't nightmares. Nor was she cleverly triumphant over him. Her nighttime dreams were sensual fantasies in which he wove his pagan, masculine spell over her. She would awaken with her blood beating in her temples, with her body aching with a pulsing void that cried for fulfillment. She would lie awake for hours, wanting him and despising herself because she did.

At first he'd tried to telephone her, but she only hung up on him every time she heard his voice on the other end of the phone. She'd been just as brutal on the fishing pier when he'd tried to talk to her face-to-face.

She'd been watching Juan and Pedro load the conveyor belt with shrimp. Suddenly she'd grown aware of Rex standing behind her. There had been no time to prepare herself.

She turned, and there he was, towering over her. The unexpected shock of his presence sent a thrill of sensation through her body.

Beneath his golden hair, his handsome face was unsmiling, his blue eyes brooding.

Never had he been more charismatic. Never had she been happier to see anyone.

"Rex—"

"Kate," he said at the same time. "Are you all right?" he asked gently.

He reached out to touch her, but she deftly backed away.

She nodded her head as memories of their last night together made her insides churn with warm sensations. Oh, why couldn't she feel indifferent toward him? What chemistry operated between them to ignite this storm of dangerous feelings that made her a stranger to herself?

She was supposed to be tough Kate Andrews, an independent woman who didn't crave the companionship of a man the way other members of her sex did.

So why did his sheer masculinity raise this traitorous fever in her blood?

He had asked her how she was.

"Never better," she managed with forced brightness, "since I got you out of my life."

He looked away from her, spots of dark color staining his cheeks. "I guess I deserve that," he said at last.

His blue eyes fastened on her face again with an intensity that left her breathless.

"Kate, I'm sorry about that night. I came on a little strong."

"A little—" Even her voice quivered.

"Let me make it up to you. I'll do anything you say."

His Southern drawl caressed her with husky sound, and her stomach did a little somersault.

She met his tense gaze. Despite herself, she found herself studying him and liking what she saw far too much.

He wore a cotton shirt of faded blue that intensified the color of his eyes. Faded denim molded his muscular thighs. His work boots were old and scratched.

The sleeves of his shirt were rolled to the elbows, and Kate noticed the sleek contours of the hard tanned muscles in his arm every time he moved them. Why did he have to be so unerringly male?

"You'll do anything I say?" she whispered.

"Anything," he murmured.

It was exciting the way he stared down at her in that hot, passionate way of his. He was offering her friendship and more. He was awakening all the old longings that made her aware of how completely vulnerable she was where he was concerned.

He had used her. He only wanted to go on using her. Still, it took all the stubbornness and pride in her nature not to melt and be friendly.

Somehow she managed.

"Rex, all I want is for you to leave me alone."

He kept looking at her as if to rip away the stubborn mask that concealed her true feelings. She was aware of the magnetic currents between them that were alternately pulling them toward each other and pushing them apart. Though he made her feel unsure of her wants and needs and uncomfortable, her rigid mask stayed firmly in place.

"All right," he replied coldly at last, his face expressionless. "Have it your way. I hope you're happy."

"That's impossible as long as you're around."

A muscle flexed along his hard jawline. "I didn't come by to quarrel with you, Kate. I came over to tell you that I'm leaving in two days to go look for the *Marta Isabella.* I was going to ask you to go with me, but I guess all that's left to say is goodbye."

He'd come over to ask her to go with him! Her heart leaped with excitement at the thought of accepting his casually offered invitation. But that would mean being with him...on *Wanderer,* his flagship, day and night, being constantly exposed to the temptation of wanting him.

"Well, you've said it, Rex," she replied with forced indifference. "I just hope it's goodbye forever."

She turned her back on him and stalked off.

After she left him, she'd wanted to die because she'd longed to make up with him so much. But no happiness could ever come from giving in to a weakness she knew was wrong. Rex had used her in the past and then left her. He was using her now.

After that day, he'd left her alone, but that only made her more miserable than ever. Despite everything, she'd wanted to go with him. She'd almost called him on the telephone that night and begged him to take her with him.

It had been three weeks since he'd left on *Wanderer* in search of the *Marta Isabella*. With her heart filled with turbulent emotions, she'd watched him leave, though he hadn't known it. He'd used her just to get information on that wreck. Why did he have to make love to her, as well? Why did he have to steal her heart all over again? And would she ever be able to forget him?

Kate walked aimlessly around the square, the heart of old maritime Key West. She forced herself to stop thinking about Rex and concentrate on the local color.

In the distance two little islands gleamed like gemstones in the bright blue Gulf waters. A teenager slouched against a wall in a hot-pink T-shirt that read, Key Wasted.

Kate was hot. Across the street she saw the tropical garden of an inviting outdoor café. The restaurant was famous for its wonderful piña coladas, and she felt as if she was dying of thirst.

When Don happened by a few minutes later, he found her there at a corner table. She was dwarfed beneath the foliage of a spreading banyan tree, sipping her piña colada, a tiny frown between her eyes marring the loveliness of her narrow face.

Don pulled out a chair and squeezed his large body under the little round table. "What's the matter, darlin'?"

She looked up, startled. In a way she was glad to see him, but she always hated it when he called her that.

"I was just thinking, Don. I've got a lot on my mind."

"By a lot you mean Rex Reynolds."

"Right on target."

"You've been seeing a lot of him lately, I hear," Don said.

Kate had no desire to talk to Don about Rex, so she just sat silently, sipping her drink through her straw.

Don signaled a waiter and ordered a beer. "Want another one of those, darlin'?"

"I'll pass."

"So are you serious about Reynolds, Kate?"

"I'd rather not talk about it if you don't mind."

"Reynolds is hardly my favorite person, either, Kate. I used to work for him, you know."

For the first time, Kate looked up from her frothy drink. In spite of herself, she was curious. "I didn't realize that."

"It's not something I go around bragging about, darlin'. I'd been diving for him for more than a year. We were after a wreck that had been part of the 1715 Spanish fleet. Well, when we started coming up with gold and artifacts that had some value, Reynolds just up and fired me."

"Without any reason? I find that a little hard to believe." She was shocked that she instinctively leaped to Rex's defense.

"He had a hell of a reason. He wanted my share as well as his."

The rum was having an effect on Kate. She felt warm and fuzzy-headed, and her guard was down. Normally she would never have talked about Rex to anyone, but suddenly it felt good to be able to talk to Don. Apparently they each had a problem with Rex, and this common interest bound them more closely together than usual. Besides it was pleasant having an old friend to talk to. Who knew? She might even marry Don someday. At the thought, she shivered. Odd, how unattractive the prospect of marrying Don seemed.

Why was that? she wondered. All the girls went for Don's dark good looks, and she'd always been proud to be seen with him. He was acting so concerned and kind, as if her feelings mattered. That was something Rex hadn't bothered to do lately.

"I haven't liked your seeing Reynolds, darlin'. How'd you get mixed up with him again?"

She took another sip from her drink. "He loaned me money, Don."

"That was worse than signing a pact with the devil and selling your soul for it."

Suddenly all her pent-up feelings boiled to the top, and it was as if once she'd started talking, she couldn't stop. "You're telling me! He made me sign a contract that ties me up in knots. I can't even take *Bright Star* out of the marina without begging permission from him. He's gone after the *Marta Isabella,* and you know it was always Jake's dream to find her. Don, he stole information from me to find her.''

"What do you mean?''

"I never told anyone this before, and I probably shouldn't be telling you, but on that last trip Jake and I made, we found some gold coins that we were almost sure were from the *Marta Isabella*. Rex saw the chart that I'd marked the location on, and he memorized the coordinates.''

"Where is she?'' Don whispered.

Kate felt so strange. The heat and the liquor combined to make her feel light-headed. She bent her head to his and murmured the answer in his ear. What did it matter if she told an old friend like Don if Rex already knew?

Don sat back, quiet and thoughtful. For a time, she did most of the talking while he half-listened. Don kept ordering beers while Kate nursed her one piña colada.

After a while, he changed the subject. "What was this I heard about you coming into a fortune, darlin'?''

Kate smiled. She'd only learned this morning that she was an heiress, but she'd told Mrs. Benson, so she wasn't surprised that Don had already heard something about it. "Not a fortune, but an aunt of mine did die. I hardly knew her, but she was fond of Jake. I just received a letter from a lawyer in Miami telling me that I'm to be one of the heirs. It isn't all that much really.''

It was enough to free her of the debt she owed Rex and then some. "It'll be a while before I actually see any money,'' she said.

"I'm happy for you, darlin'.'' Don held his bottle up, signaling for another beer.

"I've applied for some teaching jobs, too, Don.''

"That's good, as long as you don't leave Key West.''

Key West was the one place she hadn't applied, but there seemed no point in telling Don that. They would only argue.

Brilliant streaks of fire radiated across the sky, announcing the approach of a Technicolor tropical sunset, but for once Kate found it impossible to respond to the beauty of the night.

* * *

Kate's black ponytail spilled in soft disarray over her shoulders. Meeting Don had been pleasant all in all. He'd had a few too many beers, but then sometimes that was his way of relaxing on weekends.

"Just one little kiss, darlin'," Don begged, as he pressed her into the wall with his body.

They were standing in the deepest shadows of the porch in front of her apartment house. Moonlight glinted on her bicycle, which lay in a heap on the wooden planks nearby. A slight breeze stirred snowy jasmine blossoms, perfuming the air with a thick, cloying sweetness.

What did one kiss matter? Maybe it would even be therapeutic to kiss Don. It might help her forget Rex and the destructive passion she felt for him.

The edges of her mouth dimpled slightly in invitation.

"You're very beautiful, darlin'," Don whispered.

She closed her eyes when she felt the slight pressure of his mouth on hers. He drew her yielding shape against his.

There was nothing in Don's kiss to excite her, nothing to make her heart throb and her breathing race unevenly. Not that kissing him was unpleasant. It was just nothing special, and after having known the thrill of Rex's lovemaking, she felt only disappointment in Don's arms.

From out of nowhere came a steel-edged Southern drawl that Kate recognized instantly.

"Mind if I cut in, Taylor?"

Don's mouth tensed on hers as they both grew aware of the tall muscular giant lounging indolently against a gingerbread corner in the darkness. How long had Rex been there? How much had he seen and heard?

Don slowly withdrew his lips from Kate's. The taste of beer lingered in her mouth like an unpleasant aftertaste. She felt treacherously glad about Rex's unexpected interruption of their kiss, though she fought valiantly to conceal her feelings.

She glared at Rex just as fiercely as Don did. Rex only grinned back at her jauntily.

Even in the darkness, she could see that Rex's hair was a

whiter blond, that his skin was more deeply tanned, that he hadn't shaved in three weeks. His golden beard made him look like a pirate. Oh, why did he have to look so male and so magnificent?

His bold gaze swept her from head to toe. And a scalding tremor traced the same path his masculine gaze had followed. Wildly she looked away.

"I damn sure do mind, Reynolds," Don barked. "Why don't you get lost?"

Rex's grin vanished with frightening speed. "Because you're kissing my girl."

"Says who?"

"Ask Kate." Rex chuckled. "If she isn't my girl, she damned sure ought to be, after—"

"Rex," Kate hissed, her temper exploding inside her like a firecracker. "You'd better shut up."

"Whatever you say, my love," Rex replied, laughing softly.

"What's he talking about, darlin'?" Don demanded.

The grin was back in place on Rex's dark face, broader and whiter than before. Rex was clearly enjoying the havoc his insinuations were causing. The rascal! Kate wanted to kick him, but she was not going to lower herself to anything so undignified.

"Darlin'?"

The situation was growing more impossible by the second. The last thing Kate wanted to do was confess all the intimate details of her relationship with Rex to anyone, much less to Don.

"Oh, nothing, Don," she muttered furiously.

"I'd hardly call what we've been together nothing," Rex inserted silkily, stirring the pot to bring it to full boil.

"Reynolds—" Don began threateningly.

In another minute they would be fighting. Though Don was tall, his head only came to Rex's shoulder, and Rex was built much more powerfully. There was no way Kate could let Don take abuse because of her. Since Rex was too perverse to leave as long as Don was there, clearly she would have to ask Don to go.

"Don," Kate pleaded, grabbing his arm. "Why don't you

come back tomorrow? I really do need to talk to Rex about something in private, something that has to do with that loan I told you about.''

''You're sure this is what you want, Kate? I don't like leaving you alone with him.''

''Please, Don. I'll be okay.''

Don left, but only with the greatest reluctance.

As soon as he was gone, Kate attacked Rex. ''Just what did you think you were doing?''

A faint smile curved his lips. ''Eliminating the competition.''

''Don happens to be a friend of mine.''

Rex's jaw tightened and his eyes grew cold. ''Do you kiss all your friends in the moonlight?''

''What's it to you?'' Her heart was thumping wildly.

''Plenty,'' he murmured in a soft, velvety tone.

''It's hardly as if you've never had another woman.''

He delayed his answer, and she studied him. The moon touched on his handsome face and broad shoulders. His smooth brown skin gleamed in its light. The thought of him with another woman brought Kate a sudden, swift ache.

''There hasn't been anybody since you,'' he said quietly.

''What about Sue?''

''Susan.''

''You know who I mean.''

''So does every other man in town. She's dating somebody else.'' He sounded indifferent.

''Maybe that's why you keep hanging around me.''

''For your information, it isn't.''

''Well, for your information, I don't care why you do what you do. I just want you out of my life. Understand? Got the message?''

Her rejection infuriated him. With pantherlike swiftness, he bridged the distance that separated them. Then he caught her to him, his lean, hard body immensely threatening to her small frame. His eyes captured hers.

''Got it.'' His features were cold and stark. The two words were just as cold.

''Then let me go!''

He hesitated, his blue eyes freezing her. Every sense, every nerve in her body screamed of his male presence. She could feel the imprint of his fingers on her arms, smell the faint scent of his cologne. Most of all she was aware of his long body crushed intimately against hers.

Her hands struggled weakly against his chest in a futile attempt to push him away. Behind his guarded look, Kate felt the dark intensity of his gaze as he studied her face. He was searching for something, but she didn't know what.

He loosened his hold, and she fell back against the front door, feeling oddly disappointed that he had. The screen door creaked, and she prayed that Mrs. Benson wasn't peering out from some dark window and taking in the intimate scene.

''Hell, Kate, the only reason I came over tonight was because I thought you just might be interested in what I found out about the *Marta Isabella*. But since you're not, I'll leave and you can get back to whatever you were doing that was so important.''

''That's impossible. You ran him off, remember!''

A muscle twitched angrily in Rex's cheek, but he said nothing. He turned and strode across the porch, his footsteps resounding heavily on the creaky boards.

She watched his retreating figure. She should let him go. What he'd found shouldn't matter to her. He'd said he was going to take all the treasure for himself. She should be strong and resist the terrible curiosity to know. She should be coolly indifferent.

Across the darkness, his name came from her lips as a hushed velvety sound that was so soft it could scarcely be heard. ''Rex.''

But he heard.

Before she could open the car door, Rex had leaped around the front of the Cadillac and opened it for her.

'When he extended his hand to help her out, she froze. Her eyes went beseechingly to his, only to be mesmerized by those deep pools of blue. A breathless weakness fluttered through her. Self-consciously, she averted her eyes.

She could hardly refuse his assistance without betraying how even his most casual touch disturbed her.

She let the hard warmth of his fingers close over hers. His grip was gentle but firm; the contact between them, electric.

Her legs began to tremble, and she found it almost impossible to breathe. She jumped lightly from the car, and he pulled her against his body.

Oh, dear. Did he have to take advantage of every opportunity?

She was burningly aware of the masculine sweep of tense muscles against her own softer body. She tried to pull her hand free of his, but he merely tightened his grip, drawing her closer.

"I wonder what you're so afraid of, Kate." His mouth curved lazily into a half smile.

"I'm not afraid."

"Liar." The glitter in his dark eyes laughed at her attempt to deny her feelings.

Her frightened gaze went to the white mansion behind him. In the moonlight it seemed even more beautiful than the last time she'd seen it.

She remembered the night he'd brought her to his home. The night he'd made love to her. The night she'd discovered that he'd merely been using her to find the *Marta Isabella*. But most of all she remembered the wanton ecstasy of being pressed beneath that male length of granite-hard muscles.

Oh, she should never have come!

"I wish I hadn't agreed to come here with you," she said faintly.

He touched her cheek tenderly. "There's nothing to be afraid of, Kate."

He'd said that before.

He bent his index finger and rubbed his knuckle across the softness of her bottom lip.

"Rex, don't torture me," she moaned.

"Believe me, honey, that's the last thing I have in mind."

He lowered his head. His mouth touched hers, at first very softly. His beard grazed her cheek. Then their lips clung hungrily.

His arm tightened around her waist. "Kate, you've nearly driven me mad these past few weeks."

His tongue sought hers and found it. Her fingertips crept up his chest and closed around the soft fold of his collar. She leaned into his body, standing on her tiptoes. He held her even tighter, and their kiss deepened. She felt boneless as he tipped her head back and gained freer access to her lips and throat. She gasped as his mouth slid up to her earlobe, and desire licked through her arteries at the darting flick of his tongue. Her fingers curled into his broad shoulders for support. She felt dizzy and light-headed. Wild drums seemed to pound in her ears.

"Do you remember the way it was ten years ago? We couldn't ever get enough of each other."

"Yes," she murmured, the memory as vivid as if it were only yesterday.

After a long time, he let her go. "I guess it's about time we went inside and took a look at the artifacts."

She gazed at the tantalizing temptation of his mouth only inches from hers.

"Hmmm?" she questioned dreamily, unable to concentrate on anything but her desire for another kiss.

He chuckled. "You remember, the reason I brought you here."

"Oh, yes."

"Of course," he murmured with a telling grin, "if you came over here with some other purpose in mind, we could skip all that and I could suggest something more interesting to do."

She only glared back at him, annoyed with herself for having kissed him so enthusiastically.

In silence he led her up the stairs to the veranda and then inside his home. Double-height doors and an extra wide staircase formed a dramatic entryway. She could scarcely help admiring the beauty of the house's soaring vertical spaces, its immense span of windows that welcomed in the beautiful moonlit night.

Rex flipped on the light and she saw that the walls were painted snowy white while the furnishings and carpets were done in blues and tans.

"The artifacts are out in my shop," he said, leading her through the den to the kitchen and then through a heavy door that he had to unlock.

His shop was panelled in dark wood. There were bookshelves along one wall that were filled with artifacts from other wrecks. Kate's attention was momentarily drawn to a stack of ominous copper bracelets known to historians as manillas. In exchange for these ornaments, once manufactured by the hundreds of thousands in Europe, African chieftans had delivered people, sometimes of their own tribes, into the hands of slave traders bound for the Americas.

"I got those off a wrecked slave ship two years ago," Rex said thoughtfully. "One thing about salvaging wrecks, you can't help but think about how costly it was to develop the new world. And not just in terms of money. I keep those manillas as a reminder of what people will do in the name of greed."

As if he needed a reminder. How odd though that Rex sounded so compassionate. Shouldn't he of all people understand the powerful motivation of greed?

Kate glanced around the shop. There were several tables, a sink and a large saltwater aquarium. A stack of the books he'd published had been piled to one side on his desk.

Rex picked up a smoky-looking bottle from the littered desk and turned it over carefully so she could see it from all sides.

She knew the smoky appearance came from a thin coating of lead oxide that could be removed by soaking the bottle in a ten percent solution of nitric acid.

"As you know, glass items are always particularly useful in dating a wreck," he said. "The glass bottles we found were definitely made in the late 1680s. Just to be sure I was right, I sent some photographs and measurements off to the Corning Glass Museum."

He set the bottle back down.

A huge, odd-looking lump of black metal sat in a tub on a large table in the center of the room. Kate knew instantly this was a mass of heavily sulfided silver coins in an electrochemical bath. On the table beside the tub, a few Spanish gold escudos glittered as brightly as the day they were minted.

In breathless excitement Kate picked up one of the irregular bits of gold and turned it over in her palm.

It was crude and misshapen, and there was no visible date. But then that was not unusual in old coins. She knew that before 1732 nearly all gold and silver coins minted in the New World were not round but of many irregular patterns.

She'd read somewhere that these irregular-shaped gold and silver coins were called cobs, that they were made by pouring molten metal out onto a flat surface in long, thin strips. When the metal cooled, pieces of the approximate size and weight of the desired coin were cut from the strip, then trimmed to their proper weight. These bits of gold and silver were then placed between two dies and struck with a heavy hammer. Since one or both sides of the coin were not always perfectly flat, the dies only marked the highest surfaces of these sides. This resulted in the majority of the cob coinage not having full die marks, and many lacked dates.

"We found those," Rex said, picking up a coin, "scattered on the ocean floor near the spot you and Jake had marked on your chart. A few of them were in deep limestone pockets and we had to use a little dredge to vacuum away the sand and loose shell."

Kate's eyes were shining. "Rex, do you think this means—"

"I think it's very likely we've found the *Marta Isabella*. If we haven't, this ship definitely dates back to the same period she was from. Kate, the ballast rocks were from Spain, and you know that ships usually carried ballast rocks from their country of origin. Anyway, we've definitely found enough so that I think it's worth the money to fully outfit a boat to do more diving. There's coral, but not too much. Some of the items are lightly encrusted."

Kate could hardly contain her excitement. How thrilled Jake would have been. If only he'd lived to go after the *Marta Isabella* himself. "Oh, Rex—"

Suddenly Kate remembered the awful reality. Rex was no

friend. He had virtually stolen information from her so that he could go after the *Marta Isabella* himself. There was no reason for her to be thrilled over the findings of a pirate.

A shadow fell across her features, the light in her eyes dying as suddenly as it had found life. Listlessly she set the coin back down beside the others.

"I don't know why I'm getting so excited," she said. "All this should have been mine. And it would have been if you hadn't tricked me out of it."

"You'll get your five percent finder's fee," he said gently, picking up the coin and putting it in her hand again. "Keep this one. I found it on my first dive."

"You said you were taking everything for yourself."

"I guess you've never said things you didn't mean when you were mad." His arm circled her shoulders. As always she liked his touching her far too much. Despite her feeble efforts to push him away, he drew her closer, and her heart began beating faster than before. "Hell, Kate, all of this is yours for the asking. You can have everything I own."

"What do you mean?" She tried to sound casual, but for some reason her voice had suddenly become light and breathless.

Relentlessly he sought her gaze and held it. "I'm asking you to marry me, you little fool," he whispered tenderly.

His hand molded itself to the slender curve of her neck, his tanned fingers sliding into the inky length of her hair at the back of her neck. His other hand cupped her chin. "And I'm not going to wait forever to get your answer. I can be stubborn, too, you know."

The low throb of his voice mesmerized her. She wanted to cry yes. Yes, yes and yes! She wanted to fling her arms around his neck and tell him she loved him. But some demon of doubt stopped her.

"Wh-why? Why do you want to, Rex? Why should I?"

What she wanted were words of love.

"Why not? Ask yourself that question, Kate."

Surely there were a thousand reasons, but at that precise moment she was at a loss to think of one.

His mouth made a slow, unhurried descent to hers. Though she knew she should fight him, she didn't even attempt to struggle. The gold coin she was holding fell through her fingers and clattered on the tabletop. All too soon his mouth was warmly devouring hers, tasting the sweetness of her lips. Her hands spread against his chest for support.

The flame of his kiss melted all her resistance. She arched her back, curving her body more closely against him, aching for his lovemaking in an inchoate, primitive way.

With a moan, she clutched him even tighter. He was kissing her throat. His mouth was honeyed fire upon her skin. His hot, panting breath made her go up in flames.

He was the one who stopped kissing her, the one who gently but firmly pushed her away. As if from a great distance, she heard his voice.

"It's really very simple, Kate. You want my money and the treasure from the *Marta Isabella*. I want you."

Kate felt deflated and sick at heart. Rex didn't love her, and he hadn't the slightest intention of pretending he did.

"There's more to marriage than sex," she began quietly. "If that's all we have, it will never be enough. We need to be friends, to like each other, to share common interests. Sexual attraction doesn't last."

His lips curled. "It's lasted ten years. Kate, no man marries a woman because of the reasons you suggest. I want something grander than friendship and common interests, something no other woman has ever given me. Only you." He shaped breast with his hand, and her nipple grew hard beneath gertips. "I find glory and joy in your body and feel or regret for doing so. You set me on fire, Kate. I wa the woman I marry. Is that so wrong?"

Was it? She didn't know anymore. Why did h to hurt so much? Her chest ached as if her he

"Think about it, Kate, but if you say y Taylor is out of your life for good. Wha for him, you'll belong to me."

"Rex, if I didn't know better, I'd think you almost sounded jealous." And that might mean—

He chuckled. "Then I'm glad you know better."

She tried to whirl out of his reach, but he pulled her back into his arms, his lips silencing her startled protests with a fierce kiss. He teased her mouth open and his tongue glided across the sensitive roof of her mouth. She felt a rush of excitement. Her legs felt as weak as melting wax.

His mouth branded her as his possession. He was deliberately stirring her to make her admit to herself that her need to have him was as great as his to have her, and it wasn't long before he had his way.

"Kate," he breathed. Then, wrapping his arms even more tightly around her, he pulled her down with him onto the floor until they were both kneeling, both trembling.

"Oh, Kate—" he buried his lips in her hair "—say yes. You have to, darling. Say it now. Say you'll marry me."

Nine

---

*R*un. Run. As fast as you can, a silent voice pounded in time to the tropical drumbeat, or was that only the furtive whisper of Kate's heart?

Much as she might long to escape, she couldn't because she'd sold herself, body and soul, to Rex. That's what it felt like she'd done anyway.

Not that there wasn't a positive side. At least she no longer had to pine for Rex. No longer did she have to hunger for his touch. He was with her constantly. Her money problems had ceased to be a constant anxiety.

But was she doing the right thing to marry him?

There are no battles more terrifying than the silent, internal ones, and Kate had been fighting a lot of those lately. Marrying Rex now seemed more complex than it had the night he'd proposed. He wanted things from her she wasn't sure she could give him.

Rex was wealthy, and his wealth was diversified in stocks, real estate and his various businesses. He never stopped working. He was writing a book, organizing the excavation trip, and plan- ning a documentary he was going to film and a book he going to write about the *Marta Isabella*. Sometimes Kate felt as if she was just another one of his many projects.

Why was it that once she had consented to become Rex's wife, he was no longer satisfied with her? It seemed he wanted to change not only superficial things like the way she dressed and the way she wore her hair but every aspect of her personality. He wanted her to be more feminine, to stop trying to be so independent. What did he want—some weak, mindless, clinging vine?

"I'm not Jake," Rex would say. "Jake wanted a son, and you always had to show him you were as good as any man. Well, you don't have to prove yourself ever again, darling. I want you to be a woman."

Sometimes when Rex said that, Kate almost believed him. At such times it almost seemed easy to be soft and to let Rex take care of her. But did that have to mean sitting back while he had all the fun?

Kate held her engagement ring so that she could examine it in the moonlight. She remembered the night he had slipped it on her finger. How filled with hope she'd been that someday he might come to love her. That was before he'd started trying to change her.

The diamond twinkled faintly. The ring was part of a treasure Rex had found several years ago off the Bahamas. It was of a gold so soft that the large three-carat diamond was almost half-buried in its crudely made setting. The diamond was cut in the shape of an uneven truncated pyramid. Though it was hardly the fiery, multifaceted gem that most women long for, Kate was crazy about it. She found herself looking at her hand constantly, and every time she did, her doubts faded. She felt again that same quiet little thrill of joy she'd known that first night he'd given it to her.

She forced her hand back to her side and began to walk softly along the upper gallery, her heels making muffled sounds on the painted wooden boards. With her black hair and black chiffon gown, she melted into the purple shadows that slanted against the pale pink walls of the house.

A coconut palm nodded faintly, its fanlike leaves scratching against the white tiled roof. The warm, sea-scented air carried with it the mingled sweetness of a thousand blossoms.

Everything was in readiness, but Kate was far from happy. The party seemed to symbolize the new rift between herself and Rex.

The lighted pool glimmered like an aquamarine jewel against the dark backdrop of the garden. Umbrella-shaded tables had been moved to one side for dancing and huge torches had been set up in the sand. Flickering yellow tongues of fire swirled from blackened sconces, licking a jet-black night sky.

Downstairs, the house throbbed with people, laughter and music. When the guests had started arriving, Kate had given in to a moment of panic and fled outside.

In the dining room, banquet tables were laden with crisp, fresh salads, tropical fruits and appetizers of roast Eleuthera chicken. Rex had forced Kate to oversee every detail personally.

"Why are you so determined to make me take care of these stupid arrangements, Rex, when I've never given a party in my life?" she had cried in frustration.

"Don't you remember what I told you when you came to me asking for money to save that old worm-eaten shrimper of yours and those reprobates you call loyal employees?" he'd murmured gently.

"You told me a lot of things," she snapped heatedly, bristling at his insults.

"I'm going to make you into a woman again, Kate Andrews. If we're going to be married, I'd better get to work."

"Your kind of woman," she erupted contemptuously.

"Wrong. My woman."

He'd smiled at her lazily, and she'd almost wished she had the courage to slap that darkly handsome face. Instead, she'd let him kiss her, and despite her anger, she'd actually enjoyed the fierce possession of his mouth claiming hers.

That horrible conversation had repeated itself again and again in her mind. Every time it had, she'd cried a silent, "Never!"

Oh, why was Rex so determined to change her?

Not that everything he'd done was obnoxious. Rex could be fun when he wanted to be. One brilliant afternoon stood out in particular. Rex had taken her with him on a business trip to Nassau. After he was through working, they'd gone shopping. She'd had such fun exploring the narrow, twisting streets with him. They'd been carried along in a sea of tourists. Together they'd laughed over the army of people in their flowered shorts, huge straw hats, transparent visors and theatrical sunglasses. Rex and she had held hands and bought inexpensive souvenirs. Most of all, they'd simply enjoyed each other. Later, he'd taken her to dinner, and they'd danced.

Rex included her in his work, as well. He'd let her help him hire additional crew for the dive trip. She'd done most of the interviews herself. She'd accompanied him on his visits to his lawyer when he'd thrashed out the legal details with the state and federal government. In fact, he'd consulted her on every detail concerning the plans for the excavation of the *Marta Isabella,* as if he'd been intending to take her with him.

Then only this morning Rex had announced that he wasn't going to let her go after all. He wanted her to stay here and concentrate on the wedding preparations while he was away.

Concentrate on her weddings plans! Was he out of his mind? How would she possibly be able to concentrate on anything other than what a monster he was for leaving her behind?

Knowing he was only telling her part of the truth, she'd been ready to explode as he'd explained that it was time she learned to be a woman. He'd gone on to say he couldn't very well work her to death as if she were some rough diver he might hire to work in dangerous conditions.

"I want to protect you, Kate, to spoil you and give you all the things you've done without. Most women would be happy to stay home."

"Maybe I'm not most women, Rex. Maybe I don't want to be spoiled. And just maybe I think you're keeping something from me. Something important." She touched his hand. "At least tell me your real reason for changing your mind about taking me with you."

He stared at her for a long time, hesitating.

"Tell me, Rex."

"All right," he muttered in exasperation. "Because it's too dangerous. My men have told me that word's out on the street that we're in for trouble."

"What?"

"There may be others set on taking that treasure away from us."

"I'm not afraid, Rex."

"No, but I will be if you're there."

"Rex, this isn't fair. You can't just leave me behind, just because I'm a woman."

He smiled at the passion in her voice, but his low tone was equally passionate when he answered her.

"Why can't you understand that I could never forgive myself if something happened to you?"

"Nothing's going to happen."

"I hope you're right, but don't you know that you're much too precious for me to take a chance?"

She'd argued and pled to no avail. Then she'd stomped, screamed and raged and gotten the same result. Rex had listened patiently and said no.

Kate paused and clutched the white wrought-iron railing that edged the veranda like a fringe of frothy lace.

Rex was going to have to accept her for the person she was. At heart she was an adventuress, not a socialite. She lived to be down in that silent blue world, using air pumps to clear away mud from ancient, coral-encrusted wrecks, surfacing only when her air ran out and she was cold and shivering because she'd been down so long. She wasn't some sissy who would shrink at the first sign of danger.

When he'd asked her to marry him, she'd envisioned a life of diving with him, exploring with him. Not jealously waiting at home for him to return from his latest adventure. She'd been independent far too long to put up with that sort of thing.

Run. Run. The voice came again. Louder. A clamoring he song. Impossible to ignore.

She gazed into the darkness at the small irregular peninsula stretching into the moonlit sea. Flames leaped like golden dancers against the dark garden. Flamboyant trees spread their bejeweled branches, shadowing the series of wide terraces that cascaded to the dark tangled overgrowth that was the garden. Red hibiscuses fringed the curving paths that meandered through the garden to the beach.

A couple came out onto the terrace and embraced. Watching them, Kate felt a pang of longing. Long ago, she too had believed in love.

Kate turned her gaze from the lovers. Suddenly she wanted to go down to the party and surround herself with people. She backed toward the house and opened the door that led into the opulence of Rex's masculine bedroom.

Kate stepped outside the bedroom onto the landing above the staircase, and the band stopped playing. She gripped the shiny brass rail and clung to it. The house was packed with Rex's friends and business associates.

Would she really ever be able to fit into Rex's life? What would she say to all these strangers? Kate longed to fly back to the safety of the bedroom, but at her appearance, a hush had fallen upon the glittering crowd. She realized with horror that Rex was standing on the bottom stair, waiting for her, and that he had just given some little speech about her. He was deliberately making her the center of attention.

A hundred champagne glasses lifted to toast her. Kate glared down at Rex. He responded by dazzling her with one of his quick white smiles. Then, with an air of jaunty mischief, he winked at her.

Her heart pitched crazily.

Tomorrow he was going after her wreck and leaving her behind. She should kill him. Why did she feel like making love to him?

Rex moved one heavily muscled leg forward and placed a polished black boot on the first step. He raised a glass frothing with champagne. Kate marveled that the fragile crystal didn't shatter in that strong brown hand.

"Ladies and gentlemen," he murmured huskily, "I'd like to propose a toast. To Kate—" his bold eyes rose to the slim woman at the top of the stairs "—my woman."

As always, his presence hit Kate with the force of a direct physical impact. In the sea of soft, spoiled faces, his roughly cut features did not belong. His body looked lean and hard in his flawlessly cut dark suit. His golden hair fell across his tanned brow. An aura of cool arrogance clung to him as he lounged indolently against the bannister. In spite of a certain worldliness in his manner, one had the feeling that there was something not quite civilized about him, but this only made him all the more dangerously charismatic.

Kate stared down at the crowd wildly. Then her eyes locked with the blue insolence of Rex's. For an instant, the air that separated them was charged with some powerful emotion.

If she married him, he believed that he would rule and she would be ruled.

It was up to her to teach him and quickly that that would never be so.

His gaze moved from her eyes to her lips and then lingeringly to her breasts. His intense inspection made her acutely conscious of just how much bosom spilled over her low-cut black gown, and blood rushed into her cheeks.

Why did he always have to look at her like that? As if he were stripping her? And why did she always have to blush and catch her breath when he did?

Rex lifted one dark eyebrow quizzically and smiled. "Darling, surely you don't prefer being alone out on the balcony to being with me," he murmured in silken challenge.

"What woman in her right mind would?" someone tossed out.

Everyone chuckled. Everyone except Kate. The color in her cheeks deepened.

She wanted to leap down the stairs and claw him for making her so conspicuous. She wanted to be enveloped in soft shadows and kiss him gently for hours.

Kate forced a smile, managing a choked, "Of course not, my love."

Several men began to laugh and joke near Rex.

"Who would have ever thought our Kate would make such a blushing bride?"

"You've turned a tigress into a kitten, old man."

"Never imagined we'd see the day when you'd act like you were serious about a woman, either, Reynolds."

"Neither did I," came that sardonic, lazy drawl.

"She must be quite a woman."

"Oh, she is," Rex purred. His white smile broadened.

Kate began to descend the staircase, her mind in turmoil. She hated being the center of attention, but she supposed that if she was going to marry a famous man, she would have to get used to it. Perhaps that was Rex's intention tonight.

Rex folded her hand tightly in his. His gaze was brilliantly intense. "Everyone expects us to dance together," he murmured against her ear, his breath the warmest of caresses. "Look like your enjoying yourself, enjoying me."

Kate's startled gaze flew to his face, and he smiled his wonderful smile. A flush of pleasure ran through her. As always when in his company, she found herself enjoying him too much. Oh, it was dangerous to love a man who professed no love in return. But she couldn't stop herself.

He led her onto the dance floor. The party was in full swing. At least, with Rex guiding her through the throng, Kate didn't have to say much to anyone else. Then she was in his arms, her body pulled tightly against his.

"Darling, you're trembling," he said. "Every time I touch you, it happens. At least you're not as indifferent as you always struggle to pretend."

"We're supposed to be engaged," she retorted crisply. "It's only natural that I should find you somewhat attractive."

"And do you find me only somewhat attractive?" he taunted in that low, husky voice.

Her heart was beating in her throat. "Since you're so sure you know how I feel, why should I answer that?" she replied on a note of asperity.

"Because I want to hear you say it." His blue eyes twinkled with amusement.

"Haven't I told you before?"

"Tell me again," he whispered seductively.

"Perhaps a bit more than…just somewhat attractive," she admitted. "Would I be like this with you now if I didn't?"

The music went on, but he stopped dancing. They were caught in the center of a kaleidoscope of swirling couples.

A brown fingertip tilted her chin, and she was forced to look into his eyes. His dark face was grave. "I wouldn't have asked, except that sometimes, Kate, I feel like I'm rushing you into something you don't really want."

"So even male chauvinists have their fleeting moments of doubt," she mocked lightly. "That's a gratifying tidbit of knowledge."

She shot him a brilliant smile, and suddenly he threw back his head and laughed.

"I'm afraid it's not very often," he admitted sheepishly.

Before she could say anything more, he swept her around with the music in a deft turn. Never had she been more conscious of the way their bodies fitted together so perfectly, of the way they moved together with such fluid ease. She could feel the heat of him through their clothes. His hard-muscled legs brushed hers from time to time. He moved with lithe, pantherlike grace. Other women's eyes followed the golden giant and the slim dark girl he swirled in his arms with more than a trace of envy. Kate found herself reveling in being his partner.

He made her feel beautiful, young and vitally alive.

Rex deliberately maneuvered them outside onto one of the terraces overlooking the glimmering ocean. In the distance she could hear the faint murmur of the waves crashing rhythmically, incessantly upon the narrow white beach. Behind her, the sound of the throbbing drumbeats of the band kept perfect time with the wild tattoo of her heart.

Rex drew her into his arms. "Darling." His voice was rich and low. Intimate.

For a breathless moment, she could only stare up into his eyes.

He was so tall and commanding in his black suit and white silk shirt, and she was so vulnerable to his golden good looks. There was such an aura of male virility about him; he dominated his surroundings. He dominated her. It was as if the mansion, the party sounds, the perfume of tropical flowers and the ocean blended together and receded into the background. Kate was aware only of him, aware only of his intense animal magnetism that drew her inexorably. She was frightened suddenly of the intensity of the emotion she felt toward him. He could hurt her, and he probably would, unbearably.

She wet her lips; they felt parched.

His eyes rested on her red mouth. He watched the enticing temptation of her pink tongue trail across the fullness of her bottom lip, wetting it.

Very slowly he smoothed his palms down over her satin-soft shoulders. There was possession in his light touch. He ran his fingers through the loose cloud of long black hair that floated down her back.

"You should have red hair," he said softly against her hair and temple. His mouth brushed across her forehead. "To go with your temper."

"I don't really have a temper," she pouted, annoyed that he had such an image of her.

"And do you always tell the truth about yourself, too?" He laughed softly when her brows drew together in annoyance.

"Of course I do."

His hands touched her breasts, cupped them, tantalizing the crests to hard little buttons of longing.

"Sure."

"Rex, you're the only person I ever get mad at." When he looked dubious, she added, "Really!"

"Maybe that's just because you like me so much."

"You're a conceited devil."

He chuckled. "The perfect companion for someone of your fiery temperament."

He pulled her against him. Then he tipped her chin back and bent his golden head to brush a soft, sweet kiss upon her mouth.

She drew a breath that was more like a little gasp. Surrender quivered through her limbs, igniting a passion so intense that it seemed to melt her bones. His mouth became harder, hotter, seeking and demanding, ravishing.

She felt dizzy and weightless in his arms. His strong hands forced her softer body to fit the hard contours of his. Her heart trembled under his demanding passion, and something quickened deep within her, something that was like a glowing spark setting a forest ablaze. She dissolved in the swift, molten flood of pleasure.

With a moan, her lips fluttered open to accept the intimate invasion of his tongue. She clung to him. Her fingers curled into the thickness of his blond hair.

She was helpless against the fire of his kiss. She felt his body against hers. He was as hard as a brick. In another minute— She had to stop him. With his guests inside, there was no way they could run away to the bathhouse and make love.

Reluctantly, she rested her head against his chest. He aroused her so much that she was panting breathlessly. Her mouth felt bruised and swollen, and she sucked in her lower lip to nurse the pain and diminish her desire.

In the morning he was leaving. She couldn't bear the thought of being parted from him.

"Take me with you, Rex," she begged.

"What?" The word was hoarse and indistinct, betraying his passion. He bent over her, brushing strands of hair from her cheek. His mouth moved below her temple.

"Tomorrow. Take me with you," she whispered.

She was aware of him tensing. The blaze of hunger in his eyes died slowly as he caught her meaning.

Then he said, "You never miss a trick, do you?" There was a trace of malice in his low tone as well as regret. "You did that deliberately, didn't you? Stirred me to fever pitch so that in a moment of weakness I'd change my mind about taking you along. You're a witch, a green-eyed enchantress. But even caught in your spell as I am, I could never agree and risk—"

"It might be weeks and weeks, Rex."

"Do you think I want that? I want you with me, Kate."

She sensed the urgency of his need for her. "Then why—"

"I told you why. Because it's going to be dangerous. Too damned dangerous to bring a woman along. If anything should happen to you—" His voice roughened. "Oh, Kate, my determined, precious darling, just this once why don't you try to understand the way I feel? Why does it have to be so difficult for you to accept my decision about this?"

His hardheadedness infuriated her, but she spoke softly. "I'm not just another of your yes-men. I'm going to be your wife, Rex. You can't just order me around as if I was some slave. I have the right to make some of my own decisions. I'm not afraid. I wouldn't hold you to blame."

"But I'd hold myself to blame." An intensity had come into his manner, and he pulled her tightly against himself as if she was very dear to him. "It's a man's instinct to protect his woman. Nothing you can do or say will change my mind."

"But—"

"Nothing, Kate."

Her brows were drawn together over green eyes that blazed mutinously. Her chin was thrust toward him at a defiant angle. She looked so stubborn, he thought, but so irresistible. His mouth curved in sudden amusement. "Though if you want to try again, I'll be glad to let you. That last attempt was certainly enjoyable."

His teasing manner only served to intensify her anger. "You low-down scamp! I wouldn't kiss you again, no matter what! And if you think I'll just meekly do what you say..."

Her fury only amused him. He chuckled low in his throat. "That's exactly what I think, Kate."

"Then you're wrong."

"We'll see."

Her eyes flashed rebelliously. She was about to say something that would take him down a peg or two when someone called to him from the house, and he turned from her and shouted jovially in greeting.

Kate reined in her temper. She smiled secretly to herself. *We certainly will see, my darling,* she thought. *We certainly will.*

There was no point in arguing with him further. He'd just tell her that she was as stubborn as a mule. Well, he was more stubborn than an entire wagon train of the ornery creatures! But she would have her way. She was sure of it.

When Rex's attention returned to her, her fury seemed to be gone. She smiled at him benignly, beguilingly, and for some reason that he didn't bother to analyze, this disturbed him far more than her burst of temper had a moment before.

"I think it's about time we enjoyed our engagement party," she whispered, taking his hand in hers.

"I thought that's what we were doing."

"You know what I mean. We shouldn't waste time quarreling on our last night together. We should..."

"Get back to enjoying each other." Rex smiled at her warmly, taking her hands in his and kissing their backs in an indescribably delicious way. "I'll bet you have a lot of good ideas."

"I have a few," she admitted softly, staring at their joined hands. "I'll show you later."

Slowly he turned a palm to his mouth, kissing it lingeringly. "I'm not sure I can wait till later," he murmured against the warmth of her cupped fingers.

"Maybe it's time a big man like you developed a little will-power," she replied tartly, snatching her hand away before she lost all will to resist him. "After all, it was your idea to give this party, and you were the slave driver who made me do all the work. I want to dance and dance and dance."

Then she ran from him, and he watched her melt into the long black shadows as she raced toward the house. Suddenly he was running after her, determined to be the only man she would dance with tonight.

He found her in another man's arms, dancing in the moonlight, and as he strode toward them, he wondered how he could stand to leave her. He simply had to. It was out of the question to take her.

For the rest of the evening, neither Rex nor Kate brought up the subject of his intention to leave the next morning, but it was never far from either of their minds. Though Kate smiled and laughed and flirted and deliberately sought to make Rex terribly jealous, she thought of nothing else.

Ten

The sky was darkening behind a gauze of high clouds as the sun sank into a gold-plated sea. Rex scarcely noticed the purr of the engine nor the roll of the gulf beneath *Wanderer*'s plunging hull as he headed across the deck.

He walked into his cabin, slammed the door and set a tray of piping-hot food on the table. Steam curled up from chicken fried steak and mashed potatoes smothered in cream gravy.

Rex was tired and hungry from the long day at sea. He planned to eat and then pass out on his bunk for a few hours of sleep.

He stripped out of his windbreaker. Then he strode across the little room, flung open the door of his locker and reached for a hanger.

He pulled, but the hanger didn't budge. He yanked ever harder.

"Ouch!" came a voice from inside the locker. "Watch it! That's my hair you're tugging out by the roots."

There was only one impertinent female who sounded like that! And she was home in Key West, planning their wedding.

Rex drew back, and watched as a slim golden hand worked to untangle a long strand of ebony hair that had become tangled in the hanger. Then the hand politely extended the hanger to him.

Kate wasn't in Key West! She was right here!

Rex was so shocked and so furious that the hanger slipped through his fingers and clattered onto the floor.

Peeking from behind his shirts was a dilated pair of bold green eyes that were shining brightly with triumph.

His face flushed darkly with anger. "Kate, what in the hell do you think—"

Kate hesitated for a split second, but only for a split second.

"I think it's about time I got out of here, if you really want to know," she interrupted him. "Don't just stand there glaring at me. Why don't you give me a hand and help—"

"Forget it." His low voice sliced across her sentence, faintly harsh yet controlled.

"My back's got a crick in it, Rex. My foot's gone to sleep. This hasn't been a picnic, you know."

With no help from Rex, Kate stepped out of the closet and took the windbreaker from him and hung it neatly in his locker. Then she began to stretch and rubbed her spine with both hands. "I don't know if I'll ever be able to stand up straight again. Now I know what a question mark feels like. And as for small dark places— Next time I'll pick a more comfortable hiding place."

His handsome face was grim. He'd been watching her every move, listening to her nervous chatter without even the faintest trace of a smile. "You think you're cute, don't you?"

"I think I'm hungry. And you could at least kiss me hello and act like you're glad to see me."

His mouth twisted with a hint of cynicism. "I'm the furthest thing from glad to see you. And there won't be any hello kisses."

"Suit yourself, but when you get around to changing your mind, I might not be in the mood. And since there aren't any other women on board, you may be sorry. In case you have forgotten, there are quite a few men. I can pick and choose."

Low in his throat, he made a sound that was almost a growl.

Prudently, she moved away from him toward his dinner and sat down in his chair. "And you'd better order more food. There's not enough for two. I wouldn't want you to go without."

"You just couldn't do as I asked and stay in Key West where you belonged, could you, Kate?"

She was busy unfurling the paper napkin from his silverware. Very methodically, she spread his napkin in her lap.

"No."

She lifted his knife and fork and sliced off a chunk of chicken fried steak.

"It never occurred to you that maybe I was right in wanting you to stay there?" he said coldly.

"Oh, I'm sure you thought you were right." She chewed a piece of steak very thoroughly, then swallowed a bite of mashed potatoes. It was hard to feel repentant when she was starving and the mashed potatoes were so delicious that they were melting in her mouth. "The cook's not bad. I wasn't all that sure he would be when I hired him, you know. His name's Cappy. He used to work for Don."

Rex refused to be sidetracked. "I don't give a damn about Cappy or anything else for that matter. All I care about is the fact that you're here, and you shouldn't be." He leaned over the table. His gaze narrowing to piercing steel. "You're so spoiled that you just had to have you way, didn't you, Kate?"

She blanched in a sudden prickling of fear. Her fingers clenched her fork so tightly that the metal edges began to cut into her skin. She mustn't let Rex get to her. She'd known he would be mad. Naturally her presence was going to take some getting used to on his part. All he needed was a little time. She just needed to remain bright and cheerful. Eventually he would come around.

"Maybe you're spoiled, Rex. Just because you're a man doesn't mean your opinions are superior to mine."

"So you see this as a battle between the sexes," Rex snapped.

"That's exactly what it is."

She looked down at her plate because she was tired of looking into the fierce unfriendliness of his glittering eyes. He refused to smile. She was through trying to be nice. Let him sulk!

A vise was suddenly clamped on her forearm, and she gasped. Her fork clanked against the metal lip of the plate when it fell. He pulled her to her feet and brought her face within inches of the dark fury of his.

"What does it take to get through to you that this isn't just some frivolous battle between the sexes, Kate? The situation is far more serious. I'm certain now that there's going to be trouble on this venture. This is the last place you ought to be."

His fingers bit into her arm. For a moment, she could only stare at him. Anger made him even more dangerously attractive than usual. Not that she dared to tell him that.

His electric-blue gaze jolted through her, charging her with the high voltage of his fury. Beneath the wayward thickness of gold hair, his face was a mahogany mask. Vitally masculine, his strength and determination were carved into his harshly drawn features. Kate was shaken by the ruthlessness she sensed in him.

"You're hurting me, Rex."

He was furious when he thought of how she'd deliberately thwarted his calculated efforts to protect her. For an instant, his grip tightened. Then he let her go, and she fell back into her chair.

A moment of stunned, tense silence passed between them.

"What did you mean when you said you were certain there's going to be trouble?" she asked hesitantly after several seconds.

"Last night, after the party, my shop was broken into, and the prowler took all my research regarding the *Marta Isabella*. Several artifacts were missing, too. Worse, now I'm sure that I can't trust my crew. This morning, sometime after we left Key West, somebody broke into my cabin and ransacked it. Nothing seemed to be missing, but I think someone's been working damned hard to reach the wreck before I do. If we do find millions of dollars in gold and silver, I feel positive we'll have unwanted company. There'll probably be violence."

"Rex, I can handle all that."

"I could, too, damn it, if you weren't on board."

"I don't see why it makes any difference—"

"Don't you? Then let me spell it out. It takes a hell of a lot to scare a guy that's been through what I have, but now that you're here, I'll be running scared all the time. I won't be able to think straight because you're on board and in danger. I've gone through my entire life alone, Kate. I've lost everyone I've ever felt close to and I can't bear the thought of losing you." His eyes filled with self-contempt. "There, is that enough for you?"

He cursed savagely under his breath. Then he threw open the door. "I need some air, Kate," he said brusquely. "Enjoy my dinner. And my bed."

"Oh, I intend to."

His dark scowl deepened.

Magnanimously she added, "But I wouldn't mind sharing."

"Thank you, but I would. I'll bunk down with the crew. The less you and I see each other, the better."

That was one thing Kate couldn't agree with.

"You could always throw me to the sharks," she tossed out, attacking his chocolate square of cake with a vengeance.

"Don't tempt me."

They reached the wreck site the next morning, and Rex sent down divers to attach steel lines to blocks of coral on the bottom, preparing several secure anchorage sites for *Wanderer.* After they'd completed the task, he went down to inspect the anchorage sites himself. The one to the west was adequate, but the one on the east had come loose and had to be changed.

During the afternoon, a team went out to install a new sling on the bottom to the north of the reef, and established, by means of radio and radar, a deep-water anchorage point to the northwest. Meanwhile a film crew was taking pictures of the entire operation.

If Kate had hoped that Rex would be in a better mood after a night's sleep, her hopes had been dashed when he'd crept silently into his cabin for a fresh change of clothes shortly before dawn. If anything he'd been even colder to her than he had been when he'd first discovered her on board.

She was in bed, sleeping lightly, dreaming of Rex. He was touching her breasts through her thin, filmy nightgown, gently circling her nipples with his fingers until they stood up hard and proud. Her longing was a fire that once ignited, grew into a firestorm.

His fingertips traced every inch of her body, expertly arousing her. How hard and callused his hands felt against her flesh, yet how gently he touched her. His mouth fell upon her lips, devouring, probing, while his hands explored every contour of her shapely body.

"Oh, Rex," she moaned incoherently and then rolled over to dream of him some more.

Metal scraped against metal as Rex wrenched open a drawer and began to rummage through it.

"What the hell?" he muttered, swallowing a furious oath as he removed a lacy garment with satin straps. Next he pulled out a pair of lace-edged nylon panties.

Snapping on the light he shouted in the direction of the blanket-covered lump in his bunk, "What have you done with my clothes, woman?"

With a yank he ripped the sheets from her body. And that was his first mistake.

For a moment, he could only stare at her in hushed silence while his heart beat like a drum against his temples. She lay in his bed, her opulent loveliness a glorious display of wanton womanliness. She stretched, and he watched the delicate play of muscle beneath satin-smooth flesh.

Kate came awake slowly, staring drowsily at the fierce, golden giant looming over her bunk who was shaking his fists from which dangled a pair of her panties and her bra.

"Good morning, Rex," she said huskily, remembering her dream.

Her features were softer than usual, prettier. She looked exquisitely refreshed, as though she'd slept deeply and well, as though she hadn't a care in the world. Beneath her tan, her creamy skin positively glowed. He'd scarcely caught a wink.

Kate's hair tumbled loosely in mussed inky waves over her shoulders. Her mouth curved into a gently, tempting smile that lured him, teasing, promising rapture. She sat up in bed, her long sable lashes fluttering languidly as she adjusted her eyes to the unexpected brilliance. She did not bother to pull the sheets back to cover her exposed body. She seemed to revel in his looking at her.

"I hope you've decided to be friendly," she murmured shyly, peering up at him through those slanting, downcast lashes.

She looked deliciously sexy in her state of charming dishabille. Her green eyes held a voluptuous, yielding expression. The curve of her red lips enticed him. Her lips parted, and he saw the tips of her white teeth.

Her presence in his bed, her unspoken invitation, her feminine softness stirred him to the point of insanity. His stomach knotted in a mixture of desire and anger. He looked like he wasn't sure which he wanted to do more, throttle her or make love to her.

His gaze fell to her smooth, silky breasts rising full and tantalizing against her transparent pink nightgown. Her waist was as narrow as a wasp's. She ran a light finger down her belly. Hypnotized, he watched the path of that finger, which invited him to follow it with his hands and lips. He could not help admiring the well-curved hips and the graceful length of feminine thigh that could be his for the asking.

He caught the gentle fragrance of her perfume. She'd never worn perfume before. Or nightgowns like that one.

Moisture beaded his brow. His body was tight with desire. Only some last feeble shred of sense enabled him to quickly turn away from her, but not so quickly that she did not guess she was having a powerful effect upon him.

As he averted his gaze, she burst out laughing, enjoying his discomfiture so much that she nearly choked on her last few giggles. When she regained herself, she managed breathlessly, "You look so silly, Rex. Just what do you think you're doing waving my underwear as if they're war flags? A girl's entitled to some privacy now, isn't she?'' When he said nothing, she added, "Why, Rex, I do believe you're blushing.''

Angrily he threw the bra and panties toward her, and she caught them in midair.

"Thank you.'' She smiled demurely. "But I don't really need them right now.''

"I'll get out of here and leave you to your privacy if you'll just tell me what you did with my damn clothes,'' he thundered.

"Maybe I don't want to be left to my privacy, darling,'' she breathed softly.

His eyes ran boldly over her luxuriant curves. What a beautiful tawny body she had, and to go with it, she possessed such an appealing, passionate nature. A soft green fire blazed in her eyes. She was seducing him. Deliberately.

His desire for her was vanquishing his ungovernable anger. He clenched and unclenched his fists as he gazed down at her, struggling for control.

"Don't play games with me, Kate,'' he growled.

"I thought you liked...playing games with me,'' she whispered in a low, erotic tone.

"Damn it,'' he groaned, "I'll find them myself.'' He turned from her and yanked open a drawer. Two of her bikinis spilled to the floor.

He was about to pull open another drawer when she stopped him. "There's no need to tear the place apart, Rex. I moved them over there,'' she replied casually, pointing to the locker on the opposite side of the cabin. "I thought it would be nice if all your things were together and if mine were, too, so I put my clothes in the drawers. Yours are in the locker.''

He grabbed what he wanted and would have left without saying another word, but before he stormed out, she said sweetly, "Please turn the light off before you go. I'd like to sleep a couple of more hours.''

He hit the switch much harder than he needed to, and the cabin melted into darkness.

"Thank you, Rex, for being sweet enough to—''

His low, icy voice came to her. "Sweetness had nothing to

do with it. I'd agree to nearly anything that would keep you out of my sight two hours.''

To that she said nothing. It would never do for him to see how he wounded her. She curled beneath the covers, feeling miserable.

Later, things were no better between them. Rex refused to let her help him. He threw himself into his work and ignored Kate completely. At first she felt so hurt and left out that she kept to his cabin. Then she decided that was exactly what he wanted. To thwart him, she made friends with the crew. Cappy, in particular, welcomed her company. He basked in her compliments about his cooking. Her one small triumph was that Rex became even angrier every time he caught one of the crew members laughing and talking to her. Her friendship with Cappy seemed to annoy him especially. At least Rex wasn't indifferent to her, although that was small consolation.

In the days that followed, the tension remained between Kate and Rex. He was the boss, and, therefore, in total control of the operation. Since he never issued her a direct order, it was difficult for Kate to take part in what was going on. Everyone but her was busy mapping the wreck site and recording all the information they gathered while she had virtually nothing to do.

She prowled the ship restlessly, and it wasn't long before she was intimately acquainted with every inch of it. *Wanderer* was a 400-ton, 160-foot reconditioned ship of World War II vintage. Kate was impressed with the way Rex had equipped it with dredges, coring devices, a submerged underwater observation chamber at the bow, and a well by which divers could go directly from the ship into the sea.

Since Kate had so little to occupy herself with, she slowly grew aware of a tension on board that had nothing to do with Rex and herself. She began to sense that beneath the surface, something was wrong. The crew was not working together. There were odd, quick quarrels that burst out over nothing and that were over as quickly as they'd arisen. The crew was nervous. Kate had the feeling that someone was waiting and watching, but for what, she couldn't be sure.

A month passed, during which the only treasure that the divers found was twenty pieces of eight, four lengths of gold chain and two anchors. But neither Rex nor the crew became disheartened. The *Marta Isabella* had broken apart, and her wreckage was spread across an expanse of coral and sand several miles long. Salvaging a wreck like her could take years.

Every find was carefully marked on a map of the wreck site, and though she wasn't allowed to dive, Kate spent many hours studying that map and thinking. Sometimes she read and reread the copy she kept of the letter she and Jake had discovered written by the Spanish captain.

One night she had a nightmare. In her dream she was a passenger aboard the doomed *Marta Isabella* as it headed on its northeasterly course toward Spain. Black seas were sweeping the bow. In the moonlight, she could see waves frothing angrily over a reef. The captain was struggling to avoid it, and it seemed for a while that he might succeed. Then, just as she was almost out of danger, the ship was hurled onto the northern tip of the reef. Kate awoke on a strangled cry as water burst into the dream ship.

She got out of bed and went to Rex's desk and looked down at the charts and the map of the wreck. Rex was concentrating on the southern tip of the reef because he thought that was where the currents would have been more likely to sweep a ship in distress. But what if the ship had almost passed safely by the reef only to nick its northernmost edge? What if...?

Her first thought was to tell Rex, but because Rex remained so cool and unreceptive to her, she found no opportunity to discuss her theory with him. He kept diving where he'd been diving.

Then a storm kept all the divers on board for two days, and the strange tension was more noticeable than ever. Sometimes Kate felt as if they were hovering on the brink of some unknown disaster.

The first sun-spangled afternoon after the bad weather, everyone was restless to get back to the salvage operation. Diving was sometimes especially good after a storm because the waves could shift tons of sand from one location to another. Sometimes storms uncovered wrecks that had been hidden beneath twenty feet of sand before the storm.

Kate begged Rex to change his mind and let her dive, but he refused. In fact Rex had been particularly cold to Kate that morning, and right before he jumped into the launch to go diving himself, he'd repeated his strict orders to her not to dive. In a rage she'd watched his launch leave.

Just who did he think he was? She'd been patient and obedient long enough, and where had it gotten her? Didn't he realize how bored she was with nothing to do other than watch the gulls and frigate birds wheel over the water and the sea turtles sound in the deep channels?

The sea was as placid as a mirror, and the more she gazed at it, the greater was the temptation to disobey him. What would he do to her if she did? He would only get mad. So what! That might even be a welcome change from his cold, silent treatment.

Within minutes she was in her skintight black wet suit, plunging over the side of the boat, while Cappy screamed she would get into trouble for what she was doing.

The water was cool, a shock at first, as it oozed into her wet suit. Soon, however, she adjusted to it. There was no sign of the other divers. Quickly she swam toward the northern tip of the reef and then down to the bottom.

For a while, she didn't notice anything of particular interest. Then, in a great coral ravine twenty feet under the sea, she saw something glistening like tiny gems at the bottom of a mine shaft. As she got closer, pinpricks of iridescent green, blue, lavender and gold flickered among the dark coral crevices.

With gloved fingers, she carefully lifted a few of the bright little bits from their coral pockets. She realized with a start that they were glass beads and that they must have been part of the cargo of the *Marta Isabella*. Excitedly she began to scoop them into the goodie bag she'd brought with her to carry up small treasure. Only when she had retrieved the last bead did she swim a few feet away to something else that had attracted her attention.

Beside a gently swaying sea fan, she saw a solitary cannon

that stood out against the white sand. It was as if a marine mortician had arranged it for burial. However, it was not the cannon that attracted her attention. Protruding from the sand was a dark rectangular shape. When she pushed against it, it didn't move. It had the feel and look of a silver ingot.

Was she right about where the ship had hit the reef?

She began to hand-fan the sand. Suddenly something glimmered against the coarse white bottom. She picked it up and realized it was a misshapen gold escudo. Sifting the sand through her fingers, she recovered one after another. There were so many that it was as if the sea floor was carpeted with gold.

Treasure! And she'd found it!

The storm must have shifted tons of sand from the wreck site. Soon her goodie bag bulged with coins and could hold no more. There was no way she could lift the silver ingot without help.

Reluctantly she surfaced, spat out her regulatory mouthpiece and pulled herself up the diving ladder by one hand.

The first thing she saw when she climbed on deck and ripped off her mask was Rex. He fixed her with a stare as merciless as a predator stalking his prey. Though her heart began to race in panic, she shook the water out of her hair with an air of studied nonchalance.

Rex was still in his wet suit, though it was unzipped to his waist. Her gaze was drawn to the bronzed V of his furred chest. Never had she been more aware of the latent power of that muscular physique. As he strode toward her, his piercing blue gaze held no softness. He looked very male and very angry, and Kate didn't know which frightened her more.

"Where in the hell have you been?" he growled, rage darkening his face.

If he'd asked her in any other tone, she might have answered him. Suddenly she was as furious as he was. She lifted her chin and looked at him down the straight length of her nose.

What right did he have to constantly tell her what to do? She'd been so excited over her find, so anxious to let him know about it, and he was ruining everything.

She met the fire of his gaze with ice in her own. "That's obvious, isn't it?" she replied, deliberately goading him.

"I gave you a direct order not to dive."

"You pushed me too far, Rex."

"Maybe you've pushed me too far." Fury flared brighter in his eyes. "From now on you're going to stay in my cabin. You won't come out on deck unless I bring you."

"Says who?" She stood there glaring at him with color cascading into her face. "I'm sick and tired of you telling me what to do and when to do it."

"I can't imagine why, since you do exactly as you please."

The dry contempt in his voice made her eyes flash with indignation.

"You're wrong, Rex. I wanted to be a part of this expedition, but you bullied me at every turn and left me out. Was it so wrong of me to want to contribute something? All I've done is sit around and wait while you and the men went diving."

"Until today."

"You weren't going to let me go down. I had to take matters into my own hands."

"Maybe it's time I took matters into my own hands." His smooth, low tone was rife with sardonic mockery.

The golden sun backlit her hair and glinted off her wet suit.

There was something in his eyes that warned her, but as she stumbled backward to escape him, he lunged. He caught her before she'd gone three steps and crushed her against his body in a powerful embrace. She was conscious of the crew's open-mouthed astonishment as Rex lifted her into his arms.

"You're going to my cabin, and that's where you're staying," he said with awful finality, "until I decide otherwise."

"Put me down," she cried, kicking at him.

All the men except Cappy began to hoot encouragement to Rex, and Kate reddened, ashamed because Rex was making them think so little of her.

Rex's hands were iron manacles; his arms felt like the arms of an iron statue. His body felt equally invincible beneath the weak blows of her clenched fist. There seemed nothing she could do to stop him from humiliating her in front of the men, and from deliberately asserting his right to rule her.

Her pride burned like a flame, obliterating her ability to think and act rationally. She remembered the heavy bag of gold she was still clutching tightly in one fist, and in a rage, she flung it to the deck.

It split in two when it thudded against the varnished planks, and gold coins went flying.

Rex didn't even notice. His hand was moving beneath the wet warmth of her hair, grasping her neck to force her face toward his. Then his lips slanted across her mouth, hurting, demanding, possessing.

The men were yelping. "Gold!" They were scrambling after the bits of brightness as the *Wanderer* lazily rode the faint swells.

"It's treasure, men! Kate's found gold!"

A fevered madness swept the crew that had nothing to do with the fevered madness between Rex and Kate.

Cruelly Rex ravaged the softness of her lips. Kate thought surely her neck would break beneath the force of his grip. He kissed her until she could hardly breathe. She felt the heavy, hammerlike thudding of his heart against her breast, and she was aware of the threatening strength of his powerful body.

She felt dizzy. Frightened. On fire. And completely his.

The world was whirling, and Rex was the only thing she could cling to. Her fingers dug into his shoulders.

His arms bound her too savagely; muscle ground against bone. His mouth and teeth bruised the soft tissue of her lips, yet his fierce, wild passion sent tremors of excitement racing through her. Her entire consciousness was stimulated by the feel, the taste, the smell of him.

Nothing mattered except Rex. No longer did it make a difference who was the conqueror and who the conquered. For the first time in her life, she was yielding helplessly to a greater will than her own. Her arms crept upward to circle his neck. Breathlessly she parted her lips and kissed him back.

She belonged to him. She always had. She always would.

To her stunned amazement, he let her go. They both just stood there, panting, looking at one another warily. His face was dark, passionate, intense. He wanted her. She knew it: he wanted her badly.

"Go to my cabin," he said, his voice angry and rough, "and wait for me there."

"Oh, Rex," she moaned softly. "I—"

"Go to my cabin," he commanded. "Now."

For once, she obeyed.

It seemed like hours that she waited before Rex came, but it was only minutes. When he entered without knocking, Kate whirled away from the little mirror where she'd been touching the red places on her mouth.

She sank weakly against the wall as he stepped inside, her pulse skittering in both eagerness and fear. He had humbled her and hurt her, and yet she had gloried in his doing so. She should be ashamed. She should hate him.

Never had she realized how wildly she was in love with him.

She felt embarrassed. Shy.

Rex winced when he saw the marks he'd made on her lips, and it made him feel even worse than before. He thought himself an animal for the way he'd treated her in front of his men. He wouldn't blame her if she despised him, and he fully expected her to tell him she never wanted to have anything more to do with him.

Just the thought made him queasy with fear. If she did that, he was prepared to go down on his knees and beg her to forgive him.

Their eyes touched briefly. Then they looked away, but that one look was enough to set Kate's heart pounding in fright.

His expression was so bleak and cold, so stern. In his anguish he looked as if he hated her.

Why had she defied him? she wondered. Had she made him the object of ridicule in the eyes of his men?

"I'm sorry for what happened a while ago," he said in a low, tense voice. "Sorry if I hurt you." He wanted to tend her lips, to kiss away the pain, but he was too afraid of her rejection to even try.

Her stomach tightened. "I'm okay," she managed through stiff, dry lips. "And I'll stay in the cabin from now on, like you want me to."

He studied her beautiful, solemn face for a long moment, her silence killing him as he waited for the inevitable storm, waited for her to demand that he get out of her life, but it didn't come.

The suspense was just as terrible for her. Her own emotions were too overwhelming to permit speech. Her lips began to quiver. She turned away from him, pretending to stare out the porthole. She fought back the scalding tears that threatened to slide down her cheeks.

He saw the white drawn knuckles of her clenched hands. Slowly it dawned on him that whatever she was feeling, she wasn't going to order him from her life, and she'd even agreed to obey him from now on.

He had won.

But so had she.

His lips curved into one of his slow, enchanting smiles that would have dazzled her with its sudden warmth had she been looking at him. "I figured you'd say something bratty like that, Kate."

"What?"

There was something in his voice that took away the chill in her heart. She turned, her white face uncertain.

His smile grew cockier. "Because that's about the most perverse thing you could do, as if you didn't realize it."

An ember of hope flickered to life. "What are you saying, Rex?"

"You found gold. If you don't put on a tank and go down and show the men where you found it, there's going to be a mutiny, and I'll be strung up by my neck."

She flew across the room to him, her face as radiant and expectant as a child's. Her shining eyes rose to his. "Rex, are you saying that I can dive?"

Gently he wrapped his arms around her and folded her into his body. Then he kissed her. It was a long, soft, undemanding kiss.

"Do I have any choice?" he murmured in amusement and wonder.

He lowered his mouth to hers, and his blood surged through his veins with the beating force of a turbulent storm at sea.

His finger hooked the zipper of her wet suit and slowly pulled it down to reveal the warm, damp body inside.

Their lips drew apart, and lifting their eyes, they met each other's gazes in breathless excitement.

She was now soft and willing, and raising her in his arms, he carried her to his bed.

"What about the men?" she murmured. "And the gold?"

"Later." And that was all he said for a very long time.

Eleven

Rex and Kate swam together through aquamarine waters, Rex leading the way through a platoon of sleek spadefish and sheepshead. As the water grew shallower, the man and the woman stood up, removed their goggles and mouthpieces, and gazed briefly at one another.

Behind them, out to sea, *Wanderer* pitched at her anchorage over the *Marta Isabella*. Kate and Rex had sneaked away together, leaving the weary crew to continue the pleasant task of raising 76-pound chunks of pure silver with air bags and winches. Each silver brick, blackened with silver oxide, was added to the growing dark mountain of silver ingots stacked amid the clutter of air tanks, hoses and archaeological tools on deck.

Rex leaned toward Kate and lifted her tank from her shoulders to carry it for her. She swallowed hard in an attempt to clear her ears, which were banging and crackling from the pressure. She swallowed again, and this second effort brought a delicious popping in the center of her head.

"You okay?" he asked gently.

When she nodded, he took her hand and led her to the beach. The deserted island was a white jewel studded with lush mangrove trees. Aeons of wind, rain and surf had ground its coral edges into a talc-soft beach and had whittled starkly beautiful shapes out of limestone outcroppings along the shore. A rock that had been carved by erosion jutted toward the open sea.

"Look, Rex," Kate cried in delight at the natural sculpture. "It's like *Wanderer*'s bow."

He cocked his blond head, and with a critical frown, he studied the pointed rock and then looked dubiously past it at *Wanderer*. His attention returned to her face, his look one of indulgent amusement. "Whatever you say."

"But you don't think it does?"

"I don't care what it looks like." Rex laughed, and the pleasant sound shivered down her spine.

"Rex, you have absolutely no imagination," she chided.

"Oh, I have an imagination," Rex countered, without taking his eyes from her radiant face.

"For example?"

His smile was lazy and warm. His gaze skimmed over her from the top of her glossy black head, down the curves of her trim, glistening body to the tips of her shiny flippers and then back again, lingering where her lush breasts swelled above the red bra of her bikini. It was not so much a stripping look as a caressing one, and her skin quivered pleasantly in feminine reaction to his masculine appraisal.

"Right now I'm imagining you and me, without these clothes and tanks, lying in the shade of that rock you're so crazy about. I'd kiss you everywhere, and you'd kiss me back. Everywhere. Then—"

She caught her breath. "That's enough."

"I haven't even gotten to the interesting part." The grooves on either side of his mouth deepened.

"You never think about anything but sex." She couldn't seem to drag her eyes from the myriad rivulets tracing glistening patterns over that big brown muscled chest of his. Why was it that every time she was with him, she ached to touch him? A dangerous sensation of intimacy raced through her. They were alone on a deserted island. It made her feel primitive and wild.

"Unlike you," he teased with a knowing smile.

She flushed at his having read her mind. But how could she not look at him when he wore nothing but those black bathing trunks that outlined his vital male body? There was too much sleek, tanned muscle exposed.

"You're a lot worse than me," she replied tartly. "Occasionally another thought flickers through my mind. You never think of anything else."

"That's not true. I've been thinking about silver ingots and Spanish escudos all morning."

"I mean besides your work."

Cupping her cheek tenderly with his hand, Rex traced the satin-smooth line of her jaw with his thumb. Then he let his thumb seek the curve of her velvet lips, outlining them. "I always thought a working man deserved a little fun."

With a toss of her head, she pulled away from him and changed the subject. "So last night you finally radioed for another salvage vessel to come out?"

"I want to send *Wanderer* back to be unloaded."

"That's okay with me as long as you let me stay."

His gaze held hers. "You know I couldn't do without you."

"It took you long enough to figure that out."

His mouth crooked in a rueful smile. "I probably should send you back."

"No way!"

"Kate, there's no doubt you'd be safer in Key West. I feel uneasy with so much treasure on board. There's always the danger of pirates."

"But nobody knows about it."

"They do now. I sent the message myself. I put it off as long as I could, but I didn't really have a choice. I'm almost out of film. And we're running short on other supplies."

"After that silver ingot this morning and that chest of silver coins last night, how much treasure have we got on board, Rex?"

"As if you didn't know, my avaricious little darling."

"I just like to count everything over and over again."

The warmth of his laughter mingled with hers. "It is fun, isn't it?"

She smiled.

"Well," he began, "there's that pile of gold coins, ten chests of silver coins, five gold bars, seventy silver ingots..."

"And that smashed golden chalice Cappy found," Kate added. "Oh, Rex, Jake would have been so thrilled. Think. Now everyone will know Jake wasn't a fake. He was right all along."

"And is that so important to you?" he asked softly.

"More important than anything."

"And I thought you were just after the treasure."

"I guess I thought I was, too, but the *Marta Isabella* was Jake's dream for most of his life."

"I've been thinking, Kate. I've decided not to sell my part of the treasure. I'm going to open a sunken-treasure museum and dedicate the exhibit to Jake."

"Oh, Rex, that would be wonderful. I loved Jake and I believed in him. If you did that, people would know what he believed in was real. I know now that the treasure and the money were never all that important to me."

Rex's jaw hardened. "Maybe not so far as your feelings toward Jake are concerned."

An awkward silence fell between them. Rex's voice became deathly quiet. "But it was the only reason you agreed to marry me."

He looked down at her, his blue eyes filled with an intense yet incomprehensible emotion.

Briefly she wondered if she only imagined that she saw fear in his eyes.

Feeling as uncertain as he, she reached out and touched his arm. Very softly she said, "That wasn't the reason, Rex."

"Then why?" He had looked away. Only his low almost rasping voice told her he was vitally attentive to her every word.

Perhaps he was as afraid as she.

She pulled at his arm, forcing him to face her again. A thousand doubts tore through her heart as his hard gaze met hers.

Should she be honest? Or should she keep hiding behind all the barriers she'd built to protect herself from her true feelings?

Some instinct warned her that there comes a time in all relationships when the moment of truth must be faced, no matter how vulnerable one feels, no matter how frightened it may be to do so.

She swallowed. Why was it so much more difficult for her to risk herself emotionally than physically? If she told him how she felt, and he laughed at her, she would die.

It was so easy to fight, so hard to love.

At last, she said hesitantly, "Because I loved you."

His dark face was grave as he stepped back a little and searched her features for the truth. Gruffly, so as not to show how much he cared, he said, "You used the past tense."

"Then I'll use the present. I love you, Rex."

"You never let on."

She remembered all the defenses she'd built around her heart after he'd left her ten years ago. He was rich, she was poor. He was famous and successful. All she possessed was a mortgaged shrimp boat and a college degree. He was handsome; he could have any woman. She was a dreamer whose dreams had never come true.

"Oh, Rex, can't you understand that it was only because I was afraid to," she whispered.

He pulled her into his arms and wrapped her closely. "You shouldn't have been." His voice was an odd, cracked sound.

She felt the heat of his body burning into her, the warmth of his lips in her hair. "You jilted me ten years ago, Rex."

"I told you why."

"I guess I was too unsure of myself as a person to believe you."

She felt his hands stroking her damp hair. Could it be that he loved her, too? She clung to him tightly, feeling safe and complete in the cradling circle of his hard arms. It was as if she finally belonged at last, to the only man she had ever truly loved.

"Believe me, Kate. It hurt me to jilt you just as much as it hurt you. I loved you then, and I love you now. And I know all about feeling unsure. I thought you were marrying me for my money because some part of me still feels that without money, I would be nothing again and despised, and that no woman would want me. Not even you. The scars of my childhood, I guess, are partly to blame.''

"Oh, Rex. I'm sorry."

"It didn't help, either, when Jake took me in and gave me a chance in life only to throw me out a year later when he realized I was falling for you. I was just beginning to believe in myself, when everything blew up in my face. It was even worse than before. The man who'd been my hero thought I wasn't good enough for his daughter. You see Jake told me about his own past which wasn't so different from mine. He felt he was a failure.''

"He wouldn't ever talk to me about his past," she whispered.

"Jake didn't say much, but the bottom line was he couldn't have any more faith in my doing well than he had in himself. He didn't want you tied to a man with no future. He loved you, Kate. You were always fighting so hard to prove yourself to him, but you didn't have to. You were the most important thing in the world to him.

"I held a grudge against the two of you for a while, but gradually I got over those feelings. I could understand Jake's wanting to protect you. That's why when he came to me for money, I loaned it to him and told him he didn't even have to pay it back. I figured I owed him. But he was a such a proud man that he insisted upon repaying it with interest.''

"And I blamed you for that."

He smiled. "Apparently there was a time when you blamed me for everything.''

"Maybe if you hadn't married—''

His eyes grew bitter. "Ah yes, my marriage. After Jake threw me out, I married Carla on the rebound because she'd been one of the only people in my hometown who would have anything to do with me. As it turned out, she didn't really love me, either. She was merely attracted to my reputation as the town's bad boy. When she discovered I wasn't interested in maintaining that aura of wildness, that I was more interested in getting somewhere in life, well she lost interest and started chasing after other men who could give her the kind of excitement she craved.''

"Rex, I nearly died when you married her."

"You never let on."

"I was too proud. I've loved you for years. Ever since I was a girl. And it's you I love, not your badness and not your money, and not your success and fame. You're so handsome. So big. So sexy. So wonderful."

He chuckled, at last believing her. "Keep talking."

"I could go on forever," she admitted softly.

"We have the rest of our lives."

"I thought I was just another woman to you. No one special."

"You're just the *only* woman for me, Kate." He loomed over her, his eyes caressing.

In the sunlight his hair was nearly white against his dark skin. His deep blue eyes were brilliant. She was conscious of a qualm—could this gorgeous man really love her?

"I do love you, Kate," he said in the tenderest of voices.

She smiled radiantly, unaware of how beautiful she was when she smiled. Her green eyes sparkled with happiness; her cheeks glowed. Her hair, which was drying in the breeze, fluttered loosely about her shoulders, framing her narrow face with inky silkiness.

Never had she seemed more beautiful to him than she did then, smiling up at him with the love she felt for him shining in her eyes.

"Do you still want to change me?" she whispered.

"No. I want you just the way you are."

She caught her breath as he lowered his head. His mouth was soft on hers, infinitely gentle, filled with loving and caring.

She felt warmly alive, young, in love. His.

Her arms went around his broad shoulders to draw him closer. Her fingers found the golden hairs that curled at his nape and lingered to explore the contrast between his hard, warm skin and cool, silken hair.

"Maybe it's time I proved to you that I do have an imagination after all," he murmured huskily as he led her slowly toward a shady, protected niche beneath the natural limestone sculpture she had admired earlier.

He lowered her hand to the scarlet strap of her bikini. His fingers burned her skin where they touched her, but he made no attempt to untie the knot at her neck.

"Maybe it is," she whispered.

His hand loosened the knot, freeing her breasts. Lovingly he lifted the ripe, aroused globes and kneaded them.

"They're so hard," he muttered thickly as he caressed the tips of her pointed nipples with callused fingertips.

"Oh, Rex. They get that way whenever I think about you."

He chuckled softly against her neck. "And you said I was the one who sat around thinking about sex."

"I wasn't thinking about sex. I was thinking about you."

"And there's a difference?"

"Someday, Rex, I'll explain it to you. Now I just want to love you."

"I want that, too. More than I've ever wanted anything." He hugged her fiercely. "Darling, there'll never be anyone but you."

She looked at him with a sudden tearing pain. It took great effort to make her voice light. "There'd better not be."

His mouth pressed hotly against hers, and she felt herself surrendering willingly. His kiss was long and hard, his lovemaking carrying her out of herself on glorious wings of fire. For half a moment they were still, each clinging to the wonder of the other. Then he kissed her again, even harder than before as he drew her down upon the soft sand. She responded to him, not only with her lips, but with her whole body, her whole being.

At last she was no longer afraid of the love and the soaring passion she'd always felt for him.

At last he felt that he'd found what he'd spent a lifetime searching for, someone to love. He would never be alone again.

Midnight was a rich velvet blackness, a moonless sky spreading over waves of liquid ink. *Wanderer* groaned and made creaky sounds as she rode the swells at her anchorage.

Curled against Rex's back in the narrow bunk they shared, Kate came awake abruptly. It was warm in the cabin. Too warm. Their bodies were perspiring and seemed glued together everywhere they touched.

She rolled over, listening to the sounds of the night: the gentle slapping of the waves against the hull, the incessant metallic noises that the ship made as it rocked and shifted. Just as she was falling asleep again, she heard the distant purr of a motor.

If another boat was approaching, the man on watch would surely alert the rest of the crew. Kate waited expectantly. The sound grew louder, and then unexpectedly it was extinguished altogether.

What did it mean? Was it only a dream?

The rhythm of the waves lulled her to sleep once more.

An hour later Kate awakened again. This time she couldn't go back to sleep no matter how she tried.

There was a funny, close stillness in the air, a strange tension. She threw off her cotton sheet. Her whole body felt warm and sticky.

It seemed even hotter than before. Rex was sprawled all over her side of the bed, as well as his. He'd even stolen her pillow. She thought fleetingly of waking him and complaining, but then she remembered all the work he'd done after they'd returned together from the island.

He needed his sleep, poor darling, though how he could sleep in this steamy furnace was beyond her. The fact that he could only proved how totally exhausted he was. He hadn't stopped diving until it had gotten too dark to see, and he hadn't gone to bed until he'd collapsed over that last cup of coffee when he'd been working at his desk.

What she needed was a breath of air, a stroll up on deck, where she could enjoy the refreshing coolness of the ocean breeze. She wiped her hair away from her damp brow.

Carefully Kate slipped out of bed. Her bathing suit was lying across a chair, so she pulled it on along with the blouse and the pair of shorts she'd been wearing over it. Then she tiptoed soundlessly across the cabin and opened the door.

A welcoming rush of cool air enveloped her. The glimmer of the stars was lovely, but the minute she stepped outside, she sensed something was wrong.

An odd shiver swept over her. The ship was eerily quiet. Slowly she made her way toward the bow where Cappy should have been standing watch.

He wasn't there.

She whispered his name, and the frail thready sound was lost in the darkness.

Frightened, she turned, and then she saw the shrimp boat tied alongside of *Wanderer.*

It was Don's boat!

She shrank inside a darkened hatch and slipped down the ladder that led to the diver's well in the center of the ship. Immediately she guessed that Don must have come after the treasure. Her heart began to pound at a frightening rate.

She thought of Rex, who was asleep and vulnerable, and she knew she had to warn him. Just as she started up the ladder she heard Don's voice from above. "We've got to take Reynolds by surprise."

Shock made Kate almost fall backward, a startled cry rising to her throat. She gripped the ladder with nerveless hands.

There was no way she could get back to Rex. In a panic, she stealthily descended the stairs. The little room was a dank black hole that smelled of mildew and stale salt air. She leaned over the well and stared at the dark water sloshing against the metal sides of the ship. In the darkness she could feel the faint vibration of *Wanderer*'s generator. Or was it just her body shaking?

Oh, what would Rex think of her when Don surprised him and Rex discovered she was gone? She remembered how many times Rex had said the thought of her being in danger was the only thing that terrified him. She was afraid now that Rex might interpret her absence as betrayal. If she went back now, at least he would know for sure she was safe and hadn't betrayed him for Don. But then what would happen to the treasure? To Rex? And to everyone on board *Wanderer*?

It was up to her to save them.

For a long time, she listened to the water bounce against the sides of the well. Then she stripped out of her shorts and blouse and felt her way in the darkness over to the shelf where she kept her flippers. She kicked off her shoes and pulled on the flippers. She picked up an air tank and her goggles.

A desperate plan had formed in her mind.

It was bold and not without risk.

She ripped a strip of cloth off the bottom edge of her blouse and tucked it into the bosom of her bathing suit. Then she slowly climbed down the ladder into the well.

As the cool water swirled over her ankles, she paused, her heart pumping double-time. It was dangerous to go down alone without anyone even knowing where she was. It was especially dangerous to swim in these waters at night. There were sharks, currents. She could have a problem with her gear. A million things could go wrong.

She shuddered involuntarily right before she plunged underwater and swam purposefully under *Wanderer*'s hull toward the stern of Don's boat.

Only when she reached her destination did she surface. In the darkness she groped for the through-hull fitting she was looking for.

Barnacles cut her fingers, which began to bleed. Silently she prayed no sharks would be attracted. The seconds ticked by, and she scraped her hands again. And again.

Where was it?

Then at last she found the opening she'd been searching for. She pulled out the strip of her blouse that she'd brought with her and wadded it up, stuffing it inside the hole.

Ten minutes later, her mission accomplished, she was pulling herself back up the ladder inside the well.

When she reached the top she sagged in a mixture of relief and fear. She shivered as water dripped from her body onto the floor. Her cut fingers were stinging with pain. The currents had been stronger than usual, and it had taken all her strength to swim back to the well. Now she had to find Rex and see if there was anything she could do to help him.

Kate stowed her diving gear and then pulled on her shorts. She wrung the water out of her long hair and pulled it back from her face.

When she came up on deck, *Wanderer* was as ominously quiet as before. She was stealing quietly toward Rex's cabin to warn him when a hand coiled out of the darkness and clamped over her mouth. She was dragged into the shadows and held closely against the man's body.

She started to bite into his fingers and scream, but the cold barrel of a gun was jammed against her temple. The beery whisper against her ear was dreadfully familiar.

"I wouldn't if I were you, darlin'."

"Don," she gasped, whirling.

"Where you been, darlin'? Out for a midnight swim?"

A quiver of fear went through her. Everything counted on his believing her when she replied.

She swallowed. "I—I was hot. I just took a shower to try and cool off."

Don seemed to accept her answer. Kate saw Cappy right behind him, and he had a gun, too.

"Where's the rest of the crew?" she whispered, fearing the worst.

Don smiled. "Below. Bound and gagged."

"Don, what do you think you're doing? You're not a pirate!"

"Settling an old score, darlin'. Reynolds cut me out of my rightful part of treasure once."

"More likely he fired you because you were drinking too much on that job."

"The devil's a liar as well as a thief, darlin'."

"No!"

"Take me to him."

Don was dragging her across the deck. She opened her mouth to scream, but he hissed, "If you yell, I just might have to kill him, darlin'. Not that's it's likely he'll wake. Cappy put something into his coffee to make sure he slept like a baby tonight.''

She stared at Don in horror as he yanked her toward Rex's cabin. Softly, Don opened the door. He pulled her toward the bunk.

In his sleep, Rex groaned restlessly.

Don grabbed the chain of the bedside lamp and pulled. Brilliant light flooded the cabin, and when Rex's eyelids opened groggily, all he saw was Kate held tightly in Don's arms. Then the barrel of Don's gun crashed down onto his head.

In an agony of pain, Rex slumped to the floor. A trickle of dark red began to pool beneath his golden hair.

Don lunged and would have hit him again, across the bridge of his nose, but Kate began to scream and to struggle in his arms and managed to push him off balance. She threw herself protectively over Rex, cradling his injured head in her lap.

Furiously Don demanded, ''Get out of the way, Kate.''

''No!'' she cried, desperate to save Rex from further injury. ''I thought it was the treasure you wanted, Don.''

''Reynolds has taken more than treasure from me, Kate. If it weren't for him, you would have married me. When I finish with him, no woman will ever want him again.''

He drew back his fist, intending to pound it into Rex's jaw.

''No,'' Kate whispered. ''If you'll just leave him alone, Don, I'll come back to you. I promise. What more do you want? You'll have taken the treasure from him. And me. You'll have everything, and he'll have nothing.''

Slowly Don lowered his fist. Then he held out his hand toward Kate.

Her heart froze. Was there no other way? Rex would believe she'd betrayed him.

She had no choice. The important thing was that Rex lived. No matter what the cost to herself.

Gently, reluctantly she placed Rex's head on the floor once more, praying silently that he wasn't injured too badly to recover.

She tried not to shudder as Don captured her hand in his. He brought his mouth down to hers and it took all her acting ability not to wrench free of his kiss.

Rex's eyelids fluttered drowsily. His head throbbed with white-hot pain. There was a deafening roar in his ears. He felt leaden, as if a great weight held him down, and it was impossible to move.

He heard their voices, and they didn't know he heard.

"I never really wanted Rex, Don," Kate was saying softly. "I only came with him because he was after my treasure."

So softly spoken, yet those were the cruelest words Rex had ever heard.

Rex squinted against the brilliant light, forcing his eyes to focus on the indistinct shapes across the room.

Then he saw her, wrapped tightly in Don Taylor's arms.

"Kate," Rex groaned aloud. "Kate—"

Her name was a smothered cry of agony wrenched from his soul. She had betrayed him for money.

He thought faintly that he'd always known it was the money she really wanted, not him.

For a second, her eyes locked with his. Her frightened face was as white as death. She seemed to be shaking, or was it he who was shaking? He would never know. A black sea was rushing over him and he was lost and drowning in its terrible power. He called out to her, but she turned her back on him and walked away, her arms laced around another man's body.

Again Rex lapsed into unconsciousness. When he came to, he was alone.

Rex dragged himself to his feet and stumbled out onto the deck. Then he went below, where he managed to free the crew before he almost fainted again. This time, the sick feeling subsided and he remained conscious.

The treasure was gone and so were Don, Cappy and Kate.

Rex remembered how meticulously Kate had hired the crew, how frequently she'd extolled Cappy's virtues as a crew member.

Obviously Kate had been in on the conspiracy from the beginning. Obviously she had stowed away expressly for the purpose of betraying him.

Was it only this morning that she'd told him she loved him and that he'd believed her?

He was a fool! All his life he'd wanted love. He'd wanted a family. And for a brief, shining moment he'd almost believed he could have them.

Never again!

He was through with Kate Andrews. This time for good.

Twelve

There wasn't a ripple on the black water as Don's shrimp boat made its way toward Key West. Swathed in the crinkly yellow plastic of Don's overlarge windbreaker, Kate sat in the cabin by herself. Her eyes were half-closed in despair. Her mind kept returning to Rex. She kept remembering how still and pale he'd been when she'd left him in a crumpled heap on the floor of his cabin.

Suddenly the red warning light she'd been waiting for came on and she placed her hand over it to conceal it.

Just a few more minutes. That's all it would take.

Outside she heard Cappy holler, "Do you smell something funny, boss?"

A shrill horn blared.

"Damn!" Kate muttered the single expletive under her breath. She pulled her hand away from the red light just as Don rushed into the cabin.

"Why didn't you holler when you saw the light, darlin'?"

She tried to look drowsy. "I must have dozed off, Don."

The horn sounded its warning a second time, and Don cut the engine.

"She's hotter'n hell, Cappy."

Now that the boat was drifting, the stench of burning-oil fumes enveloped them. Don ripped open a wooden door and began to tinker with several valves on the engine. "Hell, I just overhauled her myself. Let's start her back up and see if she's circulating water."

Cappy started the engine while Don leaned over the stern with a flashlight. "Here's our problem, Cappy. No water's coming out. A piece of seaweed or something must have gotten sucked into the cooling-water intake. You'll have to cut her off, and I'll go over and see if I can unplug her."

Kate was holding her breath. What would Don do to her when he found out it wasn't seaweed at all but a strip of material she'd torn from her blouse?

"Boss, there's lights right behind us."

"Reynolds!"

"Rex," Kate whispered, a faint hope seeping through her terror.

"There's no way we can outrun 'em, boss."

In the darkness, Kate sensed that Don had turned his attention to her.

"We won't have to," Don said slowly. "Why do you think I brought Kate along?"

Kate stiffened with horror. She wasn't going to let Don use her against Rex. With one movement she shrugged out of her windbreaker and then bolted toward the bow. Don was right behind her. Just as she was about to dive over the side, he grabbed her by the hair. She whirled and sank her teeth in his wrist. He let her go and she jumped.

The cool waters swallowed her, and she swam underwater for as long and as far as she could until her lungs screamed for air. At last she surfaced.

Wanderer was pulling alongside Don's drifting shrimp boat. Kate watched as two men sprang from out of nowhere and seized Cappy. Just as quickly, Don was overpowered by three more and then another stepped into the cabin to look for Kate.

"Kate's gone!"

The next voice was Rex's, and never had that husky, velvet

sound held more menace. "If she's hurt, Taylor, I swear I'll kill you."

"Sh-she jumped overboard."

There was a sound of a fist crunching against bone and Don cried out, "I'm telling the truth."

Kate yelled then. "Over here." She began swimming toward the shrimp boat as five flashlight beams bobbed along the surface of the water. They all found her at once, blinding her.

Two men lifted her on board.

Rex was standing behind them, his head swathed in white bandages. His dark face was gray and lined with exhaustion. She saw the bitterness and hurt in his eyes.

She longed to run into his arms, to touch him to hold him, but something in his hard demeanor stopped her.

Her gaze sought his, begging for his understanding, but his eyes were cold, blue chips of ice. His mouth curled in disgust. Then he turned and was about to board *Wanderer* again.

At his rejection, her heart felt like it was tearing in two.

"Rex," she began weakly, "you have to let me explain."

He turned, his face set and implacable. "Treasure hunting again, my love?" he whispered. There was a curious stillness in his manner, an utter indifference to her. He was a man who'd lost everything.

"No. I...love you, Rex." All the words she would have spoken clogged in her throat like a gag of dry dust. It was no use trying to defend herself. He wouldn't believe her anyway.

"You have a strange way of showing your love, Kate."

She paled. "Rex, if you'd only listen to me, I could explain."

"I'm sure you could, and fool that I am, I just might be tempted to believe in you again. I don't want to hear a single word."

A tiny sob escaped in a moan from Kate's lips.

So Rex believed the worst of her.

Duffel bags were stacked on Rex's bunk in his cabin. Kate was still cramming a tangle of blouses and jeans into the last bag. The other salvage vessel had arrived and Rex was going to send *Wanderer* back to Key West to be unloaded. He was sending Kate back, as well. Just the thought of never seeing Rex again made her heart ache.

When she got back to Key West, the check from her aunt's estate would be waiting for her. That meant she would be able to repay Rex the money she owed him. Then she would probably take a teaching job somewhere else in Florida.

Slowly Kate paced the room, her thoughts whirling. Rex had decided to be lenient with Don. Kate had seen Don early this morning after he'd sobered up. Don had said he was going to quit drinking and start a new life for himself. He'd confessed to Kate that Rex had had a good reason for firing him all those years ago.

Don was ashamed of his act of piracy. He'd said he must have gotten crazy drunk and crazy jealous to have ever done such a thing and that it was way past the time when he should stop holding grudges against other people for imagined misdeeds.

"Who knows," Don had muttered, "maybe I never would have lost you to Reynolds in the first place, Kate, if I'd taken myself in hand before."

Kate was thankful that at least Don seemed to be headed in the right direction and she felt Rex was being very generous toward him. One thing bothered her, though. How was it possible that Rex could be so fair to Don, someone who had really wronged him, but refuse to even talk to her?

It hurt that he'd condemned her without even listening to her side of the story. She swallowed against the hard, dry knot in her throat, but it refused to go down. She wondered if it ever would.

"Rex. Oh, Rex..."

She buried her face in her hands. How could she bear to lose him again? She'd loved him so wildly for such a long time and had known so little real happiness with him.

There was a faint knock at the door, and then she heard it open. When she turned, her gaze locked with the steely blue eyes of the golden man who haunted her every thought. *Rex.*

"Kate, we have to talk."

What could he possibly have to say that wouldn't make her feel worse than she already did? He despised her, and she couldn't bear his hatred. She buried her face in her hands.

"If you're worried about the money I owe you, I'm going to pay it back out of some money I inherited. Then I won't owe you anything else."

"It's always money with you, isn't it?" he snarled.

She got up and would have run past him and escaped outside, but he grabbed her by the arm and yanked her roughly against him, knocking the breath from her lungs when she collided with the granite hardness of his muscular chest.

For one long, breathless instant their eyes met, and she saw that his blazed as passionately with uncontrollable emotion as hers. She began to struggle. Her fists pounded against his chest. He only grinned, and it maddened her that he found her weakness so amusing.

He tightened his grip, making it even more difficult for her to breathe. The world began to blacken. She had no chance to draw another breath before her lips were ground against her teeth by the fierce assault of his mouth on hers. For a timeless moment, Rex plundered the softness of her lips, brutally ravishing them until she had neither the strength nor the will to push him away.

"I love you," she murmured. "I love you. I love you. Oh, Rex, please believe me," she begged desperately.

Abruptly he let her go—everything except her wrist.

Their eyes, their lips, their faces were only inches apart. She was vaguely conscious of his eyes poring over her features.

"Don't lie to me, Kate."

"Rex..." she began in bewilderment. Oh, why couldn't he believe her?

"You know just what to do, just what to say to torture me, don't you?" he hissed, his voice harsh with pain. "All night I've been going crazy, wondering what you would have said in your defense if I'd listened. I keep wondering if it's somehow possible you're innocent. Now you tell me you love me."

Pride gleamed brightly in her emerald eyes. "I am innocent, Rex."

"Maybe it's time I let you try to explain your side of the story. I can't promise I'll believe you, but I'll listen."

She didn't dare look at his handsome face for fear of weakening. So she studied the intricate markings on the chart laid out on top of the desk. "If you can't believe in me," she began quietly, "then it's got to be over for us, Rex. Marriage needs to be based on mutual trust. If we don't have that, we'll have nothing."

Slowly she arose.

"If you go, Kate, I'll never ask you to come back."

She turned, and very softly, her voice came to him, "I feel a lot of terrible things right now, Rex, but do you know what I feel most of all? I feel terribly sorry for you."

"Sorry for me?"

"Yes, because no matter how much money you go on to make, no matter how famous you become, you'll end up alone. And do you know why? It's because you're still running scared. You're still that frightened kid Jake found half-dead on the highway. You're still trying not to feel scared and trying to act tough. You're a coward, Rex Reynolds. You're afraid to love me and trust me because you don't really believe anyone can love you. It's not me you don't believe in. It's yourself."

She saw the pain in his eyes. His face went as white as if she'd struck him.

"All you have to do to verify my story is to check the cooling water intake where I stuffed part of my blouse to make Don's engine overheat. The rest of my blouse is probably on the floor by the well. But you won't do that, will you? You don't really want to trust me, do you?"

She tore her gaze from his. Her tears were blinding her as she turned and fled. He was calling her name, but she didn't stop. She was too afraid that if she did, she would never find the strength to leave him again.

Later that afternoon, he found her in the submerged underwater observation chamber at the bow of *Wanderer*. She was watching one of the divers feed a school of fish that were swimming in the aquamarine waters.

Behind her came the low-pitched huskiness of the voice Kate loved more than any other. "They're beautiful, aren't they?"

She didn't turn or even try to say anything, but she didn't pull away when Rex wrapped his hard arms around her and pressed her into the protective warmth of a tough, male body.

"Kate, darling," Rex whispered, his low tone desperate. "I was wrong...about everything."

She felt something damp and hot scald her shoulder, and she knew it was his tears. The hands upon her body trembled.

Slowly her sooty lashes fluttered.

"Kate, look at me."

Slowly she turned and focused obediently on his craggy, masculine features.

Her heart thrilled to the love she read in his eyes.

"Rex," she said weakly. "Oh, Rex. So you checked the intake."

"I didn't have to. I know you were telling me the truth. I love you, Kate. More than anything in the world."

"I never lied to you," she whispered, her voice shaking from the depth of her emotion.

"I know." He lifted her injured hands and kissed the torn places where the barnacles had bitten into her flesh. When his gaze met hers, his smile was dazzling. "You were right, darling, I was scared of love, scared of the pain of it. I needed your love so badly that I was afraid to let myself believe in you. It was easier to believe that what you really wanted was my money. I knew I could deliver on that score. I wasn't so sure of myself as a human being." His mouth moved roughly over her brow and into her hair, kissing and caressing.

She knew all about being afraid to love, so she could afford to be benevolent.

"I forgive you, darling," she murmured right before he lowered his mouth to hers and kissed her passionately on the lips.

After a long time she murmured, "When are you ever going to learn that our love is the greatest treasure of all?"

"Apparently I'm a slow learner. I hope you don't mind."

"That will only make it all the more fun teaching you."

"How about giving me a lesson now?"

"The first of many."

He pressed a kiss on her lips and then farther down, into the warm hollow of her throat.

The passion of their love made all the doubts of two lifetimes vanish forever.

* * * * *

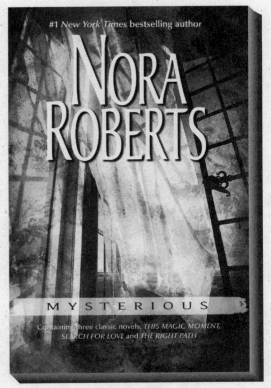
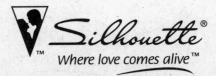

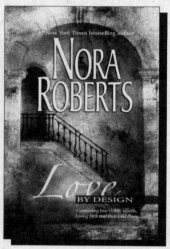

MONTANA MAVERICKS

The Kingsleys

A woman from the past. A death-defying accident. A moment in time that changes one man's life forever.

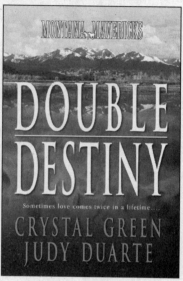

Nothing is as it seems beneath the big skies of Montana....

Return to Rumor, Montana, to meet the Kingsley family
in this exciting anthology featuring two brand-new stories!

First Love by Crystal Green
and
Second Chance by Judy Duarte

On sale July 2003 only from Silhouette Books!

Also available July 2003
Follow the Kingsleys' story in **MOON OVER MONTANA** by Jackie Merritt
Silhouette Special Edition #1550

Where love comes alive ™

Visit Silhouette at www.eHarlequin.com   PSDD-TR